ANGEL HEART

Marie Laval

Published by Accent Press Ltd 2015

ISBN 9781910939086

A mes soleils…

Chapter One

The cutter was sailing too close to the cliffs, heading straight for the Devil's Tooth.

Marie-Ange's cloak billowed in the blustery wind, the hood blew back and her hair swirled like a golden veil around her. From the cliff top, she watched the small French ship dancing wildly on the waves, its tricolour and white ensigns flapping at the top of the mast. If it carried on its course the ship would be ripped open by the reef. A man stood alone at the prow, oblivious of the danger ahead. He was too far away and the roaring of the waves crashing onto the cliffs was so loud shouting a warning to him would be useless. She unfastened her cloak, pulled her black shawl from her shoulders, and waved it above her head in the direction of the Devil's Tooth.

A ray of sunshine tearing through the clouds bathed her black-clad silhouette in a bright golden light. For a few seconds the sun was in her eyes, blinding her before the wind pushed the dark clouds across the sky and the sun disappeared once more. When she looked towards the bay again, the ship was steering east, back to the high sea. She heaved a sigh of relief. The crew must have seen her signals and spotted the reef in time. They were safe.

She resumed her walk on the cliff path to St Nectan's chapel, a small granite building sailors' wives visited to pray for the safe return of their men. Or rather, they came to the ancient wishing well at the back of the chapel. Today, like so many times before, Marie-Ange wanted to pray for Christopher.

'Six years already, my love,' she whispered, blinking

away the tears.

Six years since her husband had been lost at sea when his ship was sunk by French artillery off Corunna. She searched in her pocket for the piece of wedding ribbon she had cut earlier that morning.

'Please, come back to me.' She repeated the words like an incantation and kissed the white satin bow before leaning forward to throw it into the ancient well. It whirled as it flew down, becoming smaller and fainter as it was swallowed by the shadows.

Her dream last night still felt so real. Christopher held her in his arms while she touched his face and gazed into his grey eyes…Then he melted into the mist, leaving her cold and alone.

Damn this ship. Damn this weather. And damn Malleval. Hugo Saintclair clapped his hands together a few times and blew on them to keep them warm. Around him, the crew shouted orders and heaved on ropes in order to switch sails and change course before they hit the rocks. The Angel warned them, the sailors said, heaven was on their side. Shaking his head with impatience, he listened to their nonsensical chatter. Angels didn't exist, but the woman who waved at them from the cliff top had saved them from a certain death. The black, fierce looking rock in the middle of the bay would no doubt have torn the ship open.

It was sobering to think that having survived so many bloody battles in Europe he might have drowned in the grey, stormy waters of the English Channel while carrying out an assignment which had nothing to do with the army, and everything to do with his own foolishness.

He pulled a flask from his coat pocket and drank a swallow of rum to fight the queasy feeling in the pit of his stomach. A grimace twisted his lips as the cheap liquor burned his throat and brought tears to his eyes. The sooner they reached the shore, the better. He was a cuirassier officer, damn it, not a sailor. He tightened his lips, squared his jaw. Some cuirassier officer he was! Not only was he stuck on a ship in the middle of a storm, but he was about to play bodyguard to a rich noblewoman who would no doubt turn out to be every bit as spoilt, haughty, and demanding as the other aristocrats he'd had the misfortune to encounter so far.

Gripping the side of the boat, he took a long gulp of air. He had nobody to blame but himself. He should have held his liquor better and stopped gambling before it was too late.

It was raining when Marie-Ange finally set off on the path inland. Soon the outline of Norton Place appeared in the distance—the grey, forbidding manor house crouched in a clump of trees. She walked through the gate and sighed as she stepped over several broken slate roof tiles dislodged by the storm. There would be more holes in the roof, as if the old manor house wasn't plagued by enough leaks and draughts already…

She entered the hall, gave her wet cloak to Rosie. The maid whisked away to dry the sodden garment. Shivering and eager to stand near the fire, she opened the door to the austere oak panelled drawing room. Her fingers were raw and stiff after her long walk and she rubbed them hard over the flames.

'There you are! Any sign of our French guest?'

She turned at the sound of her brother-in-law's voice and smiled. Bewilderment hit her as he strode towards her. With his tall stature, unruly ash blond hair and grey eyes, Robert was more like Christopher with every passing day. She shook her head.

'Not yet. Monsieur Malleval wrote that Capitaine Saintclair would be with us mid-January. I wonder if…'

She recalled the cutter that sailed dangerously close to

the reef earlier in the day. It flew a French flag—two French flags, in fact—the revolutionary tricolour and the white flag of the newly-restored Bourbon monarchy. Maybe Capitaine Saintclair was on board.

'You don't have to travel to France alone with him, you know.' Robert looked at her hopefully. 'I'd be more than willing to come with you. Indeed, I believe that, as the man of the family, I should come with you.'

Marie-Ange smiled. She had trouble considering Robert anything other than a younger brother. Yet at eighteen, he was almost a man, and she would do well to remember it. He would probably get married soon and leave her alone in this draughty old house on the edge of the moors.

'No, Robert. We talked about it before. Monsieur Malleval is unable to come for me because of his old battle wound but he wrote that Capitaine Saintclair would be a most reliable escort.'

'Still, we don't know anything about him,' Robert protested.

'We know he is a distinguished officer from the Second Cuirassier Regiment,' Marie-Ange said, patting Robert's forearm. 'And as much as I would like you to come with me, you must stay here and look after the estate. I won't need more than a few weeks to settle my inheritance at Beauregard.'

Robert looked at his boots and frowned. 'But…'

'You know what this bequest means for Norton Place and for you. I will be able to get the roof fixed at last and you will join the Naval Academy.'

Robert pulled a face. His dream was to follow in his brother's footsteps and buy a commission in the Royal Navy but there had been no money for him to do so. Until now.

Two cocker spaniel puppies burst into the drawing room and jumped at her skirt.

'Rusty! Splinter! Calm down!' She laughed and knelt down to stroke the dogs' shiny coats. 'Besides, who would look after my two darlings here?'

Robert still looked disgruntled.

'Cheer up.' She grinned. 'I heard there was jelly for pudding tonight.'

This time there was something akin to anger in his eyes.

'I wish you would stop treating me like a child,' he growled before storming out.

Her breath caught in her throat. What was wrong with him? Robert was the only family she had left. They had never argued before today.

'Come on, boys, let's go out,' she called to them, hoping that taking the puppies out would cheer her up.

She headed towards the cliffs once again. Her boots were soon covered with mud, the hem of her dress drenched, but she didn't notice the rain, the puddles, or the coarse tufts of grass. This time she followed the steep path down onto the pebbly beach where, as usual, the sea spray on her face and the roar of waves crashing onto the reef made her heart beat faster. She licked the salt from her lips and took a deep breath. How she would miss these walks along the coast during her time in France…Still, it would be worth it. Even though he didn't quote an exact figure in his letter, Uxeloup Malleval had promised a substantial legacy from her mother's family estate in the Beaujolais.

The sky was darkening by the time she made her way back. Her heart skipped a beat when she came in view of Norton Place and she quickened her pace. A carriage was stationed by the front steps. They had a visitor. Perhaps it was Saintclair?

She let herself in, slipped the cloak off her shoulders and checked her reflection in the hall mirror. Lord, she looked wild. The wind had made her pale blue eyes sparkle and given her complexion a deep rosy blush. She combed her curly blond hair with her fingers, twisting it into a rough plait. It was far from perfect but it would have to do. She couldn't keep her visitor waiting any longer.

She pushed open the door to the drawing room and hurried inside. Splinter and Rusty ran under her feet, tripping her. Her cry of alarm died on her lips as two strong arms caught her. Surprised, she tilted her head up to look at the tall, dark-haired man holding her against his hard, wide chest. His intense blue eyes held her gaze and sent a shiver down her spine. One side of his weather-beaten face was barred by a long, ragged scar. The thin line of the mouth and the tightness in his jaw gave an impression of controlled anger. For a moment fear gathered in her chest. Then he smiled, a slow, confident smile, and he was transformed into the most handsome man she had ever laid eyes on.

The dogs barked at them furiously. Marie-Ange parted her lips to order them to stop but before she could speak Robert took a few steps forward, an angry scowl twisting his face, his fists clenched by his sides.

'Let her go at once, sir,' he warned, 'or …'

'Or what?' The man arched his eyebrows, a mocking smile at the corner of his mouth, as if he dared Robert to come any closer. He shook his head and released her.

'I will ask you to restrain your puppies, Madame. The three of them,' he said as he looked down at her.

'How dare you call me a puppy?' Robert's face flushed a deep red, and he took another step forward.

Marie-Ange found her voice at last.

'Rusty. Splinter. Lie down at once.' She pointed to the rug in front of the fireplace. The dogs whimpered but obeyed. 'Robert. That's enough. Monsieur was just helping me.'

Robert muttered an apology and crouched beside the dogs to stroke their wet, muddy coats.

'You must be Capitaine Saintclair,' she said, tilting her

chin up to look at him again.

The papers had been full of sketches and reports about the famous French cuirassiers and she had no difficulty imagining Saintclair in a dark blue uniform, his chest covered with shiny metal plates and his helmet topped by a black horse mane, charging onto the battlefield. His current attire of black breeches and tall leather riding boots topped by a short brown coat did nothing to dispel the heroic image conjured in her mind.

He clicked his heels together and bowed his head.

'At your service, Madame.'

'Please take a seat.' She pointed to an armchair near the fireplace and sat opposite him.

'I have a letter from Malleval for you.' He pulled a thick envelope out of the leather bag which was strapped to his belt, leant closer and handed it over.

She glanced at the red wax seal bearing the letters *A M* in the centre. She was eager to read Malleval's letter, but not wanting to appear ill-mannered, she dropped the papers in her lap.

'Did you have a pleasant journey, Capitaine?'

'Not really.' He pulled a face. 'The captain is unfamiliar with the waters in these parts. He didn't know about the currents and the reefs and our ship almost tore open on some rocks at the entrance of the bay. It was only by a stroke of luck we avoided disaster. A woman warned us from the cliff.' His lips stretched in a condescending smile. 'The crew said she was an angel descended on a ray of sunshine.'

Marie-Ange cleared her throat, embarrassed. 'It was no angel, I'm afraid, only me. The cutter was heading straight for the Devil's Tooth and I...'

Capitaine Saintclair narrowed his eyes to look at her. Her heartbeat quickened under his scrutiny and an awkward blush heated her face.

A smile stretched his lips. 'Well, thank you, Madame. I

owe you my life.'

She nodded but made no answer.

'When can you be ready to leave for France? The cutter is moored in Wellcombe harbour for now, but I want to sail back as soon as possible.'

Robert raised his head. Marie-Ange was aware of him staring at her with pleading eyes and her heart twisted a bit at the pain her leaving would cause him.

'I have been expecting you for some weeks,' she said. 'My things are ready. We can leave tomorrow if you like.'

'Not tomorrow! Not so soon!' Robert jumped to his feet, stormed out of the drawing room and slammed the door behind him.

'A hot-blooded young male,' Capitaine Saintclair remarked, arching his eyebrows.

Embarrassed by Robert's outburst, Marie-Ange looked down. The sight of her dirty boots met her appalled gaze. Whatever must the captain think of her? She shuffled her feet under her dark grey skirt, itself damp and splattered with mud, and sat upright. At least Saintclair wouldn't find fault with her demeanour and clothing. She still wore half-mourning clothes—her dresses mostly dark greys, browns and greens, with high collars and long sleeves.

'I apologise for Robert,' she said stiffly. 'He is very protective of me. He is also young and has lacked the presence of a man here. His brother—my husband—was a Royal Navy Commander and was reported missing after the battle of Corunna.' She could never say Christopher was dead. She never truly believed it was so.

'I'm sorry.' Saintclair sounded sincere.

She let out a sigh and stared out into the fire, her fingers playing with her wedding band. A tingling sensation on her skin soon made her glance up. The Capitaine was looking at her, his blue eyes serious and intense once again. Heat spread over her cheeks and throat.

'Please come with me,' she said, standing up. 'It is time

you were shown to your room.'

She rang the service bell and led him into the hallway where an elderly servant soon joined them.

'Make a fire in the green room, Francis, and have some hot water and tea brought up straight away for our guest,' she told him. The green room was Norton Place's best bedroom—at least, it was the one with the least damp patches on the ceilings, mould stains on the wallpaper and draughty windows.

As soon as the French officer disappeared up the stairs, Marie-Ange went back into the drawing room to read Uxeloup Malleval's letter.

After enquiring about her health, Malleval explained the documents concerning her inheritance were ready at Beauregard. As he was researching the history of the chateau he asked her to bring along any old family papers she might have, especially regarding her mother's godfather, Count Saint Germain. Having heard of her mother's talent as a painter, he also wished to see her sketchbook.

Marie-Ange sighed. She didn't have any family papers. In fact, she knew next to nothing about her mother's childhood at Beauregard and the traumatic events she escaped from in 1791. She died when Marie-Ange was five years old, and her father only told her the bare minimum about the French side of her family. 'What is past is past,' William Jones would always say when she asked him about the Beauregards. Since his death, there was nobody left who could answer her questions. Would Uxeloup Malleval know anything about her family? The man himself was a bit of a mystery, and so was this bequest he promised her. Maybe Capitaine Saintclair would be able to tell her more.

She went up to her room to finish packing. Opening the drawer of her writing desk, she pulled out a hard leather pouch. Inside was a dagger with a finely carved bone handle Christopher brought back from his first voyage to the West Indies as a good luck charm. He had forgotten to take it on his last mission to Spain from which he never returned. Thoughtful, she pressed it against her heart for a moment before slipping it into her bag.

Her mother's sketchbook was, as always, on her bedside table. Over the years, she had flipped so often through the pages covered with sketches and watercolours of Beauregard it seemed she already knew the place. It had all the charm of an enchanted castle with its round towers and walled rose garden, with its circular dovecote and the park surrounded by a dark forest. She traced with a finger the gold crest embossed on the book's cover—a unicorn surmounted by two *Fleurs de Lys*, Count Saint Germain's coat of arms.

'An extraordinary man,' her father once said with unusual enthusiasm. 'He was a philosopher, a scientist, and an outstanding statesman. Your mother was very fond of him.'

She slipped the sketchbook into her bag too.

When the mantel clock struck seven, she changed into a dove grey gown and went to the drawing room. Capitaine Saintclair sat in front of the fireplace, holding a glass of whisky in one hand and stroking Splinter with the other. He rose as soon as she came in but she gestured for him to sit down.

She asked if he was satisfied with his room. He replied that he had everything he needed. She cleared her throat and hesitated, suddenly shy.

'I hope you will forgive my curiosity, Capitaine,' she started, 'but Monsieur Malleval's letter inviting me to Beauregard to collect a bequest from his father came as a great surprise. May I ask you how long you have been acquainted with him?'

He nodded. 'About fifteen years. We met at the regimental barracks back in 1800 when we were both very young men. I joined the cuirassiers and Malleval, the Hussars. Since then our regiments have fought all over Europe together.' He drank a sip of whisky.

'So he was a Hussar...' She knew of the Hussars' reputation, both on, and off, the battlefield. 'I hope he isn't too seriously injured.'

Saintclair looked up, puzzled. 'Injured?'

'In his letter, he mentioned a battle wound which troubles him greatly. That's why he could not come here himself.'

'Ah. Yes. His battle wound...well, it depends on...the weather.'

The French officer's answer lacked of conviction. Maybe Uxeloup was more seriously hurt than he let on.

'In any case,' she resumed, 'it is very chivalrous of you to volunteer to escort me to Beauregard. I much appreciate it.'

'It is my pleasure, Madame,' he answered. 'I was at a loose end anyway since our new king put most officers on leave. I believe you and Malleval are related, is that right?'

She nodded. 'I am, in a way, his niece. My grandmother, Aline, married his father in 1791 after my grandfather, Philippe, was executed. She was Edmond Malleval's second wife.'

'He probably had your grandfather killed to make way for him.'

She gasped. 'Why did you say that?'

Captain Saintclair shrugged. 'As a public prosecutor in Beaujeu, then a representative of the Public Safety Committee in Lyon during the Revolution, the man sent hundreds of people to their death—not just aristocrats but commoners, too. Anyone he suspected of plotting against the Republic.' He paused. 'Or, some have said, of being in the way of his ambition.'

Marie-Ange's nervous fingers played with her wedding band again.

11

'I had no idea he was one of the revolutionaries who terrorized France and turned the country into a giant charnel house. Thank goodness these awful times are over and France is at peace. Now Napoleon has been exiled and the king is back, everything will be all right, won't it?'

His jaw tightened and his eyes flashed with anger.

'Spoken like a true royalist, Madame. You will get on well with the captain of our ship. He's a staunch Bourbon supporter. I think I should warn you however that there isn't much sympathy among ordinary French people for *émigrés* now flocking back to claim their estates and their fortunes. Neither is there much love for the British nation as a whole. Napoleon is still very much alive in French hearts.'

She raised her chin, stung by his tone.

'I don't care what people think. I am a Beauregard and I have every right to visit the chateau of my ancestors.' She stood up. 'It is getting late. Shall we make our way to the dining room?'

Like the rest of the manor house, the dining room was austere, with a damp, frigid feel that even a roaring fire in the stone fireplace could not dispel. Robert was there already, a glass of red wine in his hand, which judging by his flushed cheeks, wasn't his first. She gave him a stern look which he answered with a shrug, and took her place at the head of the table with Robert sitting to her left and Capitaine Saintclair to her right.

Francis served a plain but hearty chicken and vegetable stew. Ignoring her disapproving frowns, Robert poured himself yet more wine. She let out a sigh and turned to Saintclair.

'Are you from the Beaujolais region, Capitaine?'

'No, I'm from Lyon,' he answered curtly.

'That's a very large town, isn't it? Where is your estate?' Robert enquired.

'I don't have one,' Saintclair answered. 'My family isn't

from the landed gentry, or any kind of gentry for that matter. My father owns a small silk workshop. He has worked all his life. He still does.' He finished his plate and took hold of his glass.

'Then how did you get to be a superior officer? I thought these positions were reserved to gentlemen,' Robert insisted.

The captain's eyes glinted with heat, yet his voice was calm when he spoke.

'Napoleon allowed all men, irrespective of their social standing, access to the highest levels of command. The only things that mattered were ability and bravery. Isn't that the way it should always be?'

Robert shrugged. 'I suppose so,' he muttered before drinking another gulp of wine.

'Unfortunately, our new king is reverting back to the old ways and promoting men according to lineage rather than merit,' Saintclair carried on in sombre tones.

'You must tell us all about the battles you fought,' Robert urged, and he went on to question the French officer about his military career, exclaiming in wonder when Saintclair said he had fought at Jena, Wagram and Austerlitz, to name but a few.

'Did you ever meet Napoleon?'

'The Emperor reviewed our regiment regularly. I often saw him during campaigns but I never personally talked to him.' Saintclair's eyes clouded over and Marie-Ange wondered if the emperor was still very much alive in *his* heart.

Francis brought in a final dish of rhubarb jelly and Robert reached out for the bowl. His face was flushed, his blond hair tousled.

'Look at you, always the first one for pudding.' Marie-Ange laughed as she proceeded to comb his curls away from his forehead with her fingers, the way she had done since he was a young boy.

Saintclair leant back against his seat and looked at her, his eyebrows arched. Suddenly flustered by the intensity of his gaze, she withdrew her hand, pushed her chair back and stood up.

'I hope you do not mind if I bid you good night, Capitaine, I still have a few things to attend to before our journey.' Then turning to Robert, she said, 'Don't be too long.'

Robert shook his head. 'Don't worry. I'll come up to your room shortly.'

The noise of glass shattering made her jump. She whirled about to see Saintclair had dropped his glass of wine on the floor.

'Sorry,' he mumbled as he bent down to pick the pieces.

'Leave it, Capitaine. Francis will tidy up.'

Once in her room, she undressed and wrapped herself in Christopher's large, faded blue dressing gown. Although it no longer bore his scent, she still wore it most nights to imagine his arms around her. While waiting for Robert, she set the draught board and pieces on her desk for their nightly game, as well as sheets of paper and an inkwell for the French lesson she insisted on giving him while they played.

'I don't know why you still waste your time trying to teach me French,' he said when he joined her shortly after. 'You know how hopeless I am.'

'You will find it very useful in the Royal Navy,' she answered with a smile. 'Not to mention at balls and parties when you want to impress young ladies.'

But he was indeed so hopeless their lessons usually ended up in fits of giggles, and tonight was no exception.

'I shall miss our evenings,' he said as he lingered in the corridor, long after midnight.

'I will soon be back. Hush now, we don't want to wake Capitaine Saintclair.'

She gave him a kiss on the forehead and watched him climb the stairs to his room on the second floor. A noise at the far end of the corridor startled her. She froze and peered into the darkness, holding her breath, her heart beating uncomfortably hard. Was Capitaine Saintclair awake?

She shook her head. She was being fanciful. It was only the old manor house creaking and groaning in the blustering gale. She should be used to it by now.

Chapter Two

She didn't enjoy the Channel crossing at all. The rough seas forced her to stay in her tiny cabin, suffering from violent bouts of sea-sickness. Fortunately, after reaching Le Havre, the cutter sailed down the calmer waters of the River Seine. Despite the cold, she was able to stand on deck much of the time and watch the flat, wintry landscape unfold. For their last evening on the river, they moored at *Asnière*.

'We'll be in Paris tomorrow morning. Let's hope the river doesn't freeze,' Saintclair said as they walked on deck after the evening meal they shared with the taciturn captain of the ship. He lifted the collar of his coat. 'You'd better go in.'

'Not just yet. I don't like being cooped up in my cabin.' She sighed at the prospect of yet another uncomfortable night. 'Do you know why the captain is so unpleasant?' The man barely acknowledged their presence on board and answered Marie-Ange's questions with a grunt.

Saintclair shrugged. 'It's my fault. I demanded he fly the tricolour as well as the white flag. He doesn't like it. I told you before, he's a monarchist.'

'I see…' So she had been right about Saintclair's loyalties. He didn't support King Louis' new regime.

One of the sailors approached them and asked Saintclair if he fancied a game of cards.

Saintclair's face lit up. 'Definitely! I hope you have some of your fine rum left.' It seemed that though he might not get on with the captain, the man had no problems with the rest of the crew. They played cards, smoked and drank liquors until late every night.

Marie-Ange was left with no other choice than to retire to her cabin. She lay down in the narrow bunk for a while, tossing and turning. With a sigh of impatience, she sat up and propped a pillow behind her back. The men were laughing and talking in Saintclair's cabin on the other side of the thin partition. She thought she heard her name. They were talking about her! Curious and holding her breath, she got up and placed her ear against the wooden panel.

She heard Saintclair ask for a tumbler of rum, then another, and the game began with the clinking sounds of coins being thrown on a table and the cards being dealt out.

'Is *mademoiselle* your fiancée?' someone asked.

Saintclair let out a good-hearted laugh. 'Fiancée? Hell no. I'm escorting her to the Beaujolais where a fellow officer has some business to conclude with her. Pass me two more cards and your flask of rum, mate.'

'No, I don't believe in love, marriage, and all this nonsense,' he resumed speaking. 'What's the point of getting chained up to one woman when you can enjoy them all? I'm one of those who believe women are on this earth to be loved...for a few nights. Any longer and they turn into nags or cheats.'

The men laughed and made a few coarse comments about feminine charms. Marie-Ange gasped.

'Anyway, you wouldn't stand a chance with her,' one man said. 'She looks like a true lady.'

'And she's a widow,' another exclaimed.

'So what?' Saintclair laughed again. 'Whether they're tavern girls or ladies, they're all the same. They might put on a good show but there isn't one who can stay true to one man. Women are just like kittens, my friends. A few caresses and they purr in your arms, they just can't help it, especially where I'm concerned. So let's enjoy them while we can.' His words were drowned in laughter.

Marie-Ange put her hands to her burning cheeks. So that was what the capitaine thought of women, and of her—false, easy to seduce, and unable to be faithful. Well, what did he know, he was wrong. She would remain true to Christopher for the rest of her life. As for Saintclair, the man was boorish and arrogant, and she pitied the women who found him attractive. She certainly didn't. She stomped back to her bunk, punched the pillow a few times to soften it and lay down, arms crossed on her chest. Kittens and caresses indeed! The very thought of lying in that man's arms filled her with revulsion. Closing her eyes, she tried to ignore the rowdy laughter coming from the cabin next door and conjured up Christopher's image before drifting into a fitful sleep.

The cutter left *Asnière* at daybreak. Marie-Ange went up on the bridge as the anchor was raised and the sails hoisted. She smiled with satisfaction when she saw Saintclair, pale, unshaven and with dark shadows under his eyes, standing alone at the rail. He held a tin cup of steaming coffee and rubbed his temple with his fingers. Too much fine rum and not enough sleep, probably. Dismissing him, she turned her gaze to the French countryside slipping past as they made their way towards Paris.

The ship arrived in the capital mid-morning, sailing past tall, elegant buildings, townhouses, and churches. The quays were alive with the hustle and bustle of mariners, fishermen and traders. As if he couldn't wait to be on solid ground, Saintclair jumped onto the quay as soon as the cutter moored near the *Pont Neuf*.

He took care of the customs formalities, arranged for their luggage to be loaded into a cart, and hailed a calash to take them to the inn where he had booked two rooms.

'When we're settled at the *Le Faisan Doré*, I will hire a carriage and a driver for our journey to Beauregard,' he informed her. 'Then I'll show you around the city, if you like.'

'Oh yes, please!' The excitment of being in Paris almost made Marie-Ange forget she was annoyed at him.

There was so much to see. The cobbled-streets heaved with carriages, soldiers, peddlers, carts, and horses. On the sidewalks, stalls sold everything from flowers to live poultry, fish and wheels of yellow cheese.

Le Faisan Doré was a small, respectable establishment in the *Rue Notre-Dame des Champs*, close to the Luxembourg gardens. Saintclair checked them in, promised to return very shortly and left.

There was still no sign of him when night fell. By then Marie-Ange was bored and very cross. He had promised to take her out, and she had waited all afternoon. Where was he?

After a supper of beef stew and apple tart, she went to the landlady, a plump, dark-haired matron.

'Has Capitaine Saintclair not returned yet?'

The woman gave her a knowing grin. 'I wouldn't expect him back anytime soon, dear. He must be at his club or at a lady's house. These cavalry officers can't stay away from women, cards and drink.'

Marie-Ange pursed her lips in distaste. The landlady was probably right.

'When he comes back, please tell him that I wish to speak with him at once.'

The rest of the evening passed with excruciating slowness. How infuriating to be in Paris and confined to a room. When the mantelpiece clock struck eleven, she decided that Saintclair wasn't coming back, so she stripped down to her chemise and removed her stockings before wrapping herself in Christopher's blue dressing gown. She shook her hair loose on her shoulders and was about to snuggle into bed when there was a sharp knock on the door.

Who did the woman think he was to summon him to her room like that? A lackey, probably. His lips twisted in an angry snarl as he climbed the stairs two by two. Madame Norton might live in a ramshackle manor house on the bleak, windswept Devonshire moorland, but she was still a Beauregard on her mother's side and a member of the English gentry by marriage. He should have followed Martin's advice and stayed at the club a while longer.

He walked down the draughty corridor and drummed impatient fingers on her door.

'Who's there?' A timid voice answered from behind the door.

'Saintclair. Did you want to talk to me?' His tone was short.

The door opened just enough for Madame Norton to peer through.

He exhaled sharply to control his rising temper. 'Are you going to let me in or shall we talk in the corridor?'

She opened the door wider and he strode in.

'Is there a problem?' He looked down at her. Barefoot and swamped in an old dressing gown, the woman hardly reached his shoulder. He wondered what she wore underneath, if anything. His pulse quickened and a sudden rush of heat coursed through his veins. He stuck his hands in his coat pockets.

She stepped back and folded her arms on her chest.

'You said you would be back early, yet you left me waiting here all day.'

Her icy tone did nothing to cool his blood. In fact it had just the opposite effect. He took a deep breath and walked to the fireplace to put some distance between them. His lips stretched in a thin smile.

'Sorry. I got…distracted.' He shrugged. 'I did arrange a carriage and a driver for us. We're leaving for Lyon on Saturday.'

She looked at him again in the way a queen might look

20

at a mangy dog.

'Why wait until Saturday? Your instructions are to take me straight to Beauregard. Monsieur Malleval won't be pleased.'

If she meant to intimidate him, she had failed. She was starting to amuse him greatly—in more ways than one.

'I have things to do. Anyway, what's the rush? I thought you might like to come to town with me tomorrow and see a play in the evening.'

Her eyes flashed in anger.

'I do not go to the theatre, Capitaine. I am in mourning.'

He arched his eyebrows. 'After six years?'

'My husband was a wonderful man. I will mourn him all my life.' Her eyes filled with tears, she bit her lip.

He didn't answer. There was one thing to be said for her. She was convincing—a first-class actress. He had almost been taken in by her wistful sighs and tearful eyes, by her drab mourning dresses and the almost virginal blushing on her cheeks every time he looked her way. He had almost believed her grief-stricken widow act...until he saw young Norton leave her room in the middle of the night with a wide grin on his face. He knew better than to be fooled by a woman, especially a pretty one.

Still, the way her voice quivered with emotion, her pale blue eyes shone with tears and her lips trembled did have a strange effect on him. His throat went dry and he swallowed hard, so strong was the urge to crush her mouth under his, rake his fingers in her silky blond curls, and pull her close. The memory of her soft, pliable flesh quickened his pulse and made his body throb and grow hard.

As if she could sense the heat of his desire, a very becoming pink blush covered her cheeks and throat.

Why did he stare at her in this way? His eyes had gone dark. The red glow from the fire cast a sinister, almost evil light across his face. He walked towards her, looking like a wolf about to pounce on his prey. Uneasy, and very conscious of her state of dishabillé, Marie-Ange stepped backward until her back touched the dressing table.

'I bid you good night, Capitaine,' she said, striving to keep her voice calm despite the wild thumping of her heart. It was thundering so loudly she was sure he could hear it.

He seemed to snap back to reality. He frowned and took a deep breath. 'Of course...I have a few errands to run tomorrow morning,' he said, walking to the door. 'Be ready for ten o'clock if you want to come with me.'

Once alone, she breathed a sigh of relief. For a moment, something in his expression had made her very uncomfortable. He had come so close she could almost have touched the stubble on his cheeks or traced the outline of his mouth and the rugged line of the scar. A shiver rippled the skin on her arms and she wrapped herself more tightly in Christopher's dressing gown. She would have to be very careful where the capitaine was concerned. Despite what Uxeloup Malleval had written, she wasn't sure she could trust him. But who was there to trust here? She was on her own, in a foreign land. France might have been her mother's country, it wasn't hers.

She pushed the empty plate away, glanced at the clock with dismay and sighed. It was only eight o'clock. What would she do for the next two hours while she waited for Saintclair? Outside, what she could see of Paris was shrouded in a murky, dark grey light. Surely there could be no harm in venturing outside for a short while? She could take a stroll in the Luxembourg Gardens and return in good time to meet Saintclair. He would never know she had gone out.

Marie-Ange rushed back to her room to collect her cloak, grey bonnet and gloves. Returning to the lobby wrapped up against the cold, she stepped into the narrow, winding street and took a long breath of fresh air. It was so good to be out at last. The city was busy already despite the early hour and the bitter cold. Shutters were being taken down from shop windows, people queued for bread and pies outside bakeries. In the street, elegant *cabriolets* sped past without a care for pedestrians, and tall, sturdy horses pulled carts laden with wood, casks of ale or fresh produce.

Unfortunately the gates of the Luxembourg were shut. Disappointed, she stood a while on the pavement, reading public notices about forthcoming fairs and auctions that were pinned on the boards outside the gardens. By the time she finished, the gardens were still closed and a flurry of snowflakes drifted from the low clouds. It soon changed into heavy snow. Maybe she should go back…She stepped onto the causeway without looking.

'*Attention*,' the driver of a passing coach shouted as his horses almost knocked her over. She retreated onto the pavement to catch her breath as the carriage stopped a few metres away. A tall, blond man in a grey coat jumped down. She narrowed her eyes.

The man's face was partly hidden by the high collar of his coat but there was something disturbingly familiar about him. Was it his tall figure or his ash blond hair? She remained frozen on the spot, her mouth dry, her heart beating wildly. The man pushed open a wooden door and disappeared inside a building as the carriage drove away.

A few seconds only must have passed, but time seemed to have stopped. That man…she had to catch up with him, see his face. Marie-Ange ran across the street and pushed the door, only to find herself in an empty courtyard. Pausing to inspect her surroundings, she heaved a disappointed sigh. There was no trace of the man. She saw a sign for the concierge lodge and knocked on the door.

'*Qu'est-ce que c'est?*' A grey-haired woman asked as

she came out.

Marie-Ange swallowed hard. 'Good morning, *Madame*,' she said in French. 'A tall, blond gentleman wearing a grey coat came in a few minutes ago. Only, he lost his wallet in the street.'

She waved her father's old wallet in front of the concierge, the one she had used ever since he died.

'Tall and blond you said?'

'Yes, he had very light blond hair.' She held her breath.

'That would be Monsieur Joseph Nallay. He comes to see Monsieur Fouché almost every day. On the third floor.' The woman gestured towards the staircase. 'Turn left on the landing.'

'Monsieur Nallay?' Marie-Ange repeated, disappointed by the concierge's response. Against all logic, she had hoped for another name. 'Who did you say he comes to visit?'

The concierge narrowed her eyes in a suspicious manner. 'Monsieur Fouché, the former Minister of Police. Surely, you know of him?'

'Of course I know of Monsieur Fouché. Who doesn't?' Marie-Ange forced a smile and bade the woman good bye.

She climbed the stairs. Fouché, described in turn as a master of intrigue, a turncoat or a brilliant statesman, was one of France's most infamous politicians. How could she have forgotten his name? She was uncertain how to proceed. Should she knock on the minister's door and invent a story to get in, or wait for the blond man to come down? She heard footsteps ahead and caught a glimpse of elegant black boots and a grey coat. It was him. He glanced at her, nodded and carried on.

'Monsieur, s'il vous plaît!'

He stopped and turned.

Her pulse quickened as she stared into his face, into her beloved Christopher's face. She staggered against the stairwell banister. Her fingers gripped the handrail.

24

'Madame? Are you not well?' He asked in French as he leant towards her. She put her hand on his forearm.

'Christopher, my God, it's really you,' she answered in English, gazing into his eyes, her voice filled with wonder. 'I wasn't sure when I saw you in the street...' She let out a choked cry. 'They said you died at Corunna but I never could believe it. What happened? Why didn't you come home?' The words tumbled out. She wanted to smile but tears started falling down her cheeks instead.

'I found you at last.' She raised her hand to touch his face.

He frowned and pulled back. *'Désolé, Madame, vous faites erreur.'* There was no warmth, no flicker of recognition in his eyes. *'Excusez-moi.'* He started down the stairs.

'No, Christopher, wait! Don't you remember me?' She ran after him. 'It's been six years but surely you cannot have...Please, wait!' Her voice rose to a high pitch.

He turned around and gave her another cold, hostile stare. 'I don't know what or who you are talking about, but I'm afraid you have the wrong man. Now leave me alone. You're making a scene.' This time he spoke in perfect English, without the trace of an accent.

She didn't follow him when he started down the stairs but sat on the stone steps and buried her face in her hands. How could she have been mistaken? Her chest was so tight it felt like her heart was breaking. Maybe it was time she accepted her husband was dead and stopped chasing ghosts.

And yet... It was his face, his eyes, his voice. Heavens, she dreamt about him often enough! He was thinner, his face harder, but then again six years had passed. When she touched his arm a jolt of recognition raced through her, as if her body remembered him. What if he had been injured at Corunna and lost his memory? Those things must happen during battles. She must see him once more and make sure of his identity one way or another.

She wiped her eyes. It was time to return to the inn or she would be late to meet Saintclair. It was snowing harder when she stepped outside. She walked to the end of the street and stared at the crossroads. Where now? *Left, it was left*, she decided, starting down the street. This street was endless. Surely the *Le Faisan Doré* wasn't that far. She must have missed the turn. Had she passed that bakery, that cobblers shop on her way to the Luxembourg Gardens?

She heaved a ragged sigh. She couldn't remember anything! Men and women brushed past her, grey shadows in the snow. The blond man's face—*Christopher's face*—danced in front of her. Her eyes filled with tears again. Everything around her became a blur, she could hardly see the way ahead. She walked faster, her boots slipped on the snow and she fell on the pavement.

'*Attention, ma p'tite dame!*' A passer-by held out his hand to help her back to her feet. She thanked him and asked for directions. She had taken a wrong turn, he said. Shivering in her wet coat, she pulled her collar up against the cold, and retraced her steps.

Church bells chimed eleven when she finally pushed open the door of the *Le Faisan Doré*, limping in her wet boots.

'Where the hell have you been?' Capitaine Saintclair's thunderous voice greeted her.

'S…orry,' she stammered.

His angry expression softened immediately. He took her elbow and led her to the drawing room. 'Here, sit close to the fire. You are frozen to the bones.'

He helped her out of her cloak, then called the landlady and ordered some mulled wine. Marie-Ange's hands were shaking as she brought the cup of hot, spicy wine to her lips.

'What happened?' he asked at last.

'I got lost.' She wouldn't share anything of her encounter with the blond man. After all, she didn't know for sure he was indeed Christopher.

Saintclair frowned. 'Don't disappear like that again. The streets of Paris are never safe for a woman on her own, whatever the time of day.' He paused a moment. 'I think you'd better stay here and keep warm.'

The thought of being confined to her room for the rest of the day was suddenly unbearable.

She jumped to her feet. 'No,' she protested. 'I want to come with you. I only need to change my shoes.'

A carriage took them to the *Faubourg Saint-Honoré*. Saintclair offered his arm to walk along the avenue and pointed out elegant shops and *brasseries*. She couldn't help but stare at passers-by, hoping against all reason she would see the tall, blond man again.

Street stalls sold roasted chestnuts and fried dough sprinkled with sugar. Marie-Ange breathed in their warm, sweet smell and realised she was hungry. As if reading her thoughts, Saintclair turned to her.

'We'll get something to eat soon.' He hesitated and cleared his throat, looking a little embarrassed. 'First, I promised my sister, Lucie, new handkerchiefs from the most fashionable establishment in Paris. Would you be kind enough to help me choose? I don't know the first thing about ladies' fashion.'

So the tough, cynical capitaine cared enough about his sister to venture into a haberdasher and buy handkerchiefs…She repressed a smile.

'It will be my pleasure. How old is she?'

'Seventeen.'

'Tell me about her.'

Saintclair pushed open the door of a large shop and let her go through first. As they walked around well appointed shelves and displays of ribbons, shawls, fabric, buttons and handkerchiefs, he explained that his sister was of delicate

27

health, with dark-hair and blue eyes.

Then he shook his head. 'She spends far too long sitting in the drawing room and reading silly stories.

'Silly stories?' Marie-Ange raised her eyebrows.

'You know, stories about fair ladies and knights who play the harp with a flower between their teeth.'

She laughed. 'You mean love stories. You do not seem to rate romance very high, Capitaine. It is however essential for a successful marriage, as I well know.'

He looked down at her, suddenly serious. 'You talk like a middle-aged matron, yet you cannot have been married very long.'

'Only four months, but they were the most blissful months of my life,' she replied as a dreamy smile stretched her lips. She married Christopher a few weeks before her seventeenth birthday, on an unseasonably warm October day. Her wedding dress was silk. She had tied a long satin ribbon in her braids, which Christopher had loosened patiently that night before laying her in their bed for the first time. She shivered and let out a sigh. Hope blossomed in her chest as she remembered today's encounter and her persistent belief that he was alive.

'Yes, a man must be sensitive to be a good husband,' she whispered, stopping in front of a pile of delicate linens embroidered with lace and tiny rosebuds. 'My husband used to write poems and pick wild flowers for me.'

'Isn't romance for little girls? I thought women wanted men with courage and strength, not milksops.' Saintclair arched his eyebrows.

She looked up at him, her cheeks suddenly very hot. 'A man can be sensitive without being a milksop, Capitaine. Ask anyone who knew my husband and they will tell you how brave, how heroic he was in battle.'

How dare the man make fun of Christopher in this way? Her husband had been worth ten of the capitaine, at least. She pointed to the embroidered handkerchiefs. 'I

28

think Lucie will like those. I should know since we share the same taste in romance—or silly stories, as you put it.'

He didn't answer but picked up the fancy linens and took them to the counter.

'Come,' he said when they walked out of the haberdasher. 'I will treat you to a hot chocolate and a cake at *Café Benoit*.'

The café's windows were all steamed up. Saintclair pushed the door open and Marie-Ange was assailed with warm, rich aromas of freshly ground coffee and hot chocolate. He found a small table in a corner.

'Saintclair, you devil! Where did you disappear to last night?' A voice boomed from the other side of the crowded room.

Saintclair turned and his face relaxed into a smile. 'What are you doing here, Martin? You said you were going back to Lyon this morning.'

A giant of a man approached their table and bowed in front of Marie-Ange.

'Madame, let me introduce Capitaine Martin, a fellow officer from the Second Cuirassier Regiment.' Saintclair announced. 'Martin, this is Madame Norton. I am escorting her to Lyon to meet her relative, Malleval.'

Martin kissed Marie-Ange's hand, his eyes lingering on her. 'Now I understand why Saintclair was in such a hurry to leave last night. So, you are English?'

She freed her hand and smiled. 'Partly. My father was English, my mother was French.'

'You know Malleval, do you not?' Saintclair asked his friend.

'Yes, I do,' Martin replied. 'He fleeced me at cards more than once. I always thought he was a prize cheat, but could never prove it. I heard he got you in trouble, too.'

Martin glanced at Saintclair quizzically, but the capitaine only grunted. A waiter came over and they ordered hot chocolate and cakes.

'Do you mind if I join you?' Martin sat down without waiting for an answer.

The waiter came back with a tray laden with cups, brioches and pastries. As soon as he left, Martin leant over the table. 'Things are moving, my friend. Everybody's talking about it this morning. Fouché is sending his spies down south. So of course, is his old enemy, Talleyrand. Lyon will soon be crawling with agents, all waiting for the same thing.'

He lowered his voice. 'According to my contact at the Ministry of War, many in government are preparing to jump ship. It's a wonder the army hasn't rebelled yet. The King angered everybody by putting officers on half-pay and denying commoners any chance of promotion.'

'I am well aware of the King's actions in that regard,' Saintclair growled.

Martin nodded in sympathy. 'I still can't believe you were passed over for promotion in favour of that weasel, Comte de Mitre. Anyway, *he* will not be facing much resistance in the army. Like I said, everyone is talking about it. *He*'s coming back.'

'Of course, *he*'s coming back!' Saintclair put his cup down. Some chocolate spilled onto the saucer. He took a deep breath. 'They gave *him* a small island and a toy garrison to play with, cut *him* off from his wife and son. And now they're talking about sending *him* to an island in the Atlantic, hundreds of miles from anywhere! *He* has nothing to lose.'

Marie-Ange listened with interest. Whoever were they talking about? She bit into a brioche and drank her hot chocolate while the conversation continued as if she were not present. Suddenly her eyes widened in shock and she sat back on her chair. She knew who Capitaine Saintclair and his friend were referring to. Napoleon, of course! Since his abdication in April of the previous year, he had been in exile on Elba, a tiny island off the coast of

Tuscany.

'I thought Fouché was no longer the Minister for Police,' she interrupted.

Saintclair and his friend turned to her, looking surprised, as if they'd both forgotten about her.

'Joseph Fouché will never give up scheming,' Saintclair said. 'I believe his apartment on *Rue de Condé* is a hot-bed of intrigue. He controls a vast network of spies. Murderers. Traitors. Deserters. You name it.'

She straightened in her chair, stung by his remark. If the man she saw that morning was indeed Christopher, he might be an agent. The concierge said he was a frequent visitor. However, he was bound to have a good reason for working for Fouché. Christopher was nothing like the men Saintclair had just described.

'Some people may be forced to become spies, Capitaine. I believe they play a crucial role in politics.'

Saintclair reclined on his seat and studied her for a few moments. 'Do you have any particular knowledge of the affairs of state, Madame Norton?'

She didn't care much for the patronising tone of voice. 'No, but perhaps you should give spies more credit. They must lead a very awkward existence.'

'I wouldn't waste my pity on Fouché's spies,' Saintclair retorted. 'As I said, they're all rogues and scoundrels.'

'My friends, enough of this depressing talk.' Martin held out his hands. 'Let's go to the opera at the *Théâtre Italien* this evening.'

'I cannot possibly attend the theatre,' Marie-Ange objected.

'Don't worry, I am sure one single outing won't tarnish your impeccable reputation as a war widow,' Saintclair retorted coldly. He turned to his friend. 'Yes, we will come. Could you procure us some tickets?'

How dare he talk to her like that? She was too stunned to find a suitable reply.

'So it's settled.' Martin stood up and clicked his heels together. 'Madame, I shall look forward to seeing you later.'

He turned to Saintclair and winked. 'Don't you dare keep this charming creature to yourself. I know what you're like with ladies. After all, your record for the cuirassiers' aptitude test remains unequalled to this day.'

'Shut up, Martin.' Saintclair sounded annoyed.

Martin only laughed. 'See you tonight,' he reminded him as he left.

'What aptitude test?' Marie-Ange asked.

'It's an old story.' Saintclair stood up and pulled on his coat. 'Shall we go?'

Before he hailed a carriage to drive them back to *Le Faisan Doré*, Marie-Ange placed a hand on his arm. She so wished to return to the spot she had seen the man who resembled Christopher – the man the *concierge* had called Joseph Nallay.

'Could we please stop at the Luxembourg Gardens before we return to the hotel? It will look so pretty in the snow.'

Saintclair agreed. Marie-Ange felt a rush of excitement as the carriage stopped near the garden's black and gold gates. But the Luxembourg was closed. A notice pinned on the gates read that the snow made the lanes too hazardous.

Chapter Three

With dozens of torches burning high on the six columns of its classical façade, the *Théâtre Italien* lit up the night sky. Black cabs and private carriages lined the street. Men in dinner jackets and women adorned with sparkling jewellery and in rustling evening dresses climbed up the stone steps and made their way through the double doors. The air was full of talk about the evening's performance, *L'Amour Fugitif*, with Angelica Catalini, one of Paris' most acclaimed sopranos.

Marie-Ange held on to Capitaine Saintclair's arm as they entered the lobby. She blinked, intimidated by the scintillating lights and the even more scintillating crowd. Saintclair looked around for his friend.

'He's over there.' He gestured towards the back of the hall.

Capitaine Martin stood next to a tall, dark-haired woman. The light from the chandeliers shone on her raven black hair which was pinned in an elaborate chignon, with tight ringlets framing her face. A low-cut crimson silk gown emphasized her statuesque figure, a mink stole snaked around her creamy white shoulders. She was so beautiful, so elegant that Marie-Ange felt an unusual twinge of envy. For a few seconds, she wished she wore a fashionable gown too instead of her plain grey dress. Her fingers smoothed her hair which she wore in the simple style favoured by her mother—two tight braids twisted together and secured with embossed gold combs—the only style her mother claimed could tame their unruly, curly blond hair.

Capitaine Saintclair looked at the woman and cursed under his breath.

'Here you are at last,' Martin said with a happy smile as they approached. 'I managed to get us seats behind the orchestra.'

He turned to his female companion. 'I bumped into Caroline this afternoon and persuaded her to come tonight. Isn't that grand?'

Marie-Ange felt Saintclair's arm stiffen under her hand.

'This is a surprise,' he told the woman coldly. 'I wasn't expecting to see you so soon after you left with de Mitre for Auxerre.'

'I have just come back. Auxerre was boring and de Mitre is so…dull. How that man made Major instead of you, I really don't understand.' The woman's voice was seductively husky and her smouldering gaze darted to Saintclair.

'So this means I'm all yours. Again.' She flicked open a large black and red silk fan decorated with ostrich feathers.

Saintclair didn't reply but turned to Marie-Ange. 'Madame Norton, this is Caroline Dupin, a friend. Caroline, I am escorting Marie-Ange Norton to Lyon.'

The two women nodded politely to each other.

'Shall we go in?' Saintclair asked, taking her arm again to lead the way into the hall.

The opera was a new experience for Marie-Ange. Her only outings these past few years had been the Christmas dance at Wellcombe village hall or the spring fair on the green. There was also the occasional ball marking a betrothal or a wedding at a neighbouring manor house she was required to attend as the representative of the Norton family, but she rarely enjoyed such events. The magnificent *Théâtre Italien* concert hall made her catch her breath with its rows of seats covered with plush red velvet and the private boxes adorned with gold mouldings. Enormous glittering chandeliers hung from a blue and gold painted ceiling. A thick red curtain hid the stage. Musicians tuned their instruments in the orchestra pit. The galleries and private boxes were already filled with spectators and the buzz of conversations, laughter and music was exciting.

'This is wonderful,' she exclaimed, feeling a little guilty for enjoying the experience so much.

Next to her, Saintclair smiled and pointed out a few people in the audience.

'Général Maurice of the Fifth Hussars and over there Général George, from the Eighth Batallion of Infantry.' He turned to the right. 'Le Ministre Charette and his...ahem...lady friend, Mademoiselle Jardin, the actress. And over there, Le Duc de Richelieu, who has, I believe, just returned from Vienna.'

Next to him, Caroline Dupin waved her fan. 'Waiting for the performance is always so tedious,' she said in a bored voice. She leant closer to him. 'By the way, Hugo, I'm going back to Lyon next week. I hope you'll come and visit.'

'Maybe...' He answered, his eyes still scanning the spectators.

Loud taps resounded near the stage area. The audience hushed, the gas lights dimmed and the orchestra played the opening notes of a lively overture. When it was over, the heavy curtain slid open to reveal an elaborate set of painted Italian gardens with a castle in the background.

'It's like a fairytale,' Marie-Ange whispered.

As soon as the performance started, she lost herself in the music, and when Angelica Catalani lamented the loss of her lover, her beautiful voice stirred well-known emotions and tears streamed down her cheeks. She pulled a handkerchief from her reticule to dab her eyes.

'Are you not feeling well?' Saintclair looked concerned.

'I'm fine,' she muttered, embarrassed. 'It's the music.

I've never heard such beautiful music before.'

He arched his eyebrows but thankfully turned his attention back to the stage. At the *entr'acte*, people got out of their seats to make their way to the refreshment halls. Saintclair announced he was going for a cigar at the bar with Martin and asked Caroline to take Marie-Ange upstairs to the ladies' parlour. The woman shrugged and complained that she would much rather have a cigar, too, but she led the way to a gallery on the first floor where waiters rushed around, offering drinks to ladies dressed in a rainbow of colours. Marie-Ange chose a glass of lemonade, Caroline a champagne flute. Looking over Marie-Ange's shoulder, she then waved at someone and walked away, after promising to come back shortly.

The lemonade was too syrupy and did nothing to quench her thirst, so Marie-Ange left her glass on a table and waited patiently for Caroline to return. She soon became aware of a woman staring at her from the other side of the room. Dressed in a dark purple silk gown, the woman's brown hair was lightly streaked with grey and arranged in graceful loops above her ears in the fashion of the day. Perplexed, because she was sure she had never seen her before, Marie-Ange smiled. The woman became very pale and lifted her white-gloved hand to her throat as if she had seen a ghost before rushing across the room towards her.

'I apologise for my bluntness, *Madame*,' she said when she stood in front of her. 'You bear an extraordinary resemblance to someone I used to know, a long time ago, at the Salles Priory. May I ask if you are related to Catherine Beauregard?'

Marie-Ange let out a cry of surprise. 'Catherine Beauregard? Yes, she was my mother.'

The woman leant closer.

'*Mon Dieu!* How extraordinary. I had no idea Catherine married and had a daughter. To tell the truth, she disappeared from Salles in the most distressing circumstances. We were told she had died...' She shook her head and smiled. 'But I am forgetting my manners. My name is Louison George.'

Slightly overwhelmed and her voice hoarse wtih emotion, Marie-Ange introduced herself just as a bell rang the end of the interval. The woman took hold of her hand.

'I am afraid I cannot let you go already, my dear girl. There are so many things I want to ask you. Would you mind very much if we stayed here and talked?'

'Not at all,' Marie-Ange agreed readily. As much as she was enjoying the performance, talking to a friend of her late mother's was an opportunity she could not pass on. 'I would be delighted to talk to you, Madame George. The thing is, I don't know much about my mother's life as a girl in France. I was born in England. It's where I lived all my life, and I have never met any of my mother's French friends or relatives.'

They made their way to the sitting area, quiet now that everybody had returned to the concert hall.

'You said Catherine *was* your mother, am I to understand she passed away?' Louison asked after they sat down.

'Yes, she died of pneumonia when I was five. I was brought up by my father.'

'Poor Catherine, she led such a tragic life.' Louison sighed. 'Tell me, how did she manage to escape to England?'

Marie-Ange shook her head. 'I'm not sure. I was far too young for her to confide in me. I only know she came to Plymouth where she married my father. I was born there in December 1791.'

'December? But...' Louison George frowned and toyed with her pearl necklace.

'Please tell me how you met my mother,' Marie-Ange urged, wondering why the woman looked so uneasy.

Louison shook her head and smiled. 'Of course. I met her at Salles where I was a boarder. Catherine arrived in October 1790. She was very sad, very lonely. Her father was jailed in Beaujeu and her mother appeared to have abandoned her. I was missing my family too, so we became friends. We used to walk in the cloister gardens after our lessons or sew in the evening.' Her eyes clouded over. 'Sometimes, Catherine sang for me. She had such a lovely voice. I remember a particularly poignant song her godfather had taught her—a song about a girl weeping for her dead lover in a dovecote.'

Marie-Ange looked up sharply. She was certain this was the very song her mother sang to send her to sleep when she was little. What a shame she couldn't remember the words.

'We also enjoyed painting,' Louison resumed. 'Catherine was a good artist, much better than I was. She spent hours drawing in her sketch book. She wanted to give it to her father. Unfortunately the poor man was executed in Lyon in January 1791. Catherine was inconsolable when she heard the news.' She sighed. 'Then a couple of weeks later, her aunt, the Abbess, told her that her mother had married Edmond Malleval.' She shuddered. 'She was so angry. She couldn't understand how her mother could marry that man, that monster, especially so soon after her father was killed.' The woman sighed. 'At the time, I too thought the wedding shocking, but as I grew older I understood these were desperate times. Catherine's mother may not have been free in her choices, especially when Edmond Malleval was concerned.'

Marie-Ange's eyes welled up with tears. How her mother had suffered! It was no wonder she never talked about Beauregard and the people she had left behind.

'One day at the end of March, Malleval's soldiers came to Salles and took Catherine away,' Louison carried on.

'The poor girl hardly had time to gather some of her belongings and bid farewell to her aunt before she was bundled into a carriage. That was the last time I saw her. A couple of weeks later we were told she was dead.'

'But that wasn't true! Who told you that?'

'Edmond Malleval himself. He came to the Priory with his men to search through the things Catherine had left behind. He ransacked her room, and the whole Priory, too. I do not know what he was after but he did not find it. He was so angry he had the Abbess arrested and the Priory closed on the spot.'

'And that was in April?' Marie-Ange asked.

Louison George nodded briefly before looking away.

The blood drained from Marie-Ange's face. Now she understood why Louison George looked uneasy. The dates were wrong.

'You look so much like her,' Louison added in a kind voice. 'You have the same smile, the same hair. You even have the same hairstyle. I didn't hesitate when I saw you earlier. I knew you had to be related. So tell me, why are you in France? Are you married? Is your father here with you?'

'Sadly my father died several years ago.' It was hard to keep her voice calm as she answered. 'I did marry but...'

'I have been looking all over for you.' Capitaine Saintclair's booming voice interrupted her.

He stood in front of her, arms crossed on his chest, an angry scowl on his face.

'Why did you not go back to the hall?'

'Is this gentleman your husband?' Louison George gave Saintclair an appraising glance.

'No, Capitaine Saintclair is my escort to Beauregard,' Marie-Ange corrected. 'My husband, Commander Christopher Norton, is...was lost at sea.'

'Pleased to meet you, Capitaine.' Louison extended her hand for Saintclair to kiss. 'I am sorry to have kept Marie-

39

Ange from the opera, and from you, but we were busy talking about the past. You see, we have just established that I was a friend of her mother's.'

The French officer looked stunned. 'Really?'

'Is that not astonishing? Catherine Beauregard and I attended the Priory school at Salles together for a few months.' Louison turned to Marie-Ange in earnest. 'You said you were on your way to Beauregard. There is someone you must see when you get there. Your great-aunt, Hermine Marzac, your grandfather's sister. She came back from exile in Switzerland a few years ago.' She lowered her voice. 'She might be able to tell you more about your mother and what happened to her.'

The two women looked at each other, a current of understanding passing between them. Marie-Ange nodded. Louison was right. Her aunt might shed some light on the events of that year.

'There is something else,' Louison added in a hushed voice, pressing Marie-Ange's hand with hers. 'Beware of Uxeloup Malleval. He has a fearsome reputation.'

After taking leave of Louison, Capitaine Saintclair led the way back to the main hall for the end of the performance, but this time Marie-Ange was far too preoccupied to enjoy the music. There were things she needed to think about, alone. After the play, Martin and Caroline asked if she and the capitaine wished to join them for a late supper in a nearby *brasserie*. Saintclair declined. They would be leaving at dawn the following morning and needed a rest.

'You never let an early start get in the way of a good evening in the past,' Caroline sneered. 'Perhaps you're afraid Madame Norton will disapprove of the way we enjoy ourselves, here in Paris?' She flicked her fan open, waved it around her face.

'Of course not. I'm tired, that's all,' Saintclair replied before hailing a black cab.

They were both silent on the way back to *Le Faisan Doré*.

'Have you heard of the Salles Priory?' Marie-Ange asked at last. 'Apparently the Abbess there was a member of my family.'

Saintclair nodded. 'It was an exclusive boarding school for girls from the aristocracy. You may not realise this, Madame Norton, but before the revolution your mother's family—the Beauregards—were the wealthiest landowners in the whole of the Beaujolais. Their estates and properties were so vast they covered most of the land between Lyon and Chalons.' He let out a derisive laugh. 'In those days, I wouldn't have been allowed to ride in the same carriage as you. I would have been thrown out, beaten like a dog and left for dead in the gutter just for having the audacity to look at you.' There was bitterness in his tone.

'Things are different now, are they not?' she remarked.

'Not for much longer if our new king has his way,' he replied, sombrely.

They didn't talk again until they arrived back at *Le Faisan Doré*. He held her hand to assist her from the carriage and they faced each other a few seconds.

'Thank you for tonight,' she said at last. 'I didn't think I would, but I enjoyed the opera.' More importantly, she had found out things about her mother's past she never suspected.

He nodded and held the door open for her. 'It was my pleasure.'

'Well, good night.' Marie-Ange brushed past him as they walked into the inn. A porter was on duty in the hall but otherwise the inn was quiet. The man locked the front door behind them.

'You're the last guests to come back,' he said, pulling a bar over the door.

'I want a drink,' Saintclair decreed as he strode into the deserted drinking parlour.

41

The man let out a sigh and followed him without a word. It was wise of him, Marie-Ange thought. One look at the Cuirassier's face was enough to see that it would be pointless, dangerous even, to argue that the bar was closed.

Once in her room, Marie-Ange lit the fire and sat down, pensive as her gaze followed the flames rising in the fireplace. The dates were wrong. She had always assumed her mother had gone to England immediately after Aline's marriage to Edmond Malleval in mid-January of 1791, met her father and got married more or less straight away. Louison George revealed tonight that Catherine only escaped Edmond Malleval in April. It would have taken her several weeks to travel to England. Whoever helped her escape would have chosen roundabout routes to avoid being caught by Malleval's men or other police and army personnel looking to apprehend fleeing aristocrats.

Marie-Ange was born on the first of December that same year. So unless William Jones met her mother in France, he couldn't be her father. He had said many times he had never set foot in France, which meant Catherine was already pregnant when she arrived in England. Who then was Marie-Ange's father?

Chapter Four

They left Paris at daybreak. As soon as he climbed into the carriage, Saintclair stretched his legs, pulled his collar up, crossed his arms on his chest and fell asleep. The snow had almost completely melted and the streets were covered with brown slush and muddy puddles into which the horses' hooves and the carriage wheels splashed.

Marie-Ange stared out of the window. The grey Paris suburbs gave way to villages, and then to a very dull, flat and colourless countryside, or perhaps it just looked like that because she was tired. She had spent half the night agonising about Louison George's revelations and playing in her mind images of her childhood and of her father—the man she still thought of as her father, William Jones. Quiet and kind, if a little distant, he was a lawyer and always seemed busy at his Plymouth practice, in his study, or again in the garden where he lovingly tended his roses. The few memories she had of her parents together were of walks on the sea front, with them linking arms and smiling as she ran ahead; or of quiet Sundays afternoons when her father read to her in the drawing room while her mother worked at her embroidery. After her mother's death, William Jones had become even more quiet, even more distant. He had however never given her any cause to suspect that she wasn't his daughter. Yet he must have known. It explained why he was always so reluctant to talk about her mother's past and her family.

Her thoughts turned to Christopher. Would she see him—or the man called Nallay—again soon? The more she thought about it, the more she recalled his face, the grey eyes and the unusual colour of his hair, the less doubts there were in her heart. Nalley was her husband. Something terrible must have happened to him, for it seemed he had lost his memory. But how would she manage to find him? How did one trace a spy?

With a sigh, she leant against the padded seat and closed her eyes. The next thing she knew, her cheek rested against something warm and strong. Mixed scents of sandalwood shaving soap and tobacco tickled her nose. Still half asleep, she patted tentatively at the coarse fabric of a jacket. Her fingers touched a metal button, then another. Goodness! That thumping sound wasn't the horses' galloping hooves, but a heartbeat! She opened her eyes. And pulled out of Saintclair's arms.

'Capitaine, how could you?' she gasped. Her cheeks burning, she slid to the far end of the seat.

He shrugged. 'Next time, I'll let you fall off the seat if that's what you want.'

She picked her grey bonnet from the floor and put it back on her dishevelled hair.

'No, Capitaine, next time you will wake me up,' she corrected haughtily, gripping the side of the seat as the carriage turned yet another bend on the bumpy road.

Hugo had rather enjoyed holding the young woman against him while she slept, her fingers splayed on his chest, her head resting snugly in the hollow of his shoulder and her curly hair caressing his face. He had never seen a woman's hair so golden, so thick. He longed to unpin it, watch it fall on her shoulders and comb it with his fingers. His throat tightened and he swallowed hard. There were other things he longed to do, too…The woman was a mass of contradictions, a fascinating, tempting puzzle. Too tempting.

He shook his head. From now on, he would keep away from her. It was his responsibility to deliver her safe and sound to Malleval. It was in his interest too, and he'd better not forget it or the consequences for his family would be dire.

He would stop at the regimental barracks at Fontainebleau, pick up a horse and ride to Beauregard. They would both breathe more easily if they weren't closeted together in that carriage.

They stopped at a roadside inn to have lunch and rest the horses. He discussed details of the itinerary with the driver, leaving Marie-Ange alone to eat a bowl of soup and drink coffee in the dining room. Back on the bumpy road, he spread the map on his knees and tried to plan the route to Beauregard but the young woman was in a talkative mood. Her incessant chatter made it impossible for him to keep to his resolution and ignore her.

'Where are we stopping for the night?'

'Sens.'

'Is it a large town?'

'Not really,' he replied, not even bothering to lift his eyes from the map. Surely she would take the hint and stop talking.

She looked through the window. 'This looks like winegrowing country. Look. Another beautiful chateau! Do they produce champagne around here?'

He nodded. 'Some chateaux do.'

'I have only had champagne twice before,' she remarked, pulling a face. 'And I did not like it at all.'

This time he smiled. 'Then it wasn't real champagne. Malleval has a well appointed cellar at Beauregard. I am sure he shall be pleased to do the honours.' Hugo knew all about the wine in that cellar. It was what got him in trouble in the first place.

She was looking out of the window again. He glanced at her and held his breath, struck by the wonder and innocence in her eyes.

'Now, that's the most magnificent chateau I have ever

seen,' she whispered.

'Fontainebleau,' he announced as the carriage drove into the courtyard of army barracks. 'That's where we're stopping.'

'Why?'

He let out a sigh. 'I am picking up a horse. I'll ride for the rest of the journey.'

'Oh…' She turned away but not before he saw the look of relief on her face.

The carriage stopped and he jumped down.

Marie-Ange watched him talk and joke with his fellow cuirassiers officers and the stable lads who pulled several horses from their box to parade in front of him. Saintclair patted the animals' sides, looked at their hooves, commented on their shiny coats and well brushed manes. Fifteen minutes later he pointed to a huge charger, black like a moonless night, and highly spirited judging by the way it bucked and stomped on the cobbles. Unconcerned, Saintclair stroked its neck and kept on talking as he saddled it. Then he swung up on it in a swift, fluid movement and they set off on the road to Sens.

It was night when they reached the large, comfortable inn on the main square where they would spend the night.

'Tomorrow we'll travel through the forest,' Saintclair said when they parted for the night. He warned her of the dangers ahead. Wolves, boars, and robbers. She wasn't overly anxious though. He would protect them. He was a cuirassier, a trained killer, and he carried a pistol tucked in his belt, under his riding coat, she had seen it.

They entered the deep, dark Burgundy forest the following afternoon. The ground was frozen, the trees fluffy with silver frost. Despite the extra blanket the coach driver provided which she had wrapped around her shoulders, Marie-Ange couldn't stop shivering. Her feet were like blocks of ice and she had to keep rubbing her gloved hands together to warm them. The horses slowed to a walking pace as the road became a bumpy track and the forest closed in on them.

Daylight was fading when they arrived in a hamlet and stopped in front of a small tavern with a half-timbered black and white façade. The driver opened the door, helped Marie-Ange climb out, and carried her bag inside where they found Saintclair leaning over the counter, arguing with the innkeeper.

'My apologies, Capitaine, I only have the one room,' the innkeeper said, a contrite expression on his face. 'And it won't be available for long. A company of dragoons is heading this way. There must be trouble brewing down south, we already had two infantry battalions stopping by this week. Do you want the room or not?'

'I suppose so,' Saintclair grumbled. He took his purse out and gave the man a few silver coins. 'We require supper too, for the lady, the coach driver, and myself. And mulled wine in the room straight away.'

Marie-Ange stood in the middle of the bedroom Saintclair escorted her to. Surely she had misunderstood. He wasn't planning to share a bedroom with her, was he? While he busied himself lighting a fire, she looked around with dismay, pulling a face at the two battered armchairs, the bed piled high with quilts and blankets and the rickety washstand with its chipped bowl.

'Don't look so disgusted, it's not that bad,' Saintclair remarked, a wide grin on his face. 'At least we have a room. The coachman has to sleep in the stables with the horses.'

'What about you?' she blurted out. 'Could you not...?'

'What? Sleep in the stables, too? I suppose I could but I don't want to.' He narrowed his eyes and paused. 'I'll manage very well with these two armchairs, unless you would rather share the bed. It would be warmer and

47

certainly a lot more pleasant for both of us.'

His audacity left her speechless. His words about women purring like kittens in his arms echoed in her mind, and she didn't need to look at her reflection in the mirror to guess that her face and throat had turned crimson. She took a deep breath.

'A gentleman would never place a woman in this situation, even less so make this kind of salacious comments, Capitaine,' she said when she trusted her voice not to shake.

He stepped forward, forcing her to tilt her head all the way up to look at him. She didn't step back. He wasn't going to intimidate her so easily. When he was only a few paces away, he stared into her eyes.

'I never said I was a gentleman, Madame,' he said, his voice almost too calm.

'Very well, you can have the room to yourself. I will sleep quite comfortably in the lounge downstairs.' She crossed her arms on her chest.

He took another step towards her. 'I don't think so. Did you not hear what the innkeeper said? He is expecting a company of dragoons tonight. You will stay where I can keep an eye on you, is that clear?' His voice had a steely edge to it that brooked no disagreement.

He seemed about to add something when there was a knock on the door and a servant boy entered carrying a tray with pitchers of mulled wine.

'Good lad. I'll take that.' Saintclair placed the tray on the dressing table and gave the boy a coin.

'You should drink while it is hot,' he said, handing a pitcher to Marie-Ange.

Their fingers brushed when she took hold of it. She jerked back and tightened her lips. Sainclair shrugged, turned to the fireplace and downed his steaming hot drink in a few gulps. He then declared he had to see to his horse.

'I will meet you in the dining room in an hour,' he said

before walking out.

Heaving a sigh of relief now she was alone, she sat down near the fireplace and sipped the mulled wine. How was she going to bear the next few days travelling with such a brute? And how was she going to survive a night in the same room? She finished her drink and got up to unpack some of her clothes before going downstairs to ask the innkeeper for some hot water to be brought up to the room. After a quick toilette, she changed into a dark green dress and made her way down to the dining room, her freshly brushed hair tied loosely at the nape of her neck.

The company of dragoons had arrived. The dining room was packed with soldiers in grey and blue uniforms, eating, drinking, and getting more rowdy by the second. A few were in shirt sleeves, having thrown their coats on the floor. Others were already slumped in a drunken stupor against the walls. Saintclair waved at her from a table at the back. The dragoons stared as Marie-Ange walked across. Whistles and crude comments filled the air.

Saintclair stood up at once, his eyes cold and his face set in stone as he surveyed the room. 'Behave, dragoons, and do your regiment proud,' he said in a strong voice. Although he wasn't wearing his uniform, his air of command quelled the situation. The men muttered apologies and went back to their pitchers of wine and ale. Saintclair pulled out a chair for Marie-Ange.

'Let us get this meal over with quickly,' he said as a servant brought bowls of soup, ham, and thick slices of bread.

He glanced around the room with a preoccupied air. 'They are from the Fourth Regiment of Dragoons. Their major and half the company are stopping at a village nearby, leaving only a handful of low-ranking officers in charge here, and I'll be damned if I know where they are right now, probably dealing with supplies.' He shook his head, disgusted. 'Look at them! They're a disgrace. I wouldn't tolerate such behaviour from my men.'

Night had fallen and camp fires could be seen through the inn's small, dirty windows. There were tents, horses, men all over the courtyard, and probably all over the village, too.

'Do you understand now why you will not be sleeping in the lounge tonight, Madame?' he asked, a mocking grin on his face.

'Yes.' She sighed.

They finished their meal in silence and Saintclair escorted her to the bottom of the stairs.

'I will come up shortly. In the meantime, bar the door.'

Back upstairs, she stood in the room, wondering whether to undress or sleep fully clothed. Having decided that the thick quilts and blankets piled on top of the bed would offer enough privacy, she stripped out of her dress, stockings and underwear, and slipped her white nightdress on. She was tightening the belt of Christopher's faded blue dressing gown around her waist when Saintclair called from behind the door. There was a flicker of surprise in his eyes when he saw her nightclothes and she wondered if she had done the right thing. He dropped the pillow and blankets he was carrying on the floor.

Unsure of what to do next, she sat in the armchair and tucked her feet under her. Saintclair sat in the chair opposite. They stared into the fire without talking for a while. The noise of the soldiers' raucous laughter downstairs and in the camp outside echoed into the night.

'I fear it's going to be a long night,' he said, breaking the silence.

She bit her lower lip. There was much she wanted to ask him about Uxeloup Malleval and his father, but she wasn't quite sure how to start, especially after their unpleasant altercation earlier on.

'It was a stroke of luck to meet Madame George the other night at the opera and to hear her stories about

Edmond Malleval,' she said at last. 'He sounds like a frightful man.'

Saintclair nodded without looking her way.

'You are correct. He wasn't mourned by many when he passed away a few months ago. In fact, he was known as 'The Butcher of Lyon' and was, together with his two associates, Fouché and Collot d'Herbois, one of the most blood-thirsty and fanatical men the Revolution ever produced. Not surprising really, considering where he was from.'

'Where was that?'

'A village in the Pilat, a god-forsaken place to the south-west of Lyon, with mountains and gorges, deep forests and torrents gushing down rocky slopes. The people who live there are as harsh and unforgiving as their land. The village he came from is actually called Malleval.'

'It is a rather sinister name, is it not?'

He nodded again. 'It means 'Bad Valley'. It was for centuries the lair of brigands who rampaged through the whole region.'

He hesitated. 'Actually, I might as well tell you since you'll only hear it from somebody else. These brigands were led by the Malleval family. That's how they made their fortune, from robbing and killing.'

'Really? Then how did Edmond become such a prominent statesman during the Revolution?' Her voice was barely a whisper, her fingers tightly crossed in her lap.

'The Revolution gave opportunities to all kinds of fanatics, rogues and gold-diggers to rise to the top. Edmond Malleval was one of them. Not only did he achieve a position of power within the system but he also made his fortune by buying cheap church and *émigré* estates. And of course, he married your grandmother. When Lyon rebelled against the revolution in July 1793, he led the repression against the insurgents. Thousands were massacred. My parents sent me to an aunt in the country at the time but they later told me about some of the atrocities he ordered. Women, men, and children chained up before being shot, the guillotine working day and night on the *Place des Terreaux*. At one point, both Lyon's rivers ran red with blood.'

She turned to him. 'My God!'

'After several weeks, Malleval, Fouché and Collot d'Herbois actually signed a decree stating that Lyon was no more. They had managed to destroy the city which dared stand against them.'

'Madame George said he took my mother away by force from the Priory, and later he claimed she was dead.'

And yet her grandmother married him...Why?

'What is Uxeloup like?' she asked.

He sighed, raked his dark hair with his fingers.

'He isn't in the least like his father, if that's what you're worried about. He is far too self-absorbed and too concerned with having a good time. But for all his faults, he is a good fighter, a great Hussar.' He smiled encouragingly.

'What can you tell me about Fouché?'

He sat back in the armchair and studied her with half-closed eyes.

'I am starting to wonder why you are taking such an interest in our former Minister of Police, Madame. Are you thinking of becoming one of his spies?'

She let out an impatient sigh.

'Of course not. You said he had been an associate of Edmond Malleval. Does Uxeloup know him well, too?'

He nodded. 'I believe they are close, although I really cannot understand why any man would wish to call that snake his friend. You will be able to make your own mind up about Fouché very soon. He is attending a ball on Saturday night in Lyon where Uxeloup is invited, so if we make it to Beauregard by Thursday as planned, you will meet him there.'

Her heart made a leap. 'I will? That would be wonderful. We simply must be there on time.'

'Why do you want to meet Fouché so badly?' he asked, frowning with suspicion.

She ignored his question and jumped to her feet. 'I wish you good night, Capitaine.'

He stood up too and pointed to the dressing gown. 'Isn't that a little too big for you?'

She tilted her chin. 'It was my husband's. I always wear it in the evenings. It reminds me of him.'

'Ah. I see.'

He turned away, grabbed the pillow and the blankets and made a makeshift bed on the two armchairs. She slid into the cold, stiff and scratchy bedcovers, pulled the quilted counterpanes up to her neck and curled into a ball to keep warm. She couldn't stop thinking about what Saintclair had said. She would meet Fouché soon, and perhaps have the chance to ask him about Joseph Nallay. Even better, if the former minister of police travelled with his agents, she might even see him. This time she would establish the man's identity for sure. And if as she suspected he was indeed Christopher, she would take him back to Norton Place, where he belonged. She fell asleep, a smile on her lips and her heart filled with hope.

It was only dawn, but already raucous voices shouted orders outside, dogs barked, horses stomped and neighed in the courtyard. The dragoons were getting ready to leave. Marie-Ange sat up and yawned. Capitaine Saintclair was fast asleep, stripped down to his shirt and sitting at an awkward angle in the armchair. The blankets had fallen off in a heap on the floor.

Reluctantly Marie-Ange had to admit she was glad he hadn't left her alone in the room. It had been a noisy and troubled night, especially when a whole gang of dragoons, fired up by too much liquor, had come pounding on the door in the early hours. They hadn't known Saintclair was in the room. It had only taken him a minute to send them all back downstairs but she dreaded to think what might have happened had she been on her own.

Barefoot and in her white nightdress, her breath steaming in front of her in the freezing cold room, she tiptoed to the fireplace. She placed a handful of twigs and a couple of logs onto the grate and looked around for a box of matches. There was none. She didn't want to go down and ask the innkeeper for a light, not when there were still so many soldiers around. Then she remembered Saintclair had taken a box of matches from his coat pocket the previous evening.

She picked up the coat and tentatively slipped her hand in one of the pockets. Her fingers touched something cold and narrow, probably a folding knife, and a hard leather box, for cartridges or gunpowder. She tried another other pocket and this time felt a soft tobacco pouch and a box that made a rattling sound when she shook it. There were the matches. A piece of paper fell on the floor as she pulled the box out of the pocket. It looked like a letter. The first lines caught her eye as she recognised Uxeloup Malleval's handwriting. Curious, she raised the paper to the window to read.

'This is to certify that your debt of honour will be cancelled as soon as you have delivered Madame Norton at Beauregard. Should you fail to do so, I will call for the immediate transfer of the deeds of your St Genis house in repayment of your gambling debt, unless, that is, you can repay the five thousand Francs you owe me. UM.'

Thoughtful, she folded the note and placed it back into Saintclair's pocket.

So there was the real reason behind his trip to escort her from Devon to Malleval. He had claimed he was bored and had taken the assignment as a favour to a friend. The truth was he was indebted to Malleval. She lit the fire and stood a while in front of the flames, rubbing her hands together to warm them and pondering the new information.

Uxeloup Malleval was prepared to give up a lot of money, or the deeds of a house he had won at cards, in exchange for her presence at Beauregard, ostensively to make sure she received her inheritance. It appeared most generous of him. It didn't however tally with what she knew of him and of his father. A noise made her spin round. Saintclair was awake and looking at her.

'Good morning, Madame,' he said, his eyes skimming over her body. A slow, seductive smile appeared on his lips. 'There's nothing like a beautiful woman in her nightshirt before breakfast to put me in a good mood.'

He stood up and towered over her. The room felt suddenly very small.

'G-g-good morning,' she stammered, crossing her arms over her chest. She couldn't get Christopher's dressing gown to cover herself with because Saintclair stood between her and the bed. The fireplace behind her didn't allow the possibility of stepping back either.

Saintclair lifted a hand and gently brushed a curl off her forehead. Her breath caught in her throat. His touch burned her skin and sent shivers over her at the same time.

'Whatever are you doing, Capitaine? You forget your place,' she snapped, shocked as much by his gesture as by the way her body had responded.

'And where would that be, Madame? Of course, I forgot. The stables.' He shot her an amused glance. 'Don't worry, I'm going,' he added before she could answer. He rubbed his chin. 'I need a wash and a shave. I'll ask the landlord to have a pail of hot water brought up to you at once.'

Grabbing his boots in one hand, he unbarred the door and went out.

She stood for a moment in the middle of the room,

annoyed with the man and with her reaction to him. Around him she sounded snooty and disagreeable when she had never paid much attention to the issues of class or status. Heavens, how could she ever think she was superior to him, or to anyone else, just because her mother was a Beauregard and her husband a member of the English gentry? She lived in a run-down manor house and the only reason she was travelling across France was to collect an inheritance to enable her to fix a leaky roof.

She didn't feel superior to Saintclair at all, but it was true she didn't like him and despised his manners. However she would have to put up with him until they reached Beauregard. After that, she did not plan to ever lay eyes on the man again.

A servant girl brought the promised bucket of warm water. Although there wasn't much time to get ready Marie-Ange had a wash and got dressed. As an afterthought she pulled Christopher's dagger out of her travelling bag and slid it inside one of her boots.

When Saintclair came back, he was clean-shaven, his dark hair damp and combed back. He turned away and proceeded to peel off his shirt. Although she carried on with her packing, she couldn't help stealing a glance towards him. Her heart skipped a beat and she stifled a gasp with her hand. His broad back and powerful shoulders were criss-crossed with scars. A lifetime on the battlefields had certainly left marks on his body—on his heart and soul too, she would wager.

He pulled a fresh shirt out of his travel bag and put it on.

'I hope you're ready to face a few excitable dragoons downstairs,' he remarked as he turned to her after tucking his shirt into his breeches. 'They're so loud I gather some have already supped a cask of ale for breakfast.'

She sat on the bed and let out a sigh, realising she had been holding her breath whilst staring at him.

'Still, it was fortunate you were here last night,' she said, aware of sounding a little breathless. 'I…I am grateful.'

'That's part of my job,' he replied matter-of-factly.

Her cheeks felt too warm and her hand shook when she picked up her hairbrush and brushed her curls in fast, vigorous strokes. Watching him get dressed had given her a tight, uncomfortable feeling in the pit of her stomach. She platted her hair and tied a green ribbon at the tip.

'I had a word with the dragoons' officers in charge,' he said. 'They are en route to Lyon. There'll be no room left in the barracks by the time I get there.'

She looked at him. 'You live in barracks in Lyon? What about your family?'

'They live in my house in St Genis, a small village a few leagues to the south.'

The house he had lost at cards to Malleval.

'Lucie's physician recommended a change of air for her health, so I…ahem…acquired the house for her and my parents.' He put his jacket on. 'Ready?'

They went down to the dining room which by then was almost empty. After a quick breakfast of hot porridge and coffee, it was time to set off in the cold, grey morning on the road to Dijon.

They made good time, blessed with a mostly empty road all day, stopping only a couple of times to rest the horses and eat. When daylight started to fade, Marie-Ange reclined on the seat of the carriage, closed her eyes and started to doze off as she listened to the eerie hooting of owls in the forest. The drumming of horses' hooves on the path and men shouting close by brought her upright. The coach jerked to a stop and she was thrown onto the floor.

Chapter Five

'Nobody moves or I shoot!'

Angry shouts were followed by gunshots and sounds of a struggle.

'Damn the bastard! Hold him down and knock him out. I don't want him shooting any more of us. And get that bloody coach driver on the ground right now,' someone yelled.

They were being attacked. Marie-Ange felt for the knife she had slipped inside her boot earlier but the door of the carriage flew open before she could pull it out.

'What have we got here?'

A man wearing a dirty brown overcoat, his face partly obscured by a black large-rimmed hat leant forward, grabbed her arm, yanked her from the carriage and threw her onto the frozen ground. She cried out in pain, and panic took her breath away as she took in the scene around her. Three men lay dead on the ground, probably shot by Saintclair before he was disarmed, a couple of highwaymen stood near the coach driver who lay in a puddle of partly frozen mud, another two held Saintclair down. The cuirassier struggled but the two men kicked him until he slumped on the ground with a groan of pain.

What could she do? Her dagger was in her boot, out of reach for now. Her heart beat so hard it hurt and she didn't think she was breathing anymore. The man with the black hat pulled her to her feet, put his finger under her chin, and raised her head sharply.

'Pretty…But she sure don't look rich.' He opened up her cloak to reveal her plain green dress, pulled her hands in front of her and clucked his tongue. She wore no jewellery, only her wedding band. He turned to his acolytes and laughed. 'Too bad! I'll have to take payment in kind.'

Saintclair fought to break free again. This time the men kicked him so hard he stopped moving altogether.

'Don't damage her too much,' one of them called. 'Save some for the rest of us.'

The highwayman grinned, uncovering yellow stumps of teeth. He pushed Marie-Ange inside the coach, scrambled in beside her, and slammed the door shut behind him. She quailed away from him against the squabs of the carriage.

'Just you and me, *ma belle*,' he grunted, his eyes glinting with lust. He unbuckled his pistol belt and threw it down before giving her a hard shove.

She tried to kick him and push him away, but it was to no avail. He ripped the cloak off her shoulders, pinning her to the seat and placed his forearm across her throat. She could hardly breathe, let alone fight him off. She stopped struggling as he proceeded to fumble with her skirts and petticoats. Her only hope was to get the dagger out before he could molest her. Lulled by her apparent consent the man removed his forearm from her throat. She drew in a deep breath into her starved lungs, forced a smile, and slowly pulled her knees up towards her chest, affording him a good view of her drawers and stockings. If she distracted him she might be able to slide her hand into her boot and get the knife.

Her ploy seemed to work. The man opened his eyes wide and started panting as he thrust one hand under her skirt and groped her roughly between the legs. Fumbling with the laces on his breeches, he then climbed on top of her, inserted a knee between her thighs, and forced them wider apart. She must be quick. The men would kill her, together with Saintclair and the driver, once they had finished with her.

She forced a smiled and, playful, pushed the man's hat off with one hand. It took all her willpower not to retch when she fondled his thick neck and greasy hair whilst sliding her other hand down his body. Cautious, she moved her fingers down her leg towards her boot.

'You're a vixen, woman.' The man's words were slurred, his breathing short and raspy. He groaned when he finally managed to undo the last of his ties. The feel of his hot, bulging flesh throbbing against her bare thigh gave her heart a jolt. She would not let *that* happen to her. It was now or never.

She managed to pull the dagger from her boot and bring it up by her side. In a swift movement, she held the tip against his throat.

'Move off me,' she said, her voice barely a whisper and her hand shaking so badly she feared she would drop the dagger.

He became very still.

'What the hell?' He growled, his eyes focussed on her face.

She tightened her grip on the handle. 'I mean it. Get up, slowly.'

She would get hold of the guns he had discarded in his haste. And after that…she didn't know, she hadn't thought that far ahead.

His lips twisted into a grimace. 'Oh no, *ma belle*, I don't think so.'

Everything then happened too fast. He grabbed hold of her wrist and tried to prise the dagger off her fingers. The blade sliced through the palm of his hand. He cried out, pushed her off the seat. Her back slammed against the floor and he fell on top of her.

The dagger made a slurping sound as it went deep into his chest. His eyes opened wide in shock, blood squirted out of the wound, and he shuddered violently. With a whimper she pushed him off her, pulled her skirts down and sat up. She couldn't stop shaking as she wiped the blood off her hand on her dress, again and again. A sickening, metallic smell filled her nostrils. Her head spun, her chest heaved with fast, shallow breaths and bile rose in her throat.

But now wasn't the time to be sick or faint. The others were outside and she had to help Saintclair. She glanced around to locate the man's weapon belt, pulled his two pistols out of the holsters and extracted a couple of cartridges from his leather pouch before proceeding to arm the pistols.

Her hands still trembled but she worked fast, like Robert had shown her. When the pistols were loaded, she said a silent thank you for the shooting lessons he had given her the previous summer on the moors near Norton Place, took a deep breath, and kicked the door open.

As she jumped down, a pistol in each hand, the highwaymen spun towards her, wide-eyed and open-mouthed. She aimed at the two holding Saintclair and shot them straight through the chest. Saintclair immediately scrambled to his feet and retrieved a pistol from the ground. He checked the priming and aimed at the remaining two highwaymen.

'Come here, you two, slowly,' he ordered coldly. 'Throw your weapons on the ground and kneel down.'

The men looked at each other and shrugged before stepping forward. They placed the firearms on the ground and knelt down.

'Now, put your hands behind your head.'

They did as they were told.

'What now, Capitaine?' The coach driver enquired.

'Get something to bind them with,' Saintclair instructed. The driver searched the box next to the driver's seat, produced some rope, and proceeded to bind the brigands' hands and feet.

'Make sure it's tight. We're not taking them with us to

Dijon, they'll only slow us down. We'll leave them here for the gendarmes to find tomorrow.'

He walked past Marie-Ange, who hadn't moved since she shot the highwaymen, peered inside the carriage and cursed.

'Shame, I wanted to kill the bastard myself,' he said. He pulled the lifeless body out. It fell on the ground with a heavy thud, the carved bone hilt of Christopher's dagger sticking out of his chest.

'How the hell did you manage that?' he asked, turning to her. 'You saved us all.'

She still didn't speak but stood shivering and staring at the dead man, the pistols gripped tightly in her hands.

'If I'm not mistaken, this is the second time I owe you my life,' he added. 'I'm beginning to think the sailors were right when they said you were an angel.'

'How can you call me an angel?' she said as tears pricked her eyes and slid down her face. 'I have just killed three men.'

Saintclair frowned. He retrieved her cloak from the carriage and placed it onto her shoulders before gently easing her grip around the pistols and taking them from her. He slid them into his belt and started to turn away to deal with the dead bodies when a whimper escaped from her lips, then another, and another.

She was in his arms before she realised it, her trembling body pressed close to his own.

'It made such a horrible noise. I didn't want to kill him, but he wouldn't do as I said. He wanted to…he was going to…' She hiccupped as more tears streamed down her face.

'And the other two, I had no choice, you know that, don't you? I'm not a murderess.'

He held her more tightly and rested his chin on the top of her head. 'You were very brave. You did what you had to. They would have killed us all.'

His arms were around her, warm and strong. She buried her head against his chest and for a few moments all she heard were his heartbeat and his breathing. He rubbed her back, his touch leaving a slow, burning trail along her spine. Then he pulled away and looked down, his blue eyes overly bright as they searched her face.

'We need to set off now. Dijon is still a good distance away. Will you be all right?'

She sniffed, wiped her wet cheeks with her hands. 'Where is my dagger?'

'Here.' He stepped aside, pulled the knife from the dead highwayman's chest and wiped it on the man's coat before handing it to her.

She slid the knife into her boot without a word.

'Well done, Madame,' the coach driver called to her, a beaming smile on his face as she climbed into the carriage. Turning to Saintclair he added, 'Such a small woman, who would have thought she had it in her to dispatch three men to the devil?'

Saintclair didn't reply. He jumped on his horse and set off at the front.

'You can't leave us here all night,' the brigands protested. 'There are wolves in the forest. And bears.'

'Do not fear. They won't come near you. You stink too much.' The coach driver laughed and whipped the horses into a trot.

They reached Dijon two hours later. Immediately after checking in at an inn on the market square, Saintclair ordered a stable lad to fetch the gendarmes.

'We might as well get comfortable and order some food while we're waiting.' He took her arm to lead her to the lounge.

'You're hurt,' Marie-Ange said when she noticed the nasty bruise on his cheekbone. His posture was a little stiff too, which wasn't surprising considering the beating he had endured at the hands of the brigands.

He shrugged and pulled a chair out for her to sit on.

It wasn't long before a duty officer reported to the inn. Saintclair gave him a succinct account of the attack in the forest. The gendarme then turned to Marie-Ange for her version of events.

'The Capitaine said you killed one man with a knife and two others with a pistol, is this correct?' He sounded sceptical.

Silently she nodded and closed her eyes. The sound the knife had made when she pushed it into the highwayman's flesh, the warm, viscous feel of his blood on her hand and the startled expression in the eyes of his accomplices as she shot them would never leave her.

'Can I see your knife?' The gendarme enquired.

She bent down, lifted her skirt above the ankle and removed the dagger from her boot. She handed it to the policeman without a word.

'That is a rather strange looking knife,' the gendarme said as he returned the dagger a moment later.

'It was my husband's. He brought it back from the West Indies.'

'The West Indies? That explains it…You were very brave Madame.' He smiled and added before taking his leave, 'I will dispatch a patrol to the forest at first light but with luck, the brigands will have frozen to death. Thanks to you, they won't terrorize innocent travellers any longer.'

A servant girl appeared with some ale and two plates piled high with beef stew and vegetables. Marie-Ange protested that she wasn't hungry.

'You must eat,' Saintclair objected.

'I cannot.' She pushed her plate away.

He pushed the plate back to her. 'We have a long journey ahead of us tomorrow. I want to reach Beauregard by nightfall. The last thing I need is for you to be ill or too exhausted to travel. I promised Malleval I would look after you and I mean to do so. Even if I didn't exactly cover myself with glory back there in the forest,' he added with a grimace. 'Saved by a woman! I'll be the regiment's laughing stock if the story gets out.'

Marie-Ange remained silent and toyed with the dagger on the table.

'Where did you learn to shoot?' he asked before tucking into his meal with relish. 'You didn't hesitate when you aimed at the men and both your shots hit their mark.'

It was obvious he wouldn't let a few dead bodies spoil his appetite, she thought, watching him eat. He must have seen hundreds on battlefields all over Europe. It was different for her. She would probably have nightmares for a long time.

'Robert taught me last summer,' she explained. 'He didn't want to at first but I insisted. We made a bargain. He taught me to shoot and in return, I taught him…other things.'

She promised Robert she would never tell anyone about their French lessons. He was embarrassed at being so bad at languages. She drank a sip of ale, toyed with her food.

Saintclair stopped eating and looked at her. His blue eyes shone with curiosity.

'What kind of things?'

'Things that can help a young man both in a career and in polite society,' she replied, deliberately vague. 'We have had lessons every evening since he left boarding school.'

'Is that what you were doing the other night?'

She felt she was blushing. So he had heard them giggling. 'I am sorry if we kept you awake.'

Saintclair leant forward, his eyes intense now.

'He must have enjoyed that particular lesson very much, judging by the happy grin on his face when he left your bedroom.' He added in a low, slightly hoarse voice. 'In fact, I wouldn't mind a few lessons myself.'

She shrugged.

'Oh no, he doesn't like it, and he isn't particularly talented but I do insist he stick at it. He will thank me in the long run.' She looked up and added. 'As for you, why would you need any lessons? You *are* French. You know all about...'

Saintclair was still staring at her. The silence between them sizzled with tension. Why was he looking at her like that, so close she could see the golden specks in the iris of his blue eyes and feel his warm breath on her face? And what exactly did he believe she had been doing in her room with Robert? Her face and throat started to burn, her fingers gripped the side of the table so hard her knuckles went white as realization dawned on her.

'You cannot actually believe that Robert and I were...' She couldn't bring herself to say the word.

He didn't answer.

'How can you... Do you really think so little of me?' She almost stammered with outrage. 'Well, if you must know, I teach Robert French every evening while we play checkers in my room. He is hopeless at languages, whereas Christopher was fluent in French, German and Spanish, and as he wants to be a naval officer like his brother, he needs to speak French to improve his prospects.'

Saintclair's eyes widened. He threw his head back and burst out laughing.

'You teach him French! Well, I never... I do apologise.' He shook his head, laughed again and drank his beer but his lips were still twitching when he put the empty pitcher of ale on the table.

She threw him a furious glance and hardly realized she was gripping Christopher's dagger tightly to stop her hand shaking. Now she understood the comments he had made over the past few days. All this time he thought she was having a liaison with her brother-in-law while pretending to be a grieving widow.

'Please don't wave this thing about, you might hurt

yourself.' Saintclair gestured towards the dagger.

She hissed an angry breath between her teeth and put the dagger down, but didn't let go of it. It had saved her life today—Saintclair's and the coachman's, too. It felt like a good omen. She stiffened in her chair and tilted her chin up.

'Christopher was everything to me, Capitaine. He still is. He used to say this dagger was his lucky charm, I never knew why he didn't take it when he left for Corunna.' She paused. 'Did you fight in the Spanish wars?'

Saintclair looked taken aback by her sudden question. 'Some of them. Why?'

'Were you at Corunna in January, 1809?'

He shook his head. 'No, I was in Madrid at the time. Was your husband killed at Corunna?'

'He served on board the *HMS Amazon* which was sunk by French artillery as it moored in the harbour. No member of the crew, and none of the British soldiers they rescued, made it alive. Or so they said.'

He nodded. 'It was bad business, from what I heard.'

'In your experience, is it possible for a soldier or a sailor to be declared dead when in fact he is still alive?' She looked at him in earnest.

He shrugged, raked his fingers in his dark hair. 'It could happen, I suppose. People get lost, or disappear in the heat of battle.'

'I never believed Christopher died, you see. I never felt it, here.' She put her hand on her heart. 'And now I know he is alive.' She leant across the table. 'I saw him in Paris, two days ago.'

Ignoring the look of disbelief on his face, she carried on. 'It was in a building in *Rue de Condé*. I am almost certain it was him. Christopher had the most unusual blond hair, pale, almost like white gold.' Her eyes became dreamy and her fingers caressed the blade of the dagger, not stopping to think that a few hours before it had killed a man.

'I went after him. The concierge told me this was where Fouché lived.'

'So that was why you were so interested in Fouché and his spies,' Saintclair exclaimed. 'I will be blunt, Madame Norton. I don't think the man you saw could be…'

She interrupted again. 'Will you help me find him? You must know lots of people in the army and the government. You have contacts at the ministry of war and in many regiments. The man I saw is named Joseph Nallay.'

This time, Saintclair looked stunned. 'You actually found out this man's name?'

There was something akin to admiration in his eyes. He finished his ale and asked the servant for another pint. Then he raised his hand to stop Marie-Ange from talking.

'Hear me out, please. I think you must take time to consider the facts. The crew of the other English ships at Corunna looked for any missing sailors and officers. They would never have left without making sure there were no survivors.' He sighed. 'I don't quite know how to say this but don't you think you wanted this man to be your husband so much that you convinced yourself it was him? It has been six years after all. You were tired, confused.'

'No, Capitaine, I am almost sure it was him, this Nallay has his face, his eyes, his voice…He even spoke English without the trace of an accent! Something terrible must have happened to him, though. He doesn't remember me. He doesn't even remember his own name.'

'But why would your husband work as a spy for Fouché? Assuming that he did get injured in Spain, why did he not return to England when he was fit enough to do so? Why work for the enemy?' He frowned. 'Unless, of course, he was a spy all along, a traitor to his country.'

'No,' Marie-Ange cried. 'Christopher would never betray his country! He is an honourable man.'

Saintclair didn't answer. The servant placed a pint of ale in front of him.

'It's obvious you have turned your husband into some kind of heroic figure,' he said, lifting his pitcher to his lips. 'According to you, he was the bravest, the kindest.'

'It's because he is,' she said softly.

'Why would he work for the enemy, then, for France?' He shook his head. 'No, not even France, for Fouché. Damn it, the most despicable of all politicians, the greatest turncoat in history...unless he was one himself.'

She exclaimed in rage, 'Very well, I will find him myself since I see you have no intention of helping me.'

'I apologize, Madame,' Saintclair mumbled, looking a little contrite. 'I shouldn't have spoken so harshly.'

She picked the knife up from the table and put it in her reticule before standing up.

'No, you shouldn't have. Good night, Capitaine.'

Saintclair stood up, bowed his head slightly then took his pint and went to sit near the fire. She turned round from the doorway and saw him gazing into the flames, his legs stretched in front of him and crossed at the ankles.

Once upstairs, she locked the bedroom door behind her and leant against it. She was still reeling from what Saintclair had said. Christopher was not a traitor. He was a brave, dedicated Royal Navy officer. Yet, when her anger subsided and she could think more clearly, she had to admit that the French cuirassier had a point. It didn't make sense that Christopher hadn't made his way back home. Even if it had taken months for him to recover after Corunna, he should still have come back to England. And to her.

Chapter Six

'The chateau is at the end of the track. I'll ride ahead and announce our arrival.'

Saintclair touched his heel to the horse's side and disappeared down the lane winding its way through the forest. Despite the cold, Marie-Ange pulled the carriage window all the way down and leant out, eager for her first glimpse of Beauregard. As the road forked to the left, the chateau appeared through the trees. It seemed to glow in the fading light, ghostly white and luminous like the snow which covered the ground. On an impulse, she shouted to the driver to stop.

'I wish to walk from here,' she declared before jumping down.

Gathering the folds of her cloak, she started down the snowy track towards the iron gates marking the entrance of the estate. The forest gave way to a rolling park with a large pond in the middle, its waters still, dark and slimy, and with dead lily pads and broken reeds covering its surface.

She faced the chateau. Her breath caught in her throat, her eyes welled up with tears. This was where generations of her family had been born and brought up. This was the place her mother left when she was sixteen, never to return. The home she had painted, over and over again, like a haunting dream.

Capitaine Saintclair was waiting at the front porch and turned an impatient face towards her. Of course, he must be in a hurry to deliver her to Malleval and return to Lyon, his regiment and his family. And to make sure he had repaid his gambling debt.

They were shown inside by an elderly servant. As she walked into the hall, it was like stepping into her mother's sketchbook. Nothing appeared to have changed since Catherine had painted the chateau twenty-five years before. She almost expected her mother, as a young girl, to appear from behind a door and skip alongside her in the corridor.

'Monsieur is in the library.' The servant knocked on a door hidden behind a black velvet curtain.

'*Oui. Entrez*,' a man's voice answered.

Saintclair opened the door onto a room full of shadows which was lit only by the fire in the hearth. A man reclined on a couch. Propped on his elbow, he sucked on the tube of a strange smoking implement that made a gurgling sound, as if it was filled with water. Marie-Ange stopped in the doorway and wriggled her nose at the sweet, sickening smoke floating in the room.

Saintclair walked in. 'What are you doing hiding in the dark, Malleval?'

The other man looked up.

'Saintcair. At last! I was expecting you yesterday.' He turned his head towards the door and gestured for Marie-Ange to enter without getting up from the sofa. '*Approchez donc, ma chère.*'

She obeyed, frowning at this unconventional and rather discourteous welcome by the relative she had travelled hundreds of miles to meet. Maybe Uxeloup Malleval was too injured to stand.

'Good evening, Monsieur. I am delighted to meet you.'

In the semi-darkness she saw that Malleval was a very handsome man, despite being thin and pale. He had the most peculiar eyes, dark brown with a yellow centre and pupils no bigger than a pin. His lips stretched into a lazy smile.

'So am I, my dear Marie-Ange. I trust Saintclair took

71

good care of you?' His voice was slurred. He sounded drunk.

'Yes, he did,' she answered. Somehow she didn't think he would be interested in hearing about their encounter with bandits in the forest right now.

'*Bon*. Sophie, my housekeeper, will show you to your room.' Malleval turned to Saintclair. 'You are staying the night, of course. Sophie has your usual room prepared.'

'I was hoping to get back to my regiment tonight,' Saintclair objected, although not very strongly.

Malleval waved his hand in a dismissive gesture. 'You'll go back tomorrow. I'm sure no one is expecting you in Lyon just yet. I heard it's chaos at the barracks. Nobody knows who is in charge or who is supposed to be doing what.'

'Very well,' Saintclair acquiesced. 'I will stay the night.'

'You should go out, Malleval, get some fresh air,' he added, gesturing to the shuttered windows. 'It can't be good for you to stay in here and smoke this thing all the time.'

'You're right, my friend,' Malleval answered, 'but it's been a rotten few months for me, as you well know, and this...' He pointed at the pipe. 'This is one of the few things which brings me a little peace.' He smiled. 'I'll see you both at eight, then.'

He reclined against the back of the sofa, took a long pull on his pipe and closed his eyes. So that was it. She crossed the English Channel and most of France at his request, braved highwaymen and rowdy soldiers, suffered discomfort and Capitaine Saintclair's short temper and arrogant manners, and she was being dismissed after a five minute interview!

Saintclair sighed and took hold of Marie-Ange's elbow to lead her out of the library.

'I'm sure he will be in a more amenable disposition

later,' he remarked as they walked back to the hall.

'This wasn't the welcome I was expecting,' she said. 'What is he smoking? It has a very unpleasant smell.'

'Opium.'

'Really? Is that not a dangerous substance? Does he take it because of his battle wound?'

Saintclair tightened his mouth. 'Ah…Yes, I believe it helps with…the pain.'

A young woman was waiting for them in the hall.

'*Bonsoir*, Sophie. You are looking beautiful, as usual.' Saintclair kissed the back of the woman's hand.

'Good evening, Capitaine,' she replied, a smile lighting her pretty face and warm, brown eyes. 'It is nice to see you again. You can go straight to you room, I am sure you remember the way.' Saintclair nodded and started climbing the stairs. The young woman turned to Marie-Ange and curtsied.

'I am Sophie, Monsieur Malleval's housekeeper. Please follow me.'

The green silk of her fashionable gown whispered as she led the way across the hall.

'You must be exhausted after your journey,' she remarked, pausing at the foot of the stairs to tuck a loose strand of long brown hair into the bun at the nape of her neck. The light from the chandelier flashed on the large cabochon ruby set in the gold ring on her finger. Marie-Ange frowned, surprised. Not only was Sophie very young, but her dress and jewellery seemed out of keeping with her position at Beauregard.

They went up to the first floor, and then along a wide corridor.

'I hope you'll like your room,' Sophie said, opening a door. 'I believe it was your grandmother's.'

Marie-Ange stepped into the spacious bedroom where a welcoming fire burned in a white marble fireplace. The walls were painted white and blue and the ceiling reminded her of a summer sky scattered with wispy white clouds. Her mother had sketched the room and it too hadn't changed. Sophie ordered her trunk to be unpacked and a bath to be prepared in the adjoining dressing room, asked her if she needed anything else and left when Marie-Ange said she was fine.

Once alone Marie-Ange ran her fingers along the smooth marble mantelpiece, touched the perfume bottles, the cloisonné jewellery boxes and the delicate porcelain figurines of shepherds and shepherdesses adorning the writing desk near the window. Had these belonged to her grandmother, Aline? Had her mother admired them too, or even played with them? She lay on the blue counterpane and gazed at the intricate patterns on the ceiling. She could almost hear a long lost voice—her mother's, laughing, talking and singing to her. Tonight she felt her presence more strongly than she had in years. The mantel clock striking seven brought her back to reality.

After a quick bath in the then lukewarm rose-scented water, she wrapped herself in a soft towel and sat down in front of the fireplace to rub her hair dry. What she wanted more than anything else was to explore the chateau, open all the doors, look through cupboards and wardrobes for trinkets, clothes or books her mother or grandmother might have left behind. But that would have to wait.

She made her way downstairs. Saintclair and Malleval were talking in the drawing room. She heard her name mentioned and paused outside the door.

'When do you want me to take Madame Norton back to England?'

Malleval chuckled. 'I have no intention of letting her out of my sight just now. I have plans for her.'

'What do you mean, you have plans? I thought she was here to sign some papers regarding a bequest from your father.'

'That's what she believes, too.'

'What are you playing at, Malleval?' Saintclair sounded wary.

What did he mean indeed? She wanted to know more but she heard footsteps behind her. Someone was coming. She took a deep breath and entered the room.

Uxeloup Malleval was a different man tonight. Clad in a smart black suit with a crisp white shirt and an elaborate *cravate,* he walked towards her, a wide smile on his face.

'Here she is! *Chère* niece!' He took her hand affectionately, his peculiar brown eyes searched her face.

'I trust you find your room agreeable.'

'Yes, it's beautiful, thank you.'

He turned to Saintclair. 'What about you, old friend? I hope you'll enjoy one last night of comfort before going back to your quarters in Lyon. The barracks must be cramped by now with all the troops having recently arrived from the north. Not to mention the new recruits.'

'I'm used to it,' Saintclair replied with a shrug.

'Lucky you! I wish I was still fit enough to be part of it all.' Malleval let go of Marie-Ange's hand to walk towards a console and pour three glasses of port which he handed to his guests.

'I suspect you have many questions for me,' he said after inviting Marie-Ange to sit down.

She nodded. 'I do, indeed, but first I would like to know how you managed to trace me to Norton Place. I was very surprised to receive your letter at the end November.'

In business, there was nothing better than a direct approach. That was what William Jones used to say. Uxeloup cocked his head to one side and sighed.

'It wasn't an easy task, believe me. My father started looking for your mother a long, long time ago. His agents searched all over Germany, Belgium, Switzerland, and England without success, but he was determined not to give up. When he passed away last summer I promised him I would keep on searching. At last, a few months ago, our men stumbled upon records of your parents' wedding—July 1791, I believe—of your christening and regrettably, of your mother's death in a church register in Plymouth…After that it was only matter of days for them to pick up your trail.'

Marie-Ange closed her eyes briefly. She had not known the date of her parents' wedding. Her suspicions regarding her birth were now confirmed. William Jones married her mother in July. She was born five months later. Would she ever find out who her real father was?

She drank a sip of port and carried on. 'I apologise if I sound blunt, but I am surprised at your father's generosity. After all, nothing obliged him to leave my mother a share of the Beauregard fortune. From what I heard, he was far from being caring and sentimental.'

Uxeloup pulled a face. '*Touché*! You are correct. My father was a harsh man indeed, but he deeply regretted some of his actions and wouldn't rest until he put them to right. He had a certain attachment to your mother and wanted to do the right thing by her.'

He smiled and took her hand. 'There. Have I satisfied your curiosity?'

Although she wasn't convinced by his explanations, she nodded slowly.

'When can I sign the papers to release your father's bequest?' she asked, pulling her hand out of his.

Uxeloup laughed again. 'You certainly don't beat around the bush, dear Marie-Ange! I have always admired the no-nonsense Anglo-Saxon approach. We will visit my notary in Lyon very soon, together with Saintclair. My notary, Maitre Bernard, needs to finalise our…How shall we call it?' He turned to Saintclair and cocked one eyebrow, 'our arrangement.'

Saintclair looked distinctly uneasy as he glanced at Marie-Ange. She suspected he would be even more embarrassed if he knew she was fully aware of his *arrangement* with Malleval and of his gambling debt.

'But you wrote that the papers were ready for me to sign here, at Beauregard!' She remembered Uxeloup's most recent letter.

He arched his eyebrows. 'Did I? I don't recall. Anyway, you will enjoy Lyon. Even though it's dull and provincial compared to Paris, it's still more exciting than the Beaujolais. Apart from hunting, there's really nothing to do here. And the neighbours are all frightful old bores.'

'Actually, there is someone I would like to meet—Hermine Marzac, my great aunt. I believe she lives around here.'

Malleval snorted.

'The old battleaxe? Don't count on me to take you to Marzac. Hermine is a fossil from the *Ancien Regime*. She believes in the God-given superiority of the aristocracy whereas Saintclair and I, together with the best part of the population, are nothing but dirty peasants unworthy of cleaning her boots. And of course, she particularly hates me, seeing that my father married into her family under rather difficult circumstances.' He let out a sigh, shook his head. 'However, I can understand why you wish to meet her. After all, you and she are, I believe, the only living Beauregards left in the country.'

He stood up, impatient all of a sudden. 'I will see what is keeping Sophie. I won't be long,' he muttered before walking out.

'So what do you think of the chateau? Is it as you had imagined?' Saintclair asked when they were alone.

'It feels like coming home,' she mused wistfully. 'Or rather it feels like I have been here in dream and I remember…'

Malleval came back to say that supper was ready, and they followed him into the dining room.

He sat at the head of the table, with Marie-Ange and Saintclair on either side and Sophie opposite him. The young woman had lost her kind smile tonight. She sniffled, held a handkerchief to her red, swollen eyes all through the meal and hardly said a word, even when Uxeloup praised her for the sumptuous meal.

'If you're going to be miserable all evening, you might as well stay in your room,' he snapped at last. 'You know I cannot stand weeping females.'

Sophie let out a strangled cry and ran out, holding the handkerchief to her mouth.

'There was no need for that,' Saintclair remarked. 'She doesn't look well.'

Uxeloup laughed. 'Sophie's just being unreasonable. What is it with women? Whatever you do, you can never please them.' He cut a large piece of cake and poured cream all over it before stabbing his fork in it.

He seemed a volatile character. He drank large quantities of red wine and alternated between indolence, anger and good humour. When a maid brought a basket of fruit and a platter of cheese at the end of the meal, he leant over and wrapped his arm around her waist before whispering something in her ear. The girl giggled and swayed her hips as she walked out, casting him a provocative glance over her shoulder.

'You'll have to come hunting here again when I'm better,' he told Saintclair. 'Remember the great times we used to have? What fun! What was the name of the dark beauty who accompanied you sometimes?'

Saintclair opened his mouth to reply but Malleval raised his hand.

'Wait, I remember. Her name was Caroline, was it not? You too seemed to get along very well…a little too well at times.'

Marie-Ange looked down at her plate and tightened her lips. So Caroline Dupin and Capitaine Saintclair were lovers, and had been for some time. For some unknown reason, it annoyed her.

'Have you done much hunting this winter?' Saintclair asked.

'No. I haven't been up to much,' Malleval replied. 'But it's all about to change, thanks to Marie-Ange here.'

She looked up, surprised.

'Yes, my dear,' Malleval said cheerfully. 'You are going to make everything wonderful again.'

'I do not understand.'

Malleval drained his glass of wine and threw his napkin onto the table.

'Come with me, I want to show you something.'

He took them to the library, a lot more welcoming tonight thanks to numerous candelabras giving off a warm, bright light and a fire burning high in the hearth. Malleval's opium-smoking contraption had been removed, but the sickening smell lingered.

'Take a look at this,' Malleval gestured for Marie-Ange to join him in front of a painting, the portrait of a man.

'Count Saint-Germain,' he announced. 'The mysterious, legendary, elusive, Count Saint-Germain.'

'My mother's godfather?' She stepped closer to the painting, curious.

The painting depicted a man of average height wearing a plain dark grey suit. He had intelligent brown eyes and his mouth was stretched in a smile. He was holding a roll of parchment and a gold cross incrusted with precious gems which seemed clipped onto some kind of glass phial. Marie-Ange stepped closer and repressed a cry of surprise. Saint Germain wore a golden pendant that looked identical to a locket her mother had left her—the only piece of jewellery she had inherited from her. Could it be the same one?

'I can't read the date,' she remarked, pointing to the bottom of the painting.

'This was painted in 1783,' Uxeloup replied. 'One year later Saint Germain supposedly died at the court of the

Grand Duke of Holstein in Denmark.'

She turned to him. 'Supposedly?'

He fixed his intense brown eyes on her. 'Saint Germain did not die.'

'Come on, Malleval!' Saintclair interrupted. 'You cannot believe the tales about the man being immortal! I always thought it was a shame that legends surrounding Saint Germain out shadowed his achievements as a statesman and diplomat. All people ever remember are these silly stories about him being a Rosicrucian, an alchemist able to turn copper coins into gold, melt small diamonds to produce larger ones and, of course, being immortal.'

Marie-Ange gazed at the portrait again. Her father had never mentioned alchemy, let alone immortality.

'Saint Germain was—and still is—a mystery,' Malleval carried on, oblivious. 'He held everyone under his spell. King Louis XV was so taken by him he sent him on missions all over Europe. He valued his advice on all matters, especially occult sciences. Even a hardened sceptic like Voltaire famously said of him, and I quote, 'Count Saint German is a man who was never born, who will never die, and who knows everything.'"

Saintclair burst out laughing. 'Well, if you believe that, you will believe anything. The man had great talents—I grant you that—especially for pulling the wool over people's eyes when it suited him.'

'What is he holding on that painting?' Marie-Ange pointed to the cross.

'It is called *La Croix de Vie*,' Malleval answered. 'Like the *Crux Vaticana* which holds pieces of the True Cross, it contains a relic. A most wonderful relic.'

'That piece of white cloth here in the phial?' She pointed to the base of the Cross.

Malleval nodded. 'A long time ago, my family came in possession of documents relating to the Cross and the

80

relic.'

He walked to a glass cabinet displaying ancient manuscripts and gestured for Marie-Ange to join him.

'Have you ever heard of *Polycarpe de la Rivière*?' he asked. 'He was a prior and a famous scholar back in the seventeenth century. He discovered these documents relating to the Cross.' He pointed to the manuscripts in the cabinet. 'Coded documents written by the Knights Templar themselves as far back as the 1100's, when they were the Cross' keepers.'

Marie-Ange leant forward to examine the thick, yellow parchments. Her heart beat faster. She had seen these symbols before, on her father's desk one day when she had sneaked into his study. She recognised the strange writing—lines, circles, squares, crosses, triangles and dots...But why would William Jones have documents written in the Templar code in his possession? He was a lawyer, not a historian.

'As you can see, the scroll Saint Germain holds is written in the same code.' Malleval pointed to the portrait. 'These parchments were acquired by my family centuries ago. They relate the story of the Cross of Life and its extraordinary power.'

Saintclair raked his hair with his fingers and sighed. 'What power are we talking about now?' He sounded faintly amused. 'The faculty to change metal into gold or make a man invisible?'

Malleval's eyes shone with excitement. 'The power to give eternal life.'

'You need to ask your physician for a draught to clear your head. You're not making any sense.' Saintclair paused. 'Anyway, you said the Cross belonged to the Knights Templar...How then did it come to be in France and in the possession of Saint Germain?'

'After the fall of St Jean d'Acre in 1291, the body of Guillaume de Beaujeu, the Great Master Templar, was taken to Paris and buried in the Temple's chapel along with the Order's most precious objects and documents,' Malleval explained. 'Among these was the Cross of Life. When the Order was disbanded by Philippe le Bel in 1307, Jacques Molay—the last Great Master—asked Guichard de Beaujeu to rescue the treasure hidden in his ancestor's tomb. Guillaume's body, along with the treasure, was reburied in the family chateau in Arginy, not far from here.'

'So the Cross of Life was hidden in Arginy when the Templar Order was dissolved?'

Malleval nodded. 'Yes, until Anne de Beaujeu searched the crypt of the chateau and discovered it in the fifteenth century. I don't know how Saint Germain came to be in possession of it, but it was the Cross and its relic which made him immortal.'

'This relic…could it be the bones of a Saint?' Marie-Ange asked.

Malleval smiled. 'Oh no my dear, it's much better than that.'

'In Saint Germain's portrait, it looks like a piece of white cloth in the glass phial,' she remarked.

He leant closer to her. 'Saint Germain hid the Cross before he faked his death.' He grabbed Marie-Ange's wrists and pulled her towards him. 'Your mother knew where it was. She told you before she died, didn't she? You must tell me too. You must!' He gripped more tightly and shook her. The candlelight cast strange shadows on his face, the yellowy centre of his iris glowed and made him look deranged.

'Malleval! What on earth are you playing at?' Saintclair roared as he stepped forward with his fists clenched.

Malleval let go of Marie-Ange, who immediately stepped away towards the door.

'I'll go up to my room now, Monsieur. I don't know

what you are talking about and I regret I really can't help you.' Her head high, she turned and walked out.

'Oh, but you can, my dear, and you will.' She heard Malleval say.

The man was a lunatic, there was no other explanation. As she walked out of the library she heard Saintclair call after her. She wanted to be alone, so she ignored him and walked faster, but he caught up with her in the stairs.

'Did he hurt you?' he asked.

'A little.' She rubbed her wrist where a red mark had appeared. 'Why did you not warn me the man was crazy?'

He shook his head. 'I have never heard him talk about all this nonsense before. Do you still want to stay until you have signed the papers? If you don't, I suppose I'll have to take you back to England, but I will require a couple of days to make arrangements.'

For a moment, she thought he looked genuinely concerned. Then she shook her head. Who was she kidding? He was only worried because if she left Beauregard now, Uxeloup would demand the repayment of his gambling debt and get his hands on his family house.

She tilted her chin to look at him and replied haughtily. 'Do not worry about me, Capitaine. I can take care of myself.'

She left him in the staircase and went back to her room. But once alone, the reality of her predicament hit her. She was on her own, at the mercy of a madman. She had no idea what Uxeloup Malleval was talking about. The Cross of Life, the Knights Templar, a crypt in a nearby castle, her mother's godfather being immortal...How could anyone in their right mind believe in immortality?

She remembered her mother's locket. Pulling it out of her velvet jewellery pouch, she held it in the candlelight. It was solid gold, its cover embossed with the design of a five-petal rose, and with a heart at its centre it looked identical to the one Saint Germain wore in the painting. Thoughtful, she slipped it back inside the pouch.

What was she going to do? Was it safer to play along with Malleval and pretend she knew about this Cross, at least until he gave her the money he had promised? Or should she tell him the truth, namely that she had no idea what he was talking about?

A couple of hours later, she still hadn't reached a decision. By then, the fire had all but died down. The chateau sounded quiet, as if it were asleep. She undresed and unpinned her hair which tumbled down her shoulders. She took her time brushing it, feeling the knot of anxiety at the pit of her stomach slowly loosen with each long, soothing stroke.

The scream came from the floor above and echoed in the chateau. She dropped the brush onto the floor.

Chapter Seven

Who had screamed? Why?

Marie-Ange held her breath but there was only silence now. She tiptoed to the door and opened it. Saintclair was walking down the dark corridor, a candle in his hand. His shirt hung open at the chest, as if he too had been ready to go to bed. She stepped into the corridor to meet him, far too alarmed to notice the cold or the fact she was only wearing her nightdress.

'What was that, Capitaine?' she whispered.

He gave her a quick glance then gestured to the staircase.

'It came from upstairs. Malleval must be up to his old tricks.'

'What old tricks?'

He tightened his mouth. 'Stay here. I will go up and take a look. I'm sure there's nothing to worry about.'

'How can you say that? Whoever screamed sounded in terrible pain.'

'I said, stay here,' he instructed once again.

Just as he started going up the staircase, another high-pitched cry resounded in the chateau. Marie-Ange gasped and put her hand to her heart. There was no way she would stay down here on her own. She raced up the stairs after Saintclair.

He turned to look at her, a deep frown creasing his forehead.

'What do you think you're doing? This is no place for you. Go back down.'

'Why? What is he doing in there?'

He let out an impatient sigh.

'If you can't do as you're told, stay behind me. But I'm warning you, you won't like it,' he grunted before knocking on a double door at the end of the second floor corridor.

'Malleval! It's Saintclair. Is everything all right?'

There were a few seconds of silence, followed by sounds of a man and woman laughing inside the room. Then the door opened.

'Saintclair. Have you come to join us?' Malleval exclaimed.

Marie-Ange peeped from behind Saintclair but recoiled at the man's flushed face and feverish eyes. He was stripped to the waist and held a short leather whip. A strange tattoo of a snake biting its tail adorned his chest.

'You're here too, *chère* niece,' he added when he saw her. 'Do come in.' He opened the door wider.

'What's happening? Who is it?' A woman called.

She was lying naked on black silk sheets on the massive bed at the centre of the room. Rolling over, she stood up and walked unsteadily towards them, kicking several empty bottles of wine out of the way with her bare foot. Marie-Ange recognized the maid who served them at supper. She gripped Saintclair's arm and opened her mouth in shock. Red marks marred the maid's milky white thighs and buttocks. 'I'm sorry if I woke you, but Monsieur likes it when I scream.' The girl threw her head back and let out a drunken laugh.

'Are you not going to do anything?' Marie-Ange asked Saintclair.

The officer turned to her and sighed. 'Do what exactly?'

'She's fine, of course, there's nothing to worry about.' Malleval placed a hand on the woman's waist, another on her shoulder. The girl laughed again and snuggled close to him, seemingly oblivious to the fact she was naked in front of strangers.

'Now, shall you join us? It will be just like old times.' He cocked his head to one side and grinned again.

Disgusted, Marie-Ange turned away. She walked as fast as her shaky legs allowed but the girl's loud, cajoling voice pursued her down the corridor.

'Your friend here is a true Hussar, Capitaine,' she was saying. 'But I'm ready to wager you're not bad in bed yourself. Maybe you could let me find out?'

Saintclair muttered something and Malleval's bedroom door slammed shut. He caught up with her in a few long strides and glanced her way.

'Sorry about that,' he said, his tone casual. 'I did tell you to stay in your room.'

'So you knew what was going on up there?' She breathed out, incensed.

She didn't give him time to reply. Her cheeks burned with anger, her heart beat fast, too fast. 'Of course you knew! You must have had your fair share of that kind of...' she drew in breath as she searched for the right word, 'that kind of entertainment! After all, Malleval did talk at supper about the wild nights you two used to have during the hunting season.'

She ran down the stairs but wasn't fast enough. He caught up with her outside her door, put his hand on her arm, and spun her round to face him.

'For the record,' he said, his eyes narrowed in anger, his grip a tight vice on her arm, 'I have never treated, and will never treat, a woman like that. I can assure you that I know of more pleasurable ways to make a woman scream.'

She let out a gasp. How conceited of him! But why was she surprised? He was the man who claimed all women were helpless in his arms. He was the man who believed women were too shallow, too inconsistent to experience honest, true and lasting feelings.

They faced each other in the dark corridor, the candle throwing gigantic shadows onto the walls. He looked down at her, his eyes skimming her body from her tousled hair which covered her shoulders and breasts down to her bare feet, then back up again. Her lips parted and she breathed faster, acutely aware of the heat from his body, of the burning touch of his fingers on her arm. Her whole body tingled, tightened. She should avert her eyes, turn away. Yet, like a mouse mesmerised by a feline, she stood petrified and unable to move.

He spoke in a very low voice, breaking the spell. 'Get back in your room and lock your door. I will take you to your Aunt Marzac in the morning.' Without another word, he opened her door and left her there.

Snapping out of her trance, she did as he ordered. She wrapped herself in Christopher's dressing gown and sat in front of the dying fire. Never could she have imagined her journey to Beauregard would turn out in this way. Nightmarish images of Uxeloup played in her mind, over and over again. Images of him sucking on his opium pipe, talking about a long lost ancient relic, beating a naked woman with a black leather whip, and that strange tattoo vivid on his chest.

If only she didn't need that bequest so badly, she could leave the following morning. If only Norton Place and Robert weren't relying on her. And if only she wasn't so desperate to meet Fouché and ask him about Joseph Nallay...

It was very late when she finally slid Christopher's dagger under her pillow and got into bed.

The gentle, melodious cooing of doves on her windowsill woke her the following morning. She turned in the soft feather bed, opened her eyes and yawned. Her few hours of fitful sleep had left her with a headache and a heavy, anxious feeling in the pit of her stomach, made worse at the thought of having to face Saintclair and Malleval.

A maid came in to pull the curtains open onto a grey morning and help her get ready. Marie-Ange chose her best dress—a dark blue silk gown with white lace at the collar and at the wrists. She wanted to make a good impression on her Great-Aunt Hermine today.

She ventured downstairs, hoping Malleval was still in his room sleeping off the excesses of the night and found Saintclair in the dining room, eating eggs and ham and drinking black coffee. Without a word, he stood and pulled a chair out for her. A servant girl brought her plate and some coffee.

'I have arranged to borrow Malleval's carriage and a driver to go to Marzac this morning,' Saintclair said when the girl had left. 'Then I am going back to Lyon.'

She felt a sudden, incomprehensible, stab of sadness at the news. She might not like his arrogance and resent what he implied about Christopher, but he was the only man she trusted in this place. When he left, she would be alone with Uxeloup Malleval…

'Will you be at the ball tomorrow night in Lyon?' she enquired.

'I suppose I shall have to be,' he answered with a shrug. 'I don't care much for these events. Too much parading and prancing around for my taste, but my superiors expect me to put in an appearance. Thankfully the *Palace Saint-Pierre* is across the square from the barracks, so I can leave when I have had enough.' He hesitated, cleared his throat. 'Madame Norton, about last night…'

'I do not wish to be reminded of last night and the awful things which went on upstairs,' she retorted primly, shuddering at the memories of Uxeloup's crazed eyes, his fingers gripping the handle of the whip and the servant's white body covered with bloody marks. The young woman's drunken laugh still resounded in her ears. How could any woman submit willingly to such degrading treatment? She was annoyed to see Saintclair smile.

'I'm not talking about Uxeloup's bedroom antics but about the story he told us in the library about the Cross of Life. What do you intend to do about it?'

Should she tell him of her plan? Somehow she thought he wouldn't betray her to Malleval. She leant over the table and answered in a hushed voice.

'I never heard about it before yesterday. I don't know much about Saint Germain either. My mother died when I was little and my…father…' She swallowed hard. William Jones would always be her father since he was the man who had brought her up. 'He never talked much about Beauregard. I can't give Malleval what he wants. However, he strikes me as dangerously obsessed. It is in my best interest to pretend I can help him find this Cross. Until he has released my inheritance, that is. Then I shall return to England and never see him again.'

He raised his eyebrows and laughed. 'I admire your bluff, Madame. You would make an ideal partner at cards.' Serious again, he considered her for a few seconds. 'You are doing the right thing, of course. Go along with him for as long as you can.'

They left for Marzac after breakfast.

Located in a wine-growing valley north of Beaujeu, Marzac was an impressive medieval castle with square turrets, high walls, and a deep moat complete with a drawbridge. As the carriage drove through the gates, Marie-Ange's nervous fingers fiddled with the ties of her cloak, adjusted the ribbon of her bonnet under her chin. Hermine was the first member of her mother's family she would meet. Malleval called her a battleaxe, a woman stuck in the *old Regime*. Would she be happy, tearful or indifferent to see her? Maybe she wouldn't care at all for her long-lost great-niece.

The carriage stopped in front of the main entrance and

Saintclair jumped down from his horse to open the door. He held her hand tightly as she stepped down, glanced around, and whistled between his teeth. 'It's quite a place.'

They climbed the imposing stone porch and found an elderly servant waiting at the top of the steps. As she came nearer the man let out a loud gasp, and his face drained of all colour. When she told him her name she was sure she saw tears shine in his eyes. He coughed to clear his throat and asked them to follow him into a parlour. Soon after, a small woman with light grey hair walked in, leaning heavily on a walking stick with a carved silver pommel.

'So you are Catherine's daughter,' she declared without preamble.

Marie-Ange curtsied. 'Yes, Madame.'

The woman turned to Saintclair. 'And you are?'

Saintclair bowed. 'Capitaine Saintclair, of the Second Regiment of Cuirassiers. I escorted Madame Norton from England.'

'A cavalry officer?' Her tone was disapproving. 'Well, I suppose you needed a man for the journey.' She turned to Marie-Ange again. 'Where is your mother?'

Her cold, abrupt voice made Marie-Ange wince. 'She died a long time ago, Madame.'

'Oh...' The old woman's face seemed to crumple. She closed her pale grey eyes a few seconds. 'I am sorry, child. I must have sounded cold-hearted just then. The thing is, your arrival took me by surprise. I had no idea you existed. Last time I heard about Catherine was when she sent me a note to let me know she had reached England safely. That was in July of 1791.'

'I was not aware of your existence either, Madame, until a chance encounter in Paris with a former friend of my mother's a few days ago.'

Hermine Marzac's face softened, and she raised a hand to touch Marie-Ange's cheek.

'You have her hair and her smile, definitely. You must

tell me all about her and yourself. But before…'

She turned to Saintclair. 'You may wait in the kitchen. I am sure my servants will put up with you for a little while. They might even give you a bowl of soup if you ask nicely. But beware! I do not tolerate gambling or funny goings-on with my girls.'

Saintclair's face grew pale under the insult.

'Capitaine Saintclair has been a most valued travel companion,' Marie-Ange said quickly, embarrassed by the way her aunt had dismissed him. 'I would never have reached Beauregard safely without him.'

Saintclair walked to her. 'It was my pleasure, Madame, but now is the time for me to take my leave. As I said before, I must return to Lyon.'

She gave him her hand and he brushed it lightly with his lips. She was surprised once again at the sadness the thought of his leaving woke in her.

He bowed stiffly to Hermine Marzac. 'Madame.' And he left.

The old lady tapped her stick onto the floor.

'These cavalry officers, so many of them are lowly born ruffians. Napoleon has a lot to answer for by allowing thugs and rabble to the highest ranks of our once great army. The result was abominable. Fortunately, our royal family is back in charge. Even if they cannot undo all the harm that was inflicted on our poor country, they will rid us of the riffraff.'

She sighed. 'Now, I want to know everything about you and your poor mother.' She slid her arm under Marie-Ange's and the two women walked to a small, cosy drawing room.

Marie-Ange spent the next hour answering her great-aunt's questions about her parents, about Christopher, and her life at Norton Place. She said nothing however about her suspicions that William Jones wasn't her real father or about her brief encounter with the man she believed to be

Christopher.

After lunch and a succulent dessert of vanilla cream and sponge biscuits, she decided it was her turn to question Hermine about her family's past.

'Would you mind telling me about the winter of 1791, when my grandfather Philippe was arrested?'

Hermine heaved a shaky breath. Her hand shook and she dropped her spoon in her plate.

'Even after twenty-four years, I cannot forgive or forget what happened. My brother did not deserve to be executed. He was a good man who always tried to improve the estate and the life of his people.'

The elderly woman stood up and pulled a cord next to the fireplace. 'I will let you read Aline's letters. I still have most of them, and they will answer your questions better than I could.'

A short while later Hermine's servant walked in and gave her a bundle of papers.

'Thank you, Pierre.'

She handed the letters to Marie-Ange before walking to the door. 'Take your time, child.'

Marie-Ange untied the blue ribbon that kept the letters together and looked through the papers. The letters spanned several years and started with the announcement of her mother's birth.

Paris, 28th July 1775

Dear Hermine,

Philippe and I are delighted to let you know of the birth of our daughter, Catherine Marie-Ange, who was born ten days ago. She was christened at the Saint-Louis church yesterday. Our friend, Saint-Germain, kindly agreed to be her godfather and my aunt, Abbess Antoinette Fleury, is Catherine's godmother.

I hope you and dear Armand are keeping well and I am looking forward to seeing you again. Philippe sends his regards.

With love,
Aline R. Beauregard

The next letter had been written some years later and was addressed to Hermine.

Beauregard, 4th January 1783

Dear Hermine,

I hope that my letter finds you in good health and that you are enjoying your stay at Versailles. I am missing you dearly.

Count Saint Germain paid us a long visit at Christmas. He seems rather taken by his goddaughter. He gave Catherine a wonderful gift: a gold locket which he said was very old and has belonged to our cousins, the Beaujeus, since the reign of Philippe le Bel. He also gave her an art book. He spent many hours with her, teaching her some rudiments of drawing and watercolour, singing, talking about poetry, or walking in the park.

Saint Germain said Beauregard wouldn't be complete without a dovecote and promised to send a team of craftsmen—from Malta of all places!—to build one in the rose garden. He said these men were the best. Doves at Beauregard! How wonderful!

Yours respectfully,
Aline R. Beauregard

So her locket had indeed belonged to Saint Germain, and to the wealthy and powerful Beaujeus family before him. Uxeloup's ranting about the Beaujeu family came back to her. He had said that one of them, Guichard, hid the mysterious Cross of Life at Arginy castle in 1307 and that his descendent, Anne, retrieved it later, sometime in the fifteenth century.

Aline's next letter was dated a few months later.

Beauregard, 10th May 1783

Dear Sister,

The dovecote is finished at last. Philippe had two dozen pairs of doves sent from a breeder in Belleville. Our rose garden now echoes with the birds' cooing and I do not tire of listening to them and watching them fly around the park.

Saint Germain's Maltese builders left a few days ago. I found them most intriguing. Everything in them, the colour of their skin, their language, and their clothing was alien and exotic. There were five of them, including an interpreter, a charming young man who introduced himself as Baldassere dei Conti. The servants were rather terrified of them, but Catherine wasn't in the slightest impressed. In fact, she befriended the interpreter and they spent many hours together, although I am not sure what they found to talk about!

The men set camp in the park. It was most peculiar, a fire burnt at the entrance of their tent and a guard kept watch at all times. But they worked wonders and I never saw a more beautiful dovecote. There are one hundred and one niches for the birds, all partly closed by wooden shutters, and each shutter is carved with a different pattern. The central pole is chiselled and engraved from top to bottom. The result is simply stunning.

Philippe's plan to renovate the workers' cottages has encountered much hostility from other landowners in the region who say that he is setting a dangerous precedent, but he is determined to improve the life of his people.

I remain as always,

Yours,

Aline R. Beauregard

The following letter reminded her of Malleval.

Beauregard, 30th March 1784

Dearest Hermine,

We were all deeply aggrieved to learn that our dear friend, Saint Germain, died of pneumonia at the court of the Grand Duke of Holstein in Denmark last month. I cannot bring myself to believe this is real. He always had such a strong constitution, I never saw him ill or even unwell once in all the years I have known him. Catherine was distraught at the news and spends hours hiding away in the dovecote and drawing. Poor Saint Germain...He died abroad, without his closest friends and family. The shocking news was that there was no funeral mass held for him and he now rests in an unmarked grave somewhere in a far off Danish cemetery, making it impossible for any of us to visit his grave and pray for his soul.

Yours,
Aline R. Beauregard

Thoughtful, Marie-Ange put the letter down. No wonder Malleval, and others, believed Saint Germain hadn't really died. She read through several more letters spanning the next few years. Catherine, her mother, was growing into a vivacious young girl. With the passing of time, Aline seemed even more proud of her husband as Philippe became involved in social reforms on the Beauregard estate. He even represented the local gentry during the *Etats-Généraux* which opened in Versailles in May 1789, charged with reforming the country's finances and introducing social reforms. However he returned home in July, only days before the turmoil of the revolution. Aline and Philippe spent the following year at Beauregard. The relative tranquillity of their lives came to an end in October 1790. By then, Hermine and her husband, Armand Marzac, had fled to Neuchatel in Switzerland, and this was where Aline now wrote to them.

Beauregard, 20 October 1790
My dear Hermine,

I am concerned for our safety. Despite the terrible unrest which has engulfed the whole country this last year, we were fortunate to live a relatively sheltered existence here. The reforms Philippe started years ago won him the trust and respect of the municipal committee.

However things have changed. Moderate members of the committee were replaced recently by hateful and vindictive men. The new public prosecutor, Edmond Malleval, visited Beauregard last week, demanding a tour of the chateau and the estate.

I was not present that day but Philippe reported that Malleval was particularly critical of his reforms. There was a strange incident, too. Malleval was so taken by the portrait of our dear Saint Germain in the library he made an offer to buy it there and then. He was furious when Philippe refused.

He has now summoned Philippe to appear in front of the Tribunal at Beaujeu for treason. Philippe assures me his allies will vouch for him, but I fear I cannot share his optimism. I have heard that Malleval is a close associate of Joseph Fouché and Jean-Marie Collot d'Herbois, and that, like them, he is an ambitious, blood-thirsty brute. I sent Catherine to her godmother at Salles for her safety. I will write to you as soon as I can.

Yours,
Aline R. Beauregard

Marie-Ange stared into the flames. She knew what happened next.

Beaujeu, 26ᵗʰ October 1790
Dear Sister,

I have terrible news. Philippe's trial took place yesterday. He was found guilty of being an enemy of the National Assembly and sent to jail, awaiting execution. He was not even allowed to speak in his own defence. I am staying at the Jument Blanche Inn *for now. I fear I will be here for some time as I cannot bear to go back to Beauregard without my husband.*

Yours,

Aline R. Beauregard

Beaujeu, 28th October 1790
   Dear Hermine,
   I met with the devil today. Edmond Malleval summoned me this morning. After keeping me waiting for several hours, he finally called me into his office. The man is frightful. He stared at me in complete silence, arms crossed on his chest, refusing to acknowledge my greetings or questions. He has the strangest eyes—dark, with a peculiar dusting of gold at the centre of the iris— which remind me of a reptile. When he finally spoke, it was to make me the most abject proposition.
   He promised to spare Philippe if I became his mistress. He has given me until tomorrow night to make my decision. Should I refuse him, he will have Philippe executed at the end of the week. However I have no guarantee he will spare my husband if I give in. When this letter reaches you, I will have made my decision. Whatever it is, I will have lost my heart or my soul, or both.
   Please pray for me.
   Yours,
   Aline R. Beauregard

Marie-Ange dropped the letter onto her lap. So that was how Edmond formed his relationship with Aline. He blackmailed her.
   Beaujeu, 30th October 1790
   Dear Hermine,
   I am lost and broken. I am no more than one of these poor, degraded street girls. I have no honour left. Even if Philippe is indeed spared, I will never be able to look into his eyes again. Citizen Malleval is a brutal and lecherous man. I wonder why he hates me so much. Everything in him repulses me, from the coarseness of his manners to the cruel glint in his eyes when he 'teaches me a lesson'. How

he enjoys hurting me, making me cry with pain. He has forbidden me to leave Beaujeu and has taken away my certificate of citizenship and my travel permit.

Yours,

Aline

Marie-Ange noticed her grandmother had dropped her husband's name. Did she feel she no longer deserved to be called a Beauregard? Yet, what had she done wrong? She had sacrificed her honour in exchange for her husband's life.

Beaujeu, 17th December 1790

Dear Hermine,

Your kind words cannot soothe my broken heart, but I thank you for not giving up on me. Citizen Malleval has decided I shall reside at his Beaujeu townhouse as his official concubine. My shame is therefore public. I pray that Philippe never hears of this, or indeed my sweet Catherine at Salles.

Malleval keeps asking about Count Saint Germain. He is fascinated by our friend and wants to know everything about him. He is particularly interested in a sacred object Saint Germain had in his possession—the Cross depicted in his portrait—which Malleval says used to belong to the Knights Templar. He got very angry when I assured him I knew nothing about it.

Pray for me and for Philippe.

Yours,

Aline

So Edmond Malleval coveted the Cross of Life too!

Beaujeu, 20th January 1791

Dear Aunt,

It was all in vain. Malleval told me yesterday evening that Philippe was executed on the Place des Terreaux *in Lyon. He now insists that we wed as soon as possible and threatens to harm Catherine if I refuse. I fear Catherine will hate me when she learns of my union with the very man who sent her father to his death. Yet, what can I do? I must spare my daughter the same fate as mine.*

I do not care about myself any longer. I am following my own path to hell.

Citizen Malleval has been enquiring about Saint Germain again. For some strange reason he does not believe our friend died in Denmark. He says he was seen in Paris recently...I fear the man is mad as well as evil.

Pray for me and for the soul of my Philippe.

Yours,

Aline

When she finished reading the letter, Marie-Ange had to force herself to breathe in slowly.

Beaujeu, 31st January 1791

Dear Hermine,

The deed is done. I was married to Malleval this morning by a municipal officer. Malleval now owns the estate of Beauregard and all of Philippe's assets. He owns me and my daughter. I wonder what his fellow associates at the committee make of him becoming a wealthy land owner, one of those they have fought so hard to destroy. Mind you, many of them are now wealthy men themselves, having bought or stolen property which used to belong to the Church or to families from the gentry.

Malleval has threatened to take Catherine away from Salles and hold her captive in a secret location until I tell him what he wants to know about the Cross. He has brought a strange man to Beauregard—a physician named Karloff—to 'treat me' for memory loss. I told him it was useless since I did not forget about the Cross, I just never knew where it was in the first place.

Yours,

Aline

100

There were only two letters left.

Beauregard, 25th March 1791

Dear Hermine,

Malleval told me today he is keeping Catherine somewhere safe, but refuses to tell me where. He now believes that she is the one who holds the secret he so desperately wants. I am beyond myself with worry about my daughter. His physician, Karloff, left Beauregard after confirming that I had indeed no knowledge of the Cross of Life. He was a strange, frightening man who could control my very thoughts and my very being by staring into my eyes and talking to me with his deep, soothing voice.

I live in the hope of holding my daughter in my arms again—that is if she ever forgives me for marrying her father's murderer. My health has been poor since I came back to Beauregard. Being here, surrounded by the memories of happier times, is breaking my heart.

Yours,

Aline

Marie-Ange read Aline's last letter with tears streaming down her face.

Beauregard, 15th April 1791

Dearest Hermine,

My life is finished. Malleval told me Catherine died of illness some days ago, although he would not tell me where she was or what ailed her. The thought of my sweet daughter alone and frightened as she lay dying is more than I can bear. I have no intention of remaining Malleval's wife a day longer. Take great care, dearest aunt, and pray for my soul.

Yours forever,

Aline

Chapter Eight

Hermine walked back into the drawing room, leaning heavily on her walking stick. She glanced up at Marie-Ange and shook her head at the tears staining Marie-Ange's cheeks.

'How did my grandmother die?'

'She drowned in the pond at Beauregard.' The old lady's voice quivered.

The pond with the dead lily pads floating over dark, slimy waters. Marie-Ange shivered. Believing Catherine to be dead, her grandmother had chosen to end her life. She had nothing and no one to live for and it was all because of one man. Edmond Malleval. She clenched her fists in anger. She now understood why she was here.

'Edmond Malleval did not search for my mother all over Europe to bestow some money from Beauregard on her,' she stated. 'No! He believed she could give him what he so desperately wanted. The Cross of Life. And now his son is asking the same thing of me.'

Her great-aunt frowned. 'He asked you about the Cross?'

'Last night. He claimed the Cross made people immortal. He even insisted Saint Germain had lived for centuries and was still alive! Now I understand where he got that notion from. It sounds as if his father passed his obsession on to him.'

She glanced at the window. The sky was darkening. 'I must get back to Beauregard.'

Her heart felt heavy at the prospect of a night in the chateau now that Saintclair had left. With him around, she didn't fear Uxeloup. She didn't fear anything. She shook her head. Enough of these silly thoughts! Why should she miss the presence of the arrogant, short-tempered cuirassier? She was more than capable of dealing with Malleval on her own.

The two women hugged and promised to meet again soon.

'You do not have to return to Beauregard, you know,' Hermine said. 'You could stay here for a while. We could get to know each other.'

'I have to go back.' She didn't want to tell her aunt about the ball in Lyon where she was hoping to meet Fouché and ask him about Nallay. 'But I will come and visit you again.'

Hermine nodded. 'Next time, I will tell you what I know about the Cross of Life.'

It was pitch black when Marie-Ange arrived back at a very quiet Beauregard. She found Sophie sitting in the drawing room with some embroidery on her lap. The young housekeeper didn't look much happier than the previous evening, but at least she wasn't crying.

'Did you enjoy your visit to Marzac?' Sophie asked. 'Is your great-aunt well?'

Marie-Ange nodded. 'She is, thank you, but why is the chateau so quiet tonight and where is Monsieur Malleval?

'He left for Lyon with some of the staff this afternoon. There were final preparations for the ball to be made. His man, Rochefort, will take you to his town house in the morning.'

Marie-Ange couldn't hide her relief to learn that Uxeloup was absent. 'Are you not coming to Lyon, too?'

Sophie shook her head. 'Oh no, I never go anywhere with Uxeloup...with Monsieur, I mean,' she corrected hastily. She bent her head and toyed with the linen on her lap, looking forlorn. A servant girl announced supper was served and the two women made their way to the dining room. During the meal, Marie-Ange asked Sophie about herself.

'There's not much to tell.' The young woman put her hand on her throat. The large ruby she wore on her wedding finger glittered in the light of the candles. Surely no ordinary housekeeper wore such a beautiful jewel. Tonight again, Sophie wore an exquisite gown, this time of cream and pink silk. Perhaps the relationship between Sophie and Uxeloup was more complex than the one between a master and his housekeeper? Perhaps she was more than an employee…

Sophie confided she had started as a housemaid seven years before, as a girl of sixteen. 'I became Beauregard's housekeeper a few months ago, after Monsieur Edmond passed away. Monsieur Uxeloup was always very good to me.' She smiled and looked at her ring.

'Tell me, what was Monsieur Edmond like?'

Sophie's face contracted in a grimace. 'He was a hard master. Nothing ever pleased him.' She lowered her voice. 'He was frightening too, especially when he became obsessed with the dark arts.'

'The dark arts?'

Sophie looked around her uneasily. 'Wizardry and witchcraft…All kinds of strange men and women visited here, but out of them all, Karloff was always the worst.' She raised the glass to her pale lips and drank the red wine in one gulp.

Marie-Ange stared at her. He was the man her grandmother mentioned in her letter. 'Who is he?'

'Monsieur Karloff is a physician,' Sophie answered. 'If you ask me, he's really a wizard. He can make you do things just by looking into your eyes. He can put thoughts in your mind or make you fall asleep.' She shivered.

'Is Uxeloup involved with him too?'

Sophie nodded. 'Oh yes, Karloff is his physician, just like he was Monsieur Edmond's and he visits quite often.

Actually, I heard him talk to Monsieur about you.'

'Really?' Marie-Ange put her knife and fork down, dread creeping through her.

'It was after Monsieur Edmond's death.' Sophie lowered her voice. 'When the village priest came to talk about arrangements for the funeral, Karloff shooed him away and ordered that Monsieur's body be put in an iron cask and taken away to his village in the mountains. I heard him tell Monsieur Uxeloup that they would keep him there, in the vaults of their fortress, until the 'Beauregard girl' was found.' She looked at Marie-Ange nervously. 'That's you, isn't it?'

Marie-Ange pushed her plate away, her appetite fleeing as fear formed a hard ball in her stomach.

'You mean to say Edmond Malleval was not buried and his body is still…'

Sophie nodded and bit her lip. 'I'm sorry, I shouldn't have said anything. I didn't mean to frighten you, just to warn you about Monsieur Karloff. He may be at the ball in Lyon tomorrow.'

'The ball…Fouché will be there too, will he not? Does he ever come to Beauregard?'

Sophie nodded. 'Sometimes, for hunting, although he hasn't been here since Monsieur Edmond died. I don't like him. He is a hard, cruel man.'

Her face brightened up. 'Anyway, you will have nothing to worry about. Capitaine Saintclair will look after you. He may be a little wild but he's a man of honour.'

Marie-Ange tightened her lips. Capitaine Saintclair's notion of honour was probably very different from hers.

'About tomorrow night,' Sophie said, 'would you like me to ask the chambermaid to press your ball gown?'

'I have no ball gown.' Marie-Ange pointed to her dark blue silk dress. 'This is my best dress and it will have to do.'

'Why don't you wear one of your grandmother's

gowns? They're still in a closet in the dressing room. I am sure we could find one to fit you.'

Curious, Marie-Ange followed Sophie up the stairs.

There were rows and rows of dresses wrapped in silk covers. Sophie pulled several out and shook her head.

'What a shame, this one was eaten by moths. The light green one wouldn't suit your colouring at all. And that white gown has yellowed…Ah, this is more like it!' She held out a silk and gauze azure blue gown. Its bodice was covered with embroidered rose buds, and a white lace border ran along the low-cut *décolleté* and cap sleeves.

Marie-Ange touched the delicate fabric. 'It is ravishing but look, there is a tear in the skirt.'

'That's not a problem,' Sophie declared. 'A cousin of mine is a seamstress in Macon. I shall have her fetched this instant.'

'Oh no, do not drag a poor woman out of her home in the middle of the night on my account,' Marie-Ange protested.

'I will make sure she gets adequately rewarded. Monsieur Uxeloup leaves me in charge of the household expenses.' She gave Marie-Ange a knowing smile and leant towards her to confide excitedly. 'I know I should not speak about it just yet but…'

She showed Marie-Ange her ruby ring. 'Uxeloup gave it to me last month. He said we would get married soon, when his health improves.'

Without giving Marie-Ange time to absorb her news, she pointed to the dress. 'You should try it to see if anything else needs altering.'

The dress fitted perfectly. Its delicate fabric hugged Marie-Ange's body, emphasizing her high, slim waist and round shoulders. The colour was almost identical to the aquamarine shade of her eyes.

'Isn't it a little too revealing?' Marie-Ange frowned and tried to pull the dress up to cover the top of her breasts.

'Not at all. It looks as if it was made for you,' Sophie said, dreamily.

Was she thinking of a day when she too would wear a ball gown, maybe even a wedding gown? Marie-Ange doubted the event would ever take place. Uxeloup didn't strike her as the type of man who had any scruples discarding girls after bedding them. Having said that, he might have feelings for the girl, otherwise why would he bother giving Sophie an engagement ring?

In any case, it was obvious Sophie loved him, although Marie-Ange couldn't understand what she saw in him.

Sophie's cousin, a plump, middle-aged woman with a ready smile, arrived within the hour, and when she handed the dress back to Marie-Ange, it looked as good as new.

Eager to set off for Lyon, Marie-Ange went out early the following morning to find Malleval's carriage already stationed in front of the chateau. She paused a moment at the top of the front porch steps. The morning was still, silent. Ribbons of mist curled around the tree tops and hovered above the lawn in the park, lending Beauregard a dreamy, almost ghostly appearance. She took a deep breath. Scents of pine trees and wood smoke mingled in the frigid winter air.

A huge man dressed in a long furry brown coat appeared from behind Malleval's carriage and charged like a bear towards her. Marie-Ange recoiled, a cry of alarm escaping from her lips. The man's face was covered with a bushy beard, his small, beady black eyes shone under thick eyebrows. It was hard to see where his brown fur hat and shag pile coat started and his beard and long, grizzly hair stopped.

'Are these yours?' he grunted, pointing to her bags.

He must be Rochefort, Malleval's coachman. She nodded and he lifted her travel bags and threw them onto the rack on top of the carriage as if they were no heavier than feather pillows.

'Get in, M'ame,' he said then, flinging the door open for her. 'If we set off now, we'll be in Lyon before dinner.'

And with another grunt he climbed onto the driver's box.

The roads were busy. Stagecoaches and private carriages, army personnel and carts driven by farmers or market traders and laden with poultry, barrels of wine, and fresh produce made progress difficult. From time to time Rochefort let out a raucous shout, and even though Marie-Ange didn't always understand what he was saying, it seemed to have some affect in persuading people to move aside and let them through.

They reached the outskirts of Lyon mid-afternoon.

Uxeloup's townhouse was on *Isle Barbe*, an island on the River Saône, one of Lyon's two rivers. Covered with woodland and evergreens, *Isle Barbe* seemed an emerald in the middle of the river, with a square church tower and several large stone buildings nestling within the trees.

The coach proceeded onto a narrow wooden bridge, and then drove through a village square lined with lime trees, their branches now winter bare. They continued onto a lane with Roman arches on both sides—probably the remains of a cloister. At the end of the lane, Rochefort waited for a pair of imposing cast iron gates to be opened. They were adorned with an intricate medallion bearing Malleval's coat of arms—the letters *A* and *M* intertwined. The carriage rumbled into a cobblestone courtyard. Marie-Ange's heart sank when the tall gates closed behind them, like prison doors.

Being on the balcony outside her bedroom was like standing on the deck of a ship, cut off from the world. Malleval's house occupied the tip of the island in the middle of the Saône. The sky above was black and overcast. The river was dark too, with only a few flickers of light dancing on the surface, reflections of the windows of the buildings lining the quays on either side.

Marie-Ange shivered with cold and walked back in her room, admiring once again the green and pink silk wall coverings. Her gown lay on the elegant bed with the wooden posts rising towards the ceiling. A dark cherry wood dressing table covered with perfume bottles held her brush and mirror. The overall effect of the decor was one of beauty and refinement, not at all what she had expected from a house that had belonged to a blood-thirsty revolutionary brute. It was in fact a former Bishop's palace Edmond Malleval had acquired after Church properties were confiscated, divided into lots, and auctioned off during the Revolution.

Sinking into the chaise longue near the fireplace, she glanced nervously at the mantel clock. Time had dragged since she arrived, or was it because she felt anxious about the ball, about seeing Malleval again and meeting Fouché?

At last a maid arrived to help her dress for the evening.

'What a beautiful shade of blue,' the girl marvelled once she'd slipped the gown over Marie-Ange's head and settled it around her hips. The maid brushed her hair until it shone like gold, parted it in the middle and twisted each side into a coil secured with pins, leaving strands of golden curls to fall around her face. Marie-Ange clasped her mother's gold locket around her neck. She didn't often wear it but tonight the feel of the heavy pendant against her skin was reassuring. To finish, she slid her arms into long white gloves the maid held for her.

When she stood in front of the full-length mirror, Marie-Ange couldn't repress a gasp of astonishment. It was the first time in six years that she wore anything other than a plain, long-sleeved, dark coloured gown. She could hardly recognise herself. Tentatively, her hands skimmed over the bodice of the dress, smoothed over the folds of the skirt before touching the curls framing her face.

'You look beautiful, Madame,' the girl exclaimed with a beaming smile on her face, before leading her down the stairs into the lobby where Rochefort was waiting to take her to the ball.

Capitaine Saintclair had explained that *Palais Saint Pierre* stood in the heart of the city. A former Benedictine convent, it had been closed down at the Revolution and was now the seat of the newly-established chamber of commerce. 'Apparently, ghosts of nuns still haunt the place,' Saintclair had said, a twinkle in his eyes. 'Many of my friends who attended events there reported being groped by invisible hands. They said they found the experience rather pleasurable.'

The *Palais* did look like a monastery with its austere, grey stone walls and large gates opening onto a cloister garden. Rochefort informed her he would station along the square until she was ready to go back. Alone and slightly intimidated, she followed the crowd of gentlemen in black evening suits, ladies in ball gowns, and officers in various regimental uniforms up to the first floor.

The ballroom was ablaze with light. Crystal chandeliers glittered brightly and reflected in massive gilded mirrors on the walls. Couples danced to the music of a small string orchestra while onlookers chattered and enjoyed a glass of champagne. She stepped into the room and glanced around, unsure of what to do next.

'Madame Norton!'

Her heart skipped a beat and she could only stare as Saintclair strode through the crowd towards her, magnificent in his parade uniform. The imperial blue jacket ornamented with bright red shoulder pads and his crisp white shirt underneath made a stark contrast with his dark hair and tanned complexion. White breeches tucked into Hessian boots fitted his muscular legs snugly. The sword hanging on his side glinted under the lights.

He took his hat off and bowed in front of her. She

swallowed hard and extended her hand.

'Capitaine. I am glad to see you…Were you released from your duties for the ball?' She was annoyed to hear that she sounded a little breathless.

He nodded and lifted her hand to his lips but his eyes never left hers. The warmth of his mouth through her glove sent shivers down her spine.

'I was indeed.' He cocked his head to one side to gaze at her. 'You look different tonight,' he remarked, an intense look in his blue eyes, before taking her elbow and guiding her through the crowd.

He pointed to a closed door. 'Malleval disappeared with Fouché in the billiard room a while ago. Private meeting, I believe.'

A couple of men in cuirassier uniforms approached them.

'Saintclair! Are you keeping this lovely lady to yourself?' One of them asked, detailing Marie-Ange.

'What are you doing here, de Mitre?' Saintclair's voice was cold. 'I thought Colonel Mougeon asked you to supervise the barracks tonight.'

She remembered that name. Capitaine Martin said that de Mitre was given Saintclair's promotion because he was a member of an old, aristocratic family. Caroline Dupin also mentioned him.

De Mitre laughed. 'I delegated. One of the things I do well, I believe. I'd rather be here than in our stinky barracks with all these new recruits. Have you seen the state of them? Peasants, the lot of them! They couldn't tell a horse's mouth from its arse, never mind fight on one.'

'What a pity our old cuirassiers's test was abolished last year,' the other man said. 'Not a single one of these new recruits would pass.'

'Capitaine Martin mentioned that test before, did he not?' Marie-Ange enquired of Saintclair. 'What exactly did it consist of?'

Saintclair stared at her blankly while the other two laughed.

'Shall you tell her or shall I?' de Mitre asked Saintclair.

'I don't think it's necessary to tell Madame anything,' Saintclair replied. He turned away. 'Come, I will show you the gardens,' he said, putting his hand on Marie-Ange's forearm to lead her away.

'Not so fast,' De Mitre protested. 'Don't be so modest, Saintclair. After all, Madame has the right to know what to expect from you.' He turned to her. 'You see, dear Madame, in the good old days, aspiring cuirassiers would be given three horses, three bottles of champagne, and three willing women. The test was to cover twenty miles, drink the champagne and…well…see to the ladies in three hours, and in any order they saw fit. Saintclair here still holds the regiment's record. Two hours and…forty minutes. Was it? The ladies demanded an encore. The horses collapsed, exhausted. Saintclair asked for more champagne, and gallant as ever, he granted the three ladies their request.'

The men laughed coarsely. Marie-Ange felt her cheeks grow hot. Saintclair glanced at her, sighed impatiently and pointed to the other side of the ballroom.

'Here are Malleval and Fouché. I will take you to them now.' He sounded relieved to walk away.

Marie-Ange's first impression of Joseph Fouché was that of a snake. He surveyed the ballroom crowd with cold, unflinching heavy-lidded brown eyes, barely acknowledging the men who nodded a deferential salute to him. His thin lips didn't smile, his long face remained impassive. In fact, Marie-Ange thought as she approached, he stood very much in the superior manner of a Roman emperor—or maybe it was the image he tried to convey with the way he wore his steel grey hair, short all over with a few flicks on his high forehead.

Next to him, Uxeloup stood, very handsome in his

112

black suit and white necktie. It was hard to reconcile the image of elegance he now presented with the memory of the half-naked madman of the night before at Beauregard

'Dear Marie-Ange, here you are at last!' He took her hand and lifted it to his lips. 'You look ravishing. You do remind me of your mother tonight.'

He leant forward and stared at her pendant.

'This locket,' he whispered, 'it's the same as Saint Germain's.'

'It was my mother's,' Marie-Ange answered, uneasy, and covering the locket with her hand. Maybe it had been a mistake wearing it tonight…

'Aren't you going to introduce us?' Fouché interrupted.

Uxeloup took a deep breath and turned. 'I'm sorry, Fouché. Please allow me to introduce a long-lost relative, Marie-Ange Norton, who just arrived from Devonshire.'

Fouché bowed, his lips stretched into a thin smile which didn't reach his eyes. A shiver of repulsion skittered along her spine as his mouth brushed her gloved hand. She would be wasting her time trying to extract information from him about Nallay. This man would give nothing away. He had after all survived four successive regimes, turning from one master to another, betraying former associates—and even his emperor. He would keep his secrets close to his heart—if he had one—which, looking into his emotionless face, she very much doubted.

'Devonshire? How charming,' Fouché remarked. 'So, you are the daughter of Catherine Beauregard whom I once met at Edmond's house. You do bear an uncanny resemblance to her.'

Marie-Ange frowned. 'I had no idea you had met my mother, Monsieur. When exactly was that?'

Fouché thought for a few seconds. 'Let me think. Sometime in the winter of 1791, I suppose. Yes, it was definitely a couple of years before the Lyon rebellion.'

He turned to Uxeloup. 'Don't you remember? You were

there too. You were only a boy, though quite a feisty one.' His lips stretched into a tight smile which didn't reach his eyes. 'There was some incident between you and the young woman during which you did not particularly shine.'

Uxeloup looked uncomfortable. 'Let's not talk about it, Fouché. I do not wish to stir up unpleasant memories tonight.' The orchestra was playing a quadrille and he offered Marie-Ange his arm.

'Will you do me the honour, dear Marie-Ange?'

There was no way she could refuse without being rude so she walked with him to the centre of the parquet floor where they took their place with a dozen other couples. Throughout the dance she was aware of Saintclair's intense blue gaze on her, and even though she tried to ignore him she missed her steps a few times.

Fouché's comments confirmed her mother had been taken to Malleval's village in the mountains. She had managed to escape. Had somebody helped her?

After the quadrille, the orchestra started the first notes of a waltz. The dance had caused scandal in England a few years before. Attempts had even been made to have it banned. It was now fashionable in London but still very much frowned upon in the rest of the country and had never been played at the Wellcombe village ball. Having never danced a waltz, she asked Malleval to excuse her.

'You have never danced a waltz? What kind of barbarians do you mix with back in Devonshire?' Malleval laughed as they walked back to Fouché and Saintclair.

'Saintclair, you must show Marie-Ange how it is done.'

'How what is done?' Saintclair raised his eyebrows.

'Dancing the waltz, of course. Our dear girl has never waltzed before,' Malleval explained.

'In that case, I will be happy to oblige. Shall we?' Saintclair offered his arm and led her to the dance floor.

Her heart beat faster as he placed one hand on her waist

and started turning slowly, guiding her through the steps. Although their bodies never actually touched, she could feel the heat from his arm around her, the strength of his hand holding hers. Her cheeks burning, she concentrated on the steps, too embarrassed to look up at him. After a while however, her body responded to the music and she started enjoying swirling among other couples. She looked up and smiled.

Then she saw him. Christopher. Nallay. Or rather, she caught a glimpse of his reflection in a mirror. She stiffened in Saintclair's arms.

'What's wrong?' he asked, alarm deepening his voice.

'He's here!' She lifted her chin and pointed towards the entrance. Freeing herself from Saintclair's arms, she ran out of the ballroom, bumping into people who stood in her way. Nalley was descending the staircase. Once on the ground floor, he walked towards the cloister gardens and vanished.

The gardens gleamed under the moonlight. Breathless, Marie-Ange looked around. Where could he have gone? She ventured into the shadows. Suddenly her arm was wrenched behind her, and a hand covered her mouth. She wriggled to free herself but the man holding her was too strong. He pulled her further into the darkness.

'*Je vous connais, je vous ai déjà vue*...I've seen you before. Who are you? Why are you following me?' He spoke French, his voice a harsh whisper. He opened his hand slightly to enable Marie-Ange to answer but applied more pressure to her arm as a warning not to scream.

'Of course you have seen me before. I am...' she answered in English.

'I remember. It was in Paris, *Rue de Condé*,' he interrupted impatiently, switching to English too. 'So you're English. Who are you working for? Talleyrand?'

There was no doubt in her mind. This man was her beloved Christopher. When he leant over her shoulder, she breathed in his familiar scent.

'Christopher, it's me, Marie-Ange.' She turned her body towards him so he could see her face in the moonlight. 'Do you not recognise your wife?'

His hold slackened for a few seconds, but then he tightened his grip again.

'You're hurting me,' she protested.

'Tell me who you're working for, or I shall hurt you even more.'

He didn't seem to have heard what she said.

'Speak now, I'm warning you…'

There were footsteps in the garden and a man's voice called her name.

'Madame Norton. Are you here?' It was Saintclair's voice. He had come after her.

Christopher pressed his hand hard on her mouth and whispered in her ear.

'This isn't over. I will find you and you will tell me the truth,' he warned. He twisted her arm so tightly she gasped with pain before he released her and melted into the night.

Marie-Ange collapsed on the ground with a small cry of pain and dismay. Saintclair rushed to her side.

'Are you hurt? What did the bastard do to you?' he asked, lifting her to her feet.

The pain subsided, but the shock of her discovery overwhelmed her. Christopher was alive! Her darling husband was not dead…but he didn't know her.

Sobs shook her as she stood in Saintclair's grasp. How could Christopher have forgotten her? The capitaine touched her hair with an awkward hand. Uncertainty and worry twisted the handsome panes of his face.

And then she tilted her face towards his. Her cheeks were wet with tears. Her lips quivered and parted as she attempted to stop her sobs. Saintclair enfolded her into his arms, pressing her breasts against his chest. He buried his face in her hair. She heard him inhale harshly.

'He has f-forgotten me,' she stammered.

Abruptly, he put her away from him but still held her in the circle of his arms.

'Who has forgotten you?' His voice was a hoarse whisper. He paused. 'How could any man ever forget you?'

He lifted his hand to her cheek to wipe her tears in a soft caress which sent shivers all over her body. She didn't react when he slid a finger under her chin to tilt her face up and bent down to kiss her. All she could do was close her eyes as his mouth brushed, light and soft against hers, teasing her lips apart. With a low growl he deepened his kiss and wrapped his arms tightly around her waist.

His mouth, in turn soft and demanding, took complete possession. A dark, hot, dangerous wave of desires and sensations she was powerless to fight swept her away. She whimpered softly as her body melted, tightened, and ached all at once against his. His breathing became faster, harsher. His hands trailed down to her hips, dug into her flesh, and ground her against his hard heat. Her legs hardly carrying her, she lifted her hands to his shoulders and clung to him for support. The world around vanished, time stopped. All she could hear was the pounding of her heart, the roaring of her blood, and the rustling of their clothing as they moved against each other.

A woman's laughter and the crunching of footsteps on the gravel path nearby brought her back to reality. What was she doing in Saintclair's arms? Had she had completely lost her mind?

She tore herself from his kiss, lowered her hands onto his chest, and pushed him away with all her strength. He breathed in sharply and let his hands fall to his sides, but his fists were clenched as if he was trying to control the urge to pull her against him again.

Without a word, and thankful for the darkness hiding her burning cheeks, she gathered her skirts and fled on the path towards the stairway.

'Where do you think you're going?' Saintclair grabbed her arm and spun her round.

'I'm going to confront Fouché and ask him about my husband. Please let me go!'

'What husband?' He looked down and frowned. 'You mean that man who was there with you just then was…'

She nodded.

He cursed under his breath.

'And what exactly are you planning to ask Fouché?' he asked. 'Do you really think he will acknowledge your husband—if it's indeed him—is his spy and give you an address where you can find him?'

'I don't know what he'll say, but I have to try something—anything—to find Christopher. Now let me go!' Her voice rose to a high pitch. She tried to shake free but his hand was a grip of steel on her arm.

'Think about it,' Saintclair carried on, calmly. 'If this man is your husband and works for Fouché, then he belongs to the underworld. He is a master at hiding, concealing his identity. Fouché will never admit to employing any agents, especially when he is no longer Minister of Police. And if you think for one minute he'll take pity of you, you are sorely mistaken.'

He released her at last.

Her shoulders slumped, and she heaved a ragged sigh. He was right. Fouché was hardly likely to be swayed by her tears.

'What shall I do, then? I have been waiting for him all these years. I always knew he wasn't dead, but tonight, I actually talked to him, touched him…'

She looked up. 'Please, Capitaine, help me.'

In the dimly lit cloister, his face looked carved in stone.

'Help you do what?' His voice was harsh.

'Find him, of course. I would do anything to see him again. I want my Christopher back.'

A sardonic grin appeared on his mouth. 'Are you sure? He did not appear to be in a flower picking or ballad singing mood tonight. He wanted to hurt you.'

'It's not his fault. He lost his memory, but I shall find him and make him remember me.'

Saintclair didn't reply. Why did he stand there, impassive, when he was her only hope? Christopher was so close, yet still out of reach. The tears she had been holding broke loose again. She collapsed on her knees, buried her face in her hands. She could hardly breathe as deep raking sobs shook her body. Saintclair lifted her up and held her against him for what felt like a long time.

'You are in no fit state to be seen like this,' he said at last. 'We will go to my rooms across the square.'

Chapter Nine

Hugo nodded at the sentinel guarding the entrance to the cuirassiers barracks and led Marie-Ange across a courtyard and along the stable blocks before climbing up to the first floor of the officers' wing. He wasn't expecting to be stopped. Nobody cared these days if officers brought women in.

The barracks were almost as busy as the *Palais Saint Pierre* across the square, albeit the men looked coarser, the women more dishevelled, and the conversation was much cruder. The place was like a tavern. It made his blood boil to see what had become of the strict and well disciplined regiment under its new leadership.

He unlocked his door.

'Wait here, I will get some light,' he said as he walked in and closed the door behind them. She leant against the wooden pane while he lit an oil lamp and placed it on the table. He then took her hand, pulled a chair out, and helped her sit down. She immediately started crying again.

'I don't know what to do. I just feel so helpless.' She was crying so hard she could hardly talk.

He frowned. The woman needed to calm down. She was making herself ill. He opened a cupboard, pulled out a bottle of cognac.

'Drink this.' He gave her a glass full of liquor.

Her hand shook as she lifted the glass to her lips but she managed to drink a few sips.

'Drink it all,' he insisted. She emptied the glass. He filled it again and she drained the brandy once more.

'Better?'

She nodded and lifted her gaze to him. Her eyes were a little heavier now, but at least they were dry.

'Thank you, Capitaine. You are the only person I can turn to.' Her voice broke into a sob.

He sighed with impatience.

'*Ah non!* You're not going to start crying again! Here, let me make you more comfortable.'

He pulled her to her feet and did what he had been dreaming of for days. Slowly, almost tenderly, he took the pins out of her hair. It cascaded down onto her shoulders and into the middle of her back. He slid his fingers in the thick mass of curls. His throat was tight, his breathing fast, his body ached with the need to touch and kiss her.

She stiffened and raised her face towards his.

'Capitaine, I don't think...' she protested weakly, closing her eyes as she swayed against him.

'I have wanted to do this ever since I first saw you,' he said.

'I feel a little strange.' Her voice was slurred, her body warm and soft.

'It's the brandy.' He bent down and kissed her lips until they opened under the gentle pressure.

Damn, she tasted good, a mixture of brandy and tears and her own sweet taste. His kiss deepened, became forceful. She gasped and melted against him, as if he was taking her breath, her strength away.

She made no move to resist him as his mouth trailed along her neck to her bare shoulder, and then slowly back up again. With one hand, he undid the buttons of his jacket which he discarded impatiently on the floor. He rolled Marie-Ange's white gloves down along her forearms and took them off with a sharp pull. He looked at her. Her slightly bewildered gaze met his.

'Tell me now if you want me to stop.'

She opened her mouth to speak but didn't say a word.

So he pulled her close and kissed her again.

Tentatively, she put her arms around his shoulders, slid her hands behind his neck, and tangled her fingers in his hair. His heart about to burst, his body throbbing with need, he proceeded to unfasten the hooks at the back of her dress before pulling down the delicate muslin gown from her shoulders. His fingers stroked the swelling of her breasts above her corset, ventured lower. She shuddered and threw her head back, offering more of her to his caresses. He groaned as he pulled her chemise lower and touched the tight, pink tips of her breasts. He traced light patterns with his thumbs, teasing and caressing until she let out a moan he stifled with a long, hard kiss.

She heaved out a shaky breath.

'Christopher.'

It was like a direct hit to the chest. He pulled away, staggered back, and held her at arms' length.

Her eyes opened, dreamy, unfocused. Her lips were still parted, rosy and swollen from his kisses.

'I will be dammed if you call another man's name while you're in my arms,' he said in a low, growling voice.

He turned away and raked his dark hair with his fingers. How he wanted to punch something, or someone—preferably the man she believed was her husband… He swallowed hard, took a deep breath and sat at the table, grabbed the bottle of cognac and poured a generous measure which he drank in one gulp. He grimaced as the liquor burned his throat. Hell, he needed more than that to quell the fire in his body.

He glanced up at the woman standing, silent, in the middle of the room. Her eyes were lowered to the ground, her cheeks and throat flushed, her blond hair tousled. With her arms folded across her chest, she looked lost and vulnerable. His anger subsided at once.

'My apologies,' he muttered. 'I shouldn't have taken advantage of your distress. It won't happen again.'

He poured himself another drink.

She neither answered nor looked at him but put her dress in order with trembling hands. Desire, anger, regret stabbed at his chest—and then a flash of desire again as she pulled her dress to cover the swell of her breasts. His hand gripped his glass so tight his knuckles went white. He took a deep, ragged, breath. Sensations burned through him like a firebrand—the feel of her against him, the silk of her skin under his fingertips, her feverish abandon as he trailed kisses along her throat to the tip of her breasts. *And all along, it was her husband she pined for*. He could almost laugh. Almost.

He clenched his jaw and gestured for the woman to sit at the table opposite him.

'Tell me about Corunna.'

Her face flushed, she sat opposite him, folded her hands in her lap and closed her eyes, perhaps to collect her thoughts.

'The *HMS Amazon* moored in the bay of Corunna between January sixteenth and eighteenth of 1809. Christopher was supervising the repatriation of the sick and the wounded soldiers ordered by General Moore, and confirmed by General Hope after Moore was shot. The *Amazon* was hit by French fire at nightfall on the eighteenth. It sank rapidly and rescue attempts were hindered by the French artillery which continued firing throughout the night. Not a single member of the crew was found alive.'

'Yes. That's pretty much what I heard too,' Hugo said, thoughtful. He poured a glass of cognac which he handed to her. She left it untouched in front of her.

'I have been thinking a lot about what might have happened these past few days,' she said. 'What if Christopher was able to grab a piece of wood, a barrel, anything, and the current carried him away from the rest of the fleet further down the coast? He might have been wounded or in shock, his uniform torn, with nothing to identify him as British.'

Hugo crossed his arms on his chest. 'Go on.'

'Later he might have been sent to a French field hospital, seriously wounded and unable to remember who he was. And when he recovered, he could have been transferred to a French regiment and finished the war on the French side. He spoke perfect French, I told you before.'

'And you are positive that the man you saw, tonight and in Paris, is *your husband*?'

Marie-Ange nodded. 'I know it's him. But he doesn't,' she replied quietly.

The conviction in her voice was unmistakable. 'Yes, I suppose it's possible,' he said. 'Stranger things have happened. You said he now went under the name of…?'

'Nallay,' she replied. 'Joseph Nallay'

His mind was made up. One way or another he would get hold of this Nallay. If nothing else, he'd give the man a good beating for manhandling Marie-Ange in the *Palais Saint-Pierre*'s gardens and would get rid of one of Fouché's spies at the same time. And if the man turned out to be her husband, well, things would get complicated.

'You do realise that you may not like what we find,' he said, glancing up at her.

She nodded. 'I must know, Capitaine,' was all she answered.

'Well then…'

He stood up, retrieved his jacket from the floor, and put it back on. 'Come on, I'll escort you back to the ball and start looking for Nallay. I have a few contacts here in Lyon I can put on the man's trail.' He buttoned his jacket.

Marie-Ange stood and asked timidly, 'Please, Capitaine? I cannot manage these.' She pointed to her dress.

He gave an impatient grunt before standing behind her to fasten the tiny hooks, all the time striving to resist the

124

urge to draw her into his arms again. When he finished, he couldn't resist stroking the silky, creamy skin across her shoulders. She shivered violently under his touch, hissed a sharp breath, and pulled away as if she'd been burnt. She probably didn't trust him not to touch her again because she walked to the other side of the room to twist her hair in a plait and put her white gloves back on.

At last she said she was ready and they made their way out.

'Do you think you can find Rochefort, Capitaine? I don't want to return to the ball,' she said as they crossed the square towards the *Palais Saint Pierre.* Hugo looked for Malleval's carriage among the barouches, cabriolets, and berlins lining the square.

At last he spied the man's bulky figure. 'Rochefort is over there. He'll take you home.'

The big man was smoking a clay pipe and talking with other drivers.

'Madame Norton is tired,' Hugo told him, opening the carriage door and helping her inside.

'Very well,' Rochefort grunted, tapped his pipe against the sole of his boot, put it back into his coat pocket, and jumped up onto the driver's box.

Hugo leant inside to speak quietly with Marie-Ange. 'I will let Malleval know you weren't feeling well. I'll be in touch when I have news.' He closed the door and stepped aside.

As soon as the carriage pulled away, he strode off towards the Saint Paul district. With its seedy taverns frequented by men from all walks of life, from army personnel, municipal officers and professionals in search of illicit thrills, to larceners, pickpockets and hardened criminals, it was the place to fish for information about Joseph Nallay.

Chapter Ten

Marie-Ange reclined on the seat and attempted to marshal her whirling thoughts and emotions and bring the night's events into some semblance of order. Christopher was alive, but he was amnesic and so changed it was hard to reconcile the man who handled her so roughly this evening with the gentle husband who treasured her. Her throat tightened with pity and sadness. Heavens knew what life he had led, what terrible sufferings he had endured since Corunna. She pressed her hand against her heart and took a deep breath. Well, she would find him and do everything in her power to help him remember his past.

And then what? Would they go back to Wellcombe as man and wife? The prospect of resuming her married life which would have filled her with joy a few weeks ago now made her uneasy. The man she had encountered tonight was cold and cruel, with an almost inhuman harshness in his eyes. What if he didn't change once he got back to Norton Place? Or worse, what if he never regained his memory? She shook her head. She was being silly. Of course, he would remember, and then everything would be fine.

There was however the burning issue of Capitaine Saintclair. She closed her eyes and swallowed hard. She couldn't deny any longer that she was attracted to him. Shame heated her cheeks as she recalled how quickly she had forgotten her husband tonight in the arms of the French officer. How she yearned for him to touch and kiss her and make her body alive. She let out a sob, clenched her fist, and brought it to her mouth.

Christopher's face had floated in her mind like a reproach when Saintclair was kissing her earlier, yet she hadn't even torn herself away from the French officer's embrace! She was weak and pathetic. She had to get a grip on herself and fight the attraction. Saintclair might have set her senses on fire but he did not have her heart. Her heart would always belong to Christopher.

The island looked dark and foreboding in the middle of the river, but there were still lights inside Malleval's mansion. The young maid who had helped her get ready before opened the front door.

'A visitor is waiting for you in the study, Madame,' she announced

'Who is that?'

'Monsieur Karloff.'

Fear tightened Marie-Ange's chest. Karloff! The physician employed by Edmond Malleval to induce her grandmother to talk about the Cross of Life and Saint Germain. The man who had denied Malleval a Christian burial and who eagerly waited for her arrival from England...

Entirely clad in black in the manner of a priest, Karloff sat in an armchair near the fire, holding a book with long, bony hands. He appeared so absorbed in his reading he didn't raise his head when she walked in and all she could see of his face was his sharp, beaky nose and the grey hair he wore loose and so long it brushed the pages of the book.

'Monsieur?' She approached cautiously, remembering Sophie's warnings and her grandmother's reservations.

He looked up. She hardly took in his features—the lean face, hollow cheeks and thin lips—so intense were the dark brown eyes fixed upon her.

'Madame Norton, it is a pleasure to meet you at last. I am Gustave Karloff, an old friend of Monsieur Malleval.' He stood up and bowed in front of her before gesturing to one of the armchairs positioned near the fireplace. 'Will you sit down?'

She couldn't think of an excuse to refuse, so she took a seat in the armchair opposite his.

'There is no point wasting time in formalities.' He smiled. 'I believe Uxeloup has already told you we are interested in an object which used to be in your family's possession. The Cross of Life.'

'He did indeed.' So there it was again. The mysterious Cross of Life and its links to her family.

Karloff suddenly frowned. He bent forward and pointed to her throat, a covetous gleam in his eyes.

'*Tudieu*! Your locket! It looks remarkably similar to the one Saint Germain is wearing in his portrait at Beauregard. Could I take a look at it, please?'

Marie-Ange's response was instinctive. Her hand flew to her throat, her fingers closed protectively over the pendant, and she shook her head.

'Very well,' he muttered, tightening his thin lips.

He reclined in his chair, crossed his long legs, and entwined his fingers. 'I know your mother had a rare talent as a painter and kept her watercolours and drawings of Beauregard in a sketchbook she took with her when she left for England.'

'You mean when she escaped from Edmond Malleval's fortress where he kept her a prisoner?' Marie-Ange snapped. Even though she didn't want to openly confront the physician, she was unable to hide her hostility. Together with Edmond Malleval, the man facing her had instigated her grandmother's death and caused great harm to her mother, too. 'Yes, she did have a sketchbook. Why should you be interested?'

'I would like very much to see it. I believe the drawings hold clues as to the location of the Cross.'

'Why would they?' she asked. 'And more to the point, why should I help you and Uxeloup Malleval get hold of this Cross? If it is as precious as you suggest, it should belong to the Church.'

She stood up. 'Now if you will excuse me, I wish to retire to my room.'

She moved to the door but Karloff was faster and blocked her way out.

'You don't understand how important the Cross is for me, for Malleval. For all of us,' he said, staring into her eyes. 'You must help me. You must hand over your mother's sketchbook and the locket.'

Marie-Ange parted her lips to breathe but there was no air in the room. Karloff's eyes became darker and so large it felt as if she was being sucked into two bottomless pits with everything around her blurred like in a dream—or a nightmare. Tingling sensations, like pins and needles, crept onto her face and neck, and her body felt suddenly heavy and limp.

Fear made Marie-Ange's heart pound so hard it hurt. It took all her willpower to tear herself away from his deep gaze. Immediately her heartbeat returned to normal and the room came back into focus. She swallowed hard.

'I regret I cannot help you, Monsieur Karloff, and I can assure you there is nothing in my mother's paintings that can be of interest to you.'

She tilted her head up and added. 'Now please let me through or I shall call for help.'

Karloff reluctantly stepped away from the door. 'Very well, but you know something, and I will find out what it is,' he warned before opening the door.

She made her way to her bedroom through dark and quiet corridors. Dealing with Karloff after her encounter with Christopher and her sensual duel with Saintclair left her drained and nauseous. The physician was odd and intense, and just as obsessed as Uxeloup. Once in her room, she stripped off, bathed her face with cold water and slipped into her nightdress. She opened her travel bag to pull out her mother's art book and settled into bed. Why were both men so certain her mother knew about the Cross of Life and had passed on her knowledge to her? And why did Karloff believe there were clues in the drawings?

Even though she had no idea what she was looking for, she studied every one of the sketches and watercolours until late into the night. She didn't discern anything new. What was she missing?

Sighing, she closed the book shut. On an impulse, she wrapped it in one of her chemises, and together with the locket, hid it at the bottom of the bag under a pile of undergarments and clothing. She slid into bed and blew out the candle. Through the open curtains the city lights flickered in the distance on either sides of the river, which was now as black as a precipice. She closed her eyes and drifted to sleep.

She had no idea how long she had been dozing when she became aware of a presence in the room.

'Do you remember the words, Marie-Ange?' a man's voice said close to her. She cried out. Her heart hammering against her ribs, she sat up to glance around the room. It was empty.

She heaved a sigh of relief. So it was just a dream.

She lay down and fell asleep again.

'Tell me the words of the song your mother taught you, and then give me the sketchbook and the locket.' The voice intruded on her dreams, this time with more insistence.

Startled, she opened her eyes to find she wasn't lying in bed any longer but sitting against one of the bed posts. A tall, lean man stood facing her. Karloff! Why was he there? How did he get in? She tried to move but her body didn't respond, and when she opened her mouth to protest, no sound came out.

Karloff bent down. His dark brown eyes shone like diamonds and locked on hers like a serpent's compelling gaze. This time, Marie-Ange couldn't look away.

'You want to remember, don't you? You want to tell me the words.' His voice was smooth and persuasive.

Strangely, Marie-Ange knew exactly what he meant.

'Yes,' she said. 'I do.'

A tiny, childlike voice rose from deep within her and she started singing, using old French words.

Ma mie, ma rose de mai
Ma rose aux cinq pétales,
Qui dans la tour aux colombes
Pleure ton amant dans sa tombe.

'This is lovely. This is what I want. Carry on, Marie-Ange.'

A disturbing, persistent sound, like the rattling of tree branches against the window broke the spell he held on her. She looked away from him for the briefest moment and the words of the song seemed to vanish from her memory like clouds of mist evaporating under the sun.

Karloff got up from the bed and cursed under his breath.

'*Tudieu!* I almost had it.' He stalked across the room, opened the door, and sneaked out like a shadow.

Marie-Ange collapsed on the bed. Her eyes closed and she slid into a deep sleep…

She woke to the sounds of water washing against the rocks under her window, river fowl splashing in the rushes, and birds calling in the evergreens. The room was bathed in a grey and pink light. She stretched, enjoying the sensual feeling of the fine linen sheets against her skin, but immediately images from her dream came flooding back—Karloff, in her room, asking her about a song while she sat on the bed, unable to move…

She frowned. What a disturbing, unpleasant dream it had been, probably caused by the strain of the past few days and her meeting with the physician the evening before. And yet it seemed so real.

A winter sun rose over the city, staining the sky with a bloody, fiery glow. She got out of bed, opened the window and breathed in the cool morning air which carried the silt scent of the river. The morning might look tranquil, yet she felt anything but peaceful. She dressed and went downstairs to the dining room where two maids were setting the breakfast table. They placed a basket of bread rolls and brioches, a plate of eggs and ham and a cup of coffee in front of her.

'Did Madame sleep well?' One of the girls enquired.

'Yes, thank you,' Marie-Ange lied. 'The house is very quiet this morning.'

'Monsieur Uxeloup didn't return until dawn. He'll sleep until lunchtime now. Monsieur likes his sleep, especially when he's been smoking his pipe.'

'Justine! Shh…Don't be so indiscreet,' the other maid scolded.

'What about Monsieur Karloff?' Marie-Ange hoped she wouldn't see him this morning.

The girl called Justine shrugged. 'He already left. He said he had patients waiting for him. He's a well-known physician, you know. People come from all over France, Europe even, for his treatments and potions.' She shuddered. 'My grandma says he's one of those hypnotists who can make you do things just by looking into your eyes.' She lowered her voice. 'She also says he belongs to some secret society…'

'Justine!' the other maid remonstrated forcefully. 'You'll never keep your place if you gossip about Monsieur and his guests.'

'I'm only speaking the truth,' Justine grumbled before going out.

Over breakfast, Marie-Ange pondered what the girl had said. So Karloff knew how to hypnotise people, like Anton Mesmer, a doctor who had caused a scandal some years ago for claiming he could treat his patients with the power of suggestion alone. Wasn't that exactly what her grandmother had written about in her letter and what Sophie had mentioned at Beauregard?

She sat back in her chair. How had she failed to understand before? She hadn't dreamt the incident with Karloff last night. The man had actually come into her bedroom. A sudden, fierce anxiety constricted her throat and tightened her chest. Her hand shook so much she had to put her cup of coffee down. What intrigue had she gotten herself mixed up with? By coming here, she had fallen into a trap set by Uxcloup and his physician. Last night Karloff wanted the words of a song, the very same song her mother used to sing to send her to sleep. A song Marie-Ange had all but forgotten. Until now.

My sweet rose of May
My rose with the five petals,
You cry in the dovecote
For your lover, cold in his tomb.'

What about the rest? She frowned with concentration, but it was no good, she couldn't remember any more.

She had been so young when her mother died. Sometimes she wasn't sure if her memories were real or mixed with dreams and stories she had made up later. One thing however was certain. The song had been important. Her mother had sung it to her in the evening, over and over again.

She pushed her chair back and sprang to her feet. She needed some air, and a place to figure out what to do next. A walk on the island or into the city would clear her head. She rushed up to her room to fetch her cloak, bonnet and gloves, and ran back down again.

'I'm going out,' she informed Justine as they passed in the hall.

The young maid looked panic-stricken. 'You can't! I mean Monsieur said you weren't to leave the house. Let me call Rochefort, he's in the cellar.'

Marie-Ange shook her head. 'No, I want to be by myself.'

She opened the front door and walked to the gates. They were locked, a thick metal bar across them. Disappointed, she turned round. There must be another way out of the estate. She would walk along the park's stone wall until she found it.

'Wait!' Rochefort hailed her. He strode her way with a determined look on his thick, brutish features. 'You're not to go anywhere, M'ame, not without me.'

Marie-Ange leant against the gates and pressed her hands against her throat to fight a wave of nausea. She wasn't Malleval's guest any longer. She was his prisoner.

Chapter Eleven

Glancing around uneasily for fear of being discovered eavesdropping on Malleval's and Capitaine Saintclair's conversation, Marie-Ange tiptoed outside the study's closed door.

'I hope you're not going back on your word. You can't do that to her, not after she came all this way.' Saintclair sounded angry but Malleval only laughed.

'What I do with Marie-Ange Norton is none of your business, so keep well out of it. Don't force me to review our arrangement, Saintclair. You owe me five thousand Francs, remember? You don't want to cross me and have the bailiffs knocking at your door in St Genis and dragging your family out into the street at dawn. Think about poor Lucie's health, your mother's tears and your father's shame if they found out their son lost their lovely house in a game of cards. Actually I find the whole thing is rather ironic, since that's how you got the damned house in the first place.'

'Don't you dare threaten my family with eviction,' Saintclair replied in a low, growling voice. 'I will pay you back every *sou* I owe you, but you will have to give me a little time.'

Malleval laughed. 'And where the devil will you find five thousand Francs?'

Saintclair muttered something Marie-Ange didn't hear. She stepped closer to the door but voices nearby announced people were coming this way. Her heart fluttering, she pulled away from the door and walked to the drawing room.

Standing near the fireplace she waited for Capitaine Saintclair, anxious for news about his search for Christopher. Three days had passed since the ball. Three days, during which she had been in virtual house arrest, allowed only to take short walks in the park, always with Rochefort on her heels. Malleval had kept to his room, claiming the old battle wound was causing him too much pain to visit his notary and formalise her inheritance. Marie-Ange now doubted the existence of this mysterious injury—he had after all been well enough to dance at the ball.

She stifled a yawn. She hadn't slept much the night before, haunted once again by strange and terrifying images and voices. The dreams always started in the same way. Karloff's deep, soothing voice intruded into her sleep and asked her to remember the words of her mother's song, which she never could. She saw a tall, round tower with strange symbols carved on its walls. One side of the wall opened onto a staircase descending into the bowels of the earth, to a place filled with obscurity, horrid whistling, thudding noises, and distant screams. There were shadows down there, entities that sought to snatch something from her.

Every time, she woke shaking with fear and drenched in sweat.

She shivered and wrapped her shawl more closely around her shoulders. Outside the windows, a thick fog floated above the greenish water, hiding the banks of the river. It seemed she was sailing alone on a ghost ship, lost on a faraway sea.

Footsteps in the corridor made her turn and look expectantly towards the door. She hadn't seen Saintclair since the evening of the ball. She hoped she would be able to pretend nothing had happened between them but doubted very much her ability to do so. The memories of his caresses and her own unbridled desire still made her blush with shame. Even now as she put her hands to her cheeks she could feel they were burning.

Saintclair entered. His expression was sombre and tired. The scar on his face stood out starkly. He bowed silently, his blue glare filtered through his black eyelashes.

'Malleval was always a wastrel but at least he used to keep his word,' he declared without preamble, anger bubbling in his voice. 'I fear he has now lost the last threads of decency he possessed.' He took a deep breath. 'I don't think he has any intention of giving you what he promised—what you came all this way for.'

'I see…' She twisted her wedding ring around her finger.

'He said he was in no hurry to settle your bequest, that he had plans for you, whatever that means.' He sighed. 'I am sorry I ever agreed to escort you to France. I never thought…'

She had herself reached the same conclusion—Malleval lured her to France under a false pretence when all he wanted was the Cross of Life. Hearing Saintclair voice his opinion was the catalyst she needed and in a flash her resolve to flee solidified.

'Will you help me get away from here?' she asked, her voice barely a whisper. 'If you take me to a coach terminal in Lyon, I will buy a passage to Beaujeu. I have enough money left. After that, I shall ask my great-aunt for help.'

'Are you sure that's wise?' Saintclair's face was impassive. 'If you leave now, there'll be no chance at all of any money coming to you.'

'There was never an inheritance,' she retorted. 'Malleval fooled me. I need to get away from this house but Rochefort follows me everywhere.' She moved closer and put her hand on his forearm. 'Please, Capitaine. I know you have an agreement with Malleval about a gambling debt but…'

He glanced at her, startled. 'Did he tell you that?'

'No. Never mind how I found out,' she replied, unwilling to reveal she searched his pockets and read his correspondence while he slept, as well as eavesdropped on his private conversations.

She bit her bottom lip as she waited anxiously for his response. She was asking him to betray a fellow cavalry officer—a man he had known and fought beside for years—and to jeopardise any chance of wiping his gambling debt off. Yet it only took Saintclair a few seconds to make his decision.

'Get a few things together, only the essentials, and not your travel bag. We don't want to arouse anyone's suspicions,' he instructed.

Marie-Ange nodded and went to her room. She put her mother's sketch book, a couple of undergarments, and what was left of her travel money into her reticule before clasping the gold locket around her neck and grabbing her cloak, hat and gloves. She glanced at Christopher's dressing gown with a twinge of regret, started towards it, hesitated. There was no room for it in her small bag. She had to leave it behind.

She returned to the drawing room quietly, anxious to avoid any member of Malleval's household staff, especially Rochefort.

'Ready?' Saintclair took her arm and they made their way from the house.

Marie-Ange's heart sank when she saw Rochefort grooming a horse in the courtyard. The big man stared at them suspiciously and dropped his bristle brush in a bucket of water.

'Where are you going, Capitaine?' he asked.

'I'm taking Madame Norton to a seamstress in town for a dress fitting. Malleval's orders. I will bring her back later,' Saintclair replied with a tone that suffered no questioning. 'Bring my horse now, please.'

Rochefort frowned but fetched Saintclair's horse from

the stable block. The capitaine lifted Marie-Ange up and helped her sit side-saddled. He mounted behind her, loosened the reins, and touched the horse with his leg to send it forward and out of the courtyard.

'We'd better hurry,' he said, spurring the horse on as soon as they were on the lane. 'Malleval will probably send his men after us as soon as he finds out we're gone. He knows the only place you can go is your aunt's castle in Marzac, so his men will check the inns where coaches depart for Belleville and Beaujeu first.' He paused. 'Which is why we're not going there.'

'Where are we going, then?' Marie-Ange's face brushed against his shoulder as she turned to speak to him. She sat uneasy, her back stiff against his chest. The warmth of his body brought back sensations she had tried to forget since the night of the ball. She wriggled and attempted to shift forward, away from him.

'I am taking you to my family in St Genis.' His arms closed in tightly around her.

'Will I be welcome? They do not know me and...' She stuttered and shuffled uncomfortably on the saddle again.

'My family may be of humble origin, Madame, but they know how to welcome guests,' he retorted, tightening his grip around her. 'Now, will you sit still? You're going to get us both thrown.'

'Sorry,' she muttered.

They rode in silence until they crossed the bridge over the River Saône. Soon they were on the main road leading to the town centre.

'I met Uxeloup's doctor, Gustave Karloff, the other night after the ball,' Marie-Ange said. 'He asked me about the Cross of Life. He too seems to believe I can find it.'

'I wish I understood what this business of the Cross was all about. Karloff is a strange man who fancies himself as some sort of wise man or mage. I know Malleval trusts him with his...ahem...condition. I don't. I am always suspicious of fanatics.'

'Yes, he is very peculiar,' she agreed, 'and just as obsessed as Uxeloup.' She wondered whether to tell him the old man had intruded into her bedroom and tried to hypnotise her, and that she heard his voice in her sleep every night. She came to the conclusion she should wait until she understood what it all meant.

The fog was lifting over the city, but it was still bitterly cold. The quays of the river Saône were lined with boats being loaded with cargo, sacks, and crates. Shops lined the other side of the street. Milliners' windows displayed colourful hats and fabrics. Smells of freshly baked bread and pies escaped from bakeries. Outside *brasseries* and taverns lingered tantalising aromas of coffee, stew, and roast meats. Most of the buildings along the embankment were painted attractive shades of ochre, cream and light pink. Tall church spires lifted majestically towards the sky. A wooded hill with chateaux and elegant houses rose on the other side of the river. It was her first glimpse of the town in the daylight and it was beautiful.

'Have you heard anything about my husband?' she asked.

Saintclair tensed against her.

'Not yet. I sent word that I'm looking for a man who calls himself Nallay. I wrote to my friend, Martin, requesting he do the same in Paris. We have to wait for his move now. If Nallay is indeed one of Fouché's men, he will get in touch, one way or another.'

They reached the *Place Louis le Grand*. The flower market in the square bustled with traders and passers-by. He halted and dismounted in front of *La Gargote*, a large inn at the corner of the square. In one swift movement he swung Marie-Ange to the ground and set her gently on her feet. She grasped his arm for a moment until her legs were steady.

'I will procure a place on the coach to St Genis for you

and follow on horseback,' he said before handing control of his mount to a stable boy. He held the door open and followed her into the inn. They were in luck. A coach was ready to leave for Vienne, stopping at various towns and villages on the way, including St Genis.

The coach pulled onto St Genis' market square just over an hour later. They walked through the village's narrow cobbled streets, with Saintclair leading his horse by the reins. It was after lunch and the village was quiet, apart from the immediate surroundings of a small tavern where several drunkards were causing a disturbance. One of them shouted as they walked past. He was short and stocky, with matted straw blond hair and bloodshot blue eyes. He wore filthy rags and clogs far too large for his bare feet.

'*Oye*, Saintclair! Remember me?' he called. 'You threw me out of your regiment six months ago. You said I wasn't good enough, even to scrub horse dung from your boots!' He spat on the floor.

Saintclair ignored him and walked on, which served to make the man even more belligerent.

'You think you're so high and mighty, don't you? But you'd better beware. I'll show you and your family what I can do.'

'Wait here,' Saintclair told Marie-Ange.

He didn't seem in any hurry as he tied the reins of his horse to a post and walked towards the drunk who suddenly appeared to lose all his bravado and cowered against the wall. Saintclair grabbed the collar of his dirty shirt, lifted him up effortlessly and pinned him against the wall. The man's feet wriggled above the ground, he waved his arms about but couldn't break free from the cuirassier's iron grip.

'Don't you ever threaten my family again,' Saintclair said in a low, growling voice. 'Or I'll slice you open and leave your carcass to rot in the gutter. Understood?'

The drunk nodded, his bloodshot blue eyes bulging, his

face turning beetroot red. Saintclair released him and he fell in a heap onto the cobbles. Saintclair wiped his hands on his breeches and turned round. The man picked himself up and scampered away after shooting the Capitaine a look so filled with hatred it sent a shiver with fear down Marie-Ange's back.

'That man wishes you harm,' she remarked.

The officer shrugged. 'He's a drunk. He'll be dead in a matter of months, in a brawl if not from the bottle.' His tone was dismissive, but she couldn't help looking over her shoulder.

'Here we are.' He stopped outside a garden wall and pushed a freshly-painted green gate open. A gravel path led to an elegant, two storey house covered with ivy. The door opened onto a middle-aged woman dressed in a simple grey dress and a white pinafore. Her dark hair was neatly tucked under a white bonnet and she had the same piercing blue eyes as Saintclair.

'Hugo! You never sent word that you were coming. Two visits in less than a week. We are lucky,' she exclaimed, her face radiant.

She turned towards Marie-Ange. 'And you brought a guest, too. Good afternoon, Madame. I am Hugo's mother, Emilie Saintclair.'

She curtsied briefly. Saintclair introduced Marie-Ange and disappeared with his horse towards the back of the house.

'Please come in.' Madame Saintclair gestured to the open door.

Marie-Ange entered the black and white tiled hall. Rust coloured paper adorned the walls, house plants on a sideboard and a couple of landscape paintings near an oak staircase gave the hallway a welcoming, if unpretentious, appearance. Emilie Saintclair took Marie-Ange's coat and gloves and hung them on the tall hall stand. There were cleaning cloths and some polishing balm on a console.

'Hugo decided I should have a maid and a cook but I just can't get used to it,' she explained, her voice apologetic and her cheeks a little flushed as she folded the cloths and screwed the top back on the pot of polish. 'It is so tedious to sit in the parlour, being waited upon all day. I much prefer to do my own chores.'

Saintclair came back, shook his boots on the mat and took his riding jacket off. He bent towards his mother and kissed her cheek.

'How are you, Mother? And how is Lucie today?'

'I am fine, my love, but your sister hasn't been very well. Her cough has been troubling her again and her eyes…' She didn't finish but a heavy sigh escaped her lips. She led the way to a room at the back of the house.

Marie-Ange's first impression of Lucie was of a fragile lily. The pale and slender girl was lying on a chaise longue near the window overlooking a large garden.

'Hugo. What a lovely surprise.' She tried to get up but was overcome by a fit of coughing and reclined onto the cushions, a handkerchief pressed to her pale lips. Saintclair rushed to her side and took her hands.

'Don't get up, darling.' He kissed her forehead and arranged a few cushions around her. He turned towards Marie-Ange. 'Lucie, this is Madame Norton. She is going to stay here a few days.'

Lucie's face lit up. 'You are the lady who helped Hugo choose these lovely kerchiefs in Paris for me!' She showed Marie-Ange the delicately embroidered white and pink linen square she was clutching in her slim hand. 'Come closer so I can see you.' Lucie blinked a few times. Her eyes were inflamed and swollen.

'You are as beautiful as Hugo said.'

Marie-Ange felt she was blushing.

'Please come and sit near me. Hugo said you lived in England near the sea. I wish to know all about your house, and all about you.'

'Of course.' Marie-Ange sat next to the girl and took her hand, feeling an instinctive sympathy for Saintclair's sister.

'Can I leave you two ladies to chat while I ask *Maman* to get us something to eat? I'm famished.' Saintclair walked towards the door, but lingered just inside the room for a moment.

'So do you really live in an old castle?' Lucie asked.

Marie-Ange shook her head. 'It isn't a real castle. It is so old tiles fall off the roof almost every day, the chimneys don't work properly, and the doors don't shut right. It's always cold and draughty too, as we are on the moors. Having said that, the coast is beautiful.' Marie-Ange smiled wistfully as she spoke of Norton Place.

She turned to Saintclair. His expression was so tender and loving as he looked at his sister her throat tightened and tears pricked her eyes. He wasn't the cynical cuirassier officer any longer but a deeply caring man, a loving brother.

'I won't be long,' he promised before walking out.

Later in the afternoon, after a collation of hot chocolate and cakes for the ladies and thick slabs of bread, roast meat, and a pitcher of ale for Saintclair, Madame Saintclair showed Marie-Ange to her room. It was small but comfortable, with dark green curtains framing two windows overlooking the garden, and a large double bed covered with a thick pink and white counterpane.

'Please make yourself at home, dear. I know this isn't what you're used to…'

'This is perfect. You have such a lovely house, Madame Saintclair.'

'Hugo works very hard for us all. Quite how he has managed to buy this property on an officer's pay, I'll never know.'

She gave a resigned smile. 'Or maybe I'd rather not

know. He was adamant that Lucie should move from our house in the old weavers' district of Lyon. He was right, of course. It was far too damp for the girl, being so close to the river.'

The woman walked to the window and added quietly, 'He is a good son, and a devoted brother.' She turned to Marie-Ange, a little hesitant. 'He told me you were in a spot of trouble. I want you to know that you are welcome to stay here for as long as you need.' She curtsied again.

'I am grateful for your hospitality, Madame Saintclair,' Marie-Ange replied, her chest tight with guilt. Because of her, the Saintclairs risked losing the house which meant so much to them.

She put her reticule on the bed and proceeded to take out the few items she managed to cram in before fleeing *Isle Barbe*. She could do with more clothes and toiletries. All her things were either at Uxeloup's mansion on the island or at Beauregard and who knew if she would be able to go back there anytime soon? She asked Madame Saintclair to recommend a laundry woman to help with her washing and a seamstress who could turn out a dress or two quickly.

'Not to worry, dear. Give me your things and I will see that they are laundered. As for a seamstress, look no further. It was my occupation before we came to live here. My husband, Horace, has a small silk workshop in Lyon.' She let out a sigh. 'He always entertained the hope that Hugo would resign from the army and learn the trade, but I don't think my son will ever consider becoming a *soyeux*. He is far too keen on travel and adventure.' She sighed. 'At any rate, I used to make dresses and ladies accessories and it would please me very much to make a dress for you.'

'Oh, no, I really couldn't let you,' Marie-Ange protested.

'I would be delighted. We will ask my husband to bring

some samples from the workshop. For now, I will leave you to rest. You must be tired.'

Madame Saintclair closed the door softly behind her and Marie-Ange lay down on the bed. For the first time in days, she felt safe—safe enough to close her eyes and fall asleep in a matter of seconds.

She dreamt of her mother and it was her voice she heard, not Karloff's. It was her beautiful face she saw instead of frightening shadows, and the warmth of her arms she felt around her instead of the cold, damp darkness.

Ma mie, ma rose de mai
Ma rose aux cinq pétales,
Qui dans la tour aux colombes,
Pleure l'amant dans la tombe....
Ecoute moi, Ne pleure pas,
Ton bel amour tu reverras,
La rose sur le coeur, tourne cinq fois,
Lève les yeux et l'aile tu trouveras.
Mais choisis bien, prudente et sage,
Si l'aile de la colombe
Est blanche comme celle de l'ange,
Elle n'ouvre pas les tombes.

The voice faded away. Her mother's face became fainter.

Marie-Ange opened her eyes. That was the song. She remembered it now, all of it! She sang the words aloud a couple of times to make sure she memorised them. What a strange song it was, about a girl called Rose who cried for her dead lover. The girl went into a dovecote to retrieve an angel wing that would make her lover come back to life. This was the song Karloff so desperately wanted her to remember—a song about eternal life.

A rush of excitement surged through her. Perhaps the song referred to the Cross of Life and its relic? If so, they were hidden in a dovecote. She put her hand on her pounding heart. Could it be the dovecote at Beauregard, the one Count Saint Germain ordered a team of craftsmen to build? Feverishly, she took the sketchbook and turned the pages. There it was! She had always been fascinated by the drawings of the dovecote and the intricate carvings of roses inside it. Dozens and dozens of roses. Now that she looked more closely, she noticed that they were all very similar to her locket. She unclasped the pendant from her neck and held it in front of her.

'*Ma rose aux cinq pétales,*' she whispered. The rose embossed on the locket had five petals, too.

She knew a little about roses as they had been her father's passion. William Jones had grown them and tended to them lovingly in the garden of their Plymouth townhouse. He had collected paintings, etchings, and writings about them and naturally, Marie-Ange had taken an interest in the flowers, too. Roses were powerful, conflicting, symbols of life and death, desire, passion and virginity; and because their heart was hidden in their fragrant folds, of esoteric knowledge and secrecy.

She recalled a medieval pamphlet she had read about the depiction of roses. A five petaled rose symbolised life, a six petaled rose represented love. The rarest was a flower with eight petals and it represented mystery. The roses on the locket, in the dovecote, and in the song all had five petals. They stood for the Fifth Element. Life force. Immortality.

Marie-Ange sang the song to herself again. How did the girl in the song get hold of the relic? She placed a rose on a heart and gave five turns. Were these supposed to be a real flower, a real heart? She looked down at the locket which Saint Germain had given her mother during his last visit at Beauregard, shortly before the dovecote was built and a few months before his death. It was important. She could sense it, but why?

She pressed it against her own heart and sighed. She

was missing something. She leant over the drawing of the dovecote again. After several minutes of intense scrutiny she finally saw it. In the middle of the central beam, hidden among carvings of roses, was a heart shape.

The locket, the rose and the heart… She thought about it for a while. There was only one way to find out if she was right. She had to go to Beauregard.

A knock on the door startled her.

'Supper is ready, dear,' Madame Saintclair informed her.

Saintclair and Lucie were playing a game of piquet at the dining room table.

'Hugo! You should be ashamed of yourself. Put these cards away! You are not in your officers' canteen,' Madame Saintclair reprimanded, a smile belying the severe tone of her voice.

Lucie laughed when she saw her brother put on a contrite expression.

'Yes, Mother.' He gathered the cards and slipped them in his pocket.

A tall and strongly built man with steel grey hair entered and took his place at the head of the table. He bowed to Marie-Ange.

'Madame, we are honoured to have you as our guest.' His voice was deep and pleasant. He bent his head and joined his hands to say grace. They were rough and calloused, probably because of his work with silk weaving looms.

During dinner, they talked about Lyon and the silk industry which was experiencing a revival in peace time.

'My son and I disagreed about Napoleon for a long time,' Monsieur Saintclair said. 'Hugo was enthralled by him but I always had my doubts. He did our country a great deal of harm. All these wars almost ruined me and my fellow guild members, not to mention the hundreds of thousands of dead on the battlefields.'

Hugo nodded. 'I have come to agree with you, Father. I'll never be a royalist but have come to recognise that Napoleon's wars cost far too many lives, caused too much destruction.' He looked down and added in a low voice. 'I shall never forget the horrors I saw during the Russian campaign. My men forced to slaughter and eat their horses; then force-marched in ragged uniforms on frozen roads for days, suffering from frostbite, crying with hunger and pain, hallucinating in the white hell.' His voice was flat and distant, as if he was reliving terrible nightmares.

'Hugo, my love,' Madame Saintclair said quietly. 'Not now.'

'Sorry, Mother.' He shook his head, let out a long sigh, and looked up.

Marie-Ange tightened her grip on her knife and fork to fight the overwhelming urge to touch the side of his face and soothe away the pain in his eyes.

'Why don't you leave the army and join Father at the workshop?' Lucie asked brightly. 'You know how much it would mean to us all, we wouldn't have to worry about you getting killed or wounded anymore. And you could live nearby all the time. Maybe even marry.'

'Lucie, please. The army is my life, you know that,' Hugo said, his voice stern.

'But I miss you so much when you are away.'

Hugo leant towards her and kissed her cheek. 'I miss you too, sweetheart. Well, maybe one day…'

But Marie-Ange could see he didn't mean it.

To lighten the mood, Madame Saintclair asked Marie-Ange about the latest fashion in England.

'I am definitely not the right person to ask about fashion,' Marie-Ange replied, pulling a face. 'Most of my dresses are very dull. I never go to any elegant gathering. I did not even know how to dance the waltz before your brother showed me at Fouché's ball the other night!'

She looked at him and the words died on her lips. Her cheeks became painfully hot as she remembered what had happened after the dance, both in the cloister gardens and later at the cuirassiers' barracks.

Saintclair held her gaze. A mischievous smile appeared on his lips. 'I thought you managed very well, for someone so inexperienced,' he said.

She looked down and fussed with her napkin.

'You saw Fouché, then?' Hugo's father asked.

'Yes, he was there.'

'At least we have always agreed on that man. He is despicable, without honour or loyalty. How Napoleon tolerated him for so long is beyond me.'

'He is a snake, I'll grant you that,' Hugo agreed. 'His strength lies in the fact that he has no loyalty except to himself, and in the network of spies he has built over the years. Ministers, generals, members of the royal family and the emperor's former entourage, everybody is afraid of him and of the information he holds on them.'

He didn't look her way, but Marie-Ange knew it was for her benefit he spoke. She heaved a sigh. She didn't like being reminded that Christopher was probably one of Fouché's spies, even though he must have his reasons.

After supper, Lucie decreed that she was weary and wished to retire and her parents went upstairs with her, leaving Saintclair and Marie-Ange to sit alone in the drawing room.

'You are lucky to have your family. They are kind and loving people.'

She spared a thought for Robert who must be waiting anxiously for news at Norton Place. She should write to him but was reluctant to mention her meeting with Christopher. She didn't want to raise his hopes about his brother being alive just yet.

She leant towards Saintclair and whispered.

'I think I know where to find the Cross of Life.'

Saintclair arched his eyebrows. 'Go on.'

She explained about the song, the drawings of the dovecote, and about Aline's letter. 'My grandmother wrote that Saint Germain sent a team of craftsmen to build the dovecote. That was back in 1783, a few months before his death. Maybe he sensed it was time he hid the Cross.' She paused and looked into the flames. 'Perhaps he knew he would soon die.'

She closed her eyes, trying to remember more details of the letters. 'Aline wrote that the men worked relentlessly day and night. They camped in the grounds of Beauregard. One man guarded the entrance to the tent at all times. My grandmother wondered what they had in there that was so valuable. What if they had the Cross with them?'

'Among the hiding places he had access to all over Europe, why would Saint Germain choose to build a dovecote at Beauregard to hide the Cross?' He sounded sceptical.

'I'm not sure but it fits with the words of the song. Doves, a rose garden, the wing of an angel...'

Saintclair stared at her. 'Your name, Marie-Ange, is rather unusual,' he remarked.

'My mother was called Catherine Marie-Ange, too. It was Saint Germain, her godfather, who named her.'

'So Uxeloup may not be that mad after all. You do know how to retrieve that mysterious Cross and its relic, whatever that is.'

'The song says it's an angel wing.' She smiled. 'Well, obviously, it can't be—angels don't exist.'

Saintclair poked the fire and turned to gaze at her, his eyes smouldering and so caressing she felt her body respond.

'Don't they?' he said, with a low voice.

Her lips parted, her breath quickened, her skin prickled all over. He stepped closer, took her hand and turned it over to caress her palm and then her wrist with his lips. It was so soft, so light and yet so powerful her breath left her in a gentle sigh. Desire shot through her veins. She threw her head back and closed her eyes.

He let go of her hand and she was jerked back to reality.

'I am returning to Lyon tonight,' he said. 'I won't be able to visit for a few days but when I come back, I will take you to Beauregard. We will go into the dovecote and resolve once and for all the mystery of the Cross of Life.'

He bowed in front of her. 'Good night, Marie-Ange,' he said. It was the first time he had called her by her first name. His voice and the way he looked at her made her shiver all over again.

'Thank you for your help,' she said with a tight smile. 'And thank you for letting me stay with your family.'

He nodded and left. She sat in the drawing room a long time. Would he find news of Christopher waiting for him when he got back tonight? As she stared into the dying flames of the fire, she realised with a twinge of shame that the feelings Christopher's name aroused in her heart tonight had faded and were no longer those of an all consuming love.

Chapter Twelve

The following days were happy and peaceful. Capitaine Saintclair's family seemed to have adopted her unreservedly, and she found herself growing attached to them, particularly Lucie. The night terrors had stopped, and she was even considering the future with more optimism. She didn't need Malleval's money at all. Her great-aunt would probably help with her expenses while she waited for news of Christopher. And when she was reunited with him, he would sort out all her worries, and she would forget all about the Cross of Life.

She spent her time with Lucie and Madame Saintclair, mostly in the cosy drawing room overlooking the garden. In the mornings she helped with Lucie's medication. She brewed her ginseng tea, prepared eyebright poultices that the young girl had to keep on at least an hour every day to help reduce the inflammation of her eyes. Emilie Saintclair had confided that the doctors feared her daughter would lose her sight before she reached her twentieth birthday.

One day, Marie-Ange was sitting at the kitchen table, grinding the yellow medicinal flowers on a wooden board. Next to her was a jug of boiled water, ready to mix with the flower powder to form a paste she would then spread onto pieces of cloth. She heard a man shout outside the garden door.

'Give me more money, Martine. This is no way near enough for a crust of bread and a pitcher of wine.'

The voice sounded familiar. She stopped what she was doing to listen.

'I need at least two Francs. I know the Saintclairs pay

you well, the least you can do is help me out since it's their son who threw me out of the army.'

It was the drunken soldier who had threatened Saintclair outside the tavern.

'Stop this racket or someone will hear you,' the woman answered back. There, I'll give you one Franc. Try not to waste it all at the inn. Hurry now!'

The door opened and the scullery maid entered, dishevelled and her cheeks bright red. She looked surprised to see Marie-Ange in the kitchen and mumbled a greeting.

'Why is that man coming here, Martine?' Marie-Ange asked. She hadn't forgotten the soldier's threats against Saintclair and his family.

The woman put her fists on her hips and retorted defiantly, 'Antoine is my cousin. I help him out sometimes. Give him scraps of food, a bit of money…'

'I don't think Capitaine Saintclair would approve of him coming into the garden or the house,' Marie-Ange remonstrated. In fact, she was sure he would be irate if he ever found out. He would probably send the maid away too.

Martine approached and tugged at her arm. 'Please Madame, don't tell him. I promise I won't let Antoine in ever again.'

Marie-Ange hesitated, bit her lower lip. 'I don't know…All right then, but you must give your word.'

Martine swore Antoine would not come in ever again. 'Not even in the garden,' she added.

Still uneasy, Marie-Ange resumed preparing Lucie's poultices. It didn't feel right to hide the drunken soldier's visits from the Saintclairs. They were such kind people. Her thoughts turned to the dresses Madame Saintclair was making for her. Lucie and her mother had ordered silks in soft shades of periwinkle and coral from Horace Saintclair's workshop. Marie-Ange had suggested more muted colours, but Madame Saintclair had shaken her head.

'These shades of blue and pink suit you. Surely, you can now put an end to your mourning. In France, nobody would have any objections to a widow wearing bright colours after six years.'

So Marie-Ange had relented. After all, she wasn't a widow any longer.

In the afternoon, when a pale sunshine pierced the clouds, she usually took Lucie for a stroll in the garden. They would link arms and walk along the gravel lanes. The girl had submitted her to a thorough interrogation. She now knew all about Wellcombe, about Norton Place and its occupants, including Robert, the servants and the two spaniels, Rusty and Splinter. Marie-Ange hadn't said much about Christopher, only that he had been lost at sea. Lucie however wasn't in the least interested in Christopher. She much preferred talking about Hugo, her hero.

'It has been wonderful to have him at home these past few months,' Lucie said during one of their walks. 'I, for one, am glad peace has been restored and Napoleon sent into exile. Before, we would spend months without any news and Maman was worried sick about him. Hugo has been on so many campaigns, so many battlefields, all over Europe. I know that the worst one was Russia. He was much changed when he came back.'

One afternoon, they ventured outside the walled garden into the village. Lucie had talked about getting a dog and Martine mentioned a lady who lived near the church who had puppies for sale.

'We will go today,' Lucie had decreed. It was cold, grey and misty, but she was determined to take a look at the puppies.

As they walked through the winding village streets, she spoke about the ambush in the forest. 'Hugo said you were the bravest woman he ever met.'

Marie-Ange tutted. 'He shouldn't have told you about the highwaymen. I am not proud of what I did.' In fact, she was positively angry at Saintclair for telling his young sister she had killed three men.

'Why not?' Lucie leant towards her and squeezed her arm. 'He thinks very highly of you, you know. I do hope you will live close by when you get married. You could even live in St Genis. Wouldn't that be wonderful?' Lucie clapped her hands together and laughed.

Marie-Ange gasped. What was the girl talking about? What had given her the idea that she would marry her brother?

'Lucie, your brother and I are not getting married.'

'Of course you are,' the girl retorted. 'I see the way you two look at each other. It's just like in my romance novels. I am sure he is waiting for his promotion to major before he proposes. Hugo was always so determined to make to the top but I sometimes fear his ambition will get the better of him. It is as if he wants to constantly prove his worth to the world…or to himself.'

Marie-Ange thought Lucie's remarks about her brother's character very insightful for a young girl. Saintclair did indeed burn with ambition to pursue his military career to the very top. However, she couldn't be more wrong about him wanting to marry her or being in love with her. The man had made it clear he didn't believe in romance or marriage. As for her, she would never marry him, even if she wasn't already married. The capitaine possessed too many undesirable traits. And of course, she did not love him.

She looked around uneasily. A thick fog had descended and covered the village roofs. The church spire had already disappeared.

'We should go back, Lucie.'

The girl ignored her.

'I wonder what your brother-in-law will say when he

reads your letter. I hope you told him that Hugo was the bravest, the most honourable of men.'

Marie-Ange had at last written to Robert about the developments of her travel to France—or at least about some of them. It was only fair he should know there would be no inheritance, and therefore no prospect of him going to the Naval Academy just yet. She had not, however, mentioned Christopher.

'Lucie, I don't know why you think...'

The streets were very quiet now that the fog had thickened further, turning houses and trees into ghostly shapes. There was nobody else but them in the street. The eerie silence was broken by the thunderous sounds of a horse-drawn carriage behind them. Marie-Ange put her arm around Lucie's shoulders to push her against the wall, out of harm's way. Instead of overtaking them, the carriage stopped and blocked the street. A man sprang up in front of them, reeking of cheap wine and unwashed rags. It was the ex-soldier.

'Here they are! The Capitaine's strumpet and his little sister.'

He walked up to Marie-Ange, so close she saw the burst veins in his eyes and winced at the smell of his foul breath. He raised a grimy hand towards her face and she stepped back in disgust.

'You sure are pretty, miss! Pretty enough to kiss.'

'Enough! Shut up and scamper!' A booming voice called from behind.

Marie-Ange turned round, her heart sinking as she recognised Rochefort. He climbed from the driver seat. He was holding a black hood and a length of rope in his hands.

'You promised me three Francs. I told you they'd be here, and here they are,' the drunkard protested.

So it was a trap. Martine had lured them to this deserted alleyway at the back of the church on behalf of her cousin.

There were no puppies for sale.

Rochefort threw a few coins on the ground which the man picked them up before running off, swallowed by the fog. Lucie held onto Marie-Ange's arm, terrified. Her breathing had become laboured and wheezy.

Marie-Ange decided to gain time.

'Good afternoon, Monsieur Rochefort,' she said with assurance. 'Do you just happen to be visiting St Genis or did you come especially for me?'

'If you come with me without making any fuss, the girl won't be harmed and I won't need to use these on you.' He showed the black hood and the rope.

'Where exactly are we going?'

'You'll find out soon enough, M'ame. Hurry now, get in.' Rochefort stepped forward.

'Marie-Ange, who is this man?' Lucie asked, her voice quivering with fear. She was deadly pale now. Her lips had taken a blue tinge. With her hand pressed against her chest as if trying to slow her heartbeats, she looked about to faint. Marie-Ange took one look at her and decided she could not put the girl in any more danger.

'It's all right, Lucie. You can go home.'

Lucie shook her head. 'No, I won't leave you alone with him.'

'Don't argue with me. Go now!' Marie-Ange almost shouted, pushing Lucie forward into the street.

She walked towards Rochefort. 'I am coming.'

He grunted and gestured for her to get into the carriage. She opened the door. The thick black curtains were pulled across the windows but she glimpsed the black-clad figure of a man sitting in a corner. He leapt forward, grabbed her wrists to pull her to him and before she could scream, pressed a cloth on her face, forcing her to breathe in a strong, acrid substance. As she lost consciousness, Marie-Ange recognised the gleaming, dark brown eyes of Gustave Karloff.

She coughed, shivered violently, and opened her eyes. Her fingers scraped the hard, wet floor on which she was lying before she managed to sit up against the cold stone wall. Her head throbbed. She licked her dry lips and took several deep breaths to control the nausea that threatened to overtake her. When she felt a little steadier and the world had stopped spinning, she looked around. She was in a cell. There were iron rings and chains fastened to the bare stone walls and a couple of old straw beds on the floor. Where had Rochefort and Karloff taken her?

She put her hands in front of her. At least she wasn't chained. Then she touched her dress. It was wet through, no wonder she was frozen to the core. She tried to get up but her legs wouldn't obey and she slumped back against the wall.

Heavy footsteps outside and the noise of keys rattling against the door sent her heart pounding and she pressed herself against the damp, cold wall. The door creaked open and Rochefort came in.

'Can you walk?' he asked, gruff and with a scowl on his face. 'I'll carry you if you can't.'

'Where am I?' She didn't move.

'Malleval,' he replied. 'I asked you if you could walk.'

'Why am I here?'

'Not my place to tell.' He marched towards her, grabbed her arm and pulled her up roughly. His thick, hairy fingers formed an iron ring around her arm. It was pointless to resist as he dragged her along a dark corridor and up two dozen roughly carved stone steps. He was too strong. He opened a thick wooden door and pushed her through it. She stumbled into a brightly lit hall, with a chequered black and white tiled floor and dark wood panelled walls covered with hunting trophies—stuffed heads of deer complete with huge antlers, snarling silver wolves and brown bears.

Rochefort gestured to a staircase.

159

'Up there.'

They climbed to the first floor. Rochefort opened a door and Marie-Ange stepped into a large, almost entirely black bedroom lit by thick, tall candles. The walls and the ceiling were painted black, too. The chimney breast was carved black granite. In a corner of the room was a four poster bed covered with black silk blankets and with black veils hanging down. It was the most sinister place she'd ever seen.

'Sit down over there,' Rochefort ordered.

Marie-Ange crossed her arms on her chest. 'First I want to know why I'm here. And then I want you to take me back to St Genis,' she said haughtily. Her voice faltered when she saw the mocking grin on Rochefort's face.

'Do as you're told or I'll give you another dose of medicine.' He pointed to a basin of water near the fireplace. 'There's hot water and a change of clothes, if you want.'

He left, a key grated in the lock.

As soon as Rochefort was gone, she walked to the windows and lifted the black curtains. The windows were encased in thick iron bars. She pressed her face to the pane but it was too dark outside to see anything. Saintclair had said the village of Malleval was located in a small mountain range, with nothing but precipices and forests for miles around. She might as well be alone in the world.

She prayed Lucie had arrived home safely and raised the alarm, and that Monsieur and Madame Saintclair had alerted their son of her abduction by now. Capitaine Saintclair was her only hope.

Shivering, she turned back into the bedroom. Heavens, this place was ghastly! She walked to the washstand and dipped her fingers into the warm, fragranced water. She washed her face and her hands, but refrained from undressing and slipping into the black robe which was draped on the back of the armchair.

She stood in front of the fire in an attempt to dry her dress. The spicy scent of the water in the washstand was becoming overpowering, and the heat of the fire made her lethargic and sleepy. She sat down, closed her eyes and rested her head against the soft cushions of the armchair.

She had no idea how long she slept. When she woke up, Karloff and Uxeloup were sitting opposite her, conversing in very low voices. She straightened up. The room seemed to move in front of her as if she was at sea.

Karloff bent over, frowning with concern. He put his hand on her forehead and turned to Malleval. 'She's burning with a fever. I think we should let her rest now. I'll give her something.'

'No, we will proceed as planned,' Uxeloup retorted sharply.

Marie-Ange tried to focus her eyes on his face. He looked paler, thinner tonight.

'How dare you keep me against my will? I want you to take me back to St Genis.' Her voice sounded weak, barely more than a whisper.

'What happens next depends on you, dear Marie-Ange,' Uxeloup replied. 'And what you will tell us. Hopefully our conversation will be fruitful, and painless.'

He nodded to Karloff, who produced a gold pocket watch from his waistcoat pocket. Leaning towards her the physician dangled the chain in a slow, regular movement in front of her face.

'Last time, we were interrupted by the noise of branches rattling on the window,' he explained. 'I hope we will be able to reach the desired conclusion tonight.'

He gazed deep into Marie-Ange's eyes and started talking with the soothing, monotonous voice she remembered only too well from her nightmares.

'Have you been hearing my voice in your dreams? I have been calling to you every night. I hope it helped you remember the words.'

The gold pocket watch glistened in the light of the fire, the flames reflecting on its smooth, shiny cover.

'You are tired, Marie-Ange. You are so tired. Your limbs are heavy. You are unable to move. You desperately want to close your eyes and sleep. But you can't. Not yet. First you must tell us what we want to know, and then you will be able to sleep for as long as you wish.' Karloff's voice became soft and caressing. 'Your reward is to sleep, in a nice, warm bed, safe and secure.'

His pocket watch rocked with a regular pendulum motion from left to right, catching the light of the flames as it moved. Marie-Ange stared, fascinated by the glittering metal and its regular, rhythmical motion. She yearned for sleep, Karloff was right about that. More than anything else she wanted to lie down, to be safe and warm.

'Remember the words, Marie-Ange. The words of the song your mother taught you. The words her godfather Saint Germain taught her. The secret words.'

Karloff repeated his instructions several times, until Marie-Ange's lips opened as if of their own accord and she sang the first verse. There was only one thought in her mind. All she had to do was tell them the words, and then she would be able to rest.

Ma mie, ma rose de mai
Ma rose aux cinq pétales,
Qui dans la tour aux colombes,
Pleure l'amant dans la tombe....

'This is all very well, but we already know the first verse,' Uxeloup cut in, impatient.

'Shh!' Karloff turned towards him. 'Don't interrupt again or she might wake up.'

He kept his voice even and soothing but it was too late. The spell was broken. Just like in her bedroom on *Isle Barbe*, Marie-Ange managed to snap out of her trance. She had been about to reveal the secret. With the song, Uxeloup and Karloff would find the Cross of Life in the dovecote. Her mind was racing now. Maybe she could change a few of the words whilst pretending to be still under Karloff's spell.

She sang the last verses very slowly.

Listen to me, don't despair,
Your lover you'll see again,
Place your hand *on the rose, give* one *turn,*
Lower *your eyes, and the wing you will find.*
But you must choose wisely,
For if the wing of the dove
Is as white as the angel's
It will not open your lover's tomb.

Exhausted, Marie-Ange reclined against the back of the armchair. She had managed to change what she considered to be the most important words. She had turned the instruction 'put the rose on the heart and turn five times' into 'put your hand on the rose and turn once'. Then, she had said that they had to look down instead of up to find the wing.

Would the two men notice her subterfuge? And would these little changes make any difference in preventing them from finding the Cross?

Uxeloup finished scribbling the words on a thick piece of paper, put his quill down, and blew on the sheet to dry the ink.

'There, that wasn't so hard, was it?' Karloff whispered, putting his watch back in his pocket. 'Now you can rest, as promised.'

He turned towards Uxeloup, a little anxious.

'Will that be all for now? The girl needs to sleep or she will be useless to us for the rest.'

Uxeloup didn't answer but came to stand behind her armchair. He leant slightly forward. His fingers touched her hair and played with her golden curls. Suddenly they slid down to her throat and pressed hard. Unable to breathe, she tried to wriggle out of his grip as he pinned her against the back of the armchair.

'Don't move,' he instructed coldly. 'A word of warning, my dear. Never, ever, make a fool of me again. I really didn't appreciate your escaping from *Isle Barbe* with Saintclair.'

He pressed his fingers harder against her neck until her vision dimmed and blurred. 'As for my good friend, the man is as good as dead,' he finished.

He released her suddenly. She gasped and panted, in a desperate attempt to catch her breath.

'You are mad! Mad and dangerous,' she managed to say.

Uxeloup chuckled. He walked across the room and opened the door.

'Give her something for the fever and let her sleep, Karloff. We don't want her to be ill for Beauregard. We will leave as soon as the snow stops.'

A look of triumph lit up his face. 'Soon, my father will be proud of me.' And he went out.

Karloff got up and pulled Marie-Ange from the chair. She was too weak to walk so he carried her to the bed and laid her down. With one hand he swept her hair away from her face in a gentle gesture.

'I have been trying to get into your mind for days, or rather nights, but you are very strong. Much stronger than I thought. Anyway, I was right. You are the one. You are of the true blood of the Keepers. It was written in your stars and in your mother's stars that you would find the Cross for us.'

'Did you send me the shadows?' she whispered.

'Which shadows?'

'The shadows in my dreams. They want to take something from me. They are angry. They want it back...' Her head was burning. She closed her eyes.

'There are no shadows. You are delirious. I will ask a chambermaid to get you out of these wet clothes, and I shall come back with a draught. You have caught a nasty chill.'

His footsteps receded and then a key turned in the lock.

Chapter Thirteen

Huge ravens shrieked as they circled the grey skies outside the grilled window. The mountains and pine forests clinging to their steep slopes were covered in a thick carpet of snow. All morning Marie-Ange had hoped to see a tall figure riding through the village, but Saintclair hadn't come. Did he know she had been taken? Did he even care? May be he had second thoughts about helping her out of Malleval's clutches and decided to put his family's interests before her.

Another thought troubled her. What if Uxeloup had already carried out his threat and Saintclair was dead? She closed her eyes and conjured up an image of the cuirassier officer, with his bright blue eyes, in turn frosty or smouldering, and the quick smile that so often appeared on the corner of his mouth. Catching her breath, she recalled for the hundredth time the sensual caress of his lips over her mouth, of his hands over her skin, the way she felt the night of the ball, out of control and wanting more. She hated herself for it. What kind of woman longed for a man she had only just met, and who had ideas and values so different from her own? The only man she should be thinking of was her husband.

She turned towards the bedroom which had become her prison. Three times a day a servant woman brought her food and a tonic Karloff prepared to help her recover from her fever. Now she was better they would probably set off for Beauregard. When Uxeloup realized she had lied about the song, he would be angry. He might even hurt her again. She touched her throat where his tight grip had left painful bruises.

Karloff came in, silent as always. The man slipped in and out of the room like a ghost. He was dressed for an outing, in a black pelisse lined with brown fur and a hat.

'Would you like to join me for a short walk in the village, my dear? Now that you are no longer ill, I think fresh air would do you good.' He closed the door behind him. 'Actually we should go now, while Monsieur Uxeloup is busy in his study.'

It sounded as if he was anxious to get out without Malleval knowing. Marie-Ange acquiesced, only too glad of the chance to escape the sinister black room. Rochefort waited for them in the hall. With the coat made of some animal skin he wore today, he looked more bear than man. They stepped out into the courtyard and Marie-Ange pointed to Malleval's coat of arms carved above the door— *A + M*—and asked Karloff what the letters stood for.

'*Ante Mortem*. Before Death. It's the old Malleval motto. Enjoy life before it's too late,' Karloff added, muttering to himself. 'Of course, the motto will take an entirely different meaning soon.'

Before she could ask him what he meant, he led the way down the narrow street which zigzagged through the village. She was struck once again by the wilderness of the setting. Stone houses were built directly into the rock, their grated windows commanding a view of steep precipices below and dense woods covering the mountains. From the street, Uxeloup's manor house looked as impregnable as the mountain itself.

'Impressive, is it not?' Karloff asked. 'The Mallevals built their castle like a fortress back in the 1640's.'

'They must have been very successful highwaymen,' Marie-Ange remarked.

He shot her an amused glance. 'I see you know about the family's infamous past. Well, I suppose it's no secret, they were indeed a gang of highwaymen who pillaged

167

neighbouring towns, ransomed travellers, and robbed boats and barges as far as the river Rhône.'

'Did they ever get caught?'

He shook his head. 'Nobody dared challenge them. Come along and I will show you why.'

He led her through the streets to a small, square stone house with Malleval's shield carved above the door. 'Look up.' He instructed.

Four greyish sticks stuck out of the stone wall.

'What are they?'

'Leg bones. This was the Mallevals' house before they built the fortress. The bones are rumoured to belong to the sheriff who came to arrest the leader of the gang. The man disappeared that very same day. Shortly afterwards, the Mallevals inserted these bones in the facade of their house as a warning.'

'And nobody else was brave enough to stop them after that?' Marie-Ange shivered at the thought of the man who had died and been mutilated for doing his duty.

'Nobody was *mad* enough,' Karloff corrected. He considered her for a minute.

'You can trust me with your secret, Marie-Ange,' he said. 'Sometimes men have to choose the wrong allies in order to win a just cause. I may have joined forces with the Mallevals to find the Cross but my motives are pure.'

Her heart beat faster. Had he guessed she had misled them about the song? To escape his scrutiny, she walked to a parapet from which there were breathtaking views of a rocky promontory, high up above the village. Right on top a wooden gibbet cast its sinister silhouette.

'Follow me.'

Karloff set off and stopped a little further along in front of another house, this one with a six-branched star carved above its door.

'This was the family house of Polycarpe de la Rivière, a most saintly man.' Karloff bowed his head, joined his hands together as if praying, and whispered a few words in a language Marie-Ange didn't recognise.

'Polycarpe was an outstanding but misunderstood scholar, a true man of God,' Karloff said when he looked up. He kept his voice low as if he didn't want Rochefort to overhear.

'I remember that name.' On her first evening at Beauregard, Uxeloup had shown her a manuscript written in the Templar code. He said it had been in Polycarpe's possession before his family got hold of it.

Karloff took a deep breath. 'Let me tell you about myself and about Polycarpe, then maybe you'll agree to help me.'

'I belong to an organisation called the *Société Angélique*,' he started. 'It was founded in Venice during the Renaissance, disbanded after accusations of heresy by the Vatican but later reformed in Lyon. Over the centuries, our members have been among the most talented writers and artists in France. Men such as Rabelais or Nicolas Poussin, the painter. And, of course, Polycarpe de la Rivière.'

'What exactly is this *Société Angélique*?'

'Our sole purpose is to communicate with angels. Thanks to the Cross of Life, this will soon be possible.'

'Really? How?'

Karloff smiled. 'The angel will come to us when we find the Cross.'

She wanted to retort that angels didn't exist, but asked instead.

'What about Poylcarpe? Why is he important?'

'He was the prior at *Sainte Croix en Jarez*, a nearby charterhouse, in the 1620s, where he discovered a casket of precious artefacts and scrolls in a cache behind the walls of the cloister. Although he never disclosed the exact content of the papers, he confided to a friend, Sebastien de Grief from the *Société Angélique* that they were coded

169

documents written by the Knights Templar. He managed to decipher them and found they spoke of the Templars' most treasured relic—The Cross of Life.'

Karloff breathed in and carried on. 'On de Grief's advice, Polycarpe used the decoded parchments as the basis for his most famous work, '*Angels and Immortality of the Soul*'. However, as soon as it was published the treatise was placed on the list of forbidden books and every copy seized by the Church. Polycarpe himself was demoted and sent to a remote abbey in Provence.'

'What was the book about?' Marie-Ange was intrigued. Despite shivering with cold in the freezing wind which was now blowing across the village, she had no intention of going back to Malleval's fortress just yet and wanted to keep Karloff talking.

'It related the story of the Cross of Life the Knights Templar brought back from Palestine after their ultimate defeat at *St Jean d'Acre,* and its extraordinary powers to confer eternal life and enable contact with celestial beings.' He sighed. 'As I said, every single copy of Polycarpe's book was destroyed, but his correspondence with de Grief, as well as many details about the decoded parchments and the cipher used by the Knight Templars, remained in the *Société Angélique's* archives.'

'So what happened to Polycarpe?'

'In 1639, he left his abbey with several faithful servants to take up a new post in Burgundy. He visited his family here in Malleval on the way, but he never arrived in Burgundy. He and his men disappeared in the mountains, together with the casket of precious objects he was taking to his new abbey and the scrolls he carried with him at all times.' Karloff paused and stared into her eyes. 'The Malleval clan killed him and stole his gold and his parchments.'

Marie-Ange gasped. 'What makes you think that?'

'Firstly, the family became very wealthy around that

time. They built their fortress and gave up some of their criminal activities, no doubt thanks to Polycarpe's gold and precious artefacts. Secondly, it would explain how they acquired the coded Templar scroll. When Edmond Malleval contacted me at the *Société Angélique* in the autumn of 1790 he said his family had had it for well over a century.'

'Is that the parchment which is now in the library at Beauregard?'

Karloff nodded. 'The very one. Edmond said he had forgotten all about it until he saw Count Saint Germain's portrait at Beauregard, holding a similar parchment and a beautiful, bejewelled, Cross. It so intrigued him he tried to acquire the painting straight away.'

'My grandmother wrote that he was very angry when her husband Philippe refused to sell him the painting,' Marie-Ange remarked. 'So, you were the one who decoded the parchment?'

Karloff nodded. 'I found the key to the Knights Templar's code in the *Société Angélique's* archives—each letter of the alphabet is replaced with a section of the Templar Cross. The parchment was the transcription of messages from past Templar Masters about the Cross of Life and its powers. From the moment I handed Edmond the translated document, he became obsessed with obtaining the Cross and cheating death.'

He paused again. 'As for me, I knew that at last the relic was within my grasp. Ever since Polycarpe wrote his forbidden book, members of our society have searched for it. I advised Edmond to keep a close watch on Aline Beauregard because I believed she knew where the Cross was hidden. He decided that marrying her was the best way to gain control over her as well as of Beauregard. When we realised she didn't know anything about the Cross, we turned to Catherine, your mother, with whom Saint Germain had formed a special bond.'

Marie-Ange stared at the physician coldly. '*You* are responsible for my grandfather's execution and my grandmother's suicide, and for my mother's imprisonment in this god-forsaken place.' She gestured towards Malleval's fortress. 'And now I am here too, at Uxeloup's mercy, and all that for an old cross and a far-fetched legend.'

Karloff looked embarrassed for a fleeting moment. Then he shook his head. 'Oh, but it isn't any old cross. It was the Knights Templar's most treasured possession. The relic hidden inside the Cross confers eternal life, but at one condition only.'

His dark eyes were feverish. 'According to the scroll I deciphered, it can only unleash its powers if handled by the chosen one—a pure heart, someone of the same bloodline as a Great Master of the Templar Order. Edmond Malleval wasn't a pure heart, not by a long shot. Nor was he related to any former Knight Templar. So even if he had found the Cross he wouldn't have become immortal. He needed the chosen one to help him.'

He paused. 'Your mother was the one. She was a Beauregard, a cousin of the Beaujeus who counted Guillaume as a Great Master. She was also Saint Germain's precious god-daughter. He must have told her where the Cross was hidden. Edmond went mad when she escaped. He looked for her for years and years.'

His eyes clouded over. 'When he got ill, he made Uxeloup swear he would carry on with the search. And finally we found you.'

He stepped towards Marie-Ange and took her hand. 'Your mother told you the secret, didn't she? She told you and now you must find the Cross for me.'

'What makes you so different from Uxeloup and his father? You and your fanciful stories are responsible for destroying my family,' she said, pulling her hand from his.

'Uxeloup, like his father before him, only wants the

Cross for himself. I on the other hand want to make contact with the angel who, the parchment claims, will appear when the Cross is returned to its rightful place by the chosen one—the pure heart. In other words, you, now your mother is dead.'

Marie-Ange shook her head with dismay. The man was just as crazy as the Mallevals.

'You are strong-willed, like your mother. I never could exercise enough control on her mind to make her reveal the secret...You were very clever about it but I know you changed the words of the song. If you help me, I promise you will return to England safe and sound.'

It was snowing again. Thick, fluffy flakes swirled all around them. In the corner of her eye, Marie-Ange saw two grey shadows advance silently towards them. She caught her breath. In a few seconds, they were upon Rochefort. The big man, taken by surprise, crumpled, unconscious, onto the ground without offering any resistance. Karloff turned round but one of the attackers grabbed him by the throat and he too collapsed without a sound.

'Come with me,' one of the men told her, extending his gloved hand.

'Who are you?' she asked, her heart beating wildly, but not from fear.

He loosened his scarf to uncover his face. He had a handsome, lean and weather-beaten face. The lines around his mouth, on his forehead and at the corner of his eyes indicated he wasn't a young man, but it was his eyes that held her attention. They were a pale aquamarine, the exact same colour as her own. She knew who he was before he answered.

'My name is Baldassare dei Conti. I am your father.'

Now wasn't the time for questions so she took his hand and ran with him down the street, their footsteps muffled by the thick carpet of snow.

Another man was waiting with the horses behind a wall at the entrance of the village. The man who called himself Baldassare lifted Marie-Ange up onto his horse and mounted behind her. Within a few seconds, they were galloping on the narrow road which wound its way up the mountain towards the pass. She should have been terrified. There were deep ravines on both sides and the road was covered with snow. Yet she felt elated. She was escaping Uxeloup Malleval and his prison. First and foremost, she had found her father.

They rode until dusk. They had to walk after reaching the pass because of the deep snow. Then they rode again until the track dipped into a gorge where they dismounted and walked through the dark night. After a time, the outline of a partly ruined barn stood out amongst the trees. The men opened its rickety wooden doors. One of them led the horses to a corner and took their tack off while another fetched wood and kindling in the forest to make a fire. Baldassare knelt down and gathered a pile of straw sprigs. He pulled a couple of sharp stones from a bag, rubbed them against each other until he produced a spark that set the straw on fire. He lit a candle which he handed to Marie-Ange to hold while he cleared a space in a corner of the barn to make their camp.

His companion brought several leather bags over and proceeded to pull out packets of food, utensils, and colourful woven blankets. The other man came back, his arms full of twigs and branches, and made the fire.

'Sit down,' Baldassare told Marie-Ange, arranging blankets on the ground.

Soon, flames rose towards the high beamed ceiling, the smoke escaping through the many holes pitting the roof. One man filled a tin pot with snow and placed it on the fire. When the snow had melted and the water was hot, he threw a handful of herbs into it to make some tea. Then he cut slices of bread and strips of meat, and the men took their hooded capes off to sit down for supper.

'I expect you have questions for me,' Baldassare said, as he poured steaming hot tea into a cup and handed it to her.

She nodded. She did have questions, so many of them, but where to start?

'You are one of the men who came to Beauregard to build the dovecote, aren't you? Did you hide the Cross of Life in there?'

He smiled and nodded.

Did you rescue my mother from Malleval's fortress after he took her away from Salles?'

'If you know about that, then you know everything, daughter.' He paused, poking the fire with a long stick to keep it burning high.

'No, I don't know everything. I just guessed. I don't know who you really are or where you are from. I don't know why you abandoned my mother when she was pregnant, or why you waited until now to meet me. And I don't know anything about the Cross of Life apart from a lot of ridiculous stories.'

She was so angry suddenly that the words tumbled out of her mouth. 'Why did your men hide the Cross at Beauregard? Is the relic really the wing of an angel, can it really make people immortal?' She glared at the man with the pale blue eyes who sat near the fire.

'I understand your dismay, daughter, but I cannot answer all your questions tonight. The object we are seeking is one of the most precious and powerful ever held by men. It has now exceeded its time on this earth. You were chosen to return it to its rightful place.'

'But what…?'

Baldassare raised his hand to silence her. He poked the fire again, gestured towards the other two men.

'Let me tell you about us first. My companions and I

175

are Turcopilars, members of a secret armed force serving the Order of the Knights Hospitaller, also known as the Knights of St John. We were banished from our base at *Fort Saint Angel* in Malta when Napoleon invaded the island in 1798. When they took over, the British refused to allow us back on the island, so we now wander between the Order's priories across Europe, from Paris to Sicily, from Cyprus to Russia.'

'I don't understand. Aren't the Knights Hospitaller the same as the Knights Templar?'

The three men exchanged a glance.

'No, the Hospitaller were always a distinct entity. They never provoked the ire of Philippe Le Bel or Pope Clement V and therefore were allowed to take over much of the Knights Templar's wealth when they were disbanded.' Baldassare paused. 'They also inherited their secrets, and us—the Turcopilars. Our mission is to help our brothers wherever they need us. We are an army of shadows. Nobody sees us. Nobody knows we exist.'

Baldassare looked at Marie-Ange and smiled softly. 'I first met your mother as a young man when I was entrusted with the very special mission by our Great Bailiff of building a secure hiding place for the Cross of Life. Our brother Saint-Germain feared he could no longer guarantee its safety.'

'Why Beauregard?'

Baldassare smiled again. 'It was Saint Germain's idea. Beauregard was close to Arginy castle where the Cross must be returned eventually. He also knew it would be safe there with his goddaughter—your mother.'

A tender expression appeared on his face. 'She was wise, brave, and talented beyond her years. Saint-Germain taught her the secret words she would need to retrieve the Cross when the time came. She never betrayed his trust.'

The men finished eating and drinking. They exchanged a few words in a language which sounded a little like

Italian, and one of them walked out.

'First watch,' Baldassare explained. 'We should rest now. We have a long ride ahead of us tomorrow.' He wrapped a blanket around his shoulders but Marie-Ange would not let him sleep just yet.

'How did you rescue my mother from Malleval's fortress?'

He stared into the fire, a look of sadness on his beautiful, chiselled, features.

'Catherine's godmother, the Abbess at Salles Priory, knew about us. She sent her man servant, Pierre, to warn me your mother had been taken by Edmond Malleval and to give me Catherine's sketchbook and the locket she had managed to hide—it was lucky because Malleval later searched the Priory and as you may have gathered, both the locket and the sketchbook hold clues as to the Cross' hiding place.'

Baldassare paused. 'I rode to Malleval and watched the fortress for days but Edmond kept your mother under tight supervision. Finally, I had my chance. One night, an important visitor came to Malleval, a man with a face as sharp as a knife and cruel, cold eyes.'

'Joseph Fouché,' Marie-Ange said.

Baldassare nodded. 'There was a banquet, and the guards got very drunk. I managed to get into the fortress and reach Catherine's bedchamber in the tower. I got there just in time to stop that viper, Uxeloup, as he was trying to force himself on her. He was only fourteen or fifteen I guess…he wanted to prove himself, as a man.'

Baldassare's voice became harsh. 'I knocked him out, tied him up, and shoved him in a closet. Then your mother and I escaped. We rode day and night for weeks towards the North coast. Catherine and I became…close…during our long journey. She was beautiful and kind. She was a treasure.'

'So why did you abandon her? You must have known

177

she was expecting a child.' Marie-Ange wasn't angry anymore. She could see the sadness in her father's eyes and hear the regret in his voice.

'I was a Turcopilar. Having sworn a vow of allegiance to my order, I wasn't a free man. Catherine knew it, she understood. It was arranged she would board a ship for England and that one of our brothers would meet her in Devonshire and look after her…'

'My father? William Jones?' She was confused. 'You mean he was one of yours?'

Baldassare nodded. 'I knew he would take good care of Catherine and of our baby. And he did, didn't he?' He smiled.

Marie-Ange shook her head in disbelief. William Jones, the quiet and taciturn Plymouth lawyer, had been part of a secret brotherhood charged with protecting the Knights Templar's secrets all over Europe.

Neither of them spoke for a while. They listened to the crackling of the fire, the hooting of the owls in the woods and the light snoring of the man who had fallen asleep, wrapped up in his blanket, next to them.

'How did you find me today?' she asked, breaking the silence.

'Pierre again. He is an old man now. You met him at Marzac where he has been in your great-aunt's service for some years. He sent a message to our Prior in Paris after your visit to Marzac. He was worried about your safety. He was right. As we arrived in Lyon we heard reports about your escape from *Isle Barbe*, and then about you being abducted by Rochefort in Saint-Genis. I guessed you were at the fortress in Malleval and we travelled with God's speed to reach you. I am sorry it took us so long.'

There were tears in his eyes when he took hold of her hand and brought it to his lips. Moved with the sudden realisation that this man was her father, she leant closer to him and rested her head against his shoulder. He still had much to explain, particularly about the Cross, but for now she was content just to be close to him.

Baldassare smiled. 'By the way, I must thank the French officer who has been looking after you. Capitaine Saintclair…'

She glanced at him, anxious. 'Uxeloup wants to kill him.' And she explained how Saintclair assisted her to escape from *Isle Barbe*.

'I'm sure the man can take care of himself,' Baldassare said reassuringly. 'You must rest now. We will talk some more tomorrow.'

There were still many questions Marie-Ange wanted to ask her father, but all her strength seemed to desert her all of a sudden. She wrapped a blanket around her, lay down, and was about to close her eyes when she remembered something.

'The locket. It is at Saintclair's house in St Genis. I need it to open the secret cache in the dovecote, don't I?'

Baldassare nodded. 'You do indeed. We will get the locket and your mother's sketchbook on our way to Beauregard, don't worry. Go to sleep now.'

Surprisingly, despite the hard cold ground, her aching limbs, and the extraordinary events of the evening, she fell asleep in minutes and slept soundly until dawn.

'Daughter. You must wake up.' Baldassare shook her shoulder gently and handed her a cup of hot tea.

She smiled and sat up to drink the hot, fragranced drink which tasted of mint and spices. Then she stood up and stretched her aching limbs as the first glimmers of daylight broke the darkness in the east.

The dawn quiet was suddenly broken by men voices shouting outside. Baldassare put his hand to his side and pulled a long, curved dagger. He gestured to Marie-Ange to stay inside and sneaked out of the barn. Looking through the barn's broken shutters, she saw three men fighting on the frozen ground, two of them her father's companions. The third man, their assailant, was dark-haired and looked tall and strong. Through his torn coat, the golden buttons of his brown jacket glinted in the first rays of the rising sun.

Her heart jumped in her chest. She rushed out as her father was about to join in the fighting.

'Don't! It's Capitaine Saintclair,' she shouted.

Baldassare froze. Still holding his dagger, he gave a short command for his men to get up.

Saintclair glared at them as they released him, jumped to his feet, and blinked with disbelief when he saw her standing next to the barn door.

'What the hell are you doing here?' he bellowed as he rushed to her side.

'Are you all right?' He held her at arms' length to look at her before wrapping his arm around her waist to pull her against him.

'I'm fine,' she answered.

He turned to glare at her father and his companions. 'If you hurt her, I swear I'll…'

'I said I was fine,' she said, struggling to breathe against his chest and dizzy with relief. He was safe, he had come for her.

She closed her eyes, inhaled his scent of leather, shaving soap, and tobacco and listened to his thundering heartbeat. A warm, heart-clenching feeling flooded her. A thought flashed through her mind. This is where she wanted to be, where she was meant to be—in his arms.

Someone coughed behind them, bringing her back to reality.

'So, this is Capitaine Saintclair,' her father said.

Her cheeks hot, Marie-Ange tried to pull away but Saintclair's arm was like a band of steel around her waist.

'Who are you?' he asked Baldassare, putting his hand on his holster and cursing when he found it empty.

'Is this what you're looking for?' Her father didn't reply but handed him his weapon, a smile on his face.

With a growl, Saintclair took the pistol from him.

'Capitaine, this is my father, Baldassare dei Conti,' Marie-Ange said matter-of-factly, taking advantage of the cuirassier putting his pistol back into his holster to step out of his grasp. 'He and his men rescued me from Malleval yesterday.'

'Your father?' Saintclair puzzled, a deep frown creasing his forehead. 'How is it possible? You said your father was dead, you said he was…'

'English?' she finished. 'I thought he was, too, until very recently.'

He scowled at her. 'He could be lying, for all you know.' Turning to her father, he asked, 'Where are you from, and what do you want?'

'This is a story my daughter will tell you later,' her father answered, a calm smile on his face. 'For now you will have to trust me. We have a long way to go to reach Beauregard and it looks as if it's going to snow again.'

'Why Beauregard?'

'We are going to find the Cross,' Marie-Ange replied.

'Very well. I'm coming with you,' Saintclair declared. 'Many of the passes and roads are closed because of the snow. I had to cut through the woods, pulling my horse behind me.' He rubbed his bristly face and let out a deep sigh. 'I was preparing myself for a very unpleasant argument with Malleval, a fight even, to get you out of his fortress,'

'He wishes to do more than argue or fight with you,' she remarked, sombre. 'He said he would kill you.'

He shrugged. 'He's all talk these days…'

'We will get ready to leave now,' Baldassare said. His men went back into the barn, kicked some soil onto the fire, packed up their bags, and set off. The path was treacherous in places, the snow so deep it reached up to their knees. Marie-Ange's dress was soon soaking wet but she never complained. After a couple of hours, however, her legs were sore and heavy, her feet numb with cold. She stumbled and fell in the snow, exhausted. Saintclair pulled her up. He rubbed her frozen hands in his, looked at her with concern and decreed they should rest.

'Not now,' she protested bravely. 'There is no time.'

'She is right,' Baldassare said. 'We will stop later, when we get out of the forest.'

So they carried on and thread through the woods until at last they reached open farmland. They sat on tree stumps and shared a quick, tasteless meal of cold meat and hard bread before starting on the road to Vienne. Saintclair said they could reach the town before nightfall. He knew where they could safely spend the night.

'Blanchard, a former lieutenant of mine, bought a tavern in Vienne when he left the cavalry. He won't ask any questions.'

They reached the town as night drew in, rode across the main square which featured the ruins of an impressive Roman temple. They left their horses in a stable block at the back of the temple and carried their bags into a small inn tucked away in a narrow street.

'Capitaine! What brings you here?' A tall, large man exclaimed when Saintclair walked in, followed by Marie-Ange, her father and his two companions.

The two men shook hands and gave each other a few resounding slaps in the back as greeting. Saintclair then imparted some news of his regiment before taking his former lieutenant to one side.

'We need board and lodging for tonight,' he said. 'And we don't want anyone else to know we're here, if you catch my drift.'

'No problem, Capitaine, I'll shut the inn for tonight, you will be my only patrons.'

Baldassare and his two Turcopilars climbed up to their

rooms. Marie-Ange was about to follow them when Saintclair put his hand on her arm to stop her.

'We need to talk,' he said with a low voice. 'It's about your husband.'

Chapter Fourteen

Blanchard showed them into an empty parlour after Saintclair asked for a quiet place. Marie-Ange sat near the fireplace, Saintclair pulled a chair opposite her. Despite shivering in her wet clothes and water-logged boots, she longed to hear what he had to say.

'There was a note for me when I came back from St Genis the other night.' He produced a crumpled piece of paper from his pocket and handed it to Marie-Ange.

Her fingers shook as she unfolded it.

'The man you want will be at the Mère Vitry Inn on Saturday evening. 21h00'

That was all.

'Is it your husband's hand?'

She dropped the note in her lap and shook her head. 'I don't recognise it. We must go to Lyon for the meeting.'

She put her hand on her heart. It was beating too fast. Her head was spinning. Tomorrow night, she would see Christopher. She would have the chance to speak to him and help him remember who he was, at last. She would...

'What about this relic?' Saintclair's voice interrupted her thoughts. 'What if Malleval and Karloff are already on their way to Beauregard. Do you want to run the risk of them getting there before you?'

'They can't find the Cross on their own,' she said with confidence. 'What is more important right now is that I meet Christopher tomorrow night.'

'You will do no such thing,' Saintclair cut in. '*I* will go to the *rendez-vous* and *you* will wait in my quarters. The man is dangerous. He already tried to hurt you once, remember?'

'That was because he did not know me. When I explain…'

'I will do the explaining and you will wait in a safe place. Is that understood?' His tone brooked no contradiction.

Marie-Ange bowed her head and muttered a vague agreement. It was easier to pretend to go along with his instructions for now.

'Thank you, Capitaine, for all you have done for me. You cannot imagine how grateful I am. You helped me escape from Uxeloup and welcomed me in your family. You came to my rescue at Malleval, and now you may have found my husband. I will be forever in your debt.'

He showed no sign that he heard her but stared hard at the flames, his face set in stone. He turned to her suddenly and asked.

'Who are these men upstairs? How can you be sure their leader is really your father? He could be an impostor.'

'He is my father, there is no doubt about it,' she said softly, recalling the extraordinary feeling she experienced when she set eyes on Baldassare dei Conti for the first time. Somehow, she had recognized him for who he was.

'Of course, there are still many things I don't know or don't understand, especially about the Cross of Life and about my father. He says that he is a Turcopilar.'

Saintclair almost jumped out of his seat.

'A Turcopilar? That's impossible! They were disbanded centuries ago when the Templar Order was broken down.'

'What—or who—exactly are these Turcopilars?'

'They were the light cavalry for the Crusader armies, mostly mercenaries recruited among Christian populations rescued from Ottoman provinces. At one time, in the twelfth and thirteenth centuries, they numbered hundreds of thousands. The Crusaders couldn't have fought any battles without them. They were disbanded in the fourteenth century, or so I believed.'

He smiled dreamily. 'They are the stuff of legend. But how did he meet your mother? What can a French aristocrat and a secret fighter from the Knights Hospitaller possibly have in common?'

'My father came with the men who built the dovecote at Beauregard. Years later, when my mother was abducted by Edmond Malleval's men, he rescued her and helped her reach the north of France where she boarded a ship to England. On the way, they fell in love and…' She bent her head and sighed.

There had been a poignant sadness in her father's eyes when he had told her how he had let Catherine board the ship to England. He must have known he would never see her again, and would probably never meet their child.

'Did your father explain about the relic?'

'Not really.' She sighed. 'It appears it is indeed the wing of an angel…' she hesitated, 'which can make people immortal.'

Saintclair whistled between his teeth, and then let out a short laugh.

'Angels and eternal life! Is that all? I need a stiff drink.'

He got up and came back a few minutes later with two pitchers of mulled wine. He handed one to Marie-Ange.

'Go on. Tell me all about angels.' He directed his bright blue eyes at Marie-Ange, his lips stretched into a smile. Her pulse quickened under his gaze and she drank a sip of mulled wine to hide her confusion.

'Well, let me see…Angels do God's work on earth. Some bring messages. For example, Uriel warned Noah about the flood; Gabriel appeared to Mary and told her she was going to have a baby. Others carry out special missions, Raphael, for example, has healing powers and Michael does God's justice on earth.' She shrugged. 'I am afraid that's all I know.'

'Hmm…' Saintclair stretched his legs and sighed contentedly. She couldn't tell if that was because of what she had said or because he was enjoying his spiced wine. She suspected it was probably the latter.

'Oh, yes! I forgot about the seraphims and cherubs who guard the gates of the Garden of Eden.'

'The Garden of Eden? Is that where Adam and Eve cavorted naked, blissfully happy until Eve succumbed to the urge to eat an apple and got poor Adam into trouble?' He looked at her, a grin on his face and her cheeks became hot again.

A voice called from the doorway. 'Angels are sublime beings, spirits of love. They guide humans through ordeals and take them to Paradise.' Baldassare entered, he was dressed in an austere dark grey jacket and breeches. 'I see you are not a believer.' He regarded Saintclair severely.

Saintclair shrugged. 'I'm afraid not. I have seen too much suffering on the battlefields of Europe to believe in a benevolent God. Anyway, what is it about this relic?'

Baldassare pulled a chair and sat next to Marie-Ange. 'The Cross must be returned with the Keepers as soon as possible. We cannot let Malleval get hold of it.'

'What Keepers?' Sainclair asked.

'Those who brought the Cross over from Palestine.'

'You mean the Knights Templar? Aren't they all dead?'

Baldassare nodded. 'The Keepers are the souls of eleven Knights Templar who guard the vaults at Arginy.'

Turning to Marie-Ange, he added, 'Since your mother is no longer with us, you are the one chosen to find the Cross and put it back where it belongs.'

'No!' She stood up so abruptly her chair fell behind her.

Her father's words had conjured up nightmarish images of a dark chamber filled with distant screams and whimpers of suffering, of ghostly, faceless shadows crowding around her.

'I don't want to do it. I don't want to go down there.'

Baldassare got up and took his daughter's hands in his. 'You have to, daughter.'

Marie-Ange put her hands to her throat, struggling for breath as panic welled up inside her. Saintclair sprung to his feet and scooped her in his arms. She rested her head against his shoulder, too exhausted to protest.

'I'll take you to your room.' Holding her tight, he looked at Baldarasse sternly. 'And let's have no more talk of angels, ghostly Knights Templar, or holy relics for now. She needs to get warm and to rest.'

He carried Marie-Ange to her room and laid her gently onto the bed. 'Your dress is soaking wet. No wonder you're not feeling well,' he remarked, his voice gruff. 'I will ask Blanchard's wife to lend you some clothes.' With a last look at her, he went out.

Baldassare entered as Saintclair left. 'I am sorry if I frightened you, Marie-Ange.'

She closed her eyes and whispered, 'I had nightmares about that place, the vaults at Arginy. I saw the shadows, I heard the screams.' She took a deep breath, opened her eyes, and gestured for her father to come closer. 'Father, there is something you must know, something which will delay my journey to Beauregard.' It was time to tell him about Christopher.

She could sense her father's mounting disbelief as she explained how her English husband, who had been lost at sea off the coast of Spain six years previously, was alive and, she suspected, working as a spy for Fouché.

'I will know for sure tomorrow night when we meet him at the inn in Lyon,' she finished.

'Then I shall come with you. The man sounds dangerous.'

'He is my husband. He will not harm me,' she protested feebly. She wasn't so sure about that any longer.

'Head injuries can change people, turn them into

somebody else entirely,' Baldassare said. 'I have known men who were of a generous and cheerful disposition become so cruel and mean-spirited it seemed they had lost their heart and soul. From what you said, that is what seemed to have happened to your husband...if the man you met is your husband.'

A knock on the door announced the entrance of a plump, red-cheeked woman holding a selection of underclothes and dresses.

'Capitaine Saintclair asked me to bring you these, Madame.'

She put the clothes on a chair. 'I'll have a tub and some hot water brought up for you right away,' she added.

Marie-Ange could think of nothing she wanted more than a hot bath and dry, clean clothes.

'I shall leave you now. We will talk during dinner.' Baldassare squeezed her hand and left.

A short while later, Marie-Ange discarded her wet clothes and got into the tin bath Blanchard and two servants had brought up and filled with warm water for her. She didn't want to think any longer, not about the Cross, not about Christopher, and certainly not about Saintclair. Yet as soon as she closed her eyes and reclined in the tub, her thoughts drifted towards the Capitaine again. She had been so happy when she saw him outside the barn that morning. What she felt for him then had been overwhelming, exhilarating, almost like...she stopped the silly, unwelcome thought which popped into her mind.

No. She was feeling grateful, that was all. Saintclair came to rescue her, braving the snow storm and the Pilat mountains' inhospitable terrain. He had been prepared to face Malleval and his henchmen alone. And tomorrow, he would take her to Christopher. She owed him a lot, more than she could ever say.

Christopher...Would she be able to make him remember her? She heaved a sigh and said a silent prayer.

189

hoping that the kind, gentle man she married was still there, underneath the harsh and ruthless exterior of the agent he had become.

When the water had gone tepid, she stepped out of the bath and scrubbed herself dry until her skin was bright pink and her hair shone and curled on her shoulders. The clothes Madame Blanchard had left for her were all too big, but at least they were dry and clean. She chose a linen chemise and a corset made for a much more generous bosom than hers; grey stockings that she rolled up and tied around her thighs and a blue dress with a white petticoat. She left her damp hair to dry loose on her shoulders. By the time she was dressed, she was ravenous.

Saintclair, her father and his two companions were already sitting at a table in the dining room. Baldassare gestured to Marie-Ange to sit next to him and scooped a generous helping of chicken and root vegetable stew onto her plate. The men resumed their conversation about travel arrangements for the following day. Saintclair persuaded Baldassare that he was more than capable of seeing to his daughter's safety in Lyon and it was decided that the Turcopilars would ride straight to Beauregard, where Saintclair and Marie-Ange would join them after meeting Christopher.

'Uxeloup may take a few days to get there anyway. He can't travel as fast as he used to. He isn't well,' Saintclair remarked.

'I don't understand. He wrote he was wounded, yet he was dancing the other night at the ball,' Marie-Ange said.

Saintclair put his knife and fork down on his plate. 'There was no battle wound, I'm afraid. Malleval caught syphilis two years ago from Spanish brothels,' he declared.

Marie-Ange put her hand to her mouth, shocked. There was no known cure for syphilis. Uxeloup would die in terrible pain, and he would probably lose his mind, too. What would happen to Sophie, his fiancée, and the servant girl he'd been with the other night?

'So that's why he wants the Cross, he knows he is lost,' Baldassare remarked. 'Who was that old man you were with in the village? I have the feeling I have seen him before.'

'You may have, years ago, when you rescued my mother from Edmond Malleval. He is known as Karloff and belongs to the *Société Angélique*, a secret organisation.' Marie-Ange went on to explain about Polycarpe de la Rivière and the coded parchments stolen by the Malleval clan almost two centuries ago and which Karloff had deciphered for Edmond Malleval. She shook her head. 'The man is completely deluded. He thinks an angel will appear when we get hold of the Cross. Isn't that just crazy?'

She waited for her father to agree but he didn't say anything.

'How did you manage to find out so much?' Saintclair looked at her, a faint smile on his lips.

'Karloff wants the Cross as badly as Uxeloup. He tried to hypnotise me twice but I managed to hold on and not reveal the words of my mother's song. The first time, he came to my bedroom one night on *Isle Barbe* and it was...'

Saintclair put his pitcher of wine down on the table with such force that some wine spilt out onto the table. 'He came into your room at night?'

Marie-Ange blushed as she remembered the way Karloff sat on her bed while she was clad only in her nightdress. She nodded and stammered as she explained what had happened. 'He tried to hypnotise me, but there was some noise and I woke up. It is very odd this ability he has to make you tingle all over and to send you into a trance just by looking into your eyes. His voice is so persuasive...' She shuddered. Karloff said he had reached out to her through her dreams. Even though she knew it was impossible, she had heard his voice over and over again in her nightmares.

'What happened at Malleval?' Saintclair asked with a low voice, leaning towards her. There was concern in his eyes and a deep line at the corner of his mouth.

'Uxeloup and Karloff wanted the words of my mother's song. I managed to give them the wrong words, but they guessed that the Cross was in the dovecote, even if they have no idea how to get to it.'

Baldassare put his hand on her shoulder. 'You did well. You were very brave.'

'Oh no, I wasn't brave. I was terrified.'

Saintclair gestured to her neck. 'I couldn't help but notice…'

She put her hands to her throat to hide the ugly bruises Uxeloup had left, and swallowed hard. 'Uxeloup was angry we had escaped and made a fool of him.'

Saintclair narrowed his eyes and clenched his fists. 'Wait until I lay my hands on him. Sick or not, he has no right to hurt you,' he growled.

When they finished their meal, Saintclair decreed they should retire as he wanted to leave early the following morning.

'We will call at my house in St Genis first. I want Lucie to see that you are safe. She has been sick with worry about you.'

'I was very concerned about her, too. Poor Lucie, she was so scared I thought she was going to faint. I will get my bag and my locket from your house before we go to Lyon.' Marie-Ange put her hand on her heart, and a smile stretched her lips. 'Oh, Capitaine, I cannot believe that tomorrow night I will be reunited with my husband, and it is all thanks to you!'

Saintclair glared at her.

'I think you should wait before thanking me. You don't know what we'll find in Lyon,' he retorted before slamming his empty pitcher down on the table and hailing Blanchard for more wine.

She stared at him, puzzled. Why was he so disgruntled all of a sudden, when all she had done was express her gratitude for his help? She sighed and bid him good night. He didn't even reply.

Chapter Fifteen

'Thank God you're safe.' Lucie greeted her with a huge smile.

Marie-Ange rushed across the drawing room to take her in her arms. The girl felt frail, she looked ill, too. There were dark circles under her red, swollen eyes, her skin was so pale it was almost transparent, and her breathing was laboured and wheezy.

Emilie Saintclair invited her guest to sit down before leaving the drawing room to organise some refreshments.

'Where were you? Who was that horrible man driving the carriage?' Lucie squeezed Marie-Ange's hand. 'It was awful to watch you disappear into the fog and not being able to help.' She turned to her brother and gave him a tender look. 'Luckily, there is nothing Hugo cannot do. I knew he would bring you back to us.'

'We cannot stay long,' Saintclair said. 'We have to be in Lyon tonight.'

Lucie's face crumpled with disappointment. 'Why so soon?' She turned to Marie-Ange. 'You haven't even tried the dresses *Maman* made for you. They are beautiful, I am sure you will love them.'

'I promise I will be back soon.' The moment she spoke, Marie-Ange bit her lips, wishing she could take the words back. It wasn't true. She may never return to St Genis. For a moment she longed to stay here, surrounded by the warmth and affection of Saintclair's family. Her future however depended on the outcome of tonight's meeting with Christopher and her quest for the Cross at Beauregard.

Saintclair glanced at her but said nothing. He was probably thinking the same thing.

His mother returned to the drawing room, followed by a young maid carrying a tray with cups of coffee, hot chocolate, and a two-tiered cream cake. The girl was new. On their way to St Genis, Saintclair explained he had dismissed Martine as soon as he found out she had helped her cousin lure Marie-Ange and Lucie into a trap. 'She tried to deny it at first but she broke down eventually and admitted the man forced her to lie about the puppies for sale in the village. As for him, he won't be hanging around here anymore,' he had said without offering further explanations.

Madame Saintclair poured hot chocolate for the ladies and black coffee for Hugo. 'What an ordeal this has been for you, poor Marie-Ange.' She patted her hand. 'You don't mind if I call you Marie-Ange, do you? You must call me Emilie too. After all, you are practically family now. Lucie told me your wonderful news.'

'What news?' Saintclair and Marie-Ange asked in one voice.

'Your engagement, of course!' Madame Saintclair was beaming. 'I knew there was something Hugo wasn't telling me. You are the first lady he has ever brought home and I can see by the way he looks at you how much he loves you.'

'Mother,' Saintclair interrupted, a little shortly. 'Marie-Ange and I are not engaged. In fact…'

Marie-Ange sat very still, holding her cup of cocoa, hardly daring to breathe.

'It appears that her husband, a Royal Navy Commander who was reported missing in action some years ago, is still alive.' He paused and looked at Marie-Ange, his expression unreadable. 'We are meeting him in Lyon tonight. If everything goes to plan, Marie-Ange will return to England with him.' He drank his coffee and put the cup

195

back onto the table.

The only sound in the drawing room was the tic-tock of the clock on the mantle piece. Then Lucie started crying, quietly, holding her handkerchief against her mouth.

'My poor Hugo,' she whispered. She turned to Marie-Ange and shot her an angry glance. 'You lied to me, to us,' she hissed before running out. Her mother shook her head in dismay and went after her, leaving Marie-Ange alone with Saintclair.

'I did not realise Lucie entertained such fanciful ideas about you and I...' He sighed. 'I keep telling her real life is nothing like her silly romantic stories but she won't believe me.' He got up and walked to the door. 'Get what you need from your room. I want to leave as soon as possible.'

She nodded. 'Of course.'

But she didn't move. She needed a few moments alone to think about what Emilie Saintclair had said before Hugo interrupted her. That her son loved her. She put her hand on her heart. She couldn't understand why she suddenly felt like crying and laughing at the same time.

The door opened and Madame Saintclair entered the room. She closed the door and turned towards her hesitantly. 'I am so sorry, my dear, for what just happened. Lucie and I got it all wrong. Of course, had we known about your husband...' She sighed. 'In any case, it was presumptuous of me to think that you would ever contemplate marrying my son. He does not deserve a proper lady like you.'

Marie-Ange could not stand the apologetic tone of her voice. She owed her the truth.

'I am no lady, Madame Saintclair,' she confessed. 'I made several shocking discoveries these past few weeks, one of them being that I am the illegitimate daughter of a Maltese soldier who seduced my mother when she was sixteen and abandoned her once she was pregnant. So, please, do not call me a lady.' She took Emilie Saintclair's hands in hers and carried on with a passion she was hardly aware of. 'Your son helped me well beyond the call of duty. He has shown great courage, loyalty and honour. He is a strong, brave and wonderful man. Any woman would be proud to be his wife and I…'

The words died on her lips. The true nature of her feelings for Hugo Saintclair hit her like a blow to the heart, so hard she gasped and had to close her eyes. She couldn't hide from the truth any longer. What she felt wasn't just physical attraction. She loved him. With all her heart. With all her soul.

Madame Saintclair patted her hand and smiled. There was sympathy in her eyes.

'I see…Well, if things don't turn out the way you expect in Lyon tonight, you will always be welcome in our house. But for now, I think you had better get ready. Hugo is waiting outside.'

Marie-Ange nodded, her throat tight and went up to her room to gather her things. She thrust her mother's sketchbook and the few garments she had left behind in her reticule. She slipped Christopher's dagger into her boot before finally clasping her locket around her neck. Grabbing her small bag, she closed the door with a heavy heart. Would she ever come back to Saintclair's house? Before going downstairs, she knocked on Lucie's door. There was a muffled response and she walked in.

'What do you want?' Lucie stared at her, a hostile frown on her face.

'I came to say good bye. I want to thank you for being such a kind and loving friend. Whatever happens now, I will never forget you,' she said softly.

'Well, I hope *we* forget you,' Lucie cried angrily. She crossed her arms on her chest and turned away.

There was no coach leaving St Genis for Lyon that

afternoon so Saintclair decreed they would ride his horse. It was no easy journey. She sat side-saddled in front of him, the warmth of his arms around her, the feel of his broad, hard chest against her cheek a sweet torture, giving her goose bumps and making her body tight with longing. Impatient and bad-tempered, Saintclair didn't speak a word to her. He spurred his horse on to gain speed or pulled at the reins, cursing under his breath, when travellers got in his way.

As they made their way into the city she was increasingly anxious about the forthcoming meeting at the *Mère Vitry* and about her feelings. She no longer knew what she wanted. Too preoccupied with her quest for Christopher, she had failed to grasp the true nature of her feelings for Saintclair and had ignored all the signs. Now she was about to be reunited with her husband, thoughts whirled in her mind…What if Christopher had lost his memory for good and didn't want to resume his life at Norton Place? Her throat tightened and she closed her eyes in anguish. What if he *wanted* to resume their married life?

As soon as they arrived at the cuirassiers' barracks, Saintclair called for his batman and gave him instructions to bring some wine and a collation.

'Will mademoiselle be staying here tonight?' the man eyed Marie-Ange up and down. His impudence brought a flush to her cheeks and made her look away. It was obvious the man assumed she was his Capitaine's latest conquest.

Saintclair waved his hand in a dismissive gesture. 'I'm not sure yet, but make the spare bed up, just in case, will you? And not a word about Mademoiselle to anyone, do you understand?'

The batman winked at her before clicking his heels.

'Oui, mon Capitaine!' Later he brought them soup, a loaf of bread, and a pitcher of wine and they sat at the table to eat.

'The *Mère Vitry Inn* is in the old district on the other side of the Saône, in a street off *Place Saint Paul*,' Saintclair explained, darting his cold blue eyes towards her. 'Once I have spoken with…your husband,' he paused, 'and I'm sure it's safe, I will come back for you.' He finished his meal and looked towards the clock on the mantel piece. 'It's time.' He got up, put his coat on, and went to the door.

'Capitaine,' Marie-Ange called. She walked up to him, tilted her face. They exchanged a long, intense look. 'Please be careful.'

He nodded. 'Of course. Lock the door behind me.' And he left.

Marie-Ange had no intention of waiting for his return. She wrapped herself in her cloak, covered her head with the hood, and slipped out of the room. As well as wishing to speak to Christopher straight away, she feared for Saintclair's safety. The meeting at the *Mère Vitry* might be a trap. If Christopher was indeed one of Fouché's men, a ruthless spy and killer, she had to watch Saintclair's back. She couldn't let the officer get hurt because of her. She was armed. She had her dagger.

Marie-Ange hastened towards the inn, keeping her head down so as not to attract the attention of passers-by. The streets teamed with soldiers on leave, with merchants selling hot roasted chestnuts and mulled wine. Ignoring the beggars who pleaded for a few *sous* at every corner along the way, she kept her eyes on Saintclair's tall silhouette ahead. He walked very fast and she had to run to keep up with him as he crossed the bridge over the River Saône, and then reached the far side of *Place Saint Paul*.

The old district was even more crowded and echoed with the sounds of bawdy songs, shouting, and fighting. Men spilled out of taverns to fall over the cobbles. Some slumped in a drunken stupor on house porches while others relieved themselves against the walls. She pulled the hood forward over her face. A drunken soldier sprawled in a doorway grabbed her ankle as she walked past.

'Belle demoiselle, un baiser,' he bellowed.

She kicked him off and caught a glimpse of Hugo as he walked in the *Mère Vitry,* which judging by its two steamed up windows and the racket coming from inside, was packed. She looked for somewhere to hide and elected an empty doorway with a deep recess from where she could keep watch. She didn't have to wait long. Two familiar figures soon emerged into the street.

Christopher wore a long grey coat. A black hat covered his pale blond hair. He came out first and looked around with suspicion. Saintclair followed and they started down the street, with Marie-Ange close behind. She couldn't afford to lose them and made sure she kept them in her sight at all times. They turned into a narrow alley and disappeared into a doorway. It wasn't the entrance to a dwelling but a long passage dimly lit with torches which seemed to go on forever. It was probably one of the *traboules* Madame Saintclair told her about. Silk workers used the covered passages to carry their wares across the district without getting them wet with rain.

She couldn't see the men or hear their footsteps any longer. Fearing she had lost them, she started to run. When she reached the end of the *traboule* she was back on *Place Saint Paul.* She spotted Saintclair and Christopher just as they disappeared around the bend of a steep alley climbing towards *Fourvière,* one of the hills overlooking the city. Her heart beating fast, she started after them. The alley was full of shadows. A cat dashed across the cobbles with a loud meow. She bit back a startled cry. Half-way up the hill, Saintclair and Christopher took a fork to the right into a small public garden. She slid, unseen, behind a tree to listen.

'We'll stop here. Now tell me why you're looking for

me and who you're working for,' Christopher said.

'I'm not working for anyone. I'm helping out a young lady who wants to meet you,' Saintclair answered calmly. 'She believes you are…'

'Wait! Do you mean you are associated with that English woman, the pretty blond who claims I am her husband? That woman is mad.'

Marie-Ange's heart was beating so hard it hurt. She resisted the urge to step out and speak with Christopher herself.

'No, she isn't mad,' Saintclair replied, still calm.

'Who is she? And more importantly, who does she think I am?'

'Her name is Marie-Ange. She says you are Christopher Norton, from Norton Place in Devonshire. Six years ago, you were Commander on *HMS Amazon*, which sank off the coast of Corunna.'

Christopher laughed. 'Me, an English naval officer? Impossible! I don't believe a word of this nonsense.' He cursed loudly. 'You're lying. You both work for Talleyrand or the Police Prefect Bourienne. You seek to sabotage my mission here in Lyon.'

'What mission?' This time Hugo's voice was strained. There was a silence and he resumed. 'At any rate, you are mistaken about Marie-Ange. She wants to talk to you, that's all. What shall I tell her? Will you at least agree to meet her? It's the least you could do.'

Christopher didn't answer straight away. 'Very well,' he replied at last. 'If it will get you off my tail, tell her to be at the *Mère Vitry Inn* at midnight. I'll be in the yard near the back door.'

Saintclair nodded. 'That's settled, then. We will meet you there.'

He turned and made for the exit. The pale moonlight flashed on the knife Christopher pulled from his coat. In a swift movement he caught up with Saintclair and stabbed him in the back. The French officer stumbled to the ground with a grunt of pain. Christopher delivered a hard kick to the fallen man and raised the weapon to strike again.

'Christopher! Stop,' Marie-Ange cried, bolting from the shadow of the tree. She threw herself down next to Saintclair, touched the side of his neck to feel for a pulse. He was unconscious, but alive. Christopher loomed above her.

'You!' He snarled before grabbing her arm. He pulled her up roughly.

'Listen to me,' she implored. 'You have to believe me. I am your wife, Christopher.'

'This was a trap, wasn't it? Where are the others?' He looked around, and then glared at her with a look of pure hatred on his face.

Marie-Ange breathed in deeply. This man was a stranger, a cruel, harsh stranger. Still she went on. 'You are so very wrong. There is no trap. All I want is for you to remember.' She carried on talking. 'You are thirty-three years old. Your parents were Lady Susan and Sir George Norton. Sadly they both passed away. You have a younger brother, Robert, who is now eighteen and dreams of becoming a naval officer like you. You were a Commander on the *HSM*.'

'So your friend said.' He interrupted, pointing to the unconscious body of Saintclair. He pulled Marie-Ange against him and pinned both her arms behind her back. 'So, my darling, tell me, how long were we married?'

She could tell he didn't believe her but carried on regardless. Maybe one tiny detail would jolt his memory. 'We were married on October the twelfth, 1808 in Plymouth. It was a beautiful and warm, almost like a summer day. We were so happy together at Norton Place, but we only lived there together for four months. In January you boarded the *HMS Amazon* bound for Corunna. They said your ship sank, that you were dead, but I always knew you were alive.' Marie-Ange tried to find a glint of recognition, of warmth, in his eyes. There was nothing.

'The only problem, my darling, is that I am not your Christopher.'

'Who are you then? Do you even know?' she cried in desperation. 'What do you remember of your childhood? What is your earliest memory? I bet it's that of a battlefield or a French military hospital in Spain.' A spasm of surprise crossed his face before he could hide it.

'I knew it! You can't remember anything of your life before Spain, can you? You were found unconscious near Corunna by Spanish fishermen or farmers or perhaps by the French army. Maybe you were in possession of another man's coat, or carried a French soldier's identification, a man called Nallay. Am I right? Did you ever wonder why you speak such good English? That's because you are...'

Christopher twisted her arms even tighter, and she let out a whimper of pain.

'Stop this, you are driving me insane. I'll tell you what, darling. Since you say we are married, I might as well use you. I could do with a woman tonight.' His voice was hoarse and his eyes burned with an unholy hunger. Panic rose inside her and she tried to wriggle out of his grip.

'No! You cannot mean to...'

'You wouldn't deny me my conjugal rights, would you?' He snarled.

She faced him, defiantly. 'I won't leave Saintclair. He will die if he stays out here in the freezing cold.'

Christopher looked down, a cruel smile on his thin lips. 'You don't have a choice.' He produced his knife and walked next to Saintclair's body. 'Come with me now, or I finish him off.'

He grabbed her arm and led her, shaking with fear, out of the garden. She stole a last glance at Saintclair's inert body before starting on the steep lane down the hill. This was a nightmare, not the loving reunion she'd been dreaming of for the past six years. Christopher didn't remember anything. He didn't *want* to remember anything. He was a dangerous man, a killer. And at this moment, she hated him.

They walked back to *Place Saint Paul*, then on the embankment along the Saône, across a bridge, and down a series of narrow streets until Christopher stopped in front of a porch. Marie-Ange looked up but couldn't see a plaque with the name of the street. Christopher pushed open a heavy wooden door and she found herself in a courtyard with a staircase at the far end.

'This way, up to the second floor.'

A short while later he pushed her into a small but comfortably furnished apartment. He closed the front door but left the key in the lock.

'Get in.'

Shivering with fear, she followed him into the drawing room where he proceeded to take his coat and jacket off. He smiled, loosened his black *cravate* and untied the top of his shirt and sat on the sofa.

'Come here, wife, remind me of the old times,' he said, patting his knees. 'That's what you wanted, wasn't it?'

Marie-Ange didn't move. There was no love, no warmth for him in her heart. There was nothing but desolation and fear.

'Come here, I said,' he repeated, louder.

'What happened to change you so much?' she whispered. 'You were the gentlest, the more honourable of men.' At last she found the courage to cross the room and kneel in front of him. 'Christopher. Why do you not remember? We used to walk along the cliffs and on the beach. I collected shells and wild flowers, you recited poetry.'

Christopher grabbed her arms and pulled her into his lap. She struggled but he wrapped his arms around her to keep her still. 'Shut up. I didn't bring you here to talk. If you really want me to remember you, you'll have to show me a bit more.'

He laughed, lifted his fingers to her throat and ripped the collar of her dress to expose her chest. Marie-Ange cried out and tried to hide her breasts, but he laughed again. Pulling her hair back, he kissed her mouth hungrily, forcing her lips open and biting her. She struggled to get away but his grip was too strong.

'What's the matter? Don't you like your husband anymore?' he uttered harshly. His breath was short, his eyes heavy as he looked down at her quivering breasts. The locket glittered in the light.

'I've seen this before.' He frowned. 'Where did you get it?'

He toyed with the chain a few seconds and held the pendant closer to his face to examine it.

'It was my mother's,' she answered, hope surging inside her. Maybe he was starting to remember at last.

But he let the pendant drop. 'You're beautiful, I'll grant you that.' He groaned with desire as his fingers brushed over her breasts before gripping and kneading the soft flesh. He bent down to bite at her throat, his lips sliding down towards her breast to suck and nip hungrily. She winced in pain. She wouldn't let him rape her, at least not without putting up a fight. She bent sideways, just enough to reach into her boot and pull the dagger out. Quick as a flash, she brought the blade up and pressed the tip on his throat.

'Let go of me,' she ordered, panting. Her hand shook as the memory of the highwayman flashed through her mind and she almost dropped the dagger.

He laughed but there was surprise in his eyes. He lifted his hands in the air. 'Careful, woman. I don't want you perforating my neck by accident.'

'If I stab you it won't be an accident,' she promised. Still holding the blade in front of her, she got up and walked backward across the room, away from him. 'I realise now it was a waste of time. There is nothing left in you of the man I loved.' She lifted her chin, willing her voice to stop trembling. He was Nallay, not Christopher. He was a monster.

She retreated to the front door, grabbing her cloak on the way. He stood up and advanced on her, his face twisted with fury. She had to be fast. The key was still in the lock. She turned it, pulled it out, and opened the door. She slipped through and slammed it shut behind her. As she locked the door from outside, Nallay's fists pounded the wood.

'Let me out, *garce*! I'll find you and teach you a lesson you won't soon forget. That's a promise!'

She threw her cloak onto her shoulders and haphazardly fastened the ties whilst running down the staircase, where in her haste she dropped the key. The crash of Nallay's blows echoed behind her. Thankfully his apartment was on the second floor, too high for him to jump from the window without risking an injury.

Once in the street, she sprinted in the direction of the embankment and crossed the bridge to *Place Saint Paul*. The streets were quieter now. Her footsteps and the sound of her breathing echoed in the night. She ran across the square and started on the steep alley up to the gardens where Saintclair lay wounded. Would he still be there or had he managed to drag himself back to his barracks? It was so dark she didn't see him and almost stumbled onto his body.

'Capitaine, wake up!'

She touched his face. It was cold. She put her hand onto his chest and felt it move ever so slightly. He was breathing. She slapped his cheek until his eyes opened, focussed onto her face.

'Capitaine, we must leave,' she said. 'Nallay is after us and this time, he will kill us both.'

Saintclair grunted with pain as consciousness returned and he attempted to move. '*Bon sang*! That bastard stabbed me in the shoulder.' He winced and raised his hand to his head. 'He knocked me out, too.' He looked at her. 'What are you doing here?'

'I'll explain later. Come on.'

'Help me up,' he ordered.

He stood up and she put her arm around his waist to steady him. Their progress down the hill was slow but eventually they crossed the bridge and made it to the barracks.

'Get me the physician,' Saintclair instructed the sentry when they staggered into the courtyard.

Marie-Ange opened his door and helped him out his coat and jacket. He sat on a chair, holding his right hand to his wounded shoulder.

'Take your shirt off, too,' she said. 'It's soaked with blood.'

He shook his head. 'No, I'll wait for the physician. In the meantime, please get me some brandy.'

She retrieved the bottle of cognac from the sideboard and handed it to him. He took hold of it and drank a long gulp, then another.

When the doctor came, he instructed Marie-Ange to boil some water over the fire and rip strips of cloth from a sheet she found in a cupboard. He cut Saintclair's shirt off and dabbed some of medicinal alcohol to clean the wound.

'How did you come to be injured?' he asked.

'A brawl in a tavern,' Saintclair replied dismissively.

'You were very lucky,' the doctor concluded after examining his shoulder. 'The blade missed the lung. There shouldn't be any lasting damage but you must rest. No riding, no drills for two weeks at least.' He finished dressing the wound and checked Saintclair's head. 'Lucky you have a thick skull too,' he remarked.

He turned to Marie-Ange at last. 'Will you see that the

capitaine does as I say, *mademoiselle*? I know him, he will be on horseback before I reach home.' Before he packed his bag, he handed Saintclair a small vial. 'Laudanum, for the pain,' he explained. 'One spoonful now. Then one in the morning and another at night if needed.' Saintclair protested he didn't want any but the physician was adamant. In fact he refused to leave until Saintclair swallowed the medicine.

'I will let you get into bed now,' Marie-Ange said once the doctor left. She moved towards the smaller room where his batman had prepared another couch.

'Not so fast,' Saintclair said in a gruff voice, moving to block her retreat. 'There are a few things you need to explain first.'

'I think you should follow the doctor's instructions and get some rest.' She tilted her chin up to look at him

'Well I don't.' He stepped closer. 'I want to know how you found me tonight.'

She blinked and took a few deep breaths. 'I followed you.'

'I specifically told you to stay here.'

'It is just as well I did not obey, Capitaine,' she argued, staring him in the eye. 'You would have bled or frozen to death had I not been there.'

He sighed. 'Perhaps. Where is your husband now?'

She bit her lip and bent her head in an attempt to hide the tears gathering in her eyelashes. 'I left him in his apartment,' she whispered. 'He…forced me to go there with him but I managed to lock him in and run back to you.'

He frowned. 'I don't understand. Did you not talk to him?'

She toyed with the fastening of her cloak. With his free hand, he lifted her chin up. Tears welled in her eyes in spite of her best efforts to quell them.

'What happened?' Saintclair asked once more. This

time, his voice was softer. 'What did the bastard do to you?'

She pressed her hand to her collar. His fingers slid down her throat and swiftly unfastened her cloak. It dropped on the floor and revealed the ripped dress.

'Damn. Did he…?' His lips tightened.

She shook her head and he breathed a sigh of relief. 'My father was right. You were right. The man I knew as Christopher Norton might as well be dead.' Her voice trembled. She pulled on the fabric to cover her throat.

'He didn't believe you, then?'

'No.'

'None of it? Even when you told him about…' he hesitated, 'your married life?'

'He thinks I am some agent out to get him.' She looked down at her hand, at the wedding ring that glittered in the candle light and with a heart-rending sob pulled it off and put it on the table. 'My marriage is over.'

Hugo's eyes went to the ring and back to her face. She let the tears fall silently down her cheeks. He lifted his uninjured arm and with the pad of his thumb wiped them away gently, one by one. She cocked her head so that her cheek was cradled inside the palm of his hand.

Neither of them moved for a long minute. Finally he turned away. 'I need some sleep,' he muttered, rubbing his face roughly and walking to his bed. He sat on the mattress and bent to take off his boots.

'Let me do this, please.' She rushed to his side and knelt to help him. She positioned some cushions on the bed to support him and helped him get as comfortable as possible.

Marie-Ange placed her hand on his hot forehead and stroked the hair from his face. His eyes fluttered closed and a small smile creased his lips. She bit her lip to fend off the rush of guilt and regret that flooded her. When his breathing was slow and regular and she was certain he was asleep, she leant over him and whispered, 'I am so sorry, my love. All this is my fault. I wish I never laid eyes on Christopher in Paris. I wish he were dead.'

Chapter Sixteen

'What happened to *mon Capitaine*?' the batman asked with a low voice so as not to wake up Saintclair. He set a tray with coffee, thick slices of buttered bread, and a pot of jam on the table.

'He got hurt in an altercation between drunks in a tavern,' Marie-Ange lied, reaching out for a cup of coffee.

The batman whistled softly. 'Now I understand why two messieurs from the police were asking for him a few moments ago.'

'The police? Did they say what they wanted?' she asked, alarmed.

He snorted. 'No, and I didn't ask. I told them the capitaine had gone out. They said they'd come back later.' He winked. 'I thought you two were busy…'

Concerned about the news that the police had come looking for Saintclair, she ignored the man's lewd remark. 'Did they leave their name?'

The sergeant shook his head. 'No, but they were from the municipal police. I'd recognise their type anywhere.'

She asked him for a needle and some thread to make repairs to her dress. He came back shortly with a rusty sewing tin and a newspaper.

'I thought it might help you pass the time while the capitaine is out cold.'

It was an old copy of *Le journal de Lyon*, dated two weeks before. There was an article about the death of Emma Hamilton. The woman who had charmed the most powerful men in England and the rest of Europe, including Horatio Nelson, had died in Calais, alone and an indigent.

The paper also reported at length the recent religious ceremonies held in Paris and other French cities in commemoration of dead monarchs Louis and Marie-Antoinette. '*France begs for God's forgiveness*' was the headline. The executions of king and his queen had come to symbolize all the evils of the revolution. Yet so many other unfortunate souls had died too, caught in the turmoil of the revolution—men like her grandfather Philippe, for example, sent to his death because of Edmond Malleval's greed and obsession.

Saintclair slept through the morning. It was odd to watch over him as he lay in bed, oblivious to her presence, vulnerable for once. She put her hand on his forehead. Her fingers brushed his dark hair, slid down along the side of his face, and along the rugged line of his scar. She wondered how long ago he got it, in which battle...there was so much she didn't know about him. So much she wanted to learn.

He muttered something in his sleep. She gasped and withdrew her hand but didn't move away. The sight of his mouth, his broad chest, and strong shoulders filled her with longing and fear of what the future held for them. How she wanted to nestle against him and forget about the world, about Malleval, and Christopher—Nallay, as she would call her husband from then on.

When he woke up he would probably be sick of her and the problems she had caused him. Because of her, he jeopardised his family home in St Genis and risked his life. It wasn't only Uxeloup and his henchmen who were after him now, but Nallay and Fouché too.

Glancing at her bare hand, she was reminded of the wedding ring she had taken off the night before. It was still on the table. Such a little thing, but it had meant so much. One thing was certain, she would never wear it again. She couldn't however quite bring herself to throw it away.

After lunch, she pulled a chair next to Saintclair's bed

and sat down with the newspaper on her lap, but despite her best intentions her eyes closed and she drifted to sleep. It was late afternoon when she woke up. Saintclair was sitting up, looking at her.

'Oh…I am sorry. I wanted to watch over you and I fell asleep.' She rubbed her eyes and combed strands of hair away from her face. 'How are you feeling?'

'Like hell,' he said, wincing when he tried to lean onto his arm to get up.

'Don't try to move just now. Let me get you a hot drink and something to eat first.' She busied herself warming some soup and coffee the batman had left on the stove, and brought a tray over to him.

'I'd rather have some brandy,' he grumbled, but he tucked his spoon into the bowl and finished the hot soup in minutes. 'I won't take any more laudanum. I could never stand the stuff. I have lost most of the day thanks to that damned physician and his drug when there were so many things I needed to sort out.' He pushed the tray away and looked at her.

'I've been thinking and you can't stay here tonight. I am in no state for a fight if that husband of yours, or Malleval's henchmen, come after you. As a former Hussar, Malleval can get into the barracks as he pleases, and being Fouché's man, *your husband*', he stared at Marie-Ange, 'will find a way.'

He was right, of course. Malleval and Karloff would soon figure out she was here. As for Nallay, the threats he had shouted last night still echoed in her ears. He meant every word. She informed Saintclair about the visit by two policemen that morning. His face became even more sombre.

'They will be Fouché's men—he may not be the Minister for Police anymore, but he still has many staff in his pocket. There's really no time to lose to find somewhere safe for you.'

'I could go to Beauregard by stagecoach and try and find my father,' she suggested.

'No, it's too risky on your own.' He closed his eyes. 'I'll take you to Caroline Dupin's apartment. Nobody will think of looking for you there.'

She recalled the beautiful, dark-haired woman she had met at the *Théâtre Italien* in Paris. 'Won't she mind? She doesn't know me.'

'She will do as I ask. She always does,' he replied, with an arrogant smile.

Marie-Ange experienced a sharp, burning twinge of jealousy. She knew Caroline had been Saintclair's mistress—and very probably still was.

'No. I'd rather not go there.' She crossed her arms on her chest.

He arched his eyebrows. 'Really? And would you care to tell me why?'

She swallowed hard, and looked around, her mind blank. 'She is bound to be suspicious and ask embarrassing questions. What will you tell her?'

'I'll think of something. Come on, there's no time to waste, you need to change first. Someone might be watching the barracks on behalf of Malleval or your husband. They mustn't recognise you.'

He instructed his batman to get him a set of men's clothes of the smallest size he could find. For the first time in her life, Marie-Ange slipped into a pair of breeches and high boots, a white man's shirt and a short grey jacket. Her disguise was completed by a brown hat.

'Not bad.' Saintclair eyed her from top to toe when she walked back into the room, his eyes lingering on her legs clad in the high boots and the curves of her hips. 'But you need to cover up more. An overcoat should do.'

He got up, said he was going to get ready, and went out. When he came back, he handed her a coat that she slipped on her shoulders. He was freshly shaven and wore his cuirassier uniform—the dark blue coat with white and silver shoulder pads and white breeches tucked into black boots complimented his rugged physique. Marie-Ange forced herself to tear her gaze from him. Adjusting the long sword that hung from the right side of his belt, he sat at the table, holding himself stiffly as if he was in pain. He placed his black hat ornamented with a tall red feather and gold braids on the table in front of him, and gestured for her to sit down.

'Last night your husband said he was on some kind of mission,' he began. 'A mission Talleyrand and Police Prefect Bourienne were eager to sabotage. I have to follow this through.'

'Do you have any idea what it could be?'

'No. I am setting off for Paris as soon as I have seen to your safety. I must talk to my superiors at the Ministry of War and to Talleyrand at *Palais Vendôme*. Something is brewing. And when this something involves Fouché, it's never good news.'

'What about the physician's orders? You need to rest. You're wounded.'

He let out a short laugh. 'As if that ever stopped me.'

'But my father and his companions are waiting for us at Beauregard.'

'I will send someone to warn them of the delay.' He paused and his lips stretched into one of his sudden smiles. 'You are keeping me busy. Here was I, a few weeks ago, thinking I was doing a straightforward trip to England and back to fetch an heiress for Malleval…'

The coldness in his eyes melted away. 'I'm sorry it turned out like this. Instead of an inheritance, you found a load of…ahem…trouble.'

She put her hand on top of his. 'Capitaine, you are the one who got hurt because of me. I shall never forget it.'

The intensity of his gaze burnt through her. He leant forward, and his jaw tightened. For a few seconds, she was sure he was going to kiss her and her whole body tingled with anticipation. Instead, he sighed, withdrew his hand, and reclined against his chair.

'We need to go. Give me your bag.'

She nodded silently and pulled the man's hat down to hide the disappointment in her eyes. They walked across the courtyard towards the square which was lined with black carriages. Saintclair picked one from the middle of the queue and climbed in. He asked the coachman to drive around town for a while before giving him Caroline's address. Her apartment was located on the busy *Rue de la Charité*, an elegant street leading to the city's main square.

'I sent her a note warning of our arrival,' he explained as he stepped out of the carriage. He held his hand out for Marie-Ange and winced as the door closed on his wounded shoulder.

Caroline's welcome was as friendly as Marie-Ange expected.

'My darling, you look magnificent, as always.' Caroline smiled coquettishly and gave her hand to Saintclair. 'As for you, Madame, this is a surprise to see you dressed in such strange apparel. Are you going to a fancy dress ball or on a hunting party?' She gestured for them to sit down.

'I need your help for a few days, Caroline, a week at the most,' Saintclair informed her. 'Marie-Ange's husband has got it in his head that she is being unfaithful, which is totally untrue, of course. She needs somewhere safe to stay until he comes to his senses. He is a rather jealous chap and doesn't hesitate to use his blade instead of words to make his point.' He gestured to his shoulder.

So that was his cover story. Her husband thought they were having an affair and wanted revenge.

'I see…' Caroline pursed her lips. 'Why are you asking *me* to help?'

'Because I know I can trust you,' Saintclair replied

with a deep, cajoling voice. 'And I shall make it up to you, as I always do.'

Caroline's eyes suddenly shone with pleasure. 'In that case, Madame can stay as long as she needs. I think I am rather going to enjoy having a clandestine guest.'

Saintclair then gave a list of instructions. Marie-Ange wasn't allowed to go out of the apartment, and nobody should see her or even be told of her presence. He would leave money to buy a few indispensable items of clothing and toiletries and to cover any expenses Caroline might incur.

Caroline got up and held her hand out to him. 'Let's go into my drawing room, Hugo. We need to finalise our arrangement.'

'It will be my pleasure,' he said.

Marie-Ange threw him a cool, angry stare but he smiled, got up and followed Caroline out. Her composure crumbled as soon as they left the room. What did Saintclair mean when he promised Caroline he would 'make it up' to her? What did the woman imply by 'finalising their arrangement'? Were they making love right now, in a room next door? Of course they were. They had been lovers for a long time, several years, Malleval had said. The capitaine was even jealous of her. She recalled how annoyed he had been at the opera because Caroline had gone to Auxerre with de Mitre, the man who had obtained his promotion over him.

Marie-Ange pulled her hat off, shook her head and her hair tumbled down on her shoulders in a mass of curls. She felt she couldn't breathe with the unfamiliar necktie fastened tight so she loosened it and opened the collar of her shirt before reclining on the armchair. Closing her eyes, she tried not to think about what was going on in Caroline's drawing room.

She heard their voices as they walked back a short while later. Saintclair stopped in the doorway. They stared at each other. His gaze locked with hers, and it felt as if they were alone. Next to him, Caroline's smile faded. She hooked her hand into the curve of his arm and chuckled seductively.

'Well, that's settled then, my darling Hugo,' she said, hanging onto him. 'I shall look forward to our reunion. This little session has left me pining for more.'

Marie-Ange jumped to her feet, a hot flush on her face. She had been right. He had made love to Caroline. He shrugged Caroline off him and moved to stand before her.

'Do as you are told for once and don't leave this apartment before I return,' he said.

Now that the moment had come for him to leave, she didn't want him to go. Her chest was so tight she couldn't breathe. She gave him her hand.

'Thank you, Capitaine. For everything. I wish you a safe trip to Paris.'

He gave her hand a perfunctory kiss, bowed his head and put his hat on. 'I'll be in touch.'

Ten days passed and he didn't send any news.

What had gone wrong? Perhaps his injury was more serious than the physician had thought, or Christopher or Malleval's men had found him. The thought of him suffering any more harm was unbearable. Maybe he had discovered something in Paris which was keeping him away...

Marie-Ange paced the bedroom, feeling like a prisoner. She stopped in front of the window and lifted the heavy red and gold brocade curtain to look at the street below. For the hundredth time that day, she sighed as she observed the fashionable crowd strolling on the pavements. Men in dark coats and black hats, ladies in fur trimmed pelisses and bonnets looked at the shop windows or stepped in and out of *cafés* and *brasseries*.

How she longed to go out, too. She closed her eyes and

tried to imagine walking on the cliff path back in Wellcombe bay, enjoying the breeze and the sea spray on her face, or running free on the moors with Rusty and Splinter. It was only four weeks since she had left Devonshire. It felt like an eternity.

A pretty young maid came in and announced that lunch was ready. Marie-Ange followed her through Caroline Dupin's elegantly furnished apartment. She hated being here. She knew Caroline didn't like it any more than she did. On the few occasions they sat together, usually at lunchtime or for afternoon tea, the woman talked incessantly about her tumultuous relationship with Capitaine Saintclair. She would stare into space, a dreamy smile on her face as she recalled details of the passionate embraces '*her cuirassier*' submitted her to. Marie-Ange did her best to hide her feelings behind an indifferent smile, but every one of Caroline's words was like a dagger in her heart.

At the entrance of the dining room, she froze. Caroline and two men in uniform were sitting around the table. Yet Saintclair had been adamant nobody should know about her staying there.

'At last, dear Marie-Ange,' Caroline exclaimed. 'Come and meet my friends.'

The two men stood up and Marie-Ange nodded a polite greeting.

'Charming, utterly charming,' one of them said, holding her hand.

Caroline introduced him as Capitaine Renaud. He was very tall and looked like a Viking warrior, with blond hair and a powerful neck. He smoothed down his moustache while detailing Marie-Ange from top to toe.

'So Madame is a friend of yours?' the other man asked, his warm brown eyes glinting with curiosity. His name was Major Paulet. Without waiting for an answer, he added, 'It should be a most pleasurable afternoon, then.'

Marie-Ange blushed violently. She had heard enough these past few days to be in no doubt of Caroline's occupation.

'Marie-Ange is a good friend of Capitaine Saintclair's,' the woman said, her hard stare belying the smooth tone of her voice and the smile on her painted lips.

Renaud poured some champagne for Marie-Ange and offered a toast to Capitaine Saintclair's health. She took hold of the flute, not daring to object that she didn't like champagne.

'How is he these days?' he enquired. 'I have not seen him for at least three months. Last time was at a card game at Beauregard during which Uxeloup Malleval thoroughly fleeced him. Saintclair was in such a blind rage when he realised he would probably lose his house, he accused Malleval of cheating and challenged him to a duel. Needless to say Malleval refused. He might have gone a little strange lately, but he isn't that crazy. The man who could beat Saintclair in a duel hasn't been born.'

Marie-Ange looked up sharply and put her flute on the table. 'You were there when Saintclair gambled his house in a game of cards?'

Renaud nodded. 'Malleval is a devil at cards. That night, he seemed determined not to end the game until Saintclair had lost everything, and our unfortunate friend obliged him. Maybe it was because of the abundance of wine or spirits Malleval's pretty housekeeper was serving, but Saintclair threw all caution to the wind and got thoroughly beaten.'

'He was wounded a few days ago by Madame's husband,' Caroline said with a mocking voice. 'A domestic misunderstanding...'

'Poor Madame.' Renaud took hold of Marie-Ange's hand and lifted it to his lips. 'I promise I will make you forget all your problems with your husband, if you will allow me the pleasure.'

Paulet poured another glass of champagne and this time they toasted to Marie-Ange's health. She winced as she swallowed the wine and was about to refuse a third glass, but Caroline turned to her, her eyebrows arched and her tone ironic.

'You are not going to refuse to toast our King, are you?'

She had no choice but to drink. She was feeling light-headed by then. When Caroline urged the men to pour a fourth glass and toast to the English King George III and the regent, Prince George, she did nothing more than take a sip.

'It does feel strange to toast our old enemies.' Renaud laughed. 'God knows I fought the English in several countries over the years, but what the hell! We're at peace now.'

Caroline's maid brought in dishes of vegetable jardinière and a couple of roast chickens. Renaud and Paulet poured more champagne. During lunch, the conversation revolved around the impending journey the King and his entourage were making to Lyon.

'The King is determined to review the troops in Lyon next week. He thinks they need a boost to their morale if they are to fight efficiently against Napoleon...you know the rumours of his comeback are still raging,' Paulet commented.

'His majesty will stay at the *Hotel Lacroix-Laval*, a stone's-throw from here. My battalion is assigned to his safety.' Renaud turned to Caroline. 'We are all on tender hooks. There have been rumours of an assassination plot, and I swear my colonel's hair has turned white with worry already.'

He leant towards Marie-Ange. 'Are you not feeling well? You are dreadfully pale all of a sudden.'

'Too much champagne, that's all,' she whispered. 'Who would be bold enough to plan a coup against the King?'

Renaud shrugged. 'Napoleon's staunch supporters of course. The hardliners will never give up scheming for his return,' he answered. 'My money is on Fouché.'

'Or Marshall Davoust,' Paulet agreed. 'I heard Chief of Police Bourienne had him under surveillance in Paris because of rumours of a coup.'

'It's Fouché he should have under surveillance!' Paulet interrupted impatiently. 'He is the snake in the grass. Bourienne may officially be the new police chief but it's Fouché who still controls most of the agents.'

'Will Monsieur Fouché be in Lyon to meet the King?' Marie-Ange asked.

'I doubt it,' Paulet retorted. 'The two men can't stand the sight of each other. Fouché's attempts to get back into government were all defeated by the King, the Comte d'Artois—the King's brother—and his old enemy Talleyrand.'

Marie-Ange's mind was racing. Christopher had talked of a mission…What if he was the man charged by Fouché to assassinate the King during his visit to Lyon?

The maid took the dishes away and brought a bowl of fruit—apples, pears, and plums, together with a plate of dark chocolates topped with sugar violets.

'Try a couple of those, Marie-Ange. They are made especially for me by Lyon's best chocolatier, Monsieur Voisin.' Caroline handed her the plate of confectionary after helping herself to a handful of chocolates.

The combination of the bitter chocolate and the sweet sugar flower was sickening, but Marie-Ange forced herself to eat. The Major was staring at her with a wide grin on his face. He put a handful of chocolates into his mouth too and drained his champagne.

Caroline stood up and patted his shoulder.

'Time for a little entertainment,' she told him with a seductive smile. 'We shall have coffee in my boudoir.' Then turning to Renaud, she added. 'Please feel free to come and join us whenever you're ready.'

They walked out, leaving Renaud and Marie-Ange alone. The Capitaine pulled his chair closer to her and took her hand. She swayed in her seat, suddenly light-headed and nauseous.

'I have a confession to make,' he said, kissing the back of her hand. His moustache tickled her, but she felt too weak to protest.

'My presence here today is no coincidence. I too am indebted to Malleval. Like I said, the man is a devil at cards.'

She looked at him and tried to focus on what he was saying, aware that it was important, but Renaud's face was dancing in front of her eyes.

'Earlier this week, I heard that Malleval was looking everywhere for a young English lady who had given him the slip, helped by a cuirassier officer. He is offering a generous reward for any information as to her whereabouts, and an even more generous payout for whoever takes the female in question back to him at Beauregard. When Caroline told me she had an unexpected guest, an English woman who was under Capitaine Saintclair's protection, I put two and two together.'

He seized her shoulders and looked into her eyes.

'You are the one Uxeloup is looking for, aren't you? Well, you shall be my way out of financial ruin. I will take you to Beauregard later today, but first, I mean to get to know you better.' He pulled her up roughly and encircled her waist with his arm.

'Don't! I'm warning you, Capitaine Saintclair is coming for me, he won't be happy if anything happens to me,' Marie-Ange objected, her voice weak and slurred.

'I can't see Saintclair anywhere, can you? So for now, you're all mine...and Malleval's.' He bent down and kissed her mouth roughly before leading her out of the dining

223

room.

Marie-Ange felt like a rag doll, unable to walk unaided, let alone run away. Yet it was exactly what she should do.

'Don't worry.' They walked down the corridor and he pushed open the door onto Caroline's boudoir. Marie-Ange opened her eyes wide. It was the first time she stepped into the room. The walls were covered with red velvet wallpaper and large, gilded mirrors. A huge bed occupied most of the space together with a chaise longue scattered with scarlet cushions. Thick curtains were drawn against the daylight, and candles burnt around the room.

Marie-Ange saw the reflections of Paulet and Caroline in the mirrors. Paulet sat bare-chested on the bed. His breeches were down, his mouth open and his features heavy with pleasure as Caroline straddled his lap and he kneaded her bare breasts. She was completely naked, her hands holding on to the bed railing while her hips moved, slow and lascivious, on top of him. When she heard the door open, she turned her head towards Renaud and gave him an inviting smile.

'Are you joining us? I did promise you a foursome.'

Marie-Ange stepped back in alarm.

'No, please! Not that!' She lifted her hand to her mouth, feeling like she was going to be sick. 'I want to go to my room.'

Renaud laughed. 'Are you a little shy? Ah well, it will just be the two of us, then.'

He lifted Marie-Ange in his arms and carried her to her room.

Once they were there, he put her down, closed the door behind him, and started to take his jacket and shirt off. Tentatively, because the room seemed to move around her, Marie-Ange made her way towards the bed. Her dagger was under her pillow. She would use it to frighten Renaud off.

'I definitely don't like champagne,' she remarked, still

slurring her words. 'It makes me ill.'

'Oh, but it wasn't the champagne.' Renaud chuckled. 'Caroline put laudanum in the chocolates. Am I wrong in thinking you are not used to it?'

Laudanum! That explained why her body didn't respond to her any longer and why she felt an overwhelming urge to lie down, close her eyes, and fall asleep. She had to get the dagger, now. She extended her arms towards the pillow but Renaud intercepted her before she got there and roughly spun her towards him. She was unable to fight him while he undressed her, pulled her dress down, and unlaced her corset until it too dropped to the floor. Soon, she stood in her chemise and stockings in front of him.

'There, that's better.' He grunted, breathing hard and fast.

His fingers wandered up and down her chest and stomach, lifted the chemise up and touched between her legs.

'No,' she cried out and tried to push him away.

He laughed as he tugged at her chemise, exposing her breasts. Then he bent down, took a nipple in his mouth, and sucked hard. His hands cupped her bare buttocks and ground her hips into his.

'I'm so ready for you,' he moaned.

Part of her wanted to fight him off and scream, but another part observed the scene from a distance, calm and detached, as if none of this was really happening.

He took her hand and pressed it against the hard bulge at the top of his breeches. 'Touch me,' he ordered.

'I will do everything you want on the bed,' she whispered, fighting another wave of nausea. She had to get the dagger. It was her only hope of escaping him.

He heaved a ragged breath and looked at her.

'All right. Take this off and lie down while I get out of these clothes.'

He took his boots off, shrugged his shirt off, and started undoing his breeches.

She walked unsteadily to the bed and lay down, still in her chemise. Slipping her hand under the pillow, she felt for the dagger. She would kill Renaud if she had to. He was a big man. She hoped she would be strong enough.

The maid's voice at the door interrupted them. 'Capitaine, your sergeant's here. He wants a word.'

A man's voice bellowed. 'Sir! You and Major Paulet are needed at the barracks immediately. Colonel Dery is calling a meeting of all officers.'

'*Merde*!' Renaud exclaimed angrily.

'I'm coming!' He shouted back. Marie-Ange heard him put his clothes back on in a hurry.

Here was her chance. She closed her eyes and pretended to be fast asleep. She heard his footsteps approaching, felt his touch on her shoulder.

'I shall hold you to your promise later. I should only be a couple of hours,' he whispered. He shook her lightly to check she was asleep, then, satisfied, walked to the door and left.

She sat up as soon as the door closed. Her head felt heavy and fuzzy, the room spun in front of her eyes but she had to leave. Caroline couldn't be trusted to keep her safe any longer.

She took a few deep breaths and swung her legs to the side of the bed to get up. It took a long time to pull the man's clothes Saintclair had given her out of the wardrobe. She did the breeches up, buttoned the shirt with shaky, clumsy fingers. When she was ready, she pinned her hair at random on top of her head and pulled the hat down to hide her face. She stuffed some money in her pocket together with the locket, slipped Christopher's dagger into her boot and tucked her mother's sketchbook into her breeches, flat against her stomach. Then she put the jacket and overcoat on and slipped out of the room.

Walking along the corridor, she prayed she wouldn't meet Caroline or her maid on the way to the front door. Thankfully, the apartment was quiet and she was able to sneak out unnoticed. Weak and dizzy, she stopped several times to steady herself against the banister as she climbed down the stairs. Just how long would it be before the effects of the laudanum wore off?

Once in the street, she breathed in the cold, crisp air and directed her steps towards the *Place Louis Le Grand*. Her plan was to buy a passage for the next coach to Beaujeu and make her way from there to her great-aunt Hermine. From there, she would make contact with her father.

Chapter Seventeen

'My poor child. You look about to pass out.'

Hermine stood in her night clothes and frilly lace bonnet in the cold and dark hallway of Marzac Manor. She gave instructions for food and drinks to be brought up immediately and led the way to the drawing room where Pierre was busy lighting a fire.

Relieved by her great-aunt's welcome, Marie-Ange rubbed her arms with the palms of her hands to stave off the cold but couldn't stop shivering. During the two hours it had taken the coach to reach Beaujeu and her long walk from the town to Marzac, she had grown more and more anxious and exhausted, imagined being mauled to death by her great-aunt's guard dogs, or having to find shelter in a barn or a ditch if the gates were closed, or even being turned away by Hermine herself.

As it were, her great-aunt said she had been expecting her.

'That good-for-nothing Uxeloup Malleval paid me a visit two days ago. He said you absconded with this man— this Capitaine Saintclair who came here with you last time—and demanded I let him know immediately if I heard from you.'

She gave Marie-Ange a stern look and crossed her arms on her chest.

'So, what have you got to say and what on earth have you let yourself into? Has this *cuirassier* dishonoured you?' She almost spat the words, making it very obvious what she thought about Saintclair.

Marie-Ange sighed. She took her hat off, shook her

head, and combed her hair roughly with her fingers.

'I am afraid I have not been completely honest with you, Aunt Hermine.'

The old lady narrowed her eyes. 'As I suspected!'

Marie-Ange told her about Christopher losing his memory and working as a spy for Fouché.

'You are saying your husband survived a shipwreck and has been living for the past six years in France under a false identity while you lamented his death in England? This is extraordinary...But are you sure it's him? I mean, people's appearance can alter a lot in six years.'

Marie-Ange sighed. 'It is him. He has indeed changed very much, but not in appearance. He has become a cruel, dangerous man. He even stabbed Capitaine Saintclair in the back when he was only trying to help me.'

'Ah yes, Capitaine Saintclair. You seem to hold him in great esteem.' Hermine sneered. 'Yet he is nothing but one of those ruffian officers promoted by Napoleon.'

'You are not being fair, Aunt Hermine. He has been a great help over past few weeks and has risked much for me,' she said with passion.

'I see.' Hermine pursed her lips, still disapproving. 'What are your intentions regarding your husband, then? What happens if he doesn't regain his memory? Will you go back to Devonshire, pretend you never met him and carry on as if he were dead, marry again, maybe?'

'No, it would be bigamy.' Marie-Ange bent her head and sighed. 'Anyway, there is no man I wish to marry.' But even as she said the words, she knew it was a lie.

'Tell me, child, why does Malleval want to get hold of you so badly? Is it because of what we discussed last time—the Cross?' Hermine lowered her voice.

'Yes, he is obsessed with it. He held me captive twice, once at his house on *Isle Barbe* and later in his fortress in the mountains. He even had his physician, Karloff, hypnotise me, to reveal the words to a song my mother knew—a song that points to the location of the Cross at Beauregard.'

'Karloff! He was the physician who dealt with Aline, was he not?'

'Yes. He is involved in some kind of secret society and just as desperate to lay his hands on the Cross as Uxeloup.'

'How did you escape from Malleval?'

She took a deep breath. The moment of revealing the existence of her real father had come.

'A man helped me...' she began. 'His name is Baldassare dei Conti. He is a Turcopilar.'

Hermine opened her eyes wide.

'The name sounds familiar. Where did I hear of him? You said he was a Turk? Why would a Turk help you out?'

'Not a Turk, a Turcopilar.' Marie-Ange then explained about Turcopilars, the Order of the Knights Hospitaller, and the Knights Templar. Baldassare was the man Aline had written about, the young interpreter sent by Saint Germain with a team of craftsmen to build the dovecote at Beauregard, and who later rescued her mother from Malleval's claws.

A sleepy-eyed maid walked in with two cups of hot milk and slices of cake. Marie-Ange welcomed the interruption. She needed a little more time for the revelation that was to come. She drank the hot milk, licked her lips, and bit hungrily into a thick slice of orange-flavoured cake.

'Aunt Hermine, Baldassare told me something else...' she started again when all the cake was gone. She placed her empty plate on a side table. 'You see, I am his... Well, he is my...'

'What is it? Get on with it, girl.' The elderly lady stamped her cane on the floor.

'He is my father, my real father.' There! She had said it. Hermine would be horrified at the thought her niece

Catherine had conceived a child out of wedlock and with a mysterious foreign agent who lived the life of an errand knight.

'Oh! But how...? And what about your father, the English gentleman?' Hermine looked confused. Her hand shook as she lifted her cup of milk to her lips.

'Baldassare said he had to let my mother go to England alone because, as a Turcopilar, he wasn't allowed to have a family life.

'Pity he didn't think about that before.' Hermine put her cup down.

'Baldassare and his companions are now hiding near Beauregard. I need to find them tomorrow,' Marie-Ange added.

'I shall send my two stable lads with you although I am afraid they won't be much help against Malleval's men. I heard he has some brutes from his mountain clan with him at Beauregard. What about your capitaine? Where is he now?' Hermine sneered. 'No, don't answer that. He is probably rolling in a warm bed with some dancing girl.'

'No. He had to go to Paris, talk to people, about Christopher.'

'Hmm...'

The two women didn't speak for a while.

'Aunt Hermine,' Marie-Ange resumed. 'What can you tell me about the Cross of Life? Baldassare said I had to find it and take it back to Arginy.'

Hermine sat back in her chair and considered her a moment in silence. 'Do you know about Guillaume de Beaujeu, the Great Templar Master?'

'Uxeloup said his body was first laid in the chapel of the Temple of Paris, but that a member of his family, his nephew I think, later took his remains to Arginy, together with documents and artefacts, among which the Cross of Life.'

'That's right. Guichard de Beaujeu reburied

Guillaume's body and hid the Templar treasure in the crypt at Arginy back in 1307.'

'Uxeloup also said that at the end of the fifteenth century, Anne de Beaujeu searched Arginy and found the Cross.'

Hermine sighed. 'That is correct. Anne de Beaujeu ordered her men to go down into the crypt despite the traps Guichard had planted to protect the Templar treasure. Many of the men died a horrible death, their limbs crushed by stones, their bodies pierced by lances, their skin burned by fireballs...Some claimed the crypt was cursed by the Knights Templar. The poor man who did manage to bring the Cross back became a raving lunatic, ranting about shadows wanting to rip his soul out of his body. After the Cross was found, Anne had the entrance to the crypt walled. There is supposed to be another entrance somewhere, but nobody knows where it is.'

The more Hermine talked about Arginy, the more Marie-Ange was reminded of her nightmares. She closed her eyes, recalled her visions of a tall, round tower and an opening in the wall leading down to a slippery stone staircase and the vaults, where she heard whimpers of pain and where the shadows waited.

She whispered. 'Why do I have to take the Cross to Arginy? Why can I not just give it to the bishop, or any other church authorities, once I have found it?'

'Our family stole it from the crypt—well, it was Anne de Beaujeu but we, as Beauregards, are her nearest blood relatives, so it is our responsibility to put it back. And the legend says that only someone of the same bloodline as a past Great Master—that is a Beaujeu or a Beauregard— can handle the Cross without any risk to their life, to their sanity and soul.' She paused. 'It must be done, child, because only when the Cross is back at Arginy will the eleven Templar guardians be able to rest.'

They were the eleven shadows haunting her

nightmares, the Keepers her father told her about.

'What did Anne de Beaujeu do with the Cross?'

'Towards the end of her life, Anne believed she was cursed,' Hermine answered. 'She was plagued by horrifying visions that drove her almost insane. She only found peace after she gave the Cross to a dear friend of hers shortly before her death in the 1520s. The man was a scholar, alchemist, and a member of the Rosicrucian order which had vowed to guard the Templar Knights' secrets. She knew the Cross would be safe with him.'

'Who was he?'

'Count Saint Germain.'

'But that's impossible! How can Anne de Beaujeu know Saint Germain? She lived centuries before him.'

Hermine smiled but said nothing.

'You cannot seriously believe Saint Germain was alive in the fifteenth century and lived through to the 1780's,' Marie-Ange protested, incredulous.

'There have been too many reliable witnesses who testified meeting Saint Germain across the centuries to doubt that it is true. Some claim to have talked to him only recently.'

Marie-Ange shrugged. 'This is nonsense. Nothing can make a man immortal.'

'Something can. Don't forget the Cross' extraordinary powers, child,' Hermine said with quiet assurance.

It was useless to argue, her great-aunt would not see sense.

'Anyway what do you know about the relic inside the Cross?' she asked. 'Karloff claims it belongs to…'

'An angel,' Hermine finished in a whisper. 'That's right, child.'

'I don't believe a word of it.'

'And yet it is true, the story was passed down in our family through generations. The relic is a piece of clothing worn by a being, an angel, who appeared to two veterans

233

of the First Crusades, the French knights Hugues de Payens and Godfrey de Saint-Omer. The angel asked them to create a military order to protect pilgrims travelling to the Holy Land. They obeyed and that's how the Order of the Knights Templar was founded in 1119.'

'Angels don't exist,' Marie-Ange objected once again.

'They do, we just don't realize they wander the earth among us, undetected because they can take a human form,' Hermine declared matter-of-factly. 'The angel came to Payens and Saint-Omer as a man but his appearance changed once he had delivered his message. Witnessing the transformation, Hughes de Payens rushed to ask for his benediction but accidentally tore a piece of his clothing.'

'My mother's song refers to a wing.'

Hermine nodded. 'That's right. I was told the relic was a very fine, translucent, piece of fabric which glowed like the brightest moonlight. I believe the cloth was indeed the angel's wing as he changed back to his celestial form.'

Marie-Ange pulled a face but did not disagree. 'Why did Saint Germain choose Beauregard to hide the Cross?'

'Because it was close to Arginy and belonged to our family. Unfortunately he did not foresee that Edmond Malleval would one day own the place. That man was evil, I am glad he is rotting in the ground,' the old lady hissed the words vehemently between her teeth.

'Edmond Malleval wasn't buried, Aunt Hermine.'

Hermine gasped and put her hand in front of her mouth.

'My God. So he is waiting…'

'What do you mean, waiting? He is dead.'

'He is waiting for his son to get the Cross, and raise him from the dead.'

Marie-Ange shook her head. Clearly her great-aunt was as deluded about the Cross' powers as Uxeloup and Karloff.

Pierre walked in. He looked agitated. 'A gentleman requests an urgent interview with you, Madame. A

Capitaine Saintclair. What shall I tell him?'

'Saintclair!' Marie-Ange stood up, her heart leaped with joy. He was back from Paris at last. He had come for her. She turned a hopeful face towards her aunt.

'Please, Aunt Hermine. Let him in. He must have news.'

Hermine sighed and tightened her shawl onto her shoulders. 'Very well. I suppose we'd better hear what the man has to say.'

Marie-Ange sat down and took a few deep, calming breaths but her heart still beat wildly and her face was hot when Saintclair entered the room. His dark blue coat was dusty and covered his uniform, a leather satchel was slung across his chest. She couldn't repress a happy smile when he took his hat off and bowed deeply in front of her. Her smile however died on her lips as soon as he looked up. His eyes were cold, almost hostile.

'May I ask, Madame, why you saw fit to leave Mademoiselle Dupin's apartment in blatant contradiction of my orders?' His voice was as frosty as his blue eyes.

'Monsieur Saintclair. What brings you here?' Hermine asked before Marie-Ange gathered her wits to reply.

'The safety of your niece, Madame,' he replied shortly. 'I do apologise for the lateness of the hour but this isn't a visit of courtesy. I had to make sure Madame Norton was alive and well. She absconded earlier from my friend's apartment, leaving my poor friend understandably upset and concerned.'

There was only so much she could stand. Marie-Ange jumped to her feet and walked towards Saintclair, her face burning with anger.

'Your *poor friend* plied me with champagne, drugged me with laudanum, and threw me in the arms of an army captain while she cavorted with a major in her boudoir. The said captain intended to have his wicked way with me before taking me to Uxeloup as repayment of a gambling debt! That's why I left Lyon this afternoon.' She caught her breath and carried on. 'And what is this about you giving *me* orders? I am not one of your soldiers or your stable lads, Capitaine Saintclair.'

How dare he treat her like an unruly child acting on a whim when she had escaped from Caroline's apartment to save her own life?

'Drugged? There were men in the apartment…in the boudoir? That's not what Caroline reported.' He didn't sound so sure of himself any longer.

'Of course not. Caroline may be mean and calculating but she isn't stupid,' Marie-Ange added. 'She doesn't want you to know she had men in her apartment at any time of the day and night.'

Wild jealousy twisted her heart when she saw how pale Saintclair became then. Obviously he was so taken by the woman he hadn't realised she entertained other men.

'Marie-Ange, please, this is not appropriate,' Hermine remonstrated, looking suitably shocked.

She ignored her aunt, crossed her arms on her chest, and tilted her chin up.

'You really didn't have to come after me. I will take care of myself from now on.'

Saintclair took a deep breath and narrowed his eyes. 'I do have to protect you, Madame. I am the one who brought you to France, unwittingly throwing you into a very awkward, even deadly, situation. I now feel responsible for what happens to you.'

He felt responsible, that was all. That was the only reason why he was here. Her vision was suddenly blurred with tears.

'Well, there is really no need,' she retorted, trying to stop her voice from breaking. 'Anyway, how did you know I would be here?'

'It was easy. I came back from Paris late afternoon and went straight to Caroline's apartment, but you had already left. I noticed you had taken the men's clothes my batman gave you. When I made some enquiries at the coach stations in *Place Louis le Grand*, one inn keeper remembered a young man with a brown hat and a grey coat who bought passage for Beaujeu in the afternoon. I thought it might be you. I was sure you'd come here rather than try and find Baldassare on your own at night.'

'I am very grateful for your concern for my niece, Capitaine,' Hermine interrupted calmly. 'Let me offer you some refreshments. A little brandy maybe, or a cup of mulled wine? And please sit down and make yourself comfortable.'

Marie-Ange glanced up, surprised by her aunt's uncharacteristic politeness towards the cuirassier she seemed to despise so much. Saintclair asked for mulled wine. Marie-Ange decreed she would have some, too. When the maid brought the drinks, she drained her cup at once. The hot, spicy liquid burned a trail down her throat and she immediately asked for another. To spite Saintclair, who was looking at her, his eyebrows arched and a mocking smile on his lips, she drank her second cup in one gulp, too.

Hermine turned to him. 'I know you are a brave, honourable man, you have proved it by coming all this way to make sure Marie-Ange was safe. There is one thing I must ask of you. Please go with her tomorrow to look for the Cross of Life at Beauregard and return it where it belongs, at Arginy.'

'Dealing with religious artefacts is a little beyond my usual military duties, Madame.'

'I don't need Capitaine Saintclair, Aunt Hermine,' Marie-Ange protested. 'I have already taken far too much of his time and release him from any obligation he mistakenly believes he has towards me.' She tilted her chin up to look at him and added, 'You are free to return to your dear Caroline, Capitaine.'

Saintclair put his cup down. 'We will go to Beauregard tomorrow morning at first light.'

'I just said I didn't want you.' The mulled wine was making her cheeks too hot, it was hard to pull breath into her lungs. Or was it the way he looked down at her, in total silence?

'And I just said I was going with you,' he said at last.

'Very well, it is settled then.' Hermine sighed, satisfied, oblivious to the sudden tension in the room. 'I think we could all do with a good rest now. Where are you staying tonight, Capitaine?'

He shrugged. 'I don't know yet. I will find a tavern in Beaujeu.'

'Please be my guest. This is the least I can do now you've accepted my request to help my great-niece. I will ask Pierre to prepare a room for you. Come along, Marie-Ange,' she said, sliding her hand under the young woman's arm to lead her out. She obviously wanted to make sure she stayed well away from the officer. They walked up to the first floor where Hermine showed Marie-Ange into a bedroom.

'Sleep well,' the old lady said. 'You will need all your strength for tomorrow.'

Marie-Ange closed the door behind her and leant against the wooden pane, all her senses alert. She was waiting for Saintclair to come up. When she heard voices in the corridor, she half-opened the door and peered outside to see which room he was going into. When the house was quiet, she tiptoed out of her room and knocked softly onto his door.

'Capitaine.'

Saintclair appeared in the doorway. He had taken his overcoat and blue jacket off. A small bandage around his left shoulder was visible under his white shirt.

'Is there anything the matter?' He didn't open the door fully.

'Let me come in. I need to speak to you.'

He frowned. 'I'm tired. Can this not wait until the morning?'

Why was the man so reluctant to let her in? Marie-Ange tapped her foot on the floor, impatient. 'No, it cannot wait! There is something important I must tell you. It's about Christopher's mission in Lyon. Hurry or someone will hear us.'

Sainclair opened his door at last, and she slipped in. Pierre had lit a fire in the fireplace and brought up a tray with a pitcher of wine and a cup and some food. Now she was on her own with Saintclair, she was nervous and shaky. Maybe a glass of wine would soothe her nerves.

'Could you pour a glass out for me?' she asked.

'Haven't you had enough already?' he asked, crossing his arms on his chest and leaning against the bedpost.

'What do you care how much wine I drink?' she retorted, annoyed.

He still didn't move.

'Very well, I will pour it myself.' She walked to the table. 'I don't see why Caroline Dupin should be the only woman allowed to have vices,' she muttered under her breath.

She filled the cup and raised it to her lips, but the sharpness of the wine tickled her throat and made her cough. Without a word, Saintclair pulled out a handkerchief from his pocket and handed it to her before leaning back against the wooden bed post. She wiped her face, cursing herself and feeling like crying for making such a display of herself.

'Didn't you say you had something important to tell me?' he asked at last.

She nodded, folded the stained handkerchief, and handed it back to him.

'The King is coming to Lyon next week to review the troops. One of Caroline's *gentlemen friends* is in charge of the security and said there were rumours of an attempt on his life. He implied that Fouché would be the one most likely to mastermind such a coup.' She paused. 'I think Chris...Nallay's mission in Lyon is to kill the King.'

'I already know about the rumoured attempt on the King's person,' he said.

'Oh.' she said, slightly put out that he wasn't more impressed by her news. 'Why would anyone want to kill the King?'

'To make way for Napoleon, or replace the King with someone more amenable to certain policies or politicians? Or even to discredit forever Napoleon and his followers, who knows?' He shrugged.

'My Christopher would never have been capable of killing the King, or anyone, in cold blood.'

Saintclair laughed bitterly. 'Well, he was capable of stabbing me in the back. He is certainly no longer the sensitive soul you once married.'

She bowed her head. 'That's because he isn't Christopher anymore...And I am sorry you got hurt.'

'It wasn't your fault. I was careless. I should have been prepared,' he said with a softer voice. 'We are caught in a frightening web of intrigues. Your husband's involvement with Fouché...'

'Stop calling him my husband. I told you before. Christopher Norton is dead. The man who calls himself Nallay is a stranger to me.'

She lifted her head towards him and smiled tentatively. 'But you are right. I am frightened.'

Hugo narrowed his eyes. The way he was looking at her now reminded her of the night of the ball. Her skin tingled all over, her cheeks burned, her breathing became fast, too fast.

'You mean you wouldn't take Norton back even if he begged you to?' he asked after a while.

She shook her head slowly. 'I could never share my life

with him, ever again.'

He let out a long sigh and stepped forward.

'Now I must tell you about the Cross of Life and Arginy. I have seen terrible dangers in my dreams,' she said, flustered from his nearness.

'I don't much care about dreams.' His voice was hoarse.

He stood in front of her, so close she could feel the heat from his body. The intensity in his eyes, the tautness of his jaw warned her to keep still.

'In fact, I never dream,' he carried on. 'Dreams are a waste of time. I only care about what's real, about what I can touch, and kiss.' He slid his finger under her chin to tilt her head up, then bent down and kissed her lips.

She pulled back.

'How can you?' she protested.

'How can I...what?' he asked, this time setting his hands on her waist and pulling her close.

She stood as still as a statue, but inside she was trembling. The burning desire his touch awakened inside her, and the need to let her feelings for him flood in, terrified her.

'You are involved with another woman.'

'Is that so? And who might she be?' He lifted his hands to cup her face and stroked her cheeks, her throat, the back of her neck.

'Caroline, of course. You two are lovers, and have been for years.' She struggled to keep her voice steady as his fingers slid down her throat and into the opening of her shirt. She had to step away. Now.

'Whatever gave you that idea?' His fingers caressed the hollow at the base of her throat.

'Well, she told me about it, many...times and in...great detail,' she stammered. 'And tonight you were upset to...learn she had been seeing another man in her boudoir.'

Saintclair laughed. His eyes shone, warm, intense.

241

'Upset? The only thing I was upset about was that the stupid woman put you in any danger. Caroline and I are history and have been for a long time. She was never more than an agreeable pastime.'

She closed her eyes a brief moment, overwhelmed by a wave of relief.

He unbuttoned the top of her shirt. 'I have wanted you since I first laid eyes on you. I think you want me, too. So why don't we just enjoy the moment?'

'I'm not like you,' she said, placing her hand on his to stop him. 'I couldn't just do...this, and then forget all about it. I have feelings.'

What she really meant was she loved him. She loved him and she wanted to be his, but she knew what he thought about love and women.

'I have feelings too,' he replied lightly.

She let go of his hand. His fingers stroked her throat again.

'As I said, I want you. All of you.'

'That isn't the kind of feelings I mean.' She was too hot, breathless, blood pulsed in her veins. Her body shivered, ached, and throbbed under his touch.

He put a finger of her lips. 'Is there any other kind? Now stop talking, you're driving me crazy.'

She knew then she was lost. Unhurriedly, he kissed her mouth as he finished unbuttoning the shirt. She let out a small gasp as he opened it to reveal her chemise, buried his face in her neck, and kissed her softly. The stubble on his cheeks scraped her skin, his warm breath tickled, and his mouth sent shivers of delight that made her body tighten and melt at the same time.

He pulled her against his chest and whispered, 'All that matters is here and now.'

His warmth, his caresses were so tantalising she gave in with a shaky sigh. Her body moulded itself more tightly against his. She threw her arms around his neck and tangled her fingers in his soft, dark hair.

Her hand went down to his wounded shoulder.

'Does it still hurt?'

He shrugged. 'Sometimes. You'll have to take my mind off it.'

She nestled against him while he encircled her waist and held her tight. He kissed her again, a little harder, and waves of pleasure carried her away once more to the marvellous place where only he had the power to take her. She saw the same longing in his eyes, caressed the outline of his face, her fingers lingering on the scar that marked one side of his face. He took her hand and brought it to his lips.

She closed her eyes. The only sounds were their breathing and the crackling of the logs in the fire place. It was as if they were alone in the world.

She threw her head back to offer her throat to his lips. Her heart beat wildly, out of control, as he pulled her chemise down, dropped it to her feet. He undid the ties of her breeches before rolling them down her hips in a slow, deliberate movement as sensual as a caress.

'I want you naked in my arms.'

He took the last of her clothes off and held her against him, hot and shivery, tight and yielding, wanting him, needing him. She moaned when his fingers stroke the tender skin on the inside of her thighs. She parted her legs a little wider so he could touch and caress her and put an end to the ache and the need she felt deep inside. It was just the beginning. Shaking in his arms, she threw her head back. Her breasts jutted out and this time it was he who moaned as he bent down to kiss, lick, tease, trace slow circles around her erect nipples with his lips and his tongue, and then blow on the delicate, wet skin, only to start all over again.

Her breath became laboured. She arched her hips against him, wanting, needing to get closer still. He

243

cupped her bottom and pressed her hard against him, lifting her so she could wrap her legs around his hips. He was still dressed and the feel of his shirt against her bare breasts, and his breeches rubbing against the hot, tender skin inside her legs sent long, feverish shivers all over her body.

'Hugo,' she gasped. There wasn't a clear thought left in her mind. There were only feelings and sensations and overwhelming desire.

'Hmm…I like it when you say my name.'

He let her down, and she grabbed hold of his shoulders. His hands brushed past her hips and her stomach. She was aching for him to touch her again. As if he had understood her most intimate desires, he caressed and explored, gentle and insistent in turn, arousing sensations so wild, so tormenting she cried out loud. Her legs buckled underneath her, and he caught her in his arms.

'I must have you now or I'll go mad,' he said with some urgency as he lifted her up against him. He was about to carry her onto the bed when he pulled away.

'What's that noise?' He froze, and his eyes focused on the window.

Outside in the night, horses neighed, men shouted and banged loudly on the castle door.

He turned to Marie-Ange. 'Put your clothes back on. Quick! Something's happening.' He fastened his belt and checked his sword and his pistol and put his jacket and overcoat on.

Someone rapped on the door.

'Capitaine, there are men outside asking for you.' Pierre called.

Saintclair frowned, but he waited for Marie-Ange to put her shirt and breeches on before opening the door to let the old servant in.

'Monsieur,' Pierre was breathless. His eyes opened wide with shock when he saw Marie-Ange was there partly clothed. 'They say they are bailiffs sent by Monsieur Malleval to take you to the debtors' jail in Beaujeu. If you come with me now, I'll show you the old way out of the castle, but please hurry!'

Saintclair nodded. 'Give me a minute.' He looked at Marie-Ange. 'You're coming too.' It was not a question but a command.

Chapter Eighteen

They followed Pierre down the service staircase and along the dark and draughty corridors of the deserted servants' quarters. Pierre's candle flickered and threw huge shadows onto the walls.

'In its heyday, Marzac had dozens of servants,' he said in a low voice, 'but there are only five of us now. This way, please.'

They were in a small parlour now. Pierre asked Saintclair to hold the candle. He lifted the corner of a large tapestry that covered the better part of the wall and disappeared behind it. There were sounds of a door being unlocked.

'Hurry.'

Saintclair and Marie-Ange ducked under the tapestry and found themselves in another room.

'Where does this lead?' Saintclair looked around, holding the candle high.

'Down to the cellars and the vineyards,' the old man answered as he ushered them down a bare stone wall passage. 'Not many people know about it.'

They reached a basement filled with oak barrels and wine making apparatus. Pierre pushed open a wooden door and they walked out into the night and across a cobble-stone courtyard. At the far end was a small building that looked abandoned. Pierre opened the door and led them in.

'This was the lodge for the vineyard. It's empty now, nobody's been making any wine at Marzac for years.' He stuck the candle on a tall candelabrum on the table and gestured towards a couple of rickety chairs and a straw bed tucked into the corner of the room.

'You can wait in here until dawn. I'll send one of the lads with your horse when it's safe.'

Saintclair nodded to the old man. 'What will you tell the bailiffs?'

'That they've just missed you. I'll say I heard you two planning to ride back to Lyon.' Pierre smiled.

Marie-Ange put her hand on his arm. 'Thank you, Pierre, for all you help. I know you tried to help my mother when Edmond Malleval took her away from the Priory. And you alerted Baldassare dei Conti, my father, a few weeks ago.'

'These Mallevals, father and son, they were always wicked,' the old man said, shaking his head. 'Good night for now.'

Once alone, Marie-Ange and Saintclair stood awkwardly in front of each other. Hugo pointed to the bed. 'You'd better get some sleep.'

She sat on the couch. It was rough and stiff with dirt and grime. Straw sprouted from the ripped cover. There was no way she would be able to sleep now, not only was the bed uncomfortable, but too many conflicting emotions raged through her. Fear, love, desire.

She watched Hugo carry out a brief inspection of the lodge and check windows and doors. Her lips were still swollen with his kisses. Her body resonated with the memory of his caresses. She hadn't tried to stop him earlier even if he had made it quite clear he didn't have any feelings for her. Or at least not the kind of feelings she wished for. However, even knowing he didn't love her made no difference to her yearning for him. He, on the other hand, looked calm, almost detached, as if the feverish passion they had just shared was all but a distant memory. They were very different. She would do well to remember it, or she would get hurt.

'Tell me what happened in Paris,' she asked.

He sat down on a chair. It creaked under his weight. 'I spoke to my colonel straight after leaving you at Caroline's—which I'll admit now wasn't such a great idea after all.' He smiled. 'He instructed me to ride to Paris immediately and request an interview with Talleyrand.'

'Did you meet him?'

He nodded. 'Yes, in his office at the *Hôtel Vendôme*.'

He told her that the elderly, but still powerful Talleyrand hadn't looked in the slightest fazed by his news. There were indeed reports of intense activity from Fouché's camp to prepare the ground for Napoleon's return. Fouché himself was under surveillance. However he still controlled a secret army of loyal agents on whom there was very little information and whose movements were almost impossible to trace.

'Men like...Nallay,' Saintclair finished, 'with no past, no identity, and no country.'

Marie-Ange sighed heavily, wondering once again what could have happened to Christopher after Corunna to turn him into a spy, a ruthless killer.

'Talleyrand said sending Napoleon to Elba had been a mistake. It was not far enough. Having the emperor so close to France was like Mont Vesuvius towering above Naples, a constant and lethal threat.'

'What will you do if—when—Napoleon comes back?'

Saintclair sighed. 'I served him with undying loyalty for fifteen years. Yet towards the end, even I had my doubts. There were too many deaths, too much carnage and ruin...No, I don't want him back, not if it means that the country is engulfed in war again. But...' He looked at Marie-Ange. 'I may not have a choice.'

They remained silent for a while.

'What I really want is to be free.' His voice was so low she had to strain to hear him. 'Free from the army, from rigid social conventions, class, and status.'

He leant towards her and searched her face. 'Is there

such a place, do you think, where a man can live his life without having to answer to anyone, where he can make his own fortune, be master of his own destiny even if he wasn't born rich and titled?'

It was the first time he had opened his mind, his soul, to her. She took a few moments to answer. 'I don't know…I once read that the greatest obstacles to freedom are the ones we place upon ourselves. You say you long for freedom, but you also yearn for military honours and recognition by your superiors, otherwise you would have left the army long ago to join your father's business.'

She stopped and glanced at him tentatively. She had never before spoken so frankly with him and was unsure how he would respond. He smiled in the dim light.

'Very well spoken, Madame,' he said with a trace of irony. 'You are right. I am my worst enemy. My ambition was always to reach the top. With the Bourbons back at the head of the country it will never happen. Maybe I should do as you suggest and fulfil my father's wishes, but I can't help thinking that there is something else out there for me, somewhere…'

She would have liked to be brave enough to tell him she was there for him, but she remained silent. She wrapped herself more closely in her jacket. It was very cold in the old lodge.

He broke the silence. 'Tell me about the Cross of Life. You said it was in the dovecote at Beauregard. Our biggest challenge tomorrow will be to avoid Uxeloup and his men.'

'I'm so scared of going down into the crypt at Arginy,' she said weakly, burying her face into her hands.

He was next to her in a couple of seconds. He put his arm around her shoulders, and she snuggled against him.

'I don't understand why you have to take the Cross there. What has it got to do with you? Why can't your father do it? And why does anyone have to do anything about it at all?'

Marie-Ange told him what her great-aunt had said about family duty and the Beaujeus and Beauregards bloodline. 'My mother was meant to take the Cross back,' she added. 'She passed her duty to me. I am so afraid of what is down there.'

'Probably rats, a cold draughty room, and the tombs of former lords and ladies of the manor.'

'There are shadows and ghosts, too,' she whispered.

'Ghosts don't exist.' He stared into her eyes with such certainty that she almost believed him. 'You said you knew how to find the Cross at Beauregard?'

'I will follow the clues in the song my mother taught me. I know I need my locket to work the mechanism but I don't understand how to use it.'

Tell me the words again. I remember you said something about a rose and a heart.'

Marie-Ange recited the words slowly:

My sweet rose of May
My rose with five petals,
You cry in the dovecote
For your lover, cold in his tomb…
Listen to me, don't despair,
Your lover you'll see again,
Place the rose on the heart, give five turns,
Raise your eyes, the wing you will find.
But you must choose wisely,
For if the wing of the dove
Is as white as the angel's
It will not open your lover's tomb.

Hugo listened intently and shook his head. 'Let's hope it makes sense tomorrow when we are in the dovecote.'

He looked through the grimy window partly hidden behind thick cobwebs. It was pitch black. 'With luck Uxeloup and his men are spending the night smoking opium and drinking. They will be hung over in the morning.' He took his overcoat off and wrapped it around her shoulders.

'What is going to happen to you and your family?' she asked, placing her hands on his. 'Uxeloup seems determined to send you to the debtors' jail.'

'I will worry about that later.' He gestured dismissively. 'Now, get some sleep. I'll keep watch and wake you up at first light.'

Marie-Ange lay down and curled up on the bed, wrapped in Hugo's coat, while he sat at the table. He blew the candle out and remained immobile in the darkness.

It was barely light when they set off a few hours later. As promised, a stable lad had brought Hugo's horse to the vineyard lodge.

'Ready?' Hugo asked, taking Marie-Ange's waist in his hands and lifting her onto his horse. He then mounted behind her and spurred the horse into a trot on the road to *St Rigaud* Hill where he said her father and his men were hiding.

'Let's hope they are still there,' he said, steering the horse onto a lane leading through the forest and up the hill which was about three miles from Beauregard.

Half-way up the incline, he dismounted to guide the horse through the rocky path. Marie-Ange soon caught sight of the abandoned outbuilding where her father and his men were hopefully waiting for them. A sharp bird call, like a warning echoed in the eerie silence of the forest. A Turcopilar appeared in front of them stepping silently from behind a tree and the horse baulked in surprise, almost throwing Marie-Ange onto the ground. Hugo held firmly to the reins and managed to calm the animal.

'Steady on, man,' he growled. 'It's only us.'

'Pardon, Capitaine. Madame,' the Turcopilar mumbled when he recognised them.

'Don't worry.' She smiled. From a distance, anyone would believe her to be a man. 'Is my father here?' she asked. The man nodded and whistled again. Soon two familiar figures emerged from the sheepfold.

'Daughter! Here you are at last.'

Hugo helped Marie-Ange get down and she ran to Baldassare. He held her against him and kissed her forehead. 'We have been waiting so long for you. Saintclair's batman brought word that you were safe, but that was well over a week ago.'

Hugo advised they should leave for Beauregard without delay and Baldassare agreed. He gave instructions to his companions to get the horses ready.

'We must be vigilant,' he warned. 'I went on a reconnaissance tour yesterday and saw a dozen men patrolling the grounds.'

Saintclair decided to go into the dovecote with Marie-Ange. Hafiz, one of the Turcopilars, would guard the entrance to the walled rose garden while Baldassare and his other companion would keep watch at the edge of the forest and deal with Uxeloup's patrols. They were outnumbered but there was no other choice.

'Do you have your locket?' Baldassare asked. Marie-Ange touched the pocket of her jacket and nodded.

Saintclair tightened his girth, impatient to be on the move. 'We should go.'

Nobody talked as they made their way through the woods to Beauregard. When they reached the estate, they tied their horses to tree branches. Baldassare went ahead as scout. He came back soon after and gestured that the grounds were clear.

Saintclair, Marie-Ange, and Hafiz ran across the lawn towards the walled garden. The old gate creaked open. Hafiz took his position, Marie-Ange and Hugo made their way across the empty rose garden towards the round tower in the far right corner.

The moment of truth had come. As she put her hand on the door handle, Marie-Ange had an awful doubt. What if the whole story was a myth? What if there was no Cross and no relic hidden in there? She pushed the handle down and walked in with Hugo right behind her.

The dovecote looked very different from her mother's paintings. It was dark and filthy. The floor was covered with a thick layer of bird droppings and feathers. The wooden beams that had looked so beautiful on paper were so black and grimy no pattern or engraving could be seen on their surface at all. Marie-Ange walked around central beam. They had to remove the muck covering it for her to find the heart pattern. It was somewhere on the top half of the beam. She pulled her knife from her boot and scraped the dirt to reveal the wood below, careful however not to erase the original carvings she knew were there. Saintclair pulled his own knife and they worked in silence for a while.

'It's pointless.' Marie-Ange shook her head after a while, disappointed. They had hardly cleared a twenty centimetres section of the beam. 'It's going to take forever!'

A dove flew in through one of the circular openings in the top half of the tower, graceful as it perched on one of the beams that criss-crossed the eaves. It settled and started cooing. A pale sun ray filtered inside the dovecote onto the central beam, highlighting the carvings in a play of shadows and light. Marie-Ange held her breath. There was what she had been looking for. The pattern of a rose within a heart.

'It's up there!' She pointed to the dove, still perching on the beam, oblivious to their presence.

'I'll go,' Hugo suggested but she shook her head.

'No. My father said that it had to be me.'

'I really don't see why,' he mumbled, pulling a ladder across the floor. He held it while she climbed up towards the dove. The bird didn't move but observed her movements with great curiosity. She took her knife, and holding onto the ladder with one hand, scratched carefully at the layer of dirt to reveal the heart carving she had spotted from below. Inside the heart was indeed the outline of a rose. She traced the pattern, the five petals, with her finger.

The song said she had to fit the locket into the rose pattern and turn it five times to reveal the relic's hiding place. Would it work?

With a silent prayer, she took off her locket and inserted it into the carving on the beam. It fitted perfectly. She tried turning it to the right, but the locket refused to move.

'I can't do it.' She tried again, with more strength this time.

'Do you want me to try?' Hugo asked, still holding the ladder. 'It may be stuck.'

She was about to get down and let him have a go when she had a thought. What if she turned the locket the other way? She pressed it into the carving again and pushed it to the left, towards the heart, on the left-hand side of the body. This time, she heard a clicking sound. The locket penetrated deep into the wood. Holding her breath, she gave five turns and looked up towards the doves' nests.

'Right at the top!' Hugo pointed to the nests closest to the roof line. 'Three boxes have opened.'

The ladder wasn't high enough for Marie-Ange to reach them, she would have to climb onto the beams that criss-crossed the top of the tower.

'It's far too high for you. Get down. I'll do it,' Hugo said once again, but she refused.

'This is something I have to finish, no one else can.'

Hugo sighed with impatience.

'Take my bag then to put the…thing in—whatever it is.' He stepped onto the ladder and handed her the satchel which she slung across her body looping the long strap over her shoulder.

As she climbed to the top of the ladder and balanced on the top beam, she was glad to be wearing breeches and not a dress. Without looking down she stepped onto another joist and made her way towards the nests. The beam was wide enough for her to walk on it without too much difficulty. Nevertheless she was relieved to reach the wall. She slid her hand into one of the openings. Carefully, she explored the inside of the nest with her fingers until she touched something hard. She pulled a cylinder out and held it in front of her. She wiped its surface quickly. It was made of thick glass and inside was a beautiful, delicate, white, almost translucent object she couldn't immediately identify. She held it in the sun light. It looked like it was made of feathers, white feathers. Was this the angel wing?

She put it in Hugo's bag and walked to the next nest. This time, she pulled out a heavy, ornate box. There was a long line of symbols across the cover—the Templars' code—and the engraving of a rose and a heart in the left-hand corner. As she brushed the dirt off the cover with her hand, she realized it was made of solid gold and was decorated with dozens of rubies, emeralds, and sapphires. She placed the box in the satchel too. There was one last niche in the beam to explore. Inside was a small cloth bag. She carefully pulled it out and opened it up. It was another phial, this time with a piece of fine, dull, grey fabric inside. The second relic...Only one was the angel wing, but which one was it? There was no time to think about it now.

She was about to step onto the ladder when she heard pistol shots outside.

'Hurry!' Hugo urged. He pulled his pistol out and walked to the door.

Her chest tight with fear, she returned to the ladder and made her way down as quickly as she could. Uxeloup's men must have discovered their presence.

'Stay here.' Hugo opened the door cautiously and stepped outside. Marie-Ange heard Hafiz's breathless voice.

'I shot two men but more are coming from the chateau.'

'Behind you,' Hugo yelled.

There were more gun shots, and a lot of shouting. Standing behind the door, she held her hand to her heart in agony and desperate to find out what was happening outside.

'Let me go, you bastards,' Hugo roared at last. 'Malleval, tell them to let go of me.'

Uxeloup's oily voice sent shivers down Marie-Ange's spine. 'It's too late, Saintclair. You really disappointed me, my friend. I presume the lovely Madame Norton is inside?' He broke into a raucous cough and took a long time to catch his breath. 'I warned you to leave her alone. Look at the mess you're in now. By the way, it was clever of you to escape the bailiffs last night but it's only a matter of time before they catch up with you. I hope you warned your parents to pack up.'

'Leave me a few more weeks. I'll get the money to pay you back. You know I will,' Hugo said, a hint of despair in his voice.

Uxeloup laughed. 'You should have thought about it before helping Marie-Ange escape me. You cost me precious time, which I haven't got unfortunately. Take him away.'

What was happening out there? Marie-Ange couldn't stay in the dovecote any longer. She pushed the door open and stepped out into the pale morning light. Uxeloup, Karloff, and a dozen long haired men dressed in sheepskins, their faces covered with bushy beards and holding daggers and pistols, stood in the rose garden.

Uxeloup's face was so emaciated it looked like a skull with deep, purple bruises underneath his feverish brown eyes. A dry, raspy cough shook his thin frame. Marie-

Ange was surprised he could even stand in the cold breeze.

Hugo was slumped on the ground next to Hafiz's lifeless body, his face and jacket smeared with blood. One bandit pointed a pistol to his head. Instinctively, she rushed to his side, but a man grabbed her arm and held her back.

Uxeloup chuckled weakly. 'How touching. But don't worry, dear Marie-Ange. He'll live…for now.'

He raised his white, bony hand. 'Hand over the bag.'

She tightened her grip on the satchel and desperately looked around. Where was her father? Had he been caught too? One of the men snatched the bag from her and gave it to Uxeloup. He opened it and thrust his hand inside, gasped, and withdrew it as if he had been burned.

'Bring them both to the chateau!'

Chapter Nineteen

Hugo lunged forward and tackled the man standing closest to him. He knocked him out with a punch to the face, but before he could pick up his gun two of Uxeloup's thugs jumped on him and kicked him back onto the frozen ground.

Uxeloup turned round and narrowed his eyes in anger.

'That was a mistake, Saintclair —your last mistake, I daresay. Make sure he won't interfere with my business again,' he told his men. 'I have had enough of my troublesome friend. He is of no use to me anymore.'

He departed, hurrying towards the chateau, clutching the satchel against his frail body. One of the men clubbed Hugo in the face with the grip of his pistol until he stopped struggling.

'Hugo,' Marie-Ange cried out in anguish as his body was dragged away. Uxeloup had just signed his death warrant.

'Take her to the library,' Karloff ordered.

Marie-Ange was frog-marched through the garden, into Beauregard's hall and along the corridor. A man kicked the library door open and pushed her inside.

There was no fire in the hearth today. The pale morning sun had already disappeared behind snow clouds and a grey light now filtered through the partly drawn green velvet curtains. Marie-Ange breathed in the sickly scent of cold opium smoke which lingered in the room. She rubbed her arms with the palm of her hands to warm herself up. Her teeth chattered, and she shivered with cold as she stood in front of Saint Germain's portrait.

258

'What do I do now?' she asked aloud.

She looked at Saint Germain's gentle smile, his warm, intelligent brown eyes. Even if she didn't believe he was immortal or had lived for over two hundred years, that he was a Rosicrucian who held the key to the mysteries of the life and death, he was still an enigma. He had been in touch with the Knights Hospitaller and the Turcopilars. He believed in the relic, had kept hold of the Cross of Life for years before deciding it was time to hide it. He had given her mother his locket and patiently instructed her with the secret song to enable her to find the Cross when the time came.

She stared at the painting. If only he could answer...

What she dreaded most had happened. Uxeloup was in possession of the Cross and the relic. Rather, she corrected, he had two relics and according to her mother's song, only one of them had any power.

Hugo was in mortal danger, prisoner somewhere in the chateau. Hafiz had been killed. She felt a lump in her throat at the thought of the man lying dead in the rose garden. At least it seemed her father and the other Turcopilar had managed to avoid detection. She hoped they wouldn't be caught. They were her last chance. As for her, she was at the mercy of her sick, demented relative and his obsession.

She looked at the portrait of Saint Germain again and at the roll of parchment written in the secret Templars' code he was holding. There were similar symbols on the golden box she'd retrieved from the dovecote. Another coded message, no doubt.

A noise by the door made her jump. Karloff entered, the physician was pale. His grey hair fell in long, unkempt strands around his face. His hands shook as he unbuttoned his coat.

'I have just decrypted the message on the box. It's another warning that only a pure heart can handle the relic without risking eternal damnation.'

He turned towards Marie-Ange in earnest. 'There are two phials but only one is the angel's wing. Which one is it? You must tell me. Uxeloup is very agitated. I had to wrestle the phials from him. He is so desperate he was about to break them open regardless of the danger.'

He looked deep into Marie-Ange's eyes but this time his intense gaze had no effect on her. 'According to Polycarpe's parchment, only the pure heart can release the relics' powers. Only the pure heart knows which phial is the angel's wing. You know, you must tell me!'

She didn't reply. If she was the pure heart the Templar Knights had written about, why didn't she know which phial contained the true relic? There was only one thing she knew for sure.

'We must go to Arginy,' she said.

Karloff looked up, surprised. 'Arginy? What for?'

She would tell him part of the truth. 'The Cross must be returned to a special place in the vault,' she said. 'Only there can the relic release its true magic.'

She wouldn't explain about the Keepers, the eleven Templar entities as Baldassare and her great-aunt had called them, who waited for the relic to be returned.

Karloff remained silent a few moments. 'Yes. I suppose that makes sense. It's where Guichard de Beaujeu hid it in the first place when he retrieved it from the Temple of Paris, where most of the Templar treasure was hidden.' He turned to her. 'I don't have the faintest idea how to get into the crypt. The entrance to the underground passages was walled up by Anne de Beaujeu before she died. Do you know how to get in?'

Marie-Ange didn't want to admit she didn't know either. In her dreams, she always stood in a tall, round tower before descending underground.

'Yes, of course,' she lied, crossing her arms on her chest. 'But I will only go if Capitaine Saintclair comes too.'

She would make the most of her position. If Malleval and Karloff needed her so badly, they would have to keep Hugo alive.

Karloff sighed before walking to the door. 'I'll see what I can do. In the meantime, I will get you something to eat and drink.'

A few moments later, Sophie came in with some food and drinks. Her eyes were red, her face tear-stricken.

'I will light a fire for you. It's too cold in here,' she said with a broken voice before burying her face in her hand and sobbing loudly. Marie-Ange went over to her and put her arm around her shoulders.

'I don't understand what's happening,' Sophie said, wiping her eyes with the back of her hand. 'I don't recognise Uxeloup anymore, he frightens me. The things he talks about, the men he brought back from Malleval, the way he is treating you and Capitaine Saintclair who has always been his friend, all that is so unlike him.' She lowered her voice. 'He is obsessed with ancient papers and legends, he even had this horrid snake—an Uroboros, he calls it—tattooed on his chest. He says it's a symbol of eternal life. He claims he is going to be cured and everything will be back to normal, but…'

Marie-Ange sighed. Uxeloup's health had deteriorated so much these past few weeks there could be no doubt about his prospects. The disease caused terrible ravages, not only to patient's bodies but to their minds, too. Sometimes, as it appeared to be the case for Uxeloup, there were very little, or no physical marks for months or years even, but the disease inexorably attacked a man's insides and his brain.

'What about you? Are you ill too?' she asked with hesitation.

'No, he never…' Sophie looked up, her eyes shiny with tears. 'He said he loved me too much to take me to his bed, and that he would wait until he was cured. He bedded other women, though, even maids here at Beauregard. It used to make me miserable and jealous, even if I knew he was only sparing me.' She joined her hands. 'I want him back. I want the carefree and wild Hussar he used to be. What he has become now, it's not him anymore. He says he needs you to make him get better, but I fear he has gone...mad.' Sophie twisted nervously the ruby ring around her finger.

She got up and lit the fire. Marie-Ange was strangely touched by the young woman's admission that Uxeloup abstained from making love to her for fear of passing on his deadly disease. He must truly love her. However there was no hope he would ever recover. Nobody recovered from syphilis. She didn't believe for a second that the Cross would make him immortal. These things weren't possible, whatever Karloff, Uxeloup, or her Great-Aunt Hermine claimed.

She poured a cup of coffee, nibbled at a slice of bread covered with jam. She had to eat in order to keep her strength for the day to come. She thought about Hugo, injured, cold and alone in the cellars and put the bread back on the plate, her throat tight.

'Uxeloup is angry with Hugo,' she said. 'He helped me and now he will lose his family house...and probably his life.'

Sophie shrugged. 'He tricked him during the card game, you know.'

Marie-Ange looked at her sharply. 'Tricked him?'

Sophie nodded. 'He desperately needed a strong, reliable man to escort you back from England to Beauregard so he invited Saintclair over for a game of cards, knowing how much the capitaine likes to gamble. And...' Sophie bent her head, embarrassed.

'And?'

'He asked me to drug his wine during the game. I gave

him some draught Karloff made to cloud his mind. I couldn't refuse,' Sophie said, on the defensive.

Marie-Ange frowned. 'If Saintclair's debt towards Uxeloup was fraudulently obtained, it could be cancelled.'

'I won't say anything to the *gendarmes*. I will not betray Uxeloup,' she added, very agitated. Claiming she had things to take care of, she left.

The day passed with excruciating slowness. As time ticked on, Marie-Ange became more and more anxious about the events which were about to unfold. She may not be able to find the entrance to the crypt. And even if she did, Uxeloup would stop her from returning the Cross into the Templars' cache. How then would she and Hugo escape?

By the afternoon a strong wind started blowing which dispersed the clouds. Uxeloup came into the library. Once again she was struck by the ghastly paleness of his face, the fever burning in his yellowish brown eyes.

'We're leaving now. Saintclair is coming with us, as you wished.' He coughed and wiped his mouth with a handkerchief. 'Karloff said you were the only one who could do it…open the phial and take the true relic out. Why I can't open the bloody bottle myself, right now, I wonder? It's not as if I care about eternal damnation!'

He took a few steps towards her and dug his bony claw like fingers into her shoulders. 'You will hand the relic over to me as soon as we reach the crypt, is that clear?'

She nodded. At this point, she would agree to anything. He released her. She put her overcoat on and followed him out. Two black carriages waited in front of the chateau and half a dozen armed riders stood guard.

Uxeloup opened the door of the first coach. Marie-Ange glanced at the heavy carriage stationed behind. It looked like a hearse.

'Climb in.' Uxeloup pushed her inside.

She sat next to Karloff, who was holding the two phials

and the box on his lap, while Uxeloup took place next to Hugo on the seat opposite.

'He doesn't look so clever now, does he?' He sneered, gesturing towards Hugo who was unconscious. The bruises and cuts on his face testified to the treatment he had received, his hands were bound in front of him. Marie-Ange ached to sit next to him, touch him, and wake him up, but she knew better than provoke Uxeloup.

The strange convoy started down the road to the castle of Arginy.

'It's only half a dozen miles from here,' Karloff remarked.

The outline of the castle soon rose on the horizon, dark and sinister against the fierce, red winter sunset and the snowy ground. Arginy had four mismatched towers, with three medium-sized ones and a very tall one. Marie-Ange's heartbeat quickened. This was the place, the entrance to the crypt. She informed Karloff which tower was their destination. 'The Tower of Eight Beatitudes, I thought as much,' he whispered.

'What a strange name.' Beatitude, peacefulness and contentment, were the last things she expected to find at Arginy.

Karloff smiled tightly. 'It's the oldest tower, the only one left from the original medieval building. People round here claim it is haunted—cursed by the Templar Knights since Anne de Beaujeu broke into the sanctuary of the crypt. They talk of shadows seeping out, whimpers of pain and growling noises, stinking balls of fire, and blue lights hovering near the entrance.'

She stared at the tall tower and shivered. The carriages and the men went over the drawbridge. A nauseating stench rose from the slimy green waters and permeated the close confines of the coach.

'The current owners, the Rosemonts, live in Paris most of the time. Taking care of their house staff won't be a problem,' Karloff explained.

He cast a worried glance towards Uxeloup who had begun shaking. Two bright red spots burned on his emaciated cheeks. The skeletal man combed his dark hair back with his thin, pale, fingers, and licked his parched lips.

'Ah, we are here,' he whispered. 'This is the moment my father and I have been waiting for.'

He stepped out of the carriage with difficulty and almost tripped over the steps. Karloff followed, holding the boxes. Marie-Ange came last. She cast a look towards the unconscious Hugo and prayed he would soon recover. Outside, two men opened the back of the hearse. They pulled a grey coffin shaped box out and she was reminded of what Sophie had said about Edmond Malleval's body being removed from Beauregard in an iron cask. Karloff had later told her Edmond wasn't buried. Dear God, it must be his body in the coffin.

'This way.' One of Uxeloup's men pushed her in front.

They walked across the courtyard towards the tower. Uxeloup ordered two men to stand guard at the drawbridge, instructed two others to take care of the household staff. Only Rochefort and the two pallbearers would go down the crypt with Uxeloup, Marie-Ange and Karloff.

She climbed up the uneven steps leading into the Tower of Eight Beatitudes, her chest tight with apprehension. What if she couldn't find the way to the crypt?

Rochefort gave her a lantern which she held high in front of her as she walked around the empty tower to study the myriads of drawings and carvings on the walls.

'This is amazing,' she whispered.

'One of the Beaujeus was a keen alchemist, hence the symbols,' Karloff explained.

She held the lantern close to the walls to examine every one of the patterns. What better place to hide a secret symbol than here. She knew however exactly what she was looking for, and after a few minutes she found it. It was the carving of a rose with five petals inside a heart, the same one as in the dovecote. Without hesitation she pulled her locket out of her pocked and placed it at the centre of the carving. She turned five times to the left and sure enough, there was a loud clicking noise and the bottom half of the wall descended slowly into the ground, revealing a large black hole. She removed the locket and put it back into her pocket.

Uxeloup turned to his men. 'Get Father's coffin now.' He gestured to the entrance of the crypt and shouted to Rochefort. 'You get down there first.'

So Hermine had been right. It wasn't only himself Uxeloup was hoping to save tonight with the Cross of Life. She fought a wave of nausea as she stared at the cask with Malleval's body inside, but Rochefort was already leading the way into the dank depths, followed by Uxeloup, and then Karloff holding the box and the phials. His torch threw some light onto slimy stone walls and slippery steps. Marie-Ange reluctantly began the descent. Behind her came the pallbearers with Edmond Malleval's coffin.

As they descended deeper and deeper into the subterranean passage, the odour of putrefaction emanating from the moat waters just beyond the walls became so pungent it made her heave. Rivulets of slime ran down the stonework, giving out a constant dripping sound that echoed in the enclosed space.

At last, they reached the end of the staircase and walked on a long, straight corridor.

'What is that noise?' Rochefort stopped and held his hand up.

A hissing, grinding, creaking sound was getting louder and nearer.

'It's coming from…' Rochefort pointed to the darkness in front of him. A large stone appeared before them, swinging from the ceiling and travelling swiftly in an arc that was sure to crush any intruders.

'Get down,' he yelled, dropping his torch and crouching low against the floor

Uxeloup pulled Marie-Ange down and pressed her against the wet stone flags. The millstone passed just centimetres above their heads, carried on down the corridor and hit the stairs with a loud crashing noise. The pallbearers were still on the steps, which was the only thing that saved their lives.

'It's coming back.'

They remained in their crouching positions while the stone rolled back along the ceiling and disappeared into the darkness.

'Anybody hurt?' Uxeloup called to the men behind. They assured him they were unhurt.

'That was the first trap.' Karloff said as he stood up again. 'So the rumours are true. The whole place is booby-trapped. We'll have to be vigilant.'

'It's a wonder the devices still work,' Uxeloup remarked. 'It's been centuries since they were installed down here.'

They resumed their walk, scouring the darkness around them anxiously for any sign of danger.

'Who do you think set the traps?' Marie-Ange asked Karloff.

'Guichard de Beaujeu, acting on the instructions of Jacques de Molay, the last Great Templar Master, no doubt,' Karloff replied without hesitation. 'They had to protect the Templar treasure.'

The ground was covered with wet, uneven cobblestones.

'There's water on the ground.' Rochefort bent down. 'It smells like rotting moat water. Stay back while I have a look further ahead.' His torchlight disappeared in the darkness.

His voice called from the darkness a few seconds later. 'I think I found the crypt. There's a tomb in the middle. I'm taking a closer look.'

Just then there was a loud creaking noise, a blood-curdling scream. And silence.

'What on earth...?' Uxeloup sputtered. 'Rochefort, what's going on?'

No one answered. Marie-Ange's heart pounded in her chest. Staring towards the end of the corridor, she blinked a few times. Were her eyes playing tricks on her? She could see shadows moving.

'Damn it! He must have got caught in some trap. Let's go,' Uxeloup ordered. 'We've come this far. We'll carry on.'

They moved forward cautiously into the murk. A cold wind howled around them, threatening to blow out the torches.

'Where's that draft coming from? It's freezing,' one of the pallbearers complained.

When they reached the crypt, Uxeloup raised his torch. There were vaulted alcoves all around and a large stone tomb decorated with the Templar Cross at the centre. Rochefort was nowhere to be seen. He had vanished without a trace.

'Is this Guillaume de Beaujeu's tomb?' Marie-Ange enquired.

'Yes, this must be where Guichard placed his remains after removing them from the Temple of Paris,' Karloff affirmed. 'The treasure must be inside.'

So this was where she was expected to return the Cross. She walked to the tomb and inspected the lid. There was a carving at the centre. A five-petal rose inside the heart shape. Discreetly, she took her locket out of her pocket and inserted it into the hole. It clicked.

The pallbearers placed Edmond Malleval's coffin in front of the tomb and Uxeloup gestured impatiently to

Karloff.

'Put the box and the phials on the coffin.'

The physician obeyed reluctantly.

'Let's not waste any more time. Go on, open the phials now,' Uxeloup instructed Marie-Ange.

A gust of wind extinguished the two torch lights, plunging the crypt into darkness.

'Light the torches again,' Uxeloup ordered.

Nobody answered.

'What are you waiting for, you fools?'

As her eyes grew accustomed to the darkness, Marie-Ange could make out two bodies on the ground. Malleval took a few steps forward, tripping over one of them. He bent down and touched the man.

'He's dead.' His voice was shaky.

'What do you mean, dead?' Karloff demanded, approaching the other pallbearer. Then he added. 'They're both dead. How is that possible?'

Karloff and Uxeloup looked around the crypt and froze in front of her, an expression of utter disbelief on their faces. Slowly, she turned to her left, and then to her right. Were her eyes deceiving her again? She was surrounded by shadowy figures, darker than the darkness itself. So the Keepers were gathering. The time had come. Unlike in her dreams, she wasn't afraid. A diffuse bluish light shone through an opening in the vaulted ceiling, bathing the crypt.

'What is that light?' Uxeloup asked.

'It's the blue light people have talked about,' Karloff whispered. 'The blue light that shines through the tower sometimes, coming from the inside of the earth.'

'I must place the Cross and the relic on the tomb,' Marie-Ange interrupted. She opened the box and carefully lifted the Cross of Life out. It was heavy but smaller than she'd expected. She put it in the hole at the centre of the tomb.

'I will open Father's coffin now.' Uxeloup pulled a long knife from his belt, and with growing urgency, popped the nails of the lid. Then he lifted the cover and discarded it to the side. An abominable stench filled the room. Marie-Ange put her hand in front of her mouth and nose, trying not to gag. She had to concentrate on her next task.

Uxeloup walked towards her. 'Take the relic out of the phial and give it to me. Let me touch the angel and be saved.' He pointed to the phial with the white wing inside.

Karloff stepped forward, too. The two men stood side by side in front of the tomb. Marie-Ange could feel their tension, their eagerness. They were seconds away from the realisation of their dream, immortality for Uxeloup and proof of the existence of angels for Karloff.

Marie-Ange's fingers traced the outline of the phial with her finger. Sure enough, there was a pure white wing inside, but a voice inside her murmured this wasn't the angel's wing. She turned to the other, plainer phial containing the dull piece of fabric and clipped the Cross on top of it.

'What are you doing?' Uxeloup shouted. 'That's not...'

Suddenly, the content of the phial started glowing and changing shape.

'Look!' Karloff pointed to the piece of cloth which seemed to float inside the glass.

'Give it to me.' Uxeloup was so quick he seized the Cross before Marie-Ange could step away.

'You are not worthy of the angel,' Karloff protested. 'He won't come to you. Remember the parchment. Only a pure heart from the Keepers' bloodline can touch it.' He tried to wrestle the cross out of Malleval's hands.

It fell onto the ground, and the two men bent down to get at it.

'That's enough. Get up, both of you.' Hugo's voice echoed from a corner of the crypt.

Marie-Ange's heart leaped with relief as Hugo and her

father walked towards her. Hugo had a dagger in one hand, and a pistol in the other. He gestured to Malleval and Karloff to step aside. Baldassare picked up the Cross and placed it on the tomb.

'Where were you? I was so worried about you,' Marie-Ange squeezed her father's hand.

'I was waiting here,' he replied quietly.

'How did you get in?'

'I found the other entrance to the crypt. The one Anne de Beaujeu had walled in. The mortar had become brittle, it didn't take long to break a passage into it.'

He gestured to the Cross. 'You must hurry now.'

'I don't know what to do,' she objected.

'Who are you?' Uxeloup interrupted.

'I am here to put things right,' Baldassare answered calmly.

'You are the envoy, aren't you?' Karloff asked. 'The man from the Templar Order.'

'Don't be stupid, Karloff. There are no longer any Knights Templar. Did you kill Rochefort, and my men here?' Uxeloup's voice was raspy and breathless.

'I don't know what happened to Rochefort,' Hugo replied. He sounded puzzled. 'We were coming towards the crypt from the other side of the corridor when we heard him scream. But yes, we took care of these men when the torches blew out.' He shoved the bodies on the ground with his boot. 'And we will kill you both too if you move.'

Karloff stepped towards Marie-Ange, a pleading look on his face. 'Madame, please remember that my intentions are pure. I have nothing to do with Uxeloup.'

Malleval laughed bitterly. 'What are you talking about? We're in this together, old fool.'

'No we are not,' Karloff retorted with passion. 'I am here to talk with my angels, whereas you want the relic for yourself and for your father, this abomination over there.' He pointed to the open coffin.

'Shut up, both of you,' Hugo ordered.

He raised his hand, trying to touch the shadows which still hovered around. They were shades darker than darkness itself. A strange smell lingered around the crypt.

'This smell, it reminds me of some place I've been, some dangerous place,' he remarked. 'And the shadows, what are they? They move then disappear…'

'They are the Keepers' souls,' Baldassare said. 'The eleven Great Templar Masters.'

'Nonsense.' Hugo walked around, a thoughtful expression on his face. 'I remember. I have seen similar shadows before, in a mine in Poland where we hid during the Russian retreat. There were pockets of gas in there. We only just made it out before the place blew up. I wonder if…'

'Saintclair, I am begging you, let me have the angel,' Uxeloup pleaded. 'Without it, I am a dead man. I will give you anything you want. I will give you your house back, of course, and half my fortune. Beauregard…anything! Please.'

For a second Marie-Ange feared he was tempted to let the sick man get his hands on the relic, but he shook his head.

'Malleval, this isn't going to work, you should know that.'

'Look,' Karloff exclaimed, pointing to the tombstone.

A strong light was now coming out of the phial. The shape of the piece of cloth had changed. It was as bright as moonlight and lit up the whole crypt.

'The angel wing.' Karloff looked around expectantly. 'But where is he? According to the parchments the angel should appear now.'

Next to him, Marie-Ange placed the Cross inside the hole at the centre of the tomb and turned her locket to the left. Immediately, with a loud creaking and grinding noise, the tomb descended into the ground, faster and faster, leaving a great black gap in the ground.

'No,' Uxeloup yelled and he threw himself onto the tombstone as it disappeared into the chasm.

'Watch out!' Hugo grabbed hold of Marie-Ange and held her tight to keep her from falling in. She buried her face in his shoulder as the tomb disappeared with Malleval still clinging to it leaving only a gaping hole inside the crypt.

Hugo leant forward and peered into the pit.

'Where has Malleval gone? I can't see anything.'

'This smell again…' He turned back to Baldassare. 'I think we have to get out of here, fast.'

He pulled Marie-Ange's hand and Baldassare pushed Karloff forward. The physician didn't offer any resistance. He seemed broken, lifeless.

'Hugo, look!' Marie-Ange turned round and pointed to the shadows. They had changed shape yet again to become tall and lean, like men. They hovered in a circle in the middle of the crypt where the tomb had been.

'Hurry!' He urged. He towed her in his wake as he ran from the crypt.

'Can't you hear? The walls are giving in,' Baldassare cried. 'The moat waters are coming through.'

They finally reached the stairs. As they started climbing, there was a blinding flash of light, followed by a sucking noise. It was as if the darkness was breathing in.

'Get up the stairs,' Hugo shouted, pulling Marie-Ange behind him. 'It's going to blow up!'

The explosion was deafening and rocked the very foundations of the tower. Blocks of stone fell around them and the walls caved in under the pressure of the moat waters. Hugo was the first one to reach the entrance. He lifted Marie-Ange out, half-carrying her into the courtyard and then helped Baldassare and Karloff to safety. Seconds later, the ground shook underneath them. The Tower of Eight Beatitudes swayed in the fading evening light, but didn't fall.

'It's over,' Baldassare said. 'Nobody will find the crypt ever again.'

Chapter Twenty

'It may be over,' Marie-Ange remarked, 'but I can't help feeling I failed.' She stood next to her father. The horizon was bleeding to the west as a bright red sun set behind the castle towers where stars already glittered in a sapphire coloured sky to the east.

'What makes you say that, daughter? The Cross is back where it should be.'

'Perhaps, but the Templar tomb is destroyed along with the treasure and the crypt.' And I lost my mother's locket, she added to herself. The loss stung, it was one of the few things she possessed of her mother's.

Baldassare shrugged. 'You returned the Cross and the relic where they belonged. You fulfilled your duty.' He sighed. 'Men died tonight because of their arrogance and stupidity. Malleval thought he and his father could join the immortal beings. Become angels. He angered the Keepers and fell into the pit of hell.'

Hugo was tying his horse to the back of the carriage. He stopped and looked at the Tower of Eight Beatitudes.

'I don't believe in the mysteries, Templar ghosts, or eternal damnation,' he said. His face was stern, he looked angry. 'The explosion was caused by a trap laid by Guichard de Beaujeu centuries ago and a build up of gas. As for Uxeloup,' his voice became thoughtful, 'he was killed by his own madness. I shall never forget how he threw himself into that hole in the ground...'

He patted the horse's neck and leant against it for a moment. He straightened up. 'I'll check the grounds while there's still light. Who knows? Maybe there's a chance

Uxeloup and Rochefort survived after all.'

His tall figure disappeared into the thickening shadows.

'He will need time to accept what happened here. Malleval used to be his friend, after all.' Baldassare pointed to Karloff. 'The physician is alone now. We will have to take him back to Marzac with us tonight.'

Karloff sat, immobile, on the front steps of the castle. He looked stunned, exhausted, lost in a trance.

'Have you been at Arginy since this morning?' Marie-Ange asked her father.

Baldassare nodded. He explained he rode to Arginy with Marco, the only remaining Turcopilar, after fleeing Beauregard. They persuaded the Rosemonts' household staff to hide in the attic and laid in waiting for Uxeloup and his thugs.

'We dealt with them,' he said. 'Then went after you.'

'How did you manage to wake up Capitaine Saintclair? He was unconscious when we got here. I think Karloff drugged him.'

Baldassare smiled and pointed to a small leather pouch hanging from his belt.

'I gave him some of my very special snuff. It can raise a dead camel.'

'It stinks like one, too,' Hugo called out, a brief smile on his lips, as he came back. His face became serious again and he shook his head. 'There's no sign of them. They must be dead, swallowed by the ground.'

It was pitch black when they finally set off for Marzac. Hugo drove the carriage with Marie-Ange and Karloff inside. Baldassare and Marco rode in front. During the short journey, Karloff muttered to himself in the same language Marie-Ange heard him use once before, in front of Polycarpe de la Rivière's house at Malleval.

When they reached Marzac, Karloff leant forward and took hold of her hand. 'It wasn't supposed to be like that, you know. I was going to meet one of the celestial beings at last…Talk to him in his language.'

'The language you were using just now?'

'That's right. Over the centuries the *Société Angélique* devised a special language to communicate with angels.' He bent his head. 'I don't understand. Uxeloup disappeared into the bowels of the earth, towards oblivion. And I did not see my angel. I need to examine Polycarpe's documents again. Maybe I missed something.'

Marie-Ange had no comforting words for him. She shivered as she relived Uxeloup's last moments. She could still hear his cry of terror as he was plunged into the dark hole, holding onto the Templar's tomb and the Cross of Life. She hoped he died quickly.

'Here we are.' Hugo opened the door and helped Marie-Ange out. He held her close to him a few seconds and she sighed with contentment as his arms closed around her.

'Are you coming in?' she asked, tilting her chin up to look at him.

'Somehow, I don't think I would be welcome tonight.' He gestured towards the castle. 'Now I've served my purpose.'

'What do you mean?'

'I know what your great-aunt thinks of me. She only tolerated my presence last night because she wanted me to help you.'

'That's not true!'

He smiled. 'You know it is. Anyway, I must go back to Lyon and alert Colonel Dery about Nort…about Nallay,' he corrected. 'We can't leave him on the loose with the King's visit looming. And there's the matter of my debt to see to. As far as I know, I am still wanted by the *gendarmes* and the bailiffs. I must tell them Uxeloup is dead, it'll give me time to sort things out.'

'Sophie told me she drugged your wine during the card game,' Marie-Ange said.

He took a deep breath. 'That explains a lot…although drugged or not, I should have known when to stop that game. Well, I'll be on my way.'

'Can you not wait until…'

He interrupted her protest by a kiss. His lips caressed hers lightly. She felt the rough stubble on his cheeks against her skin, and remembered with a shiver of delight their embrace, interrupted far too abruptly by the gendarmes the previous night. Her hands clung to his shoulders.

'You're safe, now.' He pulled away.

'Capitaine,' Baldassare called. 'I will never thank you enough for your help. We may not agree on everything but it was an honour to meet you.'

The two men shook hands. Baldarasse untied Hugo's black horse from the back of the carriage and handed him the reins. After a last look at Marie-Ange, Saintclair climbed onto his horse and set off into the night on the road to Lyon. He was right, of course. Nallay was still out there, lying in wait for the right moment to kill the King. He had to be stopped.

Baldassare took her arm. 'Let's go in, daughter.'

Hermine was waiting for them in the drawing room. She hugged Marie-Ange and turned to Baldassare, her eyes shining with curiosity. It was true he looked unusual, wrapped in a dark grey cloak, his short, black hair streaked with grey and his clear blue eyes contrasting vividly with his suntanned skin. After a moment of hesitation, she held out her hand to him.

'I am delighted to meet you. Marie-Ange told me everything. I hope that you two will have time to talk.'

Baldassare sighed. 'Sadly, I must leave in the morning. I must report the outcome of my mission to my superiors in Catania.'

'So soon…' Marie-Ange cried. 'There are so many things I want to ask you, about yourself, your family, and my mother.' Her voice quivered and she bent her head, overwhelmed at the thought of losing the father she had only just found.

'I am not free of my duties, daughter,' he said gently. 'However, I will try and tell you as much as I can about my family—our family—tonight.'

'What you all need for now is a rest and a warm meal,' Hermine decreed. 'I will have rooms prepared straight away.'

She turned to Marie-Ange. 'Where is Capitaine Saintclair? I heard the commotion last night. Oh...the shame of it, having bailiffs knocking at my door to take him to debtors' jail.' She tapped her cane on the floor. 'Although I don't know why I was surprised. I shouldn't have expected any less from that man.' She sniggered.

'Capitaine Saintclair did nothing wrong, Aunt Hermine.' Marie-Ange's cheeks burnt with anger. 'He was tricked by Malleval during a game of cards.'

Hermine gave a short, derisive laugh and crossed her arms on her chest.

'A game of cards, of course...I am disappointed in you, girl. You seem to harbour certain feelings for the capitaine. You should remember that not only are you still married, but you are also the last of the Beauregards. You owe it to yourself and your family not to be compromised by a man such as Saintclair. He is a commoner, a vulgar soldier.'

So Hugo had been right. Hermine had been cordial to him last night only because she wanted his help. Now he had served his purpose, she could cast him aside. No wonder he was bitter about the arrogance of aristocrats.

'Dear Madame,' her father started, 'since when has a man's worth got anything to do with his lineage? You know as well as I do that a man needs to prove himself before he can earn respect, whatever his status in society. Saintclair has a distinguished military record. He came to Marie-Ange's rescue several times, causing himself great danger in the process. That is a good enough indication of his valour to me, and it should be the same for you.'

He turned to Marie-Ange with a smile. 'My daughter thinks very highly of him, and I trust her judgement. Now, shall we go upstairs and have a rest before the feast your great-aunt promised us?' He linked arms with her and they left the drawing room under Hermine's chastened gaze.

'Thank you,' Marie-Ange said as they climbed up the imposing staircase behind Pierre.

'Saintclair is a solid, honest man. I like him.' Baldassare smiled. 'And more to the point, *you* like him. You are a grown woman and free to make your own choices.'

After bathing and changing into one of her aunt's gowns, Marie-Ange made her way to the dining room where Hermine did the honours over a sumptuous meal. Karloff had declined to join them and remained prostrate, closeted in his room. He didn't even seem to care that the *gendarmes* would call for him in the morning to take him into custody.

At the dinner table, nobody spoke about Arginy and the abyss that had engulfed Malleval and the Cross of Life. And even though her mind often wandered to Saintclair, Marie-Ange was happy to listen to her father telling her about Malta and the dei Conti family.

'My father was a formidable man. He commanded the largest merchant fleet in Malta. My elder brother, Alessandro, is at the head of the business now,' Baldassare explained. 'As for my mother, she was a ray of sunshine, always singing and happy. You would have loved her, and she would have doted on you.'

'Do you only have one brother then?'

Baldassare smiled. 'No, there is, Agata, my sister. She had one daughter of her own.' He promised to take her to the island to meet them some day.

She enquired how he had become a Turcopilar.

'It was a great honour to be chosen, an honour my parents could not decline. I was eleven years old when the Bailiff of the Knights Hospitaller requested my presence at the *Commanderie* in Valetta. I was educated there, and then pursued my schooling in Italy and in North Africa, but I'm not at liberty to speak about it. Much of what we do is secret,' he apologised. 'I think Capitaine Saintclair explained, didn't he? We Turcopilars aren't even supposed to exist anymore, so you are going to have to keep my presence here a secret'

Marie-Ange didn't dare broach the subject of the short-lived romance between Baldassare and her mother. It was Hermine, with her usual bluntness, who asked him about it.

'What happened between Catherine and you? Well, I mean, apart from the obvious. How did you help her escape to England?'

He took time to drink a sip of wine before answering.

'Catherine was a beautiful young woman. She had such spirit! She was brave and resilient even after her father's execution, her abduction by Edmond Malleval, and her captivity in his fortress, where she was at the mercy of that snake, Uxeloup. She told me he constantly preyed on her.'

He talked about the months they were on the road, riding, walking alongside a troop of comedians before reaching the north coast of France. 'During our journey, we forgot we would have to part. I certainly forgot I wasn't a free man, but I have no regrets.'

Once again, Marie-Ange saw the sadness in his eyes. He turned to her and smiled. 'She would be so proud of you,' he said.

It was late into the night when Baldassase stood up and declared he needed to get some rest. He planned to set off on his long journey back to Sicily early the following morning.

'How will I get in touch if I need you?' Marie-Ange

asked as they went up to their respective rooms. 'Or am I supposed to forget all about you?'

He took her hands in his. 'Send a message to the Priory in Paris, *Rue de la Valette*, or directly to my superior, Monsegnori Della Vita at the *Commanderie* in Catania. They will know how to get hold of me.'

He put his hands on Marie-Ange's shoulders and looked straight into her eyes, the same pure blue as his own.

'I will be there for you when you need me. And I will take you to Malta one day. I promise.'

She got up in the early hours to wave farewell to her father and his companion, and remained in the courtyard, wrapped up against the cold long after they had disappeared in the grey dawn mists. The two men she loved and trusted more than anyone else in the world had now left her.

'Beauregard is back in our family, at last,' Hermine exclaimed at the breakfast table, spreading butter and jam on her brioche. 'Uxeloup didn't have any siblings or children, so you are now the heiress.'

Marie-Ange wanted to go there straight away and tell Sophie about Uxeloup's death, but Hermine said she must wait for the *gendarmes*.

'What shall I say about the Cross of Life, and about Uxeloup's death?'

'Tell them the truth—or rather part of the truth. The Cross belonged to our family, the Beauregards. You found it in the dovecote, but Uxeloup abducted you because he wanted to steal it from you. He took you to Arginy to perform some kind of ceremony—don't say anything more than that—the man fell into a trap and disappeared.'

Hermine finished her cup of tea. 'It is well known around here that Arginy is full of dangerous traps. As for Karloff, he was Malleval's accomplice. He will be taken to Beaujeu for interrogation.'

They didn't have to wait long before Commandant Picard and a small detachment of *gendarmes* were announced. Picard cut an attractive figure in his blue uniform decorated with white and red braiding. He took off his black hat adorned with a red feather and bowed deeply before Hermine and Marie-Ange.

'*Mesdames, c'est un honneur,*' he said.

Marie-Ange told him, almost word for word, what her great-aunt had advised. It was a shortened, sanitised, version of the truth. She didn't mention any angels or relics. She did however tell Capitaine Picard about Edmond Malleval's coffin being taken into the vault by Uxeloup and later lost in the explosion.

'You mean *Monsieur Malleval Père* wasn't buried?' Picard exclaimed, shocked. He smoothed the tips of his big moustache, deep in thought. '*Mon Dieu, mais pourquoi?*'

Marie-Ange raised her hands in dismay, as if she didn't have any idea. There was no point mentioning the Cross of Life's alleged powers in bestowing immortality.

'We shall send a search party to Arginy straight away,' Picard decided. 'We need to look for the bodies of Monsieur Uxeloup and his guard, Monsieur Rochefort. Do not worry, Mesdames, I will solve this riddle.'

He then asked to interview Karloff and retired to Hermine's study with the physician. The two men spent almost an hour in conversation, after which Commandant Picard said he wanted to speak to Marie-Ange again.

'Monsieur Karloff mentioned the presence yesterday at Arginy of several gentlemen you failed to tell me about. A Capitaine Saintclair, who, if I recall correctly, is wanted by the King's bailiffs, and two other men who he says were foreign agents—some kind of Turks, I believe. Would you care to explain who these men are?'

Fortunately, Marie-Ange had prepared her answer.

'I did not want to implicate Capitaine Saintclair because he did me a great favour in helping me yesterday when he was supposed to be on duty at the barracks in Lyon. He could get into serious trouble for defaulting from his post. As for his debt, I learned it was fraudulently obtained by Monsieur Malleval when he cheated during a game of cards.'

'I see,' Picard remarked, nodding his head.

'The other gentlemen were scouts from a foreign battalion who came with Capitaine Saintclair. I do not recall their names.'

Picard seemed satisfied with her answer. He said he needed to take Karloff to Beaujeu for further questioning.

'He seems very troubled about some old parchments which have remained in Beauregard. Do you know what he is talking about?'

Polycarpe de la Rivière's coded scrolls. The ones Uxeloup kept in the glass cabinet in the library. Karloff had mentioned he wanted to read through them again. Marie-Ange shook her head. 'They're not important', she lied. 'They're only old papers.'

The *gendarmes* came back for her in the afternoon. Picard said she could now travel to Beauregard. He reported that the chateau and the grounds had been searched and not a single one of Uxeloup's mountain thugs remained. 'They ran away like rabbits when they saw my *gendarmes*,' he laughed.

So Marie-Ange bade her great-aunt farewell. Today, she was going home.

Chapter Twenty-One

Beauregard, 20 March 1815 (three weeks later)

Jerusalem, 1230 Anno Domini
   Note to our Brothers—
   Our much revered Brother Bernard de Clairvaux wrote that a Templar Knight feared neither demons nor men because his soul was protected by an armour of Faith, just as his body was protected by an armour of steel. He will not fear death either if he kneels in front of the Cross of Life in our chapel at Temple Mount for he will live forever.
   May I remind you, Brothers, how this most sacred relic came to be in our possession; how God's messenger on earth appeared to Hugues de Payens and Saint Omer and demanded the creation of our Templar Order to protect pilgrims travelling to the Holy City; and how the celestial envoy's clothing, torn by our Brother Payens by accident, was preserved in a phial secured at the base of the Cross as an eternal reminder of God's awesome power.
   I must entreat you once again to keep its existence a secret. We have seen only recently how dangerous the relic can be when it falls into the wrong hands. An unfortunate and misguided pilgrim attempted to remove the Cross from Temple Mount two weeks ago. His quest for immortality was rewarded by the pit of eternal hell. Not only was his skin burnt, his eyes blinded, and his hair singed, his soul now languishes in atrocious sufferings. For we Templar Knights know that the holy relic can only be handled by one of us—a pure heart—and it will always

be so.
    Pedro de Montaigu, Grand Master Templar

Paris, 12 October 1307
    These are my instructions concerning the safe keeping of our most saintly relic, the Cross of Life. It will be hidden in the fief of a trusted brother and relative of one of our most respected Great Masters. It will be guarded by the souls of eleven Keepers, all past Masters who will punish with terrible torments whoever dares violate its sanctuary. Should the Cross be removed, it must be returned by a pure heart of the same bloodline as a Master Keeper. Only he can hold the Cross unscathed, be blessed by the visiting angel, and granted the eternal peace he longs for. Pity the unfortunate who attempts to claim the Cross for his own purpose for he condemns his soul to eternal damnation.'
    Jacques de Molay, Grand Master, Temple of Paris

Marie-Ange rolled the documents pensively between her hands. Her fingers played with the dark blue ribbon that kept them together and handed the parchments back to Gustave Karloff. The physician's hand shook as he took hold of them.

'So these are the translations of some of the papers Polycarpe was carrying when he was killed by the Malleval clan,' she remarked. The reference to a pilgrim being thrown to the pit of hell had a sinister echo after Uxeloup's disappearance into the gaping hole in the crypt of Arginy castle.

Karloff nodded. 'I will gather my things as quickly as I can and be on my way tomorrow morning at the latest.'

He walked to the window and stared at the rain-swept park and forest. 'I have been thinking about what happened at Arginy, and I fear all is not finished.'

'What do you mean, Monsieur Karloff? We both saw

286

the Templar tomb, Uxeloup and the cross thrown into the abyss just before the explosion. How can it not be finished?' Marie-Ange asked. 'Commandant Picard certainly thinks it is. He said he wasn't going to organise a search party.'

Karloff glanced at her with haunted eyes and turned towards the window and the forest again. Why did the man look so anxious?

He had arrived an hour before, having been released by Commandant Picard from Beaujeu prison pending further investigation. He appeared to have aged considerably during his three weeks' incarceration. The hair was wilder, his face marked with deep lines, and there was a nervous twitch at the corner of his mouth which hadn't been there before. There was nothing left in him of the charismatic and sinister man Marie-Ange had once feared.

There didn't seem to be any dark mysteries left at Arginy either.

A civil engineer appointed by Commandant Picard had established that the castle was built on ancient salt mines dating back to Roman times. Several entrances to tunnels had been uncovered, some as far away as half a mile from Arginy. The reports of mysterious balls of orange and blue light and sulphurous smells rising from the ground, of tremors and strange underground noises, which locals had put down to a Templar malediction, had in fact a very scientific explanation. They had their origin in pockets of gas trapped deep beneath the surface, causing explosions in the passages of the abandoned mine. It seemed Hugo had been right...the shadows in the crypt had nothing to do with ghosts of Knights Templar.

Commandant Picard decided it would be pointless and dangerous to call a search party to retrieve the bodies. The terrain around Arginy was too unstable after the explosion, and there could be no doubt that the two men were dead.

Marie-Ange walked out of Karloff's room and went

down to the library. The way the physician stared out of the window towards the woods made her nervous. She sat behind the desk where the accounts ledger she had been working on for the past three weeks lay open, but instead of studying the fine lines scrawled with figures, she sighed and slammed the book shut. There wasn't any point looking at the accounts now.

Her travel trunk and bag were packed. She would leave for England the following morning with an escort of *gendarmes*, like a criminal or a traitor.

It was Commandant Picard who had brought the news of her exile. Red-faced and apologetic, he stammered so much that she had failed at first to understand what he was trying to say.

'The Emperor...decrees of Lyon of 13th March...recent *émigrés* must leave French soil and abandon all claim to their property...under threat of imprisonment.'

Hermine had reacted with anger. 'The audacity, the nerve of that little man! I don't care if he calls himself an emperor. I don't care if they say that since landing near Fréjus with a garrison of a mere seven hundred men he re-conquered the country like 'an eagle flying from steeple to steeple'—an eagle! and what else? The truth is he is nothing more than an upstart. A glorified soldier! He ruined our country before, and he will do it all over again. I can't believe he is back at the *Tuileries* Palace and forced our King to take refuge in Ghent!' She punctuated her outburst with loud taps of her cane on the floor.

'The populace is so fickle,' she carried on after taking a deep breath. 'One year ago they cheered as he was exiled and now they acclaim his return! I read that an infantry regiment sent by Louis XVIII to stop him near Grenoble placed itself under his command instead. Even Marshall Ney who had promised the King to bring back the 'impostor in a steel cage' joined forces with him.'

'And once Marshall Ney changed sides, the whole army abandoned the royalist camp to support its former hero,' Marie-Ange concurred. Lyon had given the Emperor a rapturous welcome and Napoleon issued some of his first decrees as France's new ruler there.

Among those was, Picard explained, the decision to expulse all the *émigrés* who had returned to France between April 1814 and March 1815—during the reign of King Louis XVIII.

Marie-Ange was considered one of them.

'I will escort you to Chalons and then to Paris and Le Havre.' Picard looked sorry to be the bearer of such bad news. 'Please be ready by Wednesday morning.'

Hermine might rant against the injustice, the indignity her great-niece was subjected to, but being angry changed nothing. With a heavy heart, Marie-Ange packed her few belongings. She would be travelling back to Norton Place with nothing. Considered an *émigrée*, she wasn't entitled to claim any revenue from the Beauregard estate even if she was Malleval's only heir. Her great-aunt promised to hire a good lawyer to look after her interests.

'We will soon have you back here. In the meantime, I will ensure Beauregard is kept in good order for you.'

Somehow Marie-Ange couldn't share her great-aunt's optimism. If Napoleon had shown mercy towards returning *émigrés* in the past, he seemed to have radically changed his mind now.

Sophie came in with a cup of tea and a plate of sponge cake. The two women smiled at each other.

'I am sure you will be allowed back,' Sophie said, placing the hot drink and the food in front of Marie-Ange. 'Napoleon can't mean it when he ordered all *émigrés* from French soil.'

Marie-Ange shook her head. 'I don't know, Sophie. He has much to prove this time round and he is desperate for popular support. Returning *émigrés* are indeed an easy target and a fleshy bone to throw to the populace.'

'But you are not even a real *émigrée*!' Sophie was indignant. 'Napoleon targeted those who came back to claim their estates. You were invited here, by Uxeloup.' She bent her head. Her chest heaved as she tried to suppress a sob.

Marie-Ange stood and walked around the desk to take her in her arms. Sympathy twisted her heart for Sophie had loved Uxeloup with all her being. His death left her alone and bereft, but at least she would be able to stay at Beauregard. Marie-Ange had appointed her chatelaine in her absence, under Hermine's guidance.

Sophie wiped her tears, curtsied and left Marie-Ange alone with her thoughts. She stood at the window, looking at the dark clouds in the lead grey sky. It was doubtful she would be able to return to her mother's ancestral home in the near future. Her thoughts turned to Hugo, she longed to see him again, but that too was uncertain.

He had written the previous week. Napoleon had ordered him to escort the Comte d'Artois, the King's brother, to the port of Sète and ensure he embarked for Italy unharmed. The Comte had narrowly escaped an assassination attempt in Lyon and Napoleon didn't wish to start his new reign with an outpouring of Bourbon blood. Hugo was now posted to the southern provinces to quell a royalist uprising.

He also wrote he had been spared the threat of imprisonment for debt and his family was safe in St Genis. Hugo ended his short message with a promise to come to Beauregard as soon as he was discharged.

It would be too late by then, she would be gone.

'Hugo,' Marie-Ange whispered as her fingers traced his name on the window and followed the raindrops gliding down the other side like tears. She summoned the burning memory of his blue eyes and the caress of his lips on her skin. Memories were all she would have of him. She might not see him for many months now that war between France and Great Britain and its allies was, once again, on the cards. She might not see him ever again.

She gasped for air suddenly, her chest too tight for her to breathe. Wrapping herself in her cloak she went out into the garden, following the alley leading to the walled rose garden. It was, of course, too early for roses and the bushes were bare. She walked for a while in the park and around the pond, her heart as heavy as the skies. When her coat and her shoes were completely soaked, she made her way back towards the chateau.

The sound of a horse's galloping hooves made her turn towards the gates. A cavalier was approaching. She froze and waited for the rider to come nearer. He was tall, dressed in a dark grey coat, his face partly hidden by a black hat. She let out a sigh of disappointment. It wasn't Saintclair.

Then she recognised the rider, and panic welled inside her. She ran up the stone stairs of the front porch and pulled frantically at the door.

'Wait!' Christopher called as he jumped down from his horse.

She turned round and confronted him, her face hard and unwelcoming. Her hand pressed down on the door handle to open the door but she didn't seem to have the strength to manage it.

'What are you doing here?'

Christopher remained at the bottom of the steps. He took off his hat, revealing a gaunt face. Dark circles shadowed his grey eyes, and deep lines cut channels around his mouth.

'I want you to tell me about my past life.'

Marie-Ange opened her eyes wide. 'Why now?' She hissed. 'You weren't bothered with the truth that night in Lyon, when you stabbed Capitaine Saintclair and tried to…' The words died on her lips. She looked down at the man standing at the bottom of the steps, feeling like an invisible hand was gripping her throat.

Something was different about him. He looked like he used to, a long time ago. His head was cocked to one side, the haunted grey eyes thoughtful. There was a sad, bitter line at the corner of his mouth. Although she had resolved to give him up for dead, she couldn't shut him out, not when he looked so much like the man she had loved.

'I am sorry. Truly sorry. I didn't want to believe you. I didn't want to hear that I might be that man—Norton.'

'What changed your mind?' Her voice was still hard, even if uncertainty was slowly creeping into her heart.

The rain became heavier. Large drops bounced on the front porch of the chateau. Marie-Ange's hair stuck to her forehead, and cold rain slid down her neck.

'There are so many things I want to ask you.' Christopher smiled tentatively.

Her resolve weakened but she still hesitated. Even if he sounded genuine, she must not forget how dangerous he was. This could all be a ruse or a cruel jest. Just over three weeks before, he had tried to rape her and almost killed Hugo.

As if he sensed her doubts, he added. 'Please, Marie-Ange.'

She took a deep breath and opened the front door. 'Very well. Come in.' She called a servant and gave orders for the horse to be stabled. She peeled off her drenched cloak and handed it to a maid. She led the way to the drawing room where a fire was lit. She invited Christopher to take a place on the sofa opposite her.

'What do you want to know?' she asked, her voice guarded, wishing to maintain a distance between them.

He spoke slowly. 'Since the last time I saw you, in Lyon, I have had flashbacks about that place you told me about…the old manor house.'

'Norton Place.'

He gazed at the fire. 'I have been dreaming about England a lot lately. I see people's faces, but I can't remember any names.' He looked at Marie-Ange. 'And then, I have been dreaming about you…about us.'

She blushed as his eyes skimmed over her body. She remembered how rough he had been with her in Lyon and clenched her fists until the nails dug hard into the palms. Could she trust him?

Once again, he seemed to sense her doubts. 'I need your help. I want you to tell me about my life—our life together.'

She breathed in sharply. At last tonight he acknowledged she had told the truth. Even though she didn't love him anymore, she owed it to him to help him remember his past.

'I will only help you if you tell me what happened to you after the battle of Corunna and how you became a French agent.'

Christopher stiffened. He gave her a sidelong glance. 'You are aware of that? What else do you know about me?'

'Only that you go under the name of Nallay.' It was better to plead ignorance of the rest.

Christopher seemed relieved. 'Very well…My earliest memories date from a French field hospital at Lugo. I suffered a serious head injury. When I regained consciousness, I was given what was left of my uniform: a ripped jacket with a few personal possessions, a pouch of tobacco, a clay pipe, a letter from my fiancée—Jacqueline Leblanc—and my requisition orders from the Fifteenth Infantry Regiment. All in the name of Joseph Nallay, from Charenton sur Marne. This is who I believed I was…until I met you in Fouché's building on *Rue de Condé*.'

'Didn't you go back to Charenton to meet your fiancée, your family? They would have realised you weren't Nallay.'

Christopher shrugged. 'Why go back when I didn't remember her, or anyone else. I was made an offer I couldn't refuse by Marshall Soult's état-major in Spain. And then, I went on to work for…my current employer.'

Fouché, she thought.

'Did you really not know me when you first saw me in Paris, and again at the *Palais Saint-Pierre* in Lyon?'

'I thought you were one of Talleyrand's spies. He's a devil for hiring beautiful women to ensnare rival agents. But your face haunted me, your eyes especially. I started to wonder if maybe you had told the truth.'

He turned to her. 'Tell me about this place in England where I come from and about our life there.'

This time, she obliged. She spoke for a long time about his earlier life. His parents and his brother, Robert, about his successful career in the Royal Navy and how well he had got on with the formidable Admiral Jarvis while serving under his command. She recalled their meeting at a county ball, their brief courtship, and short married life before he embarked on the *HMS Amazon* for Northern Spain. Christopher listened without saying a word, his eyes staring right in front of him, his arms crossed on his chest. He was absorbing her every word.

Sophie came into the drawing room to announce supper was ready.

'Sophie, this is my husband, Christopher Norton,' Marie-Ange announced, a little awkwardly.

'Your husband? I didn't know…' Sophie stuttered, her eyes wide with surprise.

'Is Monsieur Karloff still upstairs?' Marie-Ange had an idea suddenly. When Sophie answered in the affirmative she asked her to invite Karloff down for supper.

The physician was a hypnotist. Perhaps he could help Christopher remember the missing weeks between Corunna and the day he woke up in the French military hospital? It was worth a try. She mentioned the possibility to Christopher.

'A hypnotist like this crook Mesmer? Certainly not!'

He flashed eyes of steel at her, cold and heartless, and she felt a shiver of fear snake down her spine. For the second time tonight, she wondered if she could trust the man standing in front of her. As if sensing her doubts, he smiled and his voice became conciliatory.

'I've heard Dr. Mesmer used to poke his patients—his victims more like—with iron rods as they sat in some kind of wooden bucket while he supposedly manipulated their minds…is this the kind of treatment you would like to submit me to?'

She shook her head. 'Of course, not. Monsieur Karloff does have certain abilities which could be helpful to your condition.' She didn't want to tell him about her own experience of Karloff's skills.

'At least consider it,' she said, leading the way into the dining room. 'This might be your only chance of finding out what happened after Corunna.' Then she added. 'Tomorrow will be too late.'

She explained that she was leaving for Chalons in the morning under an escort of *gendarmes*.

'Yes, I know. As an *émigrée*, you are now *persona non grata* on French soil,' Christopher said as they took their places around the dining table. 'Actually, that's partly why I came tonight.' He poured himself a glass of red wine which he downed in one gulp.

Curious, she turned to him. 'Really?'

He tipped more wine into his glass and looked at the deep ruby coloured liquid.

'I have decided to go home with you, back to Norton Place.'

She gaped at him, lost for words.

'You intend to return home?' Her voice was shaky.

He raised his eyebrows. 'That is where I belong, isn't it? And if you will assist me with remembering my former life, I should be able to slip straight back in.'

'How will you explain your years of absence to the Admiralty? Your work as an agent for Fouché?' she objected.

He shrugged. 'Let me worry about that, dear. The Admiralty need not know everything.'

'Will Fouché let you go now he has been reappointed as Napoleon's Minister of Police?'

'You don't sound very enthusiastic about the prospect of my return.' His expression was unreadable. 'And yet I thought all you wanted was to be reunited with me. Your husband.'

Karloff entered the room and regarded Christopher with undisguised curiosity. Marie-Ange invited him to sit down, introduced her husband and explained what she wanted him to do.

'I have dealt with mental traumas before, especially amnesia,' Karloff agreed. 'Battlefield amnesia can be caused not only by physical injuries but also mental scarring. Intense fear, for example, or the witnessing of atrocities.'

'All right! I will try your sorcery.' Christopher stood up. 'I suppose I do need to know what happened to me.'

He put his hand on Marie-Ange's arm. 'But you must give me your word of honour that this man will only ask me about Spain, nothing else!'

'Of course,' she replied, uneasy. 'That's all I wish to know about.'

Was he afraid of revealing any state secrets or any of Fouché's schemes, the plot to assassinate King Louis, maybe?

Karloff needed a dark room to carry out the experiment, so they settled in the library. He instructed Christopher to sit in front of the fireplace, took the place opposite him and asked Marie-Ange to stay at the back, in the shadows. The curtains were drawn against the night.

The only light in the library was the golden glow of the fire. The logs crackled in the fireplace, rain pattered against the tall windows and the clock ticked in a corner of the room.

'Breathe slowly and deeply. Let your shoulders drop and your hands fall into your lap.' Karloff spoke in the quiet, monotonous voice Marie-Ange remembered only too well. He pulled out his golden watch from the pocket of his jacket and dangled it in front of Christopher's face. The physician issued more instructions in the same dull and soothing voice. Christopher sighed with impatience several times.

'Listen to my voice. Listen to the rain outside. Concentrate on your breathing…You are at sea,' Karloff continued. 'What is the name of your ship?'

Christopher's breathing was now deep and slow. '*HMS Amazon*,' he answered quietly.

'What is your name?'

'Commander Christopher Norton.'

'What is the date, Commander Norton, and where is the *Amazon*?'

'Eighteenth January 1809. We are moored off Corunna.'

'What is happening on board your ship right now?'

'The French are firing their heavy artillery from the hill tops of San Diego. My men are still trying to ferry the wounded from the harbour walls to the ship, but the smoke is becoming too dense. They can't see where they're going. Several rowing boats have sunk already. I can hear men shout as they fall into the freezing cold water, but we can't get to them.'

'Is the *Amazon* safe?'

Christopher shook his head. 'No. We've been hit. The great mast has fallen and the sails are on fire. We need to evacuate but the men are too exhausted. Many are injured. We're sinking, fast.' Christopher brought his hands to his head.

'Are you injured, Commandant Norton?'

'Yes, a blow to the head.' Christopher winced in pain. 'I jumped into the water. It's damn cold. I won't last long if I don't get to a boat or some kind of raft.'

Marie-Ange sat on the edge of the sofa, tense and hanging on his every word. At last, he started to remember!

'My second, Wilson, is calling me. He's with Lieutenant Padiham on a raft. They're pulling me up with them. We're drifting. The currents are strong and we have nothing to paddle with. We watch the fire of the cannons on the cliffs and the *Amazon* burn and sink.'

'How long do you drift for?' Karloff asked quietly.

'All night. In the morning, there is a coastline in the distance. We must swim or we'll die at sea. I say I'll go first. It's freezing. I must swim quickly. I hear a splash behind me as Wilson and Padiham jump too but I'm not waiting for them. I have to reach the shore.'

'What happens now?'

Christopher shrugged. 'I don't know. I'm alone on the beach. I must passed out. It's night time now.' He shivered. 'I walk. I have to find food. Find people.'

'Do you meet anyone?'

'No. I'm tired, I lie down behind some rocks and fall asleep. Next thing I know there are gunshots all around. When I look, there are bodies of French soldiers on the beach. I'm wet through, so I strip down to my long johns and undress one of the dead men. I slip his jacket and his breeches on. That's better. There's blood on his jacket but at least it's dry.'

'Do you see any other French soldiers around?'

'Everybody's dead. I walk to a village. An old woman is talking to me in Spanish. God! My head hurts.' He moaned and took his head in his hands again.

'There are French soldiers in the street. They take me

away to the field hospital.'

'How long do you stay at the hospital?' Karloff asks.

'I don't know. They give me draughts for the pain. Then this man—a lieutenant—comes and speaks to me. He says I can help them with translating English messages. I work from the hospital at first. Then when I'm better I travel with the troops. They feel sorry for me because I don't remember anything of my past. Not even my fiancée in Charenton.'

'Do you stay with the army for long?'

'Several months. I've been promoted, but I'm sick of battlefields, of gore, blood and field rations. So when one of Fouché's men comes to my regiment to recruit new agents for the secret police and asks me to join, I take him up on his offer. I travel to Paris. I have an apartment. More money than I need. The job is easy enough. Fouché and I get along fine.' He snorted. 'We are alike in lots of ways. We don't have any feelings. I can snap someone's neck without...'

Marie-Ange rose hurriedly from the sofa and walked towards the fire light. 'We'll stop now. I gave him my word we would only enquire about what happened in Spain after the battle.'

The clock struck nine, its chiming melodic in the silence.

'Very well,' Karloff said. He turned to Christopher and put his watch back in his pocket.

'When I count down from ten, you will wake up and remember everything you have just told me, Monsieur Norton,' Karloff instructed. He snapped his fingers as he reached one.

Christopher kept his eyes closed for a few seconds and breathed in deeply. Then he looked at the old man in astonishment and shook his head.

'You did it! Your wizardry worked. I remember everything.'

He got up and strode across the library towards Marie-Ange. 'You were right. It was all true,' he said, taking her hands and pulling her towards him.

Marie-Ange looked at him frowning. He seemed surprised, as if he had doubts about his past *before* Karloff hypnotised him.

'Now, I am truly ready to go back home. To Norton Place.'

'But are you free to leave? What about Fouché? Your duties?' she asked again, gripped by panic. She needed time to think about what had just happened. The man wanted to pick up his life where he left it six years before, but she couldn't do that. She loved another.

'Don't trouble yourself with that. In fact, everything is turning out quite nicely for me. I shall ride on to Paris tonight to negotiate the terms of my...how shall I phrase it? Release or new assignment?' He laughed as if he had made a joke only he understood. 'Then I will join you at Norton Place.'

Still holding her hands tightly, he bent down to kiss her, but she turned away and his lips only met her cheek.

'I see,' he said, his tone suddenly frosty. He stared at her hand.

'I noticed that you no longer wear your wedding ring.'

She gave a small gasp. The ring. She'd left it behind at Saintclair's quarters in Lyon. She had vowed never to wear it again.

He let go of her and stepped back.

'I suppose we will have all the time in the world to re-establish our acquaintance. Try and find your ring and put it back on. I will see myself out.' He bowed and left the room.

'Christopher!' Marie-Ange ran after him, feeling a mixture of remorse and anger. She didn't know how to behave with him. He expected her to take him back as if six years hadn't passed, as if he was still the same man.

But he wasn't. And what was more, she had changed as well…

He was already putting his coat and his hat on to leave. He asked a servant to bring his horse to the front of the chateau and turned to meet her gaze with his cool grey eyes.

'We shall be together again soon. Should you get to Norton Place first, do not breathe a word about me. I will do all the explaining.' He touched the rim of his hat and bowed slightly. 'Farewell for now, my dear.'

She followed him onto the front porch, watched him climb on his horse, spur the animal into a trot on the path, and disappear into the night.

'You will return to England with him?' Sophie stood next to her, disbelief obvious on her face and in her voice.

Marie-Ange nodded. Her throat was so tight she couldn't speak.

'I'm not sure you are doing the right thing. He looks a harsh man.'

'Yes, he does but he is my husband,' Marie-Ange managed to say. 'I have no choice, Sophie.' She bent her head, her heart felt trapped in her chest. 'No choice at all.'

'What of Capitaine Saintclair?' Sophie asked. 'What will you tell him when he comes after you?'

Chapter Twenty-Two

It was still raining the next morning when Commandant Picard and his two *gendarmes* presented themselves at Beauregard.

'Are you ill, Madame? You look very pale.' Picard gave Marie-Ange a searching look.

'I will be fine, Commandant,' she replied with a tight smile. In reality her head throbbed and she felt drained after a night spent trying to envisage what life at Norton Place would be like now Christopher was returning. What had once been her dearest dream had become a nightmare.

She didn't think she would ever forgive her husband for stabbing Saintclair in the back or for molesting her. Every time she looked into his grey eyes she would be reminded of his past as an agent for Fouché's secret police, capable of executing his employer's enemies in cold blood when ordered to. She might never find it in her heart to respect him, let alone love him again.

If only she could stay at Beauregard a while longer, take the time to get to know him again…her husband, this stranger. He had made her uneasy the evening before, oscillating between disarming smiles and ruthless stares. He said he wanted to know all about Norton Place and his past, but never once asked her about herself and her life during his long absence. Instead, he only remarked on the fact she no longer wore his wedding ring. She looked down at her bare finger. She would have to buy another ring somewhere on the way to Devonshire.

She spent the early morning walking around the grounds, trying to commit to memory the images and sounds of Beauregard; the rose garden; the shadows made by the forest of evergreens around the park; the enchanting sounds of doves cooing and flying around the chateau.

Her luggage was loaded on the roof rack of her carriage.

'It is time, Madame.' Picard bowed in front of her.

She hugged Sophie and climbed into the coach. Numb beyond tears, she turned round for a last look at the chateau. She now understood a little of what her mother might have felt when she left. A grey shadow moved behind a window on the first floor. Karloff was watching. He had promised to leave later today.

The journey to Chalons was uneventful. They reached the small town on the banks of the River Saône in the afternoon. The outskirts of town had been taken over by army bivouacs and the town centre was heaving with soldiers. The coach driver stopped on the main square while Commandant Picard made some enquiries at several inns.

'They are going to the eastern border,' he said when he came back. 'Every single room in town is requisitioned for army personnel. We shall carry on. Hopefully we will find an inn nearer Autun.'

Marie-Ange nodded absent-mindedly. She didn't care where or when they stopped. She didn't care if they travelled all the way to Le Havre without interruption. She regarded the colourful crowd on the square. Soldiers in different regimental uniforms, market traders packing up, and town folks hurrying to buy food before the market finished. As the coach set off again, a man standing in a corner of the square attracted her attention. He looked familiar and she leant forward to take a better look at him. His dark hair was unkempt. A thick beard partly covered his face. He wore some kind of sheep-skin coat and high leather boots, just like one of Uxeloup's henchmen. A few seconds later, he walked away into the crowd and she lost sight of him.

Should she tell Commandant Picard? It was probably a coincidence. After Uxeloup's death, his men had fled Beauregard. Some would have gone back to Malleval, but others might have business to conclude elsewhere.

The next town was Chagny. It was dark when they stopped in front of a large inn on the main square. Picard found rooms for the night, arranged for Marie-Ange's bag to be taken upstairs and for a maid to bring her some supper. She forced herself to eat some soup and drink a glass of wine. Then, feeling weary of the day's travel, she put her nightdress on and took the pins out of her hair. She was just getting into bed when she heard men's voices in the staircase.

'I am very sorry Sir, but it's late. I don't think that you should…' It was Picard's voice.

'I need to see Madame Norton now. Get out of my way.'

Hugo! He was here, he had come after her. The overwhelming joy she felt at hearing him was immediately replaced with anguish. She must tell him about Christopher's visit to Beauregard. She had to tell him her husband planned to resume his former life with her in Norton Place.

He already knew.

'Tell me it's not true,' were his first words when she opened the door.

He closed the door behind him and marched straight in. He seemed to take up all the space in the room. She stepped back, alarmed by the thunderous look in his eyes.

'Tell me you're not taking your husband back, after everything you said.' He stopped a few inches from her and she had to tilt her head to look into his eyes. Her heart was beating so fast her chest ached.

'Who told you?'

'So it's true…Sophie was right.' He closed his eyes for

a few seconds. When he reopened them, they were cold as ice.

'Why?'

'He came to Beauregard yesterday evening, begging me to tell him about his past life, about Norton Place, his family, and…'

'And you were only too happy to oblige,' he interrupted. 'Sophie said you asked Karloff to hypnotise him to help him remember. So Norton told you all about his vile deeds, the men he knifed or shot in dark alleyways and the women he slept with in exchange for information. And still you found it in your heart to forgive him—even though you said he was dead to you.' He gave a short derisive laugh.

'It isn't like that!' She cried out, putting her hand on his forearm. 'I couldn't deny him the truth about his past, and Karloff didn't pry into his deeds as an agent.'

He raised his eyebrows. 'Why?'

'Before we started the mesmerising session, Christopher asked for my word that we would only ask him about Spain.'

'How convenient! What a good little wife you are.' He eyed her from top to toe, a sneer appearing on his lips. 'I'm surprised you are no longer wearing his dressing gown.'

She shook her head, folded her arms on her chest. 'I left it at Malleval's house on Isle Barbe.' She almost added that she wouldn't have worn it even if she still had it. Things had changed. She had changed.

'By the way, how do you know he's sincere?' He resumed. 'That he doesn't have an ulterior motive for this sudden need to be reacquainted with his past and return to England? I think it's all very timely.'

What did he mean by that?

'It would appear you have what you desired. Husband and wife reunited.'

His words cut as badly as his icy glare. She wanted to

cry out that he was wrong. It wasn't what she wanted. Not anymore. She loved him and only him. Surely he must understand that if her lawful husband wished to return to Norton Place, there was nothing she could do to prevent him. He owned the place. And in a way, he owned her too. She was bound to leave France under the new *émigrés* law, there was nowhere else for her to go to but Norton Place.

But she didn't know how to start, so she said nothing.

'I was released this morning and rode straight to Beauregard, hoping to see you before you left. I had a proposal for you. Not that it matters anymore.'

'What proposal?'

'I was planning to ask you to marry me…as a way of getting your deportation order cancelled, of course. It would have bought you time to settle your business at Beauregard.'

'Marry you? But it's impossible. I am already married.' A warm feeling spread through her. He wanted her to stay. He had been ready to marry her.

'Only you and I knew that, since Norton denied it was the truth.'

She bowed her head. 'Even if Christopher hadn't come to Beauregard yesterday, I couldn't have committed bigamy. No matter of how much I want to stay in France and marry you. It would be wrong.'

'Well, it's not going to happen since he now remembers who he is, so let's forget I ever suggested it.' He stepped forward and put his hands on her shoulders. 'You could still remain in France though. With me. I am owed a few favours. My name and position in the army should guarantee your freedom. I would put you up in an apartment in Lyon.'

Her cheeks flushed with the realisation of what he was implying.

'You mean, I would live with you as a mistress?' she interrupted.

He smiled. 'What else? I'm not asking you to be my stable lad.'

His fingers rubbed her shoulders gently. She breathed in, trying to quell the turmoil raging inside her. She was torn between two men, between love and duty. There was one question she needed to ask Hugo. His answer would determine her decision and her whole future.

'Why would you help me? I mean, why would you want me for your wife or your mistress?'

Hugo gazed into her eyes. 'Isn't that obvious? I told you before. I feel responsible for you—for what happens to you. It's a damned shame you came all this way only to leave with nothing. If you stay, you will have time to sort out your inheritance, which is far bigger now you are Malleval's heiress.'

'You feel responsible? Is that all?' She felt the blood drain from her face.

He didn't answer.

'You don't have any other feelings for me? You don't…love me?' She insisted, hating the pathetic, pleading, sound of her voice.

He dropped his hands by his side, and arched his eyebrows.

'What are you talking about, Marie-Ange? We have kissed a few times and yes, it was good. Very good even. I would more than gladly take things further.' His lips curled into a smile. 'I am sure our arrangement would be to our mutual satisfaction, but please don't make it any more than it is.'

His voice became harsh. 'Don't make *me* anymore than what I am. I am a commoner, a soldier, remember? Not a courtier. I kill, I organise men and I plan battles. I don't pick flowers or write poems.' He crossed his arms on his chest and leant back. 'That doesn't mean to say we can't have a good time together.'

He made it sound so coarse, so cheap. She bit her lower

lip hard to stop it from trembling. She had her answer. It was plain he didn't love her. He didn't even believe in love. They were too different. She would suffer if she stayed with him, so much that with time it would destroy her. Destroy her heart and her soul. It was better to sever her ties with him tonight.

'Thank you for your offer,' she said, trying to keep her voice cool, 'but I will return to England.

He stared at her a moment in silence.

'It's your decision,' he said at last, before turning to the fire and presenting his back to her.

She squeezed her eyes shut in an attempt to stop the tears. He was so close, and yet so much separated them. Suddenly, she remembered the warmth of his arms and the longing in his eyes as he had held her at Marzac. If they were going to part forever, she wanted a burning memory of him to last her a lifetime. He could be down to earth and ruthless, and so could she. She stepped forward and laid her hand on his back. His muscles tensed. Turning round, he grabbed her wrists and pulled her to him.

'What do you want from me now?'

She was aching for him.

His stare was intense, his breathing fast.

This was probably the only chance she would ever have to make love to him. She stood on her tiptoes and kissed his lips. He moaned and pulled her against him, so tightly the metal of his uniform buttons, and the coarse fabric of his jacket bit into her body. He kissed her mouth, her throat, while his hands gripped the curves of her hips.

'Why can't I leave you alone? Even now you have chosen another man,' he growled. 'And why do you let me touch you?'

She didn't reply but put her arms behind his neck and kissed him softly again.

He stroked the outline of her face, her throat, venturing further in the opening of her nightdress to the swell of her breasts. She shivered with the longing for his hands to explore the rest of her body. He bent forward and took her mouth in a hungry kiss, one hand tilting her head backward so he could deepen the kiss. His hands slid down her shoulders and pulled the night dress aside with such impatience the fabric ripped and the garment fell onto the floor. He raised a hand to her breasts, stroking and teasing until her nipples hardened so they almost hurt.

She heard a whimper of desire and realised it came from deep within her. With feverish haste, Hugo unbuttoned his jacket, loosened his shirt and threw them on the floor.

He raised a hand and caressed a lock of her hair which had escaped her braid and was nestling in the curve of her neck.

'I want you, damn it. Why isn't that enough for you?' his voice was barely a whisper.

He untied her hair, gave her a slow, smouldering look, hot enough to make her cheeks and her throat burn. He put his hand in the hollow of her waist to pull her against him and his fingers ran along her spine. His hands covered the curves of her hips, lingering on their velvety softness, before sliding to the front and stroking her stomach. When they ventured further down, she closed her eyes and whispered his name. Her legs couldn't support her any longer. She held onto his shoulders for fear of falling. His hands, in turn gentle and hard, seemed intent on exploring every inch of her body, on taking possession.

'Are you sure?' he asked, his voice low, his gaze burning.

She bit his shoulder lightly. 'Yes.'

He lifted her in his arms and laid her on the bed. He kissed her again, before finishing undressing and discarding his clothes. As he lay next to her, he twisted her hair in his hand and tilted her head up towards his. Then he caressed her, in slow, feather light strokes, from shoulders to breasts, her stomach to her hips. His breath quickened, became raspy, as he parted her legs and touched the hot, moist, tender skin. His eyes never left hers while she arched against his hand and moaned, overwhelmed by waves of pleasure. It was as if he was staking his claim on her body.

He withdrew his hand and kissed her throat, the line of her shoulders, nuzzled her breasts, licked the pale pink skin around her nipples, and then sucked on the hard tiny buds. The harsh stubble on his cheeks rubbing against her skin increased her pleasure tenfold.

She clasped her hands at the back of his neck, ran her fingers through his hair. There was a dull, throbbing need within her which she knew could only he could fulfil. He took her mouth again, let out a groan before settling on top of her, hard and impatient. She opened herself to him, and he thrust deep inside. He was ruthless, diving deeper and faster, his hands clasping her hips to bring her nearer and higher still. She closed her eyes.

'Look at me,' he ordered.

She stared into his burning, intense blue eyes as heat exploded inside her. Holding on to his shoulders, she arched her back and cried out, and then it was his turn. He lay on top of her, still staring deep into her eyes as if he owned her body and soul.

Later, he kissed her lips gently and moved to the side.

'Hugo,' she nestled against his body. 'I…'

He put a finger on her mouth. 'There's nothing to say. Are you thirsty?'

She wasn't. He got up and poured himself a glass of wine. She looked at him in the glow of the dying fire. It hurt so much to think that after this night, they would part forever.

He came back to bed and pulled back the sheets to reveal her naked body. His fingers ran along her arm towards her neck and throat and rested in the hollow of her waist. Her hair glowed, spread like sunrays on the pillow. He had to look at her, touch and possess her again. He would never have enough of her. He pulled her on top of him and she rested her head on his chest while he toyed with locks of her hair. It used to be so simple, so straightforward. He had never wasted much time thinking about women before. If he saw a woman he wanted, he bedded her. Then he would move on. Sometimes there were tears and recriminations, but they never worried him and they certainly never stopped him. He had never wanted to stay with the same woman for very long...until now. Then again there had never been a woman he had wanted quite as much as Marie-Ange. His lips curled into a cynical smile. He understood at last what other men had told him over camp fires, their eyes dreamy on the eve of a battle they believed would be their last. Some women, they said, a man wanted to hold, make love to, and keep. Forever. Marie-Ange was such a woman. But she didn't want him. Maybe it was justice for all his past sins.

His hands ventured along her spine and the fire between them started again, but this time there seemed to be a wilderness inside her. She kissed his face, his throat and chest, her lips as light as the wings of a butterfly, her tongue teasing and moist. He groaned when her breasts brushed against his chest as she moved. Her hand found him already hard and she stroked him, arousing him until he believed his heart would burst.

He buried his head between her breasts, tracing their outline with his fingers, feeling their soft weight against his cheeks, taking her nipples in his mouth. Pulsing with need, all he could hear was his own ragged breathing and the blood roaring in his ears. He let out a moan when she straddled him, sliding over him and caressing him while he stroked her.

This was torture. Unbearable pleasure. Surely he

wouldn't be able to hold on any longer. He gripped her hips to lift her, and she lowered herself onto him. His hands pressing firmly on her hips, they started moving together, faster and faster. Her moans filled the silence. He felt like a soul lost at sea, so intense were the sensations she aroused in him. They both cried out at the same time and she collapsed, shaking on top of him. He pressed her head against his chest, feeling the wild beating of her heart against his own.

They didn't speak. They made love again and were both wide awake when the first light of day filtered through the curtains.

Doors creaked open and shut, footsteps and voices resounded in the corridor and the smells of soup, fried sausages and freshly baked bread wafted in from the kitchens downstairs. It was time to get up. His fingers trailed down the side of Marie-Ange's waist. He pulled her closer, buried his face in her hair and breathed in her scent. She heaved a sigh and pressed her lightly curled fist against his chest, just above his heart, as if she wanted to feel the beats and capture them. He clenched his jaw. Yes, it was time. There was no point in prolonging the inevitable.

He pulled away and got up without a word, then picked up his clothes and got dressed quickly, aware of her gazing at him from the bed, her eyes shiny, her breathing fast and shallow as if she was trying to stop herself from crying. It was as if he was abandoning her when it was she who was leaving him behind. Hell, what did the woman want of him? She had chosen her man, and it wasn't him. With each layer of clothing he put back on he could feel his resolve harden, his anger forming a cold fist in his chest.

'I will ask a servant to bring you hot water and make the fire,' he said after strapping his sword belt across his hips, his voice harsher than he intended. 'I will meet you in the dining room when you are ready.' And he left the

312

room without a further glance.

He was having breakfast with Commandant Picard and his two *gendarmes* when Marie-Ange entered. She was so pale, so fragile with delicate mauve shadows under her eyes, his throat tightened. The men stood up as she approached and he pulled a chair out for her.

'Madame, we will be leaving as soon as the coach driver has harnessed the horses,' Picard announced, his face blushing a deep red. He must be aware Hugo spent the night in her room.

Hugo poured some hot coffee in a cup and handed it to her.

'I'm going back to Lyon this morning. I have been charged with reorganising the Second Cuirassier Regiment in view of forthcoming developments.'

Picard nodded and looked at him admiringly. 'I heard of your promotion. Congratulations, Colonel Saintclair. Your manoeuvres in the south were decisive in quashing the royalist rebellion. And to receive the Imperial Eagle from Napoleon himself…What a distinction!'

'You were promoted Colonel? Napoleon gave you the Imperial Eagle?' Marie-Ange raised her head, surprised. 'You never said…'

Hugo shrugged, neither seemed that important right now. 'I escorted the King's brother, the Comte d'Artois, to Sète when the mob wanted to lynch him. Apparently, Napoleon was grateful we avoided a blood bath. It wouldn't have looked good for his return to power.'

He paused and added. 'Especially after the foiled assassination attempt on the Comte the week before, in Lyon.'

He turned to Picard. 'Commandant, would you please get us some more coffee?'

'Of course, Colonel.' Picard got up.

Hugo leant over the table.

'This you might need to know,' he started, striving to

313

keep his voice matter-of-fact. 'In the end, the King decided against a visit to Lyon and sent his brother to review the troops in his place. After an evening at the opera, the Comte d'Artois was waiting for his carriage when fireworks were thrown in the street, causing a panic. In the confusion, nobody noticed a man running at d'Artois, firing his pistol. It was sheer luck the King's brother managed to open the carriage door and to jump in. The would-be killer ran off. Witnesses gave a vague description. A tall man. Very pale blond hair under a hat.'

Marie-Ange put her hand to her mouth to stifle a cry. 'Do you think it was…?'

She didn't need to say the name. Hugo narrowed his eyes and reclined back on his chair. 'I do.'

Her face drained of all colour and she closed her eyes. Did she understand now how timely Norton's decision to return to her was? The man needed a place to hide until the dust settled both for Fouché and himself, and where better than with his wife back in England? Yet Marie-Ange was so happy to have him back she didn't even question his motives.

'Why the King's brother?' she asked at last.

'What if the purpose of the exercise was not, as we thought before, to clear the way for the emperor? What if whoever gave the order wanted to throw discredit on Napoleon and turn people against him? To make him start his new reign with a cold-blooded execution people were bound to blame him for.'

Marie-Ange shook her head. 'But why would Fouché want to discredit him?'

'The man has a hidden agenda, as usual.'

'He is one of the emperor's closest allies,' she objected.

Hugo laughed bitterly. 'You are very naïve. When it comes to power, allegiances shift. I have heard Fouché was plotting for the creation of a Republic with himself as head of state. King Louis was in poor health and the

Comte d'Artois was next in line for the throne. His assassination would have killed two birds with one stone. It would have cleared the royalist camp and thrown discredit onto Napoleon.'

'Then Fouché would suggest a completely new regime and become the leader,' Marie-Ange finished.

'The man is nothing if not patient. He may yet have his chance. Napoleon may not have the support he needs to govern for very long. He will soon lose the popular vote when he brings back conscription.'

'Why? Do you think war is inevitable?'

'Unfortunately, yes. Napoleon's emissaries carrying his offers of peace weren't even received by the various governments across Europe. Austria, Prussia, Great-Britain, and Russia will soon declare war on France. Napoleon needs to rebuild the army fast.' He didn't add that it couldn't be done and that Napoleon was heading for disaster, along with tens of thousands of men. Including himself.

Picard came back with a jug of coffee. 'There you are, Colonel,' he said, pouring three cups.

Marie-Ange looked around and dropped her knife and fork on the table.

'That man again!' She pointed to the window. 'I saw him yesterday in Chalons. I think he is one of Malleval's men.'

Hugo turned to the window but whoever Marie-Ange had seen had already left. He turned to Picard. 'Did you notice anyone following you since you left Beauregard?'

Picard shook his head, looking sheepish. 'The roads were busy. I didn't pay attention to the other travellers.'

Hugo stood up. 'Let's go after him, then.' He ordered Marie-Ange to stay in the dining room and gestured to Picard and the two *gendarmes* to follow him.

As Marie-Ange finished her coffee, a boy dressed in

dirty rags ran into the dining room. He pulled her arm and slipped an envelope into her hands.

'What is that?'

The boy ran out without answering.

She ripped the paper and pulled out a thin sheet of paper. Something fell out onto the tiled floor. When she bent down to pick it up she saw that it was Sophie's ruby ring. She read the note.

'If you value the woman's life, come alone now behind the church. Don't tell anyone or we'll kill her. Hurry.'

Someone had taken Sophie. Marie-Ange looked around her, a helpless feeling gathering in her stomach. Clutching the note and the ring, she rushed out just in time to see Saintclair and the *gendarmes* riding out of the courtyard. Her shoulders sagged. She bit her lip and looked around. What should she do? She feared a trap, yet couldn't ignore the ultimatum in the note. She had to go to the rendez-vous.

She put the note and the ring back into the envelope thoughtfully and walked back inside.

'Please give this to Colonel Saintclair when he comes back in. It's very important,' she said as she handed the envelope to the innkeeper.

'Certainly, Madame.' The man put the letter in his waistcoat pocket.

She climbed the stairs to her bedroom, grabbed her cloak and her reticule, and ran back down. Chagny was a small place. The streets were almost empty so early in the morning. The bells were ringing for the morning service when she arrived on the church square. Half a dozen women crept into the building through a small wooden door.

'*Bonjour, M'ame.*' A gruff male voice spoke behind her. She swirled round and found herself face to face with Rochefort. She stepped back in shock.

'You! We all thought you were dead.'

He chuckled. 'Not so. I fell through a trap and landed in a chamber below the crypt. There were several tunnels branching out and it didn't take me long to gather I was in the disused salt mines. Monsieur was in a bad way when he crashed down on top of that stone tomb, but I managed to drag him along a tunnel far enough to avoid getting hurt by the blast of the explosion or hit by the rubble. It did take us a day or so to find our way out, but we made it.' He came closer, and she smelled the pungent odour emanating from his shagpile coat.

'You will come with me now.' He took her elbow.

'Where are you taking me? And where is Sophie?' Marie-Ange tried to gain time. She couldn't believe Uxeloup was alive. Had he managed to retrieve the Cross of Life too?

Rochefort walked quickly, pulling her along narrow, deserted alleyways. They soon left the village behind and found themselves near a farm. A black carriage with four tall horses and two men on the driver's box waited on the road. Her captor opened the door and pushed Marie-Ange inside. He climbed in after her.

'Sit down.' He sat opposite her and the carriage started.

'Where are we going?'

'Malleval. Now be quiet, or...' He showed her a flask and a handkerchief. She remembered the foul smelling cloth Karloff had put over her face in St Genis to send her to sleep.

'That won't be necessary,' she said. She needed all her wits about her. There might be a chance of escape before they reached their destination.

There wasn't. They travelled all day and part of the night, stopping at isolated inns to feed and rest the horses and use the rest room. Rochefort never let her stray far from his sight. He had bread, cheese and bottles of wine in a basket for himself and his men.

'Do you want some?' He asked her gruffly. She

317

accepted and forced some food down. She had to keep her strength up.

Rochefort drank a long gulp of wine and wiped his mouth on his sleeve. 'So the Captain and the *gendarmes* fell for our ruse it, what half-wits!' He laughed.

'What do you mean?'

'They walked straight into our trap and followed our decoy. Must be in Autun by now! Saintclair may be able to deal with royalist rebels but he's not so clever when it comes to dealing with the men from the Pilat.' He took another swig of wine.

She ignored him. 'Where is Uxeloup?'

'Waiting for us.' Rochefort narrowed his beady eyes. He shook his head with mocking pity. 'What a waste...I think I'll ask him for a little time alone with you before we get down to business.'

'What business?'

He grunted but didn't answer.

Although she tried to stay awake, she eventually gave in to the rocking motion of the carriage as night fell. A harsh jolt woke her up. Glancing out of the window, she saw that they had arrived at Malleval.

Rochefort grumbled. 'About time!'

He kicked the door open and jumped down. Marie-Ange shivered in the cold. The past couple of weeks had been mild at Beauregard, with a hint of spring in the air. Tonight however she had travelled back into winter. A snowstorm was blowing in the rugged Pilat mountains.

The wooden doors of the fortress were wide open as they approached and they entered the hall.

'Follow me.' A man holding a torch led the way down a dark corridor.

'I'll tell Monsieur you have arrived,' he said before leaving Marie-Ange and Rochefort alone in a large room dominated by an enormous stone fireplace bearing the arms of the Mallevals.

A + M. Ante Morte. Before Death. The Death both Edmond and Uxeloup refused.

The fire in the hearth was the only light in the room. Marie-Ange walked to a long table with a marble top on which a silver tray with medical instruments was placed. Long, sharp blades, lancets, curved and twisted implements, a pile of cloth and a white porcelain bowl. She felt a shiver of fear run down her spine.

'What are these for?' Her voice quivered.

'All in good time.' Rochefort pointed to an armchair positioned in front of the fireplace. 'Take your coat off and sit down.'

She wrapped herself more tightly in her cloak and remained near the table. She was in terrible danger. Last time she was here, Uxeloup and Karloff wanted something from her. The words from her mother's song to locate the Cross of Life. What did they seek from her tonight? She had nothing to offer them.

'Sit down, I said!'

This time she did as she was told. Rochefort seemed nervous. She looked around the room shrouded in shadows and gasped. In one corner, placed on a high console table, was the Cross of Life standing on the glass phial with the relic inside. So Rochefort and Uxeloup had saved it from Arginy.

'How did you travel back here after the explosion? I mean, all your men either died at Arginy or fled.'

'I waited near the main road, hidden in the undergrowth, while Monsieur rested. We were in luck. A couple of peasants drove past in their cart. It was child's play to ambush and kill them, then hide Monsieur in the back of the cart. It took us a few days to reach Malleval but we made it.'

'How is Uxeloup now?' Surely with the advancing ravages of the syphilis and his fall at Arginy, he must be in a very bad shape.

'Not good.'

'Where is Sophie? Why did you take her from Beauregard?'

Rochefort stood up abruptly and came to stand in front of her.

'Will you shut up?' He raised his big hand as if he wanted to strike her. She recoiled in her seat. He shrugged and went back to his seat.

Outside, a gale was howling, blowing freezing gusts down the chimney into the fireplace, threatening to extinguish the tall flames as if they were tiny candles. Marie-Ange tried not to move or make a sound. Time passed. Rochefort nodded off in his armchair. His head rolled forward and he was breathing loudly, making a snuffling noise. For the first time since she left Chagny, she had a chance of escape.

Cautiously, she stood up and tiptoed towards the door. There were probably guards both in the castle and outside but she had to try.

The door flung open as she was half way across the room. She froze with horror. In front of her stood a man so emaciated he was hardly more than a skeleton. His pale, transparent skin stretched over his bones and was marred with scratches and purplish bruises. His eyes were hollow and feverish.

'Here you are. At last.' He shuffled like an old man across the floor.

'Uxeloup!' She gasped, putting her hand in front of her mouth. She stepped back.

'Monsieur. Come and sit down.' Rochefort stood up. He rubbed his face roughly with his hand and tried to take Uxeloup's arm.

The former Hussar shook him off. 'No time for a rest. We need to do this now. Before my strength leaves me for good.'

'Do what?' Marie-Ange asked, feeling the blood drain

from her face.

Uxeloup gestured towards Rochefort. 'Lie her down on the table and tie her up.'

'What do you want with me?' She screamed as the big man grabbed her waist and lifted her up onto the marble table top.

Uxeloup gave her an evil glare.

'You are going to give me your heart.'

Chapter Twenty-Three

'I should have understood before,' Uxeloup said. 'The answer was there all along, in the parchments from the Knights Templar. A pure heart and the Master Keepers' bloodline were needed to unlock the relic's power.'

He turned his crazed eyes to the Cross of Life. His body was seized by a coughing fit that seemed to drain him of all his strength.

'What exactly do you mean to do?' Marie-Ange's voice quivered as panic welled inside her.

Uxeloup pointed to the surgical instruments on the table.

'Hold your heart in my hand. Drink your blood so that it runs inside my body, then I'll be able to handle the Cross and gain eternal life at last.'

She shuddered violently as she contemplated the gruesome death Uxeloup had in store for her.

'Karloff guessed what I meant to do.' He shook his head. 'Old fool…He told Sophie of my plan yesterday and turned her against me. After that he tried to run away from my men at Beauregard. He should have known better.'

'Where is Sophie now?' She had to keep him talking for as long as possible. But then what? Nobody was coming to rescue her this time. Her father and his remaining Turcopilar companion had returned to Sicily, and Hugo was off on a wild goose chase.

'Upstairs.' Uxeloup's eyes grew darker. 'She won't come with me on the journey. She won't even talk to me.'

He coughed again, and then gestured to Rochefort. 'This time I will succeed. I have to, after the fiasco at

Arginy and the way I failed my father.'

He pulled a small silver flask from his pocket and showed it to Marie-Ange.

'Don't worry. You won't feel a thing.'

It was now or never! She refused to be butchered by this maniac without attempting an escape. She darted for the door so suddenly both men were taken by surprise. She pushed two heavy chairs over to block their way. Flinging the door open, her heart thumping hard, she ran down the corridor. Rochefort's heavy footsteps resounded behind. They were getting closer.

'Damn you!' He shouted as he caught the hood of her cloak and pulled her sharply towards him.

He lifted her up as if she was just a bundle of rags. She kicked and wrestled against his chest, but he didn't seem to feel anything. Instead he pulled her hair sharply, yanking her head backward, and slapped her in the face. The force of his blow took her breath away. She stopped struggling, her strength ebbed and her mind drifted into unconsciousness. The last thought she had before darkness engulfed her was that Hugo would never know how much she had loved him.

She was floating on the angel's wing. Down below was Malleval's fortress and the village perched on the snow-covered mountains. Nobody could reach her now. She was safe. Muffled voices and the clinking of metal instruments close by intruded on her dream and she fought her way slowly to consciousness. She opened her eyes. Two blurred figures moved against the glow of the fire. Uxeloup and Rochefort. She wasn't safe at all. Bile rose in her throat. She coughed and tried to turn to her side to be sick but she couldn't move. Her hands were bound tightly on each side to the table legs. She shivered from fear and from cold. Her dress was open at the front, her chest exposed. A cold object pressed down on her stomach.

'Please, don't…' She moaned.

Uxeloup stood over her. He was holding a sharp, shiny scalpel. Through a daze she saw him lean closer. She mustered all her strength to struggle free, but it was no good. Her binds were too tight.

'She's awake. She needs more draught,' he said.

He took out his silver flask again and brought it near her lips. As he held her head to force her to drink, a loud explosion outside shook the fortress's walls. It was followed by shouting and the firing of pistols. Startled, he dropped the flask on the floor.

'What's going on out there? Where are the men?'

'A moment, Monsieur. I will investigate,' Rochefort said as he walked away.

'Damn!' Uxeloup stepped back.

Marie-Ange breathed a sigh of relief. She heard the door open and light footsteps walk across the floor.

'Sophie, *ma chérie*! Have you changed your mind?' Uxeloup asked. His voice was soft, full of hope.

'No, Uxeloup, I have not.'

Marie-Ange heard sounds of a struggle, then a whimper of pain and the thud of a body collapsing onto the floor.

'I am so sorry, my love. I couldn't let you do this,' Sophie cried out.

Marie-Ange felt fingers on her wrists, untying her binds.

'Quick, there is no time.' Sophie attempted to lift Marie-Ange's head off the table. 'The fortress is under attack. I don't know if it's the *gendarmes* or the army. We need to get out through the back door.'

Marie-Ange sat up and something rolled onto her lap. It was the glass phial with the relic inside. Uxeloup had placed it there, ready for him to handle once he'd cut her heart… She started shaking.

'So that's what it was all about.' Sophie took the phial and lifted it towards the light of the fire to peer at the piece of fabric inside. 'It doesn't look much like an angel wing, does it?'

She helped Marie-Ange stand up and put her dress back in order. Marie-Ange kept hold of the glass phial and, with a last look at Uxeloup's crumpled form on the floor, the two women walked from the study. The fortress was dark and deserted. They hurried along empty corridors through the kitchen and a pantry. Sophie pushed the door open into the snowstorm outside. The gale had not abated during the night. If anything, it was stronger. Snowflakes swirled madly all around. Gusts of icy cold wind slapped Marie-Ange's cheeks.

She breathed in deeply, suddenly intoxicated with the realisation she was alive. She had escaped the gruesome death Uxeloup had planned for her. A familiar voice shouted from outside the fortress walls.

'Surrender now!'

A warm, elated feeling spread through her. Hugo was there. He hadn't been fooled by Rochefort's trick after all. He must have guessed she was being taken to the Pilat and had followed them. It was only a question of minutes before he and his men stormed into the fortress. All the two women had to do was sneak out into the courtyard and hide in an outbuilding until they were rescued. They crept in the shadows along the wall, hoping Rochefort and the others were too busy defending the place to turn round and look behind them.

The phial was now very hot in her hand. Inside the glass, the relic glowed, iridescent like an opal catching the moonlight. Only there was no moonlight. The night sky was giving way to a murky greyish dawn.

'The stables are just behind there.' Sophie took her elbow to direct her to the stable block.

As they turned around a corner of the building, they came face to face with an armed man.

'Over here! The women are escaping!' He brought his

pistol to bear on them.

Marie-Ange and Sophie stopped dead in their tracks. Half a dozen men appeared and stood menacingly around them.

'Don't shoot!' Rochefort's voice bellowed over the clamour of shouts and gunshots. He came nearer, a fierce expression on his face.

Marie-Ange held the phial up in front of her. 'Don't come any nearer or I'll drop it.'

Rochefort turned to Sophie. 'Where is Monsieur?' he asked.

'Inside. He fainted,' she lied.

Rochefort gestured to one of his men and ordered. 'Gabet! Run to the study and see to Monsieur Malleval.'

Marie-Ange was still holding the phial up in the air. The men looked at it, fascinated by its white glow which was getting brighter and brighter.

'What is she holding? Why is it moving and changing colour? She must be a witch,' one said.

The storm gathered momentum. Ribbons of swirling snowflakes descended from the sky, wrapping themselves around the men, like slippery, ghostly figures.

'Rochefort!' The man named Gabet called. He was carrying Uxeloup, propping his limp body against him.

Rochefort narrowed his eyes and bared his teeth.

'What did you do to him? I swear if you hurt him...' He glared at the two women.

'He's still alive,' Gabet said, 'but he's bleeding.' He looked at the women accusingly. 'It looks like he's been stabbed.'

Rochefort pointed to the relic glowing in Marie-Ange's hands.

'Let's see if this really does what it's supposed to. Hand it over now or I'll kill you where you stand.' He aimed his pistol at Marie-Ange and armed the firing mechanism.

There was an explosion at the other end of the

courtyard and the large wooden gates blew open. Soldiers came running through, holding their rifles and bayonets in front of them.

Several of Uxeloup's men scampered towards the back of the fortress.

'I said, hand it over!' Rochefort held his hand out.

The wind suddenly grew stronger. The snow fell in a thick, white curtain. Marie-Ange swayed, stumbled against the wall and dropped the phial. She cried out and reached to retrieve it, but then realised the phial hadn't fallen on the ground. It swirled in the air in a flurry of snowflakes as if lifted up in ethereal white hands. It whirled higher and crashed onto the wall.

'Where the hell is it?'

Rochefort knelt down and frantically brushed the snow and pieces of shattered glass to retrieve the angel wing. He looked up, crestfallen. His hand was bleeding but he didn't seem to notice.

'It's gone. Blown away.' He turned to Uxeloup's body, lying next to him.

'Rochefort, we have to go!' Someone urged. Men were running or riding out of the courtyard to escape the soldiers. Rocherfort grunted, lifted Uxeloup over his shoulder and ran. His bulky figure disappeared in the snow storm.

'Marie-Ange.'

Hugo ran to her, a look of sheer relief on his face. She took a few tentative steps. All she wanted was to be safe in his arms but he stopped a few feet from her.

'I feared I would arrive too late,' he said.

They looked at each other and for a few moments, they were alone. The sounds of chaos vanished. Marie-Ange no longer felt the whipping wind and snow. All she wanted was to clasp her fingers behind his neck and bury her face against his shoulder. She yearned for the warmth of his arms around her, the sound of his heartbeat against her cheek. Yet she stood immobile, uncertain how to proceed. Hugo didn't step any closer either.

'What happened in there? Where is Malleval?' He asked, breaking the silence between them.

'Sophie saved me from him.' She heaved a shaky breath.

'He will be dead soon,' Sophie said, gazing towards the hills. She started crying. 'I killed the only man I ever loved, but I couldn't do it...I couldn't let him rip your heart out.'

'What did you say? What did he want to do?' Hugo walked to Sophie and put his hands on her shoulders.

She raised a tear-stricken face towards him. 'He said if he took Marie-Ange's heart and drank her blood, he could hold the relic and become immortal.'

Hugo hissed a breath between his teeth.

'Will you go after him, bring him back?' Sophie pleaded.

'We will find him, and the rest of his men,' he promised.

He turned to Marie-Ange. 'Do you still want to return to England?'

She nodded. Nothing had changed. She was still a deported *émigrée*. She was still married to Christopher. And Hugo still didn't love her.

'Then my men will take you both back to Beauregard later this morning, when we've cleared up this den of thieves and murderers,' he said, his eyes and his voice noticeably colder. 'Go inside and wait for me.' He walked away without giving her a second glance.

Marie-Ange was still curious about the phial. Kneeling down where it had broken earlier, she brushed the snow with her finger, careful not to cut her hand on the pieces of shattered glass. Rochefort was right. The piece of fabric, the angel wing, or whatever it was, was gone, blown away by the wind. Or had it been taken by the angel? She may not have believed Karloff's prophecy but she could have sworn she had seen the fluid shape of an arm, the outline of a white hand lifting the phial in the air.

'I'm so cold.' Sophie's broken voice brought her back to reality.

'Let's go in.' Marie-Ange took her hand and led her to a drawing room inside the fortress. 'Try and rest,' she said as the young woman huddled in a corner of the sofa and folded her feet under her body.

Marie-Ange was far too tense to contemplate sitting down. Standing at the window, she watched the soldiers line Uxeloup's men up in the courtyard. It stopped snowing. A brisk wind blew the clouds away. The sun coloured the sky and the snowy hills in delicate shades of pink and orange.

There had to be something she could do. She went to the kitchens, found a couple of servants hiding, terrified, in the pantry and asked them to prepare some hot food for the soldiers and their prisoners. When the food was ready, they set up tables in the great hall and gathered as many cups and bowls they could find.

'We are going to serve breakfast to the men,' she decreed.

She organised the soldiers and their prisoners, directed the servants and helped dish out hot porridge, soup, and coffee. It took over an hour to feed everybody. When there was nothing left, she cleared up the dirty bowls, spoons, and cups that cluttered the tables.

He stood watching her tidy the dirty pots off the table. Her cheeks were rosy and strands of hair escaped her plait and curled at her neck. His fingers remembered the feel of her hair. The feel of her skin. He swallowed hard.

'You would make a fetching tavern girl,' he remarked.

She raised her head and smiled faintly. He took his hat and thick grey leather gloves off and put them on the table.

'I am afraid there isn't much left to eat but we can have a look in the kitchen if you are hungry.'

'I'm not hungry,' he replied. He closed the distance separating them. 'I am leaving a small detachment of my men here for the next few days until the *gendarmes* take over. How are you?'

'Relieved this madness with Malleval is over at last, and glad to be alive, of course.'

He didn't say anything.

'Sophie is resting,' she added, wiping her hands on her dress. 'I will tell her we're ready to leave.'

Hugo grabbed her wrist and pulled her close to him. 'Don't go back to England, Marie-Ange. I want you with me. I'll sort out the technicalities. As I said before, I can have your deportation order cancelled.'

He bent down and kissed her lips. She remained cold and unresponsive.

'This is the last time I will ask you.'

Damn it, didn't she know he would look after her? He might not be from the landed gentry like her husband, but she wouldn't want for anything. And she would be his.

Tears filled her eyes. She shook her head. 'You must realize I have no choice. I can't stay with you if you don't lo…'

He didn't wait for her to end her sentence. He let go of her so abruptly she almost fell.

'There is always a choice,' he interrupted. 'Very well. My men will escort you back to Beauregard, where Picard is waiting.' He turned round. 'I almost forgot…' He searched his breast pocket and held out his hand. Inside was Marie-Ange's wedding ring. She took it reluctantly.

'You left it in my room in Lyon. It's just as well I didn't throw it away, isn't it?' He put his gloves and his hat back on. There was only cold anger in his heart now. 'Uxeloup's men were seen heading for the forest. I am going after them. I don't think we will see each other again. I wish you a safe journey back to England, Madame.'

He bowed and walked away. He shouted at a soldier to bring his horse, put his foot in the stirrup, and mounted. He galloped out of the courtyard without looking back.

Chapter Twenty-Four

As promised, a dozen of Hugo's cuirassiers escorted Marie-Ange and Sophie back to Beauregard later that day while the chase after Uxeloup, Rochefort, and what was left of their men carried on in the mountains.

A cuirassier shook his head and remarked, '*Le Colonnel est enragé!*' Others commented they had never seen Saintclair so angry and reported he had sworn not to give up until he had the fugitives at the tip of his sword, even if it took days.

Before leaving Malleval, Marie-Ange took the Cross of Life from the study and wrapped it carefully in a piece of cloth. Her great-aunt at Marzac could decide what to do with it. As far as she was concerned, the cross could be locked away in a cupboard or thrown to the bottom of a well. She never wanted to set eyes on it again.

Their sad, silent, and uncomfortable journey along bumpy, snowy, roads took two days. They arrived at Beauregard late the following morning.

'I don't want to stay here on my own,' Sophie cried when she stepped out of the carriage.

Marie-Ange helped her to her room and asked for hot food and drinks to be prepared. She then suggested Sophie invite a relative to stay with her for a few days.

'I can't think of anyone…my cousin maybe,' Sophie agreed.

One of Hugo's men was dispatched to fetch the dressmaker from nearby Macon. Another rode to Beaujeu to inform Commandant Picard Marie-Ange had arrived safely back at Beauregard.

'What a terrible ordeal, dear Madame!' The gendarme exclaimed when he arrived soon after. He danced from one foot to the other, holding his hat, a blush spreading across his face.

'I am deeply ashamed you should have been abducted while you were in my care. Colonel Saintclair and I chased after the man for almost an hour before the Colonel realized he was playing a game with us. The scoundrel even slowed down at times, as if making sure we could catch up to him.' Picard coughed. 'The Colonel told me to carry on with the chase whilst he turned back towards Chagny. Thank Heavens he did.'

'Yes, thank Heavens,' Marie-Ange agreed, shivering.

During the journey to Beauregard, she had time to reflect on how close to death she had come. There were images she would never forget. Uxeloup's crazed eyes as he explained how he would rip her heart from her chest and drain her blood. The snow swirling around the phial and lifting it in the air like an angel's arm at dawn…

She swallowed hard. 'What about Monsieur Karloff? I heard he was killed.'

Picard shook his head. 'His body was found in the forest.' He put his hat back on and informed her they must begin their journey to Le Havre as soon as possible. According to Napoleon's orders, any *émigrés* still on French soil by the end of the week would be jailed.

'Can you make sure my great-aunt at Marzac gets this?' she asked, handing the Cross over to him.

Picard nodded and promised to send someone to Marzac Manor that very afternoon.

Marie-Ange took her leave of Sophie once again and climbed into yet another carriage. This time she was on the road to exile and there would be no going back.

The rest of the journey was a blur. She looked through the window of the carriage, indifferent to landscapes, villages, and towns they drove through. Each passing hour was taking her away from the man she loved, and towards the stranger who was still her husband.

Picard left her in Paris in the care of a colleague of his. At Le Havre, she boarded a French cutter bound for Portsmouth. This time the crossing was calm and she didn't suffer as much from seasickness. She spent the journey on deck, staring at the horizon, wrapped in her cloak, her hood covering her head. The sailors called her 'the widow' and it brought a sad smile to her face. Now she was no longer a widow, she had never felt more like one.

It was dusk when she arrived at Norton Place, early one rainy evening at the beginning of April. As she climbed down from the carriage, she breathed in the scents of wet earth and fresh grass mixed with the salty breeze blowing from the sea.

'Welcome back, my Lady!' Rosie, her chambermaid, opened the door and walked out, a smile on her face. Francis followed and muttered a greeting.

'Is that Marie-Ange? Is she here?' Robert called from the doorway.

She couldn't help smiling when the young man ran towards her and took her in his arms.

'You've grown taller, Robert.' She kissed his cheeks and ruffled his hair.

'Marie-Ange, I have the most extraordinary, fantastic, incredible news! Guess what?' He jumped up and down like an overexcited puppy.

A cold fist gripped her heart and her smile froze. She knew exactly what he was going to say.

'Christopher is back! Isn't that just wonderful? My brother is alive! Your husband is here!' He took her in his arms again and squeezed her against him. Suddenly faint, she swayed against him. She had hoped for more time before facing Christopher. Hugo's revelations about the attempted coup on the Comte d'Artois' life had reignited her fears about him and her doubts that she would ever be able to believe him, let alone love him again.

'I am sorry,' Robert said, frowning. 'It was stupid of me to spring the news on you like that. I should have thought.'

'It's all right, Robert,' she replied, holding onto his arm.

Christopher's silhouette appeared in the doorway. 'Darling, at last! Welcome home.' He descended the steps, approached her casually before stopping a few feet away and opening his arms. He clearly expected her to throw herself against him. Dutifully, and without any of the joy she should have felt, she stepped into his embrace. He kissed her cheeks and whispered in her ear.

'Six long years, my darling, since I held you in my arms. We have such a long time to make up for.'

Her skin prickled with fear. It sounded like a threat rather than of a promise of love.

He stepped back and looked down at her. 'You are even more beautiful than the last time I saw you, on the quay at Southampton, that blustery January day when I left for Spain.'

She looked up, surprised. So he didn't want anyone to know about their meeting in France. Why?

'You look different, too,' she remarked, coldly. Then she put a forced smile on her face and a false, joyful note in her voice. She had to pretend to be happy. For Robert's sake.

'You must explain everything, Christopher. What happened to you? Where have you been all these years?'

'Later, my darling.' He kissed her again. She stiffened in his arms and pulled away.

That evening, Marie-Ange played to perfection the part of the quietly overwhelmed but happy wife in front of Robert and the rest of the household. During supper, she asked Christopher again to explain his long absence. With a hushed voice, he talked about undercover missions, state secrets, foreign affairs dossiers. He mentioned recent meetings at Whitehall with Lord Melville—the First Lord of the Admiralty, and Lord Castlereagh, the Foreign Secretary. Leaning towards Robert, he even confided having been entrusted with a very special, highly confidential mission by Lord Liverpool, the Prime Minister, himself.

'I'm afraid my mission will take me away from home again.' He looked up at Marie-Ange. 'As soon as tomorrow in fact.'

'So soon?' Robert protested. 'But you only returned yesterday.'

The young man was sitting next to Christopher, gazing admiringly at him and drinking in his every word. How different he would look at his elder brother if he knew the truth, Marie-Ange thought bitterly. She was curious though, very curious. How had Christopher managed to negotiate his release from Fouché's services and his return to the Royal Navy? There must be some truth in his talk of secret missions and foreign affairs secrets.

He smiled and covered her hand with his. She tried very hard not to withdraw it. Looking down at her fingers, he remarked.

'I see that you have misplaced your wedding ring.'

She stared back at him. 'So have you, Christopher. Or was being a bachelor a cover for your very secret missions?' Her tone was biting.

'Marie-Ange, Christopher already said he wasn't at liberty to explain about his work.' Robert flew in his brother's defence.

Christopher reclined on his chair and smiled smugly. 'Not to worry. We shall have new rings made.'

'That won't be necessary,' she replied. 'My wedding ring is in my jewellery box, in my travel trunk. You will see it on my finger tomorrow, if that is your wish.'

She excused herself after supper, claiming exhaustion

and a headache, and sought the sanctuary of her bedchamber. She prayed Christopher would not join her later and insist on enforcing his rights as husband. The very thought of his hands on her body made her sick with dread. After unpacking some of her clothes, Rosie prepared a bath.

'It's good to have you back, my Lady,' the girl said. 'Sir, too, of course,' she added, her voice guarded.

It felt so strange to be here. In a way, it was as if she'd never left. Her room was the same. Norton Place was the same. Robert was his usual self, a pleasant and boisterous young man. But she had changed.

She pinned her hair on top of her head and undressed. She asked Rosie to leave her when she slipped into the hot bath. She closed her eyes for a moment.

A noise nearby startled her. She must have fallen asleep. Opening her eyes, she let out a frightened cry. A shadow moved in a corner of the room.

'You are really beautiful, you know,' Christopher said, his voice hoarse. He walked into the light and knelt by the side of the tub. She sat up and tried to cover her breasts with her hands but he took hold of her wrists and pulled her arms apart.

'Let me go, Christopher,' she pleaded, breathing erratically as panic welled inside her. 'Let me get out of the bath.'

He laughed. 'All right, then.' He stood and pulled her up roughly with him. He stepped back and grabbed the large bath cloth Rosie had spread on the back of an armchair.

'You'll be wanting this.' He held it up but remained deliberately out of her grasp.

She breathed deeply and looked into his mocking grey eyes. He was toying with her. He wanted to upset and frighten her. She would show him no fear. Calmly, she stepped out of the bath, naked and dripping wet, and walked towards him. She raised her hand and he relinquished the towel, but as she began to wrap herself in the soft cloth, he seized her arm and dragged her to the bed.

Tipped off balance, she fell backward onto the counterpane, and he crashed on top of her, driving the breath from her lungs. She tried to wriggle free, but he pinned her down. There was no feeling in his eyes, just the grey coldness of steel. He raised one hand to her throat to stop her from moving.

'Now, my dear, listen very carefully,' he commanded.

'To the eyes of the world, you are my wife. I own you and I will use you as I please. This time, you won't push me away. I have all the power and you have nothing.' He gave a little grunt as his hands slid over her bare skin, still damp from the bath. She gritted her teeth.

'I know you were the French officer's harlot, and I'm going to enjoy making you pay for it. He pulled the towel off her, looked down at her breasts. 'Starting now...' He chuckled. 'In fact, it may not be such a bad thing that you slept with him. I bet he taught you a trick or two which will make our nights much more interesting.'

Although she felt sick with loathing and her heart beat like a wild bird trapped in a cage, she tried to remain as cold as a statue under his touch. She would have to beat him at his own game.

'If you don't get off me this instant, I swear I will tell everybody how we met in France. I will tell them about Karloff and the mesmerism session,' she said.

His hand stopped moving, settled on her stomach. He was listening, waiting.

She played her last card. 'I will tell them who is behind the assassination attempt on the King's brother, the Comte d'Artois, in Lyon a few weeks ago. I bet that will change your employer's prospects altogether and yours, too. I gather Fouché is still your employer, am I right? All this talk about missions for the Admiralty and the Foreign Affairs ministry is only half the story, isn't it?'

He withdrew his hand and cursed.

She carried on, pushing her advantage. 'I will go as high as necessary, to Lord Castlereagh…to Lord Liverpool himself.'

He rolled off her and she sat up, covering herself with the towel.

She gave a tight smile. 'If you force me to, that is.'

He stood up and crossed his arms on his chest.

'Well played, darling.' The words hissed between his teeth. 'There are indeed certain facts I would prefer to remain concealed for now. I am amazed at your perspicacity. What do you know about this?'

'About Lyon? And Fouché trying to get the King—or his brother—murdered to make room for the emperor…or was it to discredit the emperor? Which was it?' She pretended nonchalance, playing with the tassels of her towel. 'Either way, I am sure Fouché would find it tricky to explain himself. Napoleon made it clear he didn't want any member of the royal family harmed.'

Christopher was visibly shaken. He clearly didn't expect her to know so much and to confront him so fearlessly.

'What do the Sea Lords know about you, then?' she asked. 'Do they know how you really spent the last six years? Do they know you are still Fouché's man?'

He shrugged. 'They know some of it. Other things, like the unfortunate shamble outside the Lyon opera, I'd rather keep to myself.'

So he was admitting responsibility for the botched coup against the Comte d'Artois.

'Why were you not arrested for treason when you came back to England?'

'My superiors at the Admiralty Board and the Cabinet are aware of my involvement with Fouché. In fact, that's what makes me invaluable to them at the moment. I am their direct line into Napoleon's new Cabinet and with my help—and Fouché's—they have a chance to topple it.'

He walked to the door, but turned towards her, his hand on the door knob.

So Hugo had been right. Fouché was already scheming to get rid of Napoleon, only a few weeks into his new reign. He had plotted with the British against Napoleon in April the year before, just before the emperor abdicated. This time he had Christopher to liaise secretly with the British.

'Why did Fouché choose you for this particular mission?' she asked, shivering as she recalled the razor-sharp face of the minister of police, his heavily hooded eyes and thin lips. She was reminded of what Christopher had said at Beauregard when he was under Karloff's influence. That he and Fouché were very much alike because they had no feelings. Looking into her husband's cold grey eyes now, it wasn't hard to believe.

Christopher smiled. 'Actually, he chose me because of you. After the opera house incident in Lyon, I had to lie low for a while. He was very displeased with me for failing to carry out my mission. I was about to go into hiding when I remembered you and your fancy story about me being your long-lost English husband. I thought you could provide me with a new start. So I came to Beauregard and pretended I remembered you.'

He sneered. 'And you fell for it. It was all lies, you know. I didn't have any flashbacks to our married life or to this place. I didn't remember a thing! Fortunately, you obligingly filled all the gaps for me. I couldn't have asked for a more helpful wife.'

Marie-Ange felt her heart grow colder. 'You mean you didn't remember Norton Place or people from the past. Or even me?'

He gave a short laugh. 'Of course I didn't. When I came

to Beauregard, I thought I'd go along with anything you said. Slipping into a dead man's shoes would give me a good cover. It might make me useful to Fouché again, after the Lyon fiasco. If nothing else, it would give me a new identity, a chance to start again.'

He paused for an instant. 'Then you suggested Karloff hypnotise me, and the most incredible thing happened. I found out you had been right all along and that I actually was…myself.'

His voice held a trace of wonder. 'I must say I hadn't expected that.'

'So we can say whatever happens next in French and European politics will have a lot to do with you, my darling, and with your obstinate belief in me.'

He opened the door and bowed. 'I will travel back and forth to France under my French identity—Joseph Nallay. And I'd rather nobody else but I, the Admiralty Board, and a few carefully chosen people at the Ministry of Police *Place Cambon* know about it. So yes, you have won for now.'

His lips stretched into a thin, threatening smile. 'But only because I am letting you win, and only just for now.' He paused. 'Another thing Marie-Ange, you will remain here at Norton Place until I decide what to do with you. I can see you and my foolish brother are very close, so if you give me any reason to be dissatisfied with you, I promise I'll make him suffer. Trust me, I am very good at inflicting suffering. Good night.'

He walked out.

Once alone, Marie-Ange was consumed by uncontrollable tremors. She went to the fireplace, poked the logs to start the fire again, and stood staring at the flames until she stopped trembling. She had an important decision to take. Should she warn Hugo that, as he had suspected, Fouché was plotting against Napoleon? Or should she let Fouché bring down the emperor with the help of the British government? After all, if Napoleon was removed from the throne, there would be no more wars in Europe.

The emperor's return was doomed because of a powerful enemy from within. No wonder the Admiralty Lords, and members of the Cabinet, welcomed Christopher back without probing too hard into his past. He offered them the chance to topple their long standing enemy. Thanks to him, they would be privy to Napoleon's slightest move. As for Fouché, he would pour his poison into his emperor's ears and sabotage his government. And get on with plotting his political survival.

It was late into the night when she reached a decision. She would write to Hugo and warn him about Fouché. She must be very careful. She was in no doubt that Christopher would be watching her like a hawk. She had made an enemy of her husband tonight. He would never forgive her for blackmailing him and taking the advantage over him.

Chapter Twenty-Five

'It's all over this time. Napoleon is on board *HMS Northumberland* en route for *Sainte Hélène*. He won't be coming back to France.' Christopher smiled smugly. 'Not standing, anyway. If he had been sent there in the first place, the carnage at Waterloo would have been avoided.'

He folded his newspaper and looked at Marie-Ange. 'And what carnage it was. The latest figures have now been released. Over twenty-five thousand French soldiers dead—and almost twenty-two thousand of our own coalition forces lost. And thousands still unaccounted for. Mostly infantry, but many cavalry forces, too. Poor souls, they are probably rotting in a ditch under their horses. Do you remember Wellington's account of the battle in the London Gazette a few weeks ago, my dear? According to him, the French cuirassiers bore the brunt of the Prussian and Hanoverian artillery. They were decimated.'

He put the paper to one side and tucked into his breakfast of ham and scrambled eggs. Marie-Ange closed her eyes, hearing his voice from a distance. He was now talking about the fall of Paris to the British and Prussians forces three weeks before, about the siege of Lyon by the Austrians and the surrender *en masse* of the French army to the coalition forces. He quoted the names of French casualties from Napoleon's last campaign—the many high ranking officers who had died or suffered terrible injuries at Waterloo. There was one name she was desperate not to hear.

She had read descriptions of the Waterloo battlefield by Wellington and other witnesses. They were imprinted in her soul. The 'canons belching fire and death', 'the roaring and shouting sounded like a volcano'. A Foot Guard's captain had written that the French cuirassiers' armours *glittered like a stormy wave of the sea*' and their galloping horses sounded like thunder as they charged. Then they fell, mowed down by the Allies artillery fire.

She finished her cup of tea and looked at Christopher. Cool and perfectly at ease, he talked about the outcome of the war England and its allies had just won as if the past six years had never happened, as if he had never worked for the French side. No, she was wrong, she corrected silently. He worked for Fouché, not for France. And now Napoleon was gone, Fouché was leading King Louis's new government with a surprise ally—his old enemy Talleyrand. Both men succeeded in surviving another change of government. To his critics who accused him of turning his coat yet again, Fouché had replied, scornful, but with startling honesty, *'I am everything people say I am—a royalist or a Jacobin—depending on what happens; I am, and will always be, the servant of circumstances.'*

Christopher had good reason to be pleased with the outcome of events. He had helped his master, his 'employer' as he called him, gain a crucial position of power in France once again. He had travelled between England and France incessantly, no doubt delivering important instructions and messages from the British Cabinet to Fouché, and secret information about Napoleon's plans to the British in return.

At least, his frequent travels meant that Marie-Ange didn't have to endure his presence at Norton Place too often. If she had hoped that time would mellow him and help him become his old self, she was disappointed. He remained a cold and indifferent stranger, so much so that even Robert found it impossible to establish a brotherly relationship with him. After the first few weeks when he had been overjoyed by Christopher's return, the young man had suffered from his brother's sharp tone and constant rebukes.

'I don't know him, Marie-Ange,' the young man confided one evening, his grey eyes tearful and his lips quivering. 'Hell, I don't *like* him!'

Robert had now started his three-year training at the royal navy academy in Portsmouth where Christopher had purchased a commission. Marie-Ange was pleased for him. He was at last pursuing his dream. It also meant Christopher had less of a hold on her. She didn't fear quite so much that he would hurt the young man should she displease him.

Robert and Marie-Ange weren't alone in finding Christopher difficult to live with. She had heard Francis, Mrs. Green, the cook, and Elias the gardener, comment on their master's nasty temper. 'Don't you dare get on the wrong side of Sir Christopher,' they had urged Rosie one day in the kitchen. 'He's nothing like he was in the old days.'

The manor house had changed too in the past five months. Christopher paid for extensive repairs to be carried out. The roof was redone, one wing re-pointed and another partly rebuilt. Inside, most rooms had undergone significant refurbishment. Architects and decorators were summoned from the most fashionable houses in London. Marie-Ange had to admit that the result was striking. The manor house was no longer a foreboding, crumbling, and draughty old house but a bright and beautiful home. She did wonder about the source of Christopher's money though. Was it Fouché's money—or in other words, treason money, blood money?

She gestured towards the newspaper, folded on the table next to her husband, and asked him to hand it over.

'Are you sure it's wise? I don't want you having a

fainting fit. You already look very pale,' he answered with false concern. She knew he enjoyed telling her about the terrible losses the French, and the cuirassier regiments especially, had suffered at Waterloo. Instinctively, she placed a protective hand on the gentle curve of her belly and felt the baby move inside her. It was no more than a flutter but her lips formed a tender, secret smile. She put her hand back on the table straight away. Christopher had no idea she was expecting. The fashion for loose, high-waisted dresses had helped her conceal her pregnancy so far. However the time had come to tell him. It was the right thing to do. Especially since she also planned to inform him she was leaving him, Norton Place, and England.

Christopher put his tea cup down on the saucer. 'I must get ready. Lord Admiral Melville is expecting me at the Admiralty tomorrow. I shall not be back before the end of the week at the earliest.'

'Are there any new developments since the royalist cabinet was formed in Paris?'

She cast him a glance under her eyelashes and inwardly cursed her cowardice. She had to speak to him now, before he left for London, but she didn't seem able to say the words.

He looked preoccupied for a few seconds. 'No, I don't think so.'

Rosie came in with a tray. 'The post, sir.' The maid glanced at Marie-Ange. 'Would you like your correspondence, Madame?'

Christopher clicked his fingers, impatient. 'Bring it all to me.'

Rosie smiled apologetically at Marie-Ange, but did as she was told. As she walked towards Christopher, her foot caught into the rug and she tripped, sending the letters and tray flying off onto the ground.

'Silly girl! Look what you've done!' Christopher raged.

'Christopher, please, this isn't anything to be angry about.' Marie-Ange smiled at Rosie who scrambled to her feet and picked up the letters from the floor.

'I'm sorry, Sir,' Rosie said, her cheeks bright red, as she placed the tray in front of Christopher.

He looked through a pile of letters and stopped suddenly, holding a thin envelope adorned with an elaborate red wax seal in front of him.

'This one is for you, dear. How odd...It comes from Catania in Sicily and bears the seal of the Knight Order of St John—the Knights Hospitaller.' He leant over, arching his eyebrows. 'Any idea whom that might be from?'

He toyed with the letter. 'Maybe I should open it myself. You never know, it may be bad news.'

She stood up in protest. At last, news of her father! She had written to Baldassare at the beginning of May and had been waiting anxiously ever since for his reply.

'That is mine, Christopher.'

He held the letter up in the air. She recognized the warning in his eyes.

'I will ask you again, then. Do you have any idea of who this letter might be from?'

She sat down. She hadn't told him about meeting Baldassare in France.

'My father probably, or one of his associates,' she replied with a low voice.

Her husband dropped the letter on the table. 'What on earth are you talking about? Your father died over seven years ago. And his business partners all reside in Plymouth.'

'It's a long story, Christopher.'

He crossed his arms on his chest. 'Go on.'

She coughed to clear her voice. 'During my trip to Beauregard, I learnt my real father was not William Jones but a gentleman from Malta called Baldassare dei Conti. Baldassare belongs to the Order of the Knights

Hospitaller.'

She conjured the image of her father's face, of his kind smile, and pure blue eyes. 'I was fortunate enough to meet him. He is indeed an extraordinary, brave, and very knowledgeable man. He said he would write.'

She withheld details about Baldassare being a Turcopilar and the account of their dangerous quest for the Cross of Life.

Christopher whistled between his teeth. 'And you kept this to yourself since our return to England? Why?'

She raised her head defiantly. 'Because it had nothing to do with you.'

'You are my wife. Everything that concerns you is my business.'

She wanted to retort she was his wife in name only. Any feeling and affection had long gone from their marriage, but she held back.

'Will you give me the letter now?'

He didn't answer but tore the envelope open and read it silently, a frown on his forehead.

'This is fascinating. A Maltese family…Knights of St John…Well, I'd never…'

He shook his head, folded the letter and put it in his coat pocket.

'We will talk when I return from London.' He stood up and added he had last minute preparations to make for his trip.

Marie-Ange felt a surge of panic. Black butterflies danced in front of the eyes. She had vowed to tell Christopher about the baby before he left today. She clenched her fists and summoned her courage.

'Actually, there is something I really must tell you before you leave.'

'Can it not wait?'

She swallowed hard and stood up to face him. 'It's important.'

He closed the door again and walked back into the dining room. Then he sat down. His lips stretched in a thin grin. 'What is it?'

Now that the moment had come, the words she had carefully prepared vanished and her mind was blank.

'I am expecting a child. It will be born in December,' she blurted out, putting her hand on her stomach. Before her courage left her completely, she added, 'And I am leaving you and Norton Place. Now that I am no longer considered an *emigée*, I will return to Beauregard.'

She expected shouts of anger but only icy silence greeted her words.

Had Christopher heard what she said? His face was frozen in a grin, his eyes hard.

Eventually, he let out a long breath.

'Two, no sorry, three, revelations in the space of half-an-hour. You are not sparing my feelings today, my dear.' He leant back on his chair. 'Who is the brat's sire?' he asked, but almost immediately raised his hand. 'Actually, don't tell me! Let me guess. It's Saintclair, isn't it?'

'Yes,' she said, breathing out a sigh of relief. She had told him, at last. She dreaded this moment so much that she even contemplated running away to France like a coward while he was in London, leaving only a letter behind to explain herself.

'When was the last time you saw him?'

'In March, at Malleval,' she replied weakly, remembering the freezing cold morning, the pink skies after the storm, and Hugo riding off into the snow covered hills.

'Have you heard from him since?'

She shook her head.

'Does he know you are with child?' Christopher's questions were precise, his tone matter-of-factly.

She shook her head once more.

'So for all you know, he may have been killed on the

battlefields in June. At Quatre Bras, Waterloo, or somewhere else. Or he may be in some whore's bed and not give a toss about you.'

Her eyes filled with tears. Christopher gave voice to the very concerns that tormented her in the darkest hours of the night.

'Surely, Marie-Ange, you know the score with men like Saintclair.' He laughed. 'You were stupid to get yourself pregnant, even more stupid if you actually fell in love with him.' He stood up and came close to her.

'I will not allow you to go to Beauregard. You are my wife and you will stay here.' He put his hands on her shoulders. She tried to shake him off but he pressed down harder, hurting her.

'Beauregard is where I want to live. Where I belong,' she replied, wincing with pain. 'Don't you see we cannot carry on the way we are? I believed we might be able to live together, like man and wife again, even if we had both changed. I was wrong. This is wrong…'

'How can you say you tried to be my wife when you were carrying another man's child?' His voice was cutting. 'When you blackmailed me to stay away from your bed?'

He let go of her so abruptly she almost fell backwards. 'We will talk when I return from London. This child will be raised here as a Norton. I will not have the name of my family dishonoured by a woman who behaved little better than a soldier's trollop.' He clenched his jaws, and a vein throbbed on his temple.

'I won't be here when you come back.' She might sound assertive but inside she was shaking with fear.

'Then I promise I will come for you,' he snarled and shot her a look full of hatred. 'Someday, when you least expect it, I will come for you and your bastard child.'

He turned on his heel and left the dining room.

Marie-Ange collapsed into a chair and buried her face into her hands. She needed time to compose herself before facing the servants. The hateful tone of Christopher's voice, and his threats, were still ringing in her ears.

At least she had told him the truth. She was free from him. Her only regret was that she would not see Robert and explain her reasons for going away. The young man would be hurt, shocked, and probably angry, too.

She now had to concentrate on organising her journey to France. She would sell some jewellery in Plymouth to pay for the passage across the Channel to Le Havre and the coach to Lyon. She wouldn't take any money from Christopher. It was ironic she should struggle to pay for her journey considering she was now the undisputed heiress of Beauregard and all of Malleval's fortune.

Hermine had written in April to let her know of Uxeloup's death.

'Your colonel,' as Hermine called Saintclair, *'did an excellent job of wiping out most of the Malleval clan.'* As Marie-Ange was still considered an *émigrée* then, she wasn't entitled to inherit. The French state had made moves to appropriate all of Uxeloup's assets, but Hermine had been vigilant and put her lawyer on the case to slow proceedings down. In her last letter, dated just a couple of weeks before, she had written that Marie-Ange was free to return to France and take possession of her fortune *'now that the ghastly little caporal had been exiled forever and our beloved King is back. Beauregard belongs once more to your family. You are Beauregard's undisputed new owner and we are waiting for you.'*

Marie-Ange stood up and walked to the window. It had rained heavily during the night, but a strong breeze now blew the clouds away. The morning light emphasized the bright green of the grass and the tree foliage in the garden, the yellow hollyhocks, purple lobelias, and pink delphiniums borders. Very soon, she would leave this place, never to return…

Would she see Hugo in France? She breathed in slowly

351

to calm the wild beating of her heart and release the knot of anxiety at the pit of her stomach she always felt when she thought of him. As Christopher had rightly pointed out, she didn't even know if he was alive. If he was, would he acknowledge her and the baby? He never claimed to love her.

She had written to Lucie when she got back to Norton Place at the end of April, adding a line of warning for Hugo. *'Please tell your brother he was right about the fireworks at the opera house and everything else.'* She knew Hugo would understand.

Lucie had not replied. She was probably still angry with her. Marie-Ange had not written again. And of course, in June, there had been Waterloo...

Rosie came in and closed the door. She looked nervous.

'Madame,' she said. 'This came for you this morning.' She produced a small envelope from under her white apron and handed it to Marie-Ange. 'It was delivered by courier at dawn. The man said it was very urgent and he insisted I give it to you personally.' She lowered her voice. 'He was foreign. French.'

'What did he look like?' Marie-Ange's throat was so tight she could hardly speak.

Rosie blushed and stammered. 'He was quite tall, blond, very handsome.' She sighed. 'I'm sorry about the other letter Madame, the one from Catania. I couldn't keep both of them back. When Sir told me to bring the tray to him, I only thought about hiding this one. So I pretended to trip. I hope I did the right thing.'

Marie-Ange took the envelope with a shaky hand. 'Thank you Rosie. You did well,' she said, dismissing the maid with a tight smile.

Her heart thumped and black butterflies danced in front of her eyes. Her fingers shaking badly, she tore the envelop open and unfolded a thin sheet of paper.

'Chapel on the cliff. Today. Eleven. Come alone. H.'

He was alive! He wanted to see her! Her fingers shook as she scrunched up the paper and shoved it in the pocket of her dress.

She looked at the mantel clock. Ten o'clock already. She heard Christopher's voice in the hall and went to him. He was giving Francis instructions with his usual sharp tone of voice. When he saw her, he stopped talking and narrowed his eyes.

She walked to him, hesitant. This might be the last time they ever saw each other. He seemed calmer now, but she saw the steely glint of anger in his eyes and understood he was putting up a front. She followed him outside.

'Please give me my father's letter back, Christopher. It can be of no use to you.'

His lips stretched into a mean smile. 'On the contrary, my dear… I meant what I said earlier, you know. I will come after you, and those you love. Leave me now at your own risk.'

She didn't reply, but he must have seen the resolve on her face. He climbed into the carriage and slammed the door shut. The coachman raised his whip and clicked his tongue and the horses moved off. Christopher leant out of the window. 'I will see you again.'

The carriage turned onto the main road and drove away.

Marie-Ange heard a whimper and felt something tugging at her dress. She turned round.

'Splinter…good dog.' She knelt down next to the spaniel and stroked its black and brown coat. 'Shall we go?' The dog wagged its tail enthusiastically. If she walked fast, she would get to St Nictan's chapel for eleven. She rushed back inside the hall and took her light blue cape from the hook.

A few moments later, she was walking at a steady pace along the path towards the cliffs. Splinter and Rusty were chasing after each other. St Nictan Chapel stood in the distance.

She stopped when she saw the sea, glittering in the morning sunshine. As well as the usual fishing boats sailing back to Wellcombe harbour and a couple of bricks on the distant horizon, a magnificent frigate moored in the bay. It was flying a white flag—the flag of the Bourbon monarchy. It must be Hugo's ship.

Someone was walking on the path towards her. A tall, heavy-built man. The sun was in her eyes. She blinked. Her heart seemed to beat to the same rhythm as the roaring waves crashing onto the rocks below. The shriek of seagulls circling the cliffs echoed around her. The breeze blew her hair free from her braid. She waited, her hands twisted underneath her cape for the man to come nearer.

Chapter Twenty-Six

'Madame Norton…Marie-Ange.' Hugo bowed in front of her.

'Colonel Saintclair.' Her throat was so tight she couldn't manage more than a whisper.

For a few seconds, they stared at each other. His eyes were as bright, as blue, as the sea shimmering under the sunlight.

Then he smiled and reached out for her hand.

'You look radiant.' There was a note of wonder in his voice. He hesitated. 'Are you well? Are you happy?'

'As happy as can be expected,' she answered.

She waited, heart pounding, as he squeezed her hand. Why had he come?

'I hope my message didn't alarm you.' He let go of her hand and gestured towards the bay. 'I need to talk to you, preferably on board the *Pénélope*.'

She looked down at the beautiful three-mast warship rocking on the swell.

'Oh. Why is that?'

He bent his head and kicked some stones with the tip of his boot.

'We need your help, to rid France of Fouché for good,' he said when he looked up again.

Marie-Ange let out a long sigh. Disappointment churned inside her, so raw and violent she wanted to be sick. So this had nothing to do with him and her. He hadn't sailed to Devon to take her away. It was all about Fouché.

She adjusted her cape around her slightly rounded body and raised her chin.

'I don't understand how I can help.'

'I will explain when we are on board. It's rather important. Shall we go down to the beach? There's a craft waiting for us.'

She shrugged weakly. 'I suppose so.'

She called her dogs and knelt down next to them, ruffling their coats and scratching behind their ears. 'Go back. Go home…' she ordered, pointing in the direction of Norton Place, but the two Spaniels stayed put and wagged their tails.

Hugo found a couple of sticks he threw far away into the bushes. With a yelp, Splinter and Rusty sprinted off. He led the way, warning her about loose stones and slippery rocks as they made their way down. When they reached the beach she saw a small craft pushed onto the sand.

Two sailors were waiting. On Hugo's signal, they floated the dinghy and jumped in.

'Please allow me.' She stiffened as he scooped her in his arms and held her against him. He walked into the sea, lifted her into the boat. The small boat rocked precariously when it was his turn to climb in. His breeches and boots dripping wet, he sat on the narrow bench opposite her.

The frigate looked close enough from the beach but it took over half-an-hour of energetic rowing by the two sailors to reach it. She looked at Hugo but he stared ahead, seemingly lost in thought. The wind blew his dark hair. His face was harder, tauter than she remembered. There were new lines at the corner of his eyes.

She broke the silence. 'I read terrible accounts of Waterloo in the papers. Were you there?'

He nodded. 'Yes. I was there.'

'How did your regiment fare?'

'We lost three hundred and seventy three cuirassiers, and twenty five still haven't been accounted for.'

'Oh, my God.'

He narrowed his eyes. 'It was a blood bath.'

There wasn't much she could say after that. They didn't talk until they reached the *Pénélope.*

It was truly awe-inspiring with its two storey height, double rows of artillery portholes and high rear deck. Marie-Ange wondered how the row boat would manage to side along its massive hull without getting crushed. Then she worried about getting on board. One sailor grabbed a thick rope ladder that dangled down the side. Hugo went up first. He climbed quickly, and then it was her turn.

'*A vous!*'

She started to climb, petrified with fear. The ship swayed with the swell, the rope ladder was wet and slippery under her shaky fingers and her dress hampered her movements, but she soldiered on. She tried not to look at the waves frothing below. After what felt like an eternity, she finally reached the top deck. Looking up she saw Hugo lean over the side.

'Don't be afraid. I'll get you on board.' He put his hands under her arms and lifted her up, keeping her against him a little longer than was necessary. She breathed in his scent, felt the warmth of his hands on her back. Although all she wanted was to close her eyes and stay in his arms forever, she pulled back. She didn't want him to notice her swollen belly just yet. Now wasn't the time to tell him about the baby. She would wait until they were alone.

The booming voice of Capitaine Martin called from behind them.

'Madame Norton! How lovely to see you again!'

Hugo was still holding her arm. He let go of her.

'I need to tell you what we expect from you.' His voice sounded official, with no trace of any past intimacy between them. 'Please come with me to Commandant Janvier's cabin.'

He led her to the rear of the frigate. The deck was busy with men cleaning, scrubbing, and carrying out equipment

357

maintenance tasks. They looked up and stared as she walked past.

'This way.'

He went into the captain's quarters, pushed open a door into a spacious cabin with a large desk covered with maps and papers in the middle. Two men sat behind the desk. They stood and nodded towards her. The tallest one wore a dark navy and white uniform with red and gold braiding. He had a sharp, weather-beaten, clean-shaven face. The other man was dressed in civilian clothes. Short and slim, he had a tall forehead, dark blond hair, and inquisitive brown eyes.

'Madame Norton,' Hugo gestured to the smaller man, 'this is Pierre Deval, French consul to the Barbary States.' Deval bowed deeply. 'And this is Commandant Janvier who is taking us to Algiers.'

She started and looked at him, surprised. Did he say they were going to Algiers?

'You are leaving France?' she asked.

'I have been sent to smooth relations between France and the new Dey, Omar Agha. Now that he's been defeated by the American navy, he should be more amenable to our requests. The Deys and their pirates have been allowed to terrorise the seas for far too long. We need to make sure they respect the peace treaty this time.'

Martin laughed out loud. 'Liar! You weren't sent there, you volunteered. We have only been at peace for four weeks and you're already bored.'

Saintclair smiled at his friend. 'You may be right...At any rate, it's a worthwhile mission for France.'

'Stuff France! What you want is adventure, treasures to find, and maybe a *belle dame* with dark velvet eyes and silky smooth skin waiting for you in a camel-skin tent near an oasis. Admit it, you scoundrel!' Martin laughed good-heartedly.

Marie-Ange felt faint. She gripped Hugo's arm to

steady herself. So he had volunteered to go to North Africa, he would be there possibly for years to come. There was no point telling him about the baby now.

'Are you not well?' He leant towards her, frowning. 'There is quite a swell today.'

Commandant Janvier offered her his chair and Hugo helped her sit down. He stood behind her and left his hands on her shoulders a few moments. She breathed in deeply and closed her eyes.

'Monsieur Duval and I will leave you for now, Colonel. Please call for us when you're ready,' Commandant Janvier declared. The two men bowed formally and left the cabin.

Hugo sat behind the capitaine's desk. 'You heard, of course, that Fouché has wormed his way back in government,' he started.

She nodded.

'Together with Talleyrand, they form the backbone of King Louis's new cabinet. The man thinks he is untouchable.' He darted his blue eyes at her. 'However, you know something which will make his position untenable as a royalist minister.'

'Are you talking about the attempt on Comte d'Artois's life last March?'

'That is it, exactly. In your letter to my sister, you wrote something for my attention. Am I right in believing that Norton confirmed what I suspected?'

'Yes. He told me he had been ordered to carry out the assassination by 'his employer' as he calls Fouché,' she stated matter-of-factly.

Hugo sat back on his chair, a satisfied expression on his face. 'So we've got him at last!'

'My, my…' Capitaine Martin broke his silence. He looked in turn at Hugo and Marie-Ange, an incredulous expression on his face. 'You've known about that all along?'

Hugo ignored Martin. 'Will you write a statement? An affidavit will be his undoing. It will give us enough leverage to send him packing.'

She looked at him. What he was asking her to do would put an end to Fouché's days as a minister. It would also probably lead to Christopher's arrest, maybe even his execution. Now that France and Britain were at peace, the British government wouldn't hesitate to surrender him to the French authorities, should they ask. Although she didn't care too much about her husband, there was Robert to think about. A stain on his family name might ruin his chances of a career in the Royal navy.

'I'm not sure I can do this. I have to think about the implications,' she said.

Hugo shot a thunderous look at her. 'I see...' He toyed with a long wooden ruler, tapping it impatiently against the palm of his hand. 'Obviously I was mistaken when I thought you wanted to help. I wasn't taking into account your feelings for your husband. Feelings strong enough for you to want to save him from being punished for what he has done.' His tone was scornful.

She straightened in her chair and hissed. 'Do not talk to me about my feelings, Colonel Saintclair. My feelings are none of your business.'

He let the ruler drop on the desk.

'Damn it, Marie-Ange!' He put his hands flat on the desk. 'Why did you write to me if you didn't want me to do anything about the attempt on d'Artois' life? Your husband admitted to the attempted murder of the King's brother—and still you are prepared to cover up for him and save his neck?'

She held up his gaze without flinching. Capitaine Martin shifted uncomfortably in his chair.

'Calm down, Saintclair. Madame Norton didn't have to come on board, you know. She really doesn't have to...'

Marie-Ange turned to Martin and forced a smile.

'That's quite all right, Capitaine. I will do what Colonel Saintclair requests, but on one condition. I will write no names at all, neither Christopher's nor mine. It will be an anonymous statement. Is that good enough for you, Colonel Saintclair?'

'If it's the best you can do.' He sighed.

'Then give me some paper and a quill.'

Her voice might have been cool and composed, but her hand was shaking when she dipped the quill into the inkwell. She started writing, omitting Christopher's name out as well as any details which might incriminate him directly. When she had finished, she put the quill down onto the desk.

'May I?' Hugo took the document from her and read aloud.

'*This is to testify that in April of this year 1815, I was told in confidence by a British agent working for Monsieur Joseph Fouché that he was instructed by the same Monsieur Fouché to carry out the assassination of Monsieur le Comte d'Artois. The attempt took place in Lyon in February outside the Lyon Opera House. Upon my honour, I believe this to be the truth.*

A witness who wishes to remain anonymous.'

Hugo sighed. 'That will have to do. It will be our trump card. There is something else Fouché's enemies want to try first to encourage him to go.'

Marie-Ange raised her head. 'What is that?'

'Fouché is a regicide,' he explained. 'He voted for the execution of Louis XVI and Marie-Antoinette. The king, his brother, d'Artois, and his sister the Duchess d'Angoulême want to introduce a law banning from government all those who voted in favour of their brother's beheading.'

He stepped outside to ask Monsieur Deval and Commandant Janvier to come back into the cabin and witness and sign the statement which was then rolled up as a scroll and sealed with hot red wax. Marie-Ange stood up and demanded to be taken back to shore.

'Let me offer you some tea or coffee, something to eat perhaps?' Commandant Janvier offered kindly.

'No, thank you. I have things to attend to at Norton Place.' She arranged her cape around her shoulders. She wanted to make sure nobody could notice her slightly round belly. 'I want to go now.' She couldn't help the slightly hysterical ring to her voice.

She was possessed with a sudden, overwhelming need to be alone and far, far away from the man who gazed at her with such indifference. The man who had forgotten all about the night they shared; the man who had asked her to be his mistress; whose child she was carrying and who would never know about it. The man she loved more than ever but who had never loved her.

Now he had proof of Fouché's treason to the royalist camp, Hugo would sail to Algiers. She would try and forget all about him…if that was possible. She fought back her tears.

'Very well. We'll leave now,' Hugo decreed.

'There is really no need to trouble yourself, Colonel, I will be fine with the two sailors who brought us here.'

Hugo tightened his lips and insisted, so Marie-Ange bid Janvier, Deval, and Martin farewell and walked out onto the top deck. The descent into the small craft was even more harrowing than the climb up. However she was determined not to show her fear. All she could think of was that she wanted to be back on the cliff top.

When they were safely on board, the two sailors lifted the oars and rowed back to shore, singing in rhythm with their strokes. This time, Hugo sat next to Marie-Ange. His thigh touched hers. The heat from his body radiated into hers. He turned to her.

'Did you know that you are now the wealthy heiress of Beauregard and Malleval?'

'My great-aunt wrote to me about it. I intend to travel to Beauregard very soon,' she said. There was no need to tell him she was leaving Christopher, and England, probably later that day or the next. No need to tell him she planned to settle at Beauregard permanently.

'Whatever happened to that Cross you and your father were so concerned about? The one that was supposed to make people immortal, but which almost got us all killed down in the crypt at Arginy.' There was a humorous twinkle in his eyes.

'I sent it to my great-aunt Hermine for safekeeping. She wrote back to say she didn't want the responsibility of caring for it so she gave it to the abbey at Cluny.'

'What about the angel? Do you think he'll ever come?' he asked softly.

'He already came, that snowy morning at Malleval.' She shivered, remembering the white arms lifting the relic...or was it just snowflakes swirling around? 'I believe I saw him.'

He raised his eyebrows but didn't comment.

'What did you do when you went after Uxeloup in the mountains? Did you kill him?'

His face became sombre.

'No. The man was already dead when I got to the cave on the hillside where Rochefort and the others were hiding. With his stab wounds and the freezing cold, he didn't stand a chance.'

There was sadness in his voice. 'I killed Rochefort though, and others, when I could have spared them.' He bent his head. 'I didn't behave the way I should have. I was angry, so angry.'

She resisted the urge to put her hand on his face and caress his cheek. Instead, she folded her hands into her lap and concentrated on the sailors' singing. They were getting nearer the cliffs. Soon they would reach the beach.

'Why are you going to the Barbary States?'

'Why not? There's nothing for me in France.'

'What about Lucie? And your parents?'

What about me? She wanted to scream.

'I have provided for them. They will not want for anything. I long for something else now, for freedom and new adventures. I may not stay in the army very long.'

He shook his head. 'Make no mistake. The army has been my whole life. It gave me more than I could ever have hoped for. Now I want to carve my own destiny. Algiers looks like a good starting point. And then, who knows, I might very well disappear into the Sahara, like Martin said.' He looked towards the cliffs again.

So he was following this obsession of his—be his own man and make his own fortune. He had always felt he wasn't good enough, despite his glorious military record, his bravery, and the honours bestowed upon him. She wanted to tell him that if he didn't learn to accept himself, his quest for freedom and wealth would be futile and would never bring him happiness.

How could she tell him about the baby now? She bent her head and put her hands on her stomach, under the cape. Her child would have no father. Well, she would have to love him twice as much.

They remained silent until the craft reached the shore. There was so much he wanted to ask her. How had she fared these past few months? Despite the brave face she put on, he felt it had not been easy for her at Norton Place. He clenched his fists. If that bastard so much as laid a finger on her, he would…He tightened his lips. He would do what? He was leaving her behind along with his old life.

For weeks, months, he had tormented himself thinking about her, trying to picture her life with Norton, reliving the burning hot moments of passion he had shared with her. Every time he had to push away the memories. Every image of her was imprinted in his mind, in his soul. He would forever carry inside him every sensation she had awakened. He had thought of her clear blue eyes, her blond hair curling like a halo around her angelic face during the harrowing hell of Waterloo when his companions were falling under enemy artillery fire and he wished for death.

Well, a new life awaited him now. First he would make sure Fouché was exiled. Then he would start all over again. She had made it plain on the frigate she didn't want to expose her husband to any punishment for his role as Fouché's agent. She was still very much Norton's wife, and would always be.

The sailors jumped into the shallow water and pushed the boat towards the beach. He let himself down into the sea and opened his arms.

'I'll carry you to the beach.'

Marie-Ange nestled into his arms and clasped her fingers behind his neck as he strode in the water towards the shore. He put her down gently on the small beach, his hands brushing against her back almost like a caress when he released her.

Looking up to the cliff top, he said thoughtfully. 'You were on these cliffs when I first saw you, weren't you? There were storm clouds and a mighty strong wind. For a few seconds, you stood in a ray of sunshine, and the sailors said you were an angel.' He turned to her. 'They were probably right,' he whispered.

Pointing to the cliff top he took her hand. 'Come, I'll see you safely to the top.'

She shook her head. 'I will be fine on my own. You should go now.'

He combed his dark hair back with his fingers and sighed.

'Very well. Thank you for your statement about Fouché, although I was hoping for more details and…' He shook his head. 'Never mind. We are sailing for France now. Martin will get off in Le Havre and ride to Paris where he will submit the document to Talleyrand and the King. And then, I hope, Fouché will have no other choice than go into exile.'

'Will the King not insist on a trial—an execution even? Fouché did commission the murder of his brother.'

'I don't think the King will demand an execution. After Napoleon's defeat, the thousands and thousands of dead and wounded, the country needs peace, not another scandal and public execution.' He gave her a tight smile. 'Knowing Fouché, he will bow to the King's command and start scheming from abroad. However this time, he has run out of allies.'

He stepped forward and put his hands on her shoulders. He looked deep into her eyes.

'*Adieu*, Marie-Ange. I wish I could…'

He bent down so quickly she didn't have time to step away. His arms encircled her waist and brought her close to him and he kissed her, softly at first, then with more hunger. She put her hands on his chest and he pulled her closer still, tilting her head back to kiss her more deeply. His fingers caressed her neck and roamed through her thick, curly hair. For a few moments, there was only heat and desire and passion between them.

Then he let go of her and stepped back.

'*Adieu*,' he said again.

Her heart felt at breaking point, yet her voice was steady when she spoke.

'I hope you find what you're seeking.'

He looked surprised, then nodded. He gestured to the two sailors to push the boat back at sea, jumped into the craft, and took his jacket off. After loosening the top of his shirt and rolling his sleeves up on his forearms, he asked the sailors for a pair of oars. She watched him row towards the frigate before climbing up the path to the cliff top. When she reached the top, the frigate was getting ready to set sail. Hugo was already on board. The anchor was raised. Huge white sails were pulled up the three masts and billowed in the wind. The ship turned to the high seas.

'*Au revoir*,' she whispered. The breeze swirled around her, taking her words away towards the horizon.

This wasn't *adieu*. It couldn't be. As tears fell on her cheeks and sobs threatened to choke her, a voice deep within her whispered that they would see each other again.

Chapter Twenty-Seven

May 1818

'Is he asleep?' The marine breeze blew Giulia's brown hair around her face.

Marie-Ange nodded. 'Fast asleep.'

She smiled, recalling how small Lucas looked, curled up in the bunk bed of the cabin. Tonight, like most evenings, she had sung lullabies and rocked him to sleep. Great-Aunt Hermine said she indulged him far too much and should leave him in the care of a nurse, to which she usually replied that Lucas was her joy, her life, and she intended to bring him up herself.

'Sophie fell asleep, too,' she added. 'She can never resist my singing. By the way, your mother wants you to come down now. She said it wasn't suitable for a young lady to stay out on deck in the evening. I suspect she wants company, she didn't look very well.'

'Mother hates sailing. It's only because she wanted to meet you before the rest of the family that she agreed to sail to Catania.'

Marie-Ange stepped back from the banister as sea spray splashed onto her face and the front of her dress. The ship was sailing fast, its white sails billowing in the evening breeze. The captain reported they would reach Valetta in the early hours of the morning.

The figure of a man standing near the prow caught her attention. He seemed to be watching her. He pulled his hat down on his face and turned away when he noticed her looking at him. She narrowed her eyes. He was small and dark-haired and wore a cheap looking grey suit and a large black hat. She had seen him before, in Catania, as she strolled the boulevard with Giulia and Agata...and come to think of it, in the park where they walked in the evening. However, Catania wasn't a big town, so it wouldn't be unusual to bump into the same people over and over again.

She turned to the sea again. 'It is a beautiful evening.'

Her eyes skimmed over the receding Sicilian coastline towards the high sea and the golden sunset that was lighting the sky and the sea with fire. 'It looks as if we are sailing straight into the sun.'

'It's the corsairs' favourite time for an attack,' an elderly gentleman remarked next to them. 'Vigils cannot see what's coming at them with the blazing sunset.'

'I thought the bombing of Algiers two years ago had put an end to the corsairs' activities,' Marie-Ange said. 'Didn't Lord Edmouxth force the Dey to surrender all hostages and sign a new peace treaty?'

The elderly man snorted. 'If you believe that, you are very foolish indeed. The 'Corso' brings too much revenue to the Barbary States for them to relinquish it so easily. Algiers, Tunis, and Tripoli merely pretended to agree with the English demands to put an end the blockade. They now choose their targets more carefully, that's all. I heard that an Italian ship was captured just over a month ago.'

He stared towards the horizon, a frown on his face, bid them good night, and limped away. As always when someone mentioned Algiers, Marie-Ange closed her eyes and conjured up an image of Hugo. Her chest tightened. She often wondered if the pain would ever ease with the passage of time. It hadn't so far.

'Well, the gentleman isn't going to spoil my evening,' Giulia said, slipping her arm under Marie-Ange's. 'I am so happy. I still cannot believe that this day next week, I will be Matteo's wife. Mrs. Giula Perini…It sounds wonderful, don't you agree?'

Marie-Ange smiled and replied it was indeed a lovely name. She had met her cousin Giulia only two weeks before in Catania but had already developed a strong affection for the small, vivacious brunette. Giulia was ecstatic at the prospect of her marriage to the only son of a wealthy Maltese merchant.

'I want the whole world to be as happy as I am,' Giulia exclaimed. 'But I know you are worried about your father. Do you think that Uncle Baldassare will join us in time for the wedding?'

'I am sure he will do everything he can to be there. Monsignor Della Vita said that his assignment in Trieste must be keeping him there longer than anticipated.'

Baldassare had been released from the Turcopilar forces and now worked as ambassador for the Order of the Knights Hospitaller. Lately he had spent some time in Trieste, in Northern Italy. It was where, incidentally, Joseph Fouché had been exiled in September, 1815.

She hadn't seen her father in well over a year. He had stayed at Beauregard after Lucas was born and his strong, quiet, presence had been a great comfort in the wonderful but difficult first few weeks of her son's life. She had fallen in love with Lucas, with his bright blue eyes and mop of dark hair; with his thoughtful gaze when he looked at something new and his beaming smile when she picked him up; she even loved the way he clenched his fists tightly and howled when he was in a fit of temper. However there had been a constant ache in her heart and she wept most days and nights for the man she loved.

Her father had held her tightly in his arms before heading back to Catania and tried to soothe her pain. 'Do not torture yourself about the past,' he had said. 'You cannot change it. Enjoy what you have now. The future will take care of itself. There is your cousin Giulia's wedding next year to look forward to. You will meet the whole dei Conti clan, and you and I will spend some time together.'

However Baldassare wasn't in Catania to welcome her when she arrived, and there had been no message from him since. Even if he had done his best to hide it, Monsignor Della Vita seemed uneasy about Baldassare's absence.

Giulia slipped her arm under hers. Marie-Ange tried to shake her worries away and turned to admire the huge, blood red sunset.

'Maybe next year I will have a beautiful boy like yours,' Giulia whispered. 'Matteo would be so proud. Men do love a son as a first born, don't they?' Giulia put her hand in front of her mouth and made a slight grimace. 'Oh, sorry...'

'There is nothing to be sorry for,' Marie-Ange replied with a tight smile. She had told Giulia and Agata about Hugo. She never lied about the identity of Lucas's father. She'd rather people think ill of her than pretend Lucas was Christopher's son. She knew Aunt Agata had been shocked at the idea of a child conceived by a man who wasn't her husband. A man she had not seen for three years, and who didn't even know he had a son. 'Mama is old-fashioned,' Giulia had said. 'She doesn't understand about love and passion. Give her time and she will come to accept the situation.'

Giuila pecked a kiss on her cheek. 'I will go downstairs now. See how Mama is and get a few hours' sleep. Good night, cousin.' She moved away from the rail and Marie-Ange rushed after her.

'Wait a minute. I'll come with you.'

Downstairs in her cabin, Marie-Ange untied her hair before lying down next to Lucas, careful not to wake him. Sophie was fast asleep in the opposite bunk. The young woman had become Marie-Ange's closest friend. There had been no question of leaving her behind at Beauregard while Marie-Ange and Lucas travelled to Giulia's wedding.

Listening to Lucas' peaceful breathing, she closed her eyes.

She woke up an hour later, startled by a riot of shouts and screams, explosions of pistols firing and the thud of a vessel bumping against the hull of the ship. She sat up, her heart thumping, fear running through her veins.

'Sophie! Wake up!' She stood and shook the woman's shoulder.

'What's happening?' Sophie opened her eyes.

'I don't know. It sounds like we're being attacked.'

'Pirates,' Sophie shouted in alarm.

As she said the words, Marie-Ange heard guttural voices outside the cabin. The door was kicked open and a dark-skinned man entered. His lips curled into a smile when he looked at the two women. He said something she didn't understand and gestured for Marie-Ange to come to him. Instead she stepped backwards towards Lucas and took him in her arms. The little boy was awake and stared at the man, his eyes wide with fright.

Another man appeared in the doorway. Tall and lean, with a short brown beard, he was dressed in black from top to toe. A sabre dangled from a thick studded belt at his side. The only spot of colour was a red scarf he wore around his hips.

'More women!' He said in broken French. 'The two in the cabin next door are valuable. Dei Conti from Malta, no less. The Dey will be pleased. They'll fetch a good ransom.'

He walked across to Sophie and shook her arm. She let out a piercing scream and cowered on her bunk bed. He let go of her, and approached Marie-Ange who was still holding Lucas tightly. He raised a hand to touch her hair but she pulled back.

'This is the woman we keep for Aicha. She'll bring a good price.' He took hold of her chin between his thumb and forefinger and raised her face towards him. 'Nice eyes. Nice mouth.' He laughed. 'The boy stays, too. Women with children are always more amenable.'

He scratched his beard and faced Marie-Ange. 'My name is Rachid. I'm in charge now. You'd better not cause me any problems.' He said a few words to his companion and they left.

'What…are they going…to do with us?' Sophie stammered.

'I'm not sure.' Marie-Ange kissed the top of her son's head. He threw his arms around her neck and whimpered.

'Shh…Sleep, darling.'

Sophie buried her head in her hands and wailed.

'Don't cry, Sophie,' Marie-Ange said, a little impatiently. She didn't want Lucas to be anymore scared than he already was. She rocked him back to sleep, singing louder this time to cover the sounds of women wailing and men shouting outside. When he was asleep, she laid him on the bed.

'They said something about the Dey so they must be taking us to Algiers as hostages.'

'Surely the French, the Italians, or the English won't stand for that! We can't be made slaves. I read that the *janissaries* used to make their slaves do housework all day.'

'I fear this Aicha they talked about might have something else in store for me than housework,' Marie-Ange remarked with a frown.

Sophie gasped. 'You mean…' She turned towards Lucas. 'What about him?'

Marie-Ange clenched her fists. 'I won't let anyone hurt him. I will do whatever it takes to keep him safe.'

The ship sailed south throughout the night. At dawn, as

the sky paled to the east and a shiny line of light appeared above the sea, the anchor was dropped. The corsair, Rachid, came back into the cabin.

'I am taking you onto my ship now. Don't talk to anyone. If you call, if you scream, he's dead.' He pointed to Lucas' throat and made a crude gesture of slitting it.

She nodded and lifted Lucas in her arms before following him out. The passengers sat in a group at the prow, guarded by a dozen pirates armed with short swords and pistols. Marie-Ange scanned their tired, tearful faces but didn't see Agata or Giulia. As valuable hostages, they were probably locked up in their cabin. Rachid gestured to Sophie to join the group and pushed Marie-Ange towards the side of the ship.

He pointed at the rope ladder that hung down into a small craft below where two men sat, waiting. Another ship was anchored a short distance away. It was small and sleek, with three short masts and red triangular sails. A coastline could be seen in the distance—with a large white town built on a hillside.

She wondered how she would get down the ladder with Lucas in her arms. As if he understood her fear, the pirate said. 'Give me the boy. I'll take him to the chebec.'

She reluctantly let go of Lucas who started crying. Rachid untied his red scarf and wrapped him up in a bundle, then slid him onto his back. He went down the ladder, fast and agile. She gripped the rope ladder after him and climbed down into the craft. As soon as she sat down, two men rowed towards their ship.

The sea was calm and smooth, the dawn sky cloudless. It was warm already. A light breeze carried exotic fragrances of spices and vegetation.

She pointed to the coast. 'Where are we?'

'Algiers,' the pirate replied. 'We'll get you to shore today.'

'Where are you taking us?'

'You will find out soon enough.'

They reached the chebec and climbed on board. The man untied Lucas and handed him to Marie-Ange, then he gave some orders and his men got ready to set sail. Soon both the chebec and the Maltese ship were on their way to Algiers.

The town was built like an amphitheatre, with the harbour at the centre and forts standing guard on the hilltop. Houses with flat roofs and gardens climbed up the hill like giant steps. White, blue, and golden minarets darted towards the sky. Narrow streets snaked up and down. Oases of colour were dotted around. The hot, spicy fragrances Marie-Ange had noticed earlier became stronger.

Algiers…As they approached the town bathed in a pink and yellow sunrise, she couldn't help feeling a glimmer of hope. What if Hugo was still there?

The chebec entered the harbour. Rachid handed her a black scarf and ordered her to cover her head. The pirates got ready to dock. They lowered the red sails and threw ropes to men waiting on the quay. The anchor was dropped and a wooden plank laid down between the ship and the quayside. The captured Maltese ship moored next to them.

Some kind of official delegation seemed to be waiting for them—about twenty soldiers dressed in red pantaloons, dark blue tunic belted at the waist with a leather girdle and a sabre dangling at the side. Rachid signalled to his men on the Maltese ship to start getting the passengers down onto the quay. Women cried, men argued, some demanded to be set free immediately. The corsairs and the guards ignored them. Marie-Ange saw her Aunt Agata, her cousin and Sophie leave the ship, huddled together. She waved to attract their attention but they didn't see her. The guards shouted orders, and the line of hostages started off at a brisk pace.

Were they heading for the Dey's palace? In the heyday

of Barbary pirates, it was the Dey who ultimately decided the hostages' fate. Those from rich families would stay at the palace pending the payment of a ransom. Poorer passengers would be sold on the slave market. Marie-Ange wondered why she had not been taken along with the other passengers. Why had Rachid singled her out?

'You come with me now. We're going down,' Rachid yanked Lucas from her arms. The little boy started crying but the corsair put his hand roughly over his mouth.

'You'll get him back at Aicha's,' he said menacingly. 'If you don't cause any trouble.'

Chapter Twenty-Eight

The following morning Marie-Ange woke to melodious Arabic chanting coming from outside.

She rubbed her eyes, sat up, and looked around the small bedroom she had been held prisoner in since the day before. The bare walls were painted white and blue. Apart from the dirty mattress she had spent the night on, there was a wooden bucket and a chipped bowl with some water in it. She got up and pushed open thick wooden shutters covering the only window. The male chanting voice hovered above Algiers' narrow alleyways and flat-roofed houses. It was barely dawn but already men dressed in white and grey robes, their heads wrapped in turbans, hurried up and down the alleyways. Women, their bodies covered in long garments, carried jugs of water or baskets on their head.

The door creaked open, and a young woman entered. Her clothing was bright and colourful—a short, red and blue tunic over blue pants and red slippers on her feet. A blue veil partly covered her jet black hair and gold charms hung from chains around her neck and ankles, making metallic noises every time she moved. She said her name was Yasmin.

'Where is my son? I want to see him.' Marie-Ange rushed to her and put her hand on her arm. 'Please.'

'We go to Aicha now,' Yasmin said.

'Is he all right? Has anyone been looking after him?'

Yasmin nodded. 'The boy had milk and he ate bread and dates. He cried a lot.'

Marie-Ange's insides churned. Her need to see him, to

touch him, was so strong she felt faint.

'Come this way.'

She led Marie-Ange down a long passage, with rooms on both sides, some hidden by curtains, other behind doors with shutters and grids like in a prison. The house was quiet this morning. It had been very different the previous night, with laughing, singing, shouting, and calling in different languages among which Marie-Ange had recognised French, Arabic, English, and Spanish. From the sounds around her, she had gathered she was in some kind of tavern, or as she had feared, a brothel.

They went down a flight of steps and crossed a small courtyard. Marie-Ange barely saw the brightly coloured flowers glistening with morning dew and strange plants covered with hundreds of prickles. Yasmin pushed open a door at the back of the courtyard. They entered a spacious room decorated with mosaics, woven rugs covering the tiled floor. Lucas was sitting on the bed, playing with wooden figurines of animals. Marie-Ange rushed to him and scooped him into her arms.

'Darling, my darling.' She pressed him to her heart, breathing his scent, his skin, his hair, kissing his cheeks and the folds of his neck. The little boy smiled and clutched his arms behind her neck.

'*Kafin!* That's enough!' The harsh voice came from a corner of the room.

Marie-Ange turned round. A woman sat immobile in a large wicker chair. She was dressed in bright colours and like Yasmin, wore bracelets and necklaces that made tinkling noises when she moved. With her deep set dark brown eyes and hooked nose, she reminded Marie-Ange of a hawk.

'Put the boy back on the bed,' she ordered.

Marie-Ange sat down, her arms tightly wrapped around Lucas.

'So you're the woman Rachid brought me. Let's have a

look at you. Stand up and take your clothes off.'

Marie-Ange tightened her grip on Lucas. 'No, I can't…'

'If you and your brat want to live, you'll do as I say,' the woman hissed. 'Otherwise, he'll end up a beggar in the streets of Algiers, and you a whore in a tavern on the docks. Understood?'

Marie-Ange nodded and swallowed the lump in her throat. She undressed down to her chemise and stockings.

'Take everything off. *Fissa!*'

Marie-Ange obediently slipped out of her chemise and rolled her stockings down. When she was naked Aicha gestured impatiently for her to come closer. She raised her hands to touch Marie-Ange's breasts.

'No!' Marie-Ange stepped back.

'Yasmin, take the boy away.'

'Sorry…I'll do what you want,' Marie-Ange muttered.

Reluctantly she stepped closer to Aicha, gritting her teeth while the woman's hand slid across her buttocks, her stomach, and her breasts, pinching and kneading her flesh. She felt like cattle at the market.

'Open your legs.'

Marie-Ange swallowed hard, feeling sick as the woman prodded between her legs. There was a smile on Aicha's face, as if she was enjoying the humiliation she was putting Marie-Ange through.

'You'll do. Put your clothes back on.'

'What's going to happen to me…to us?' Marie-Ange asked as she quickly dressed. All she wanted was to grab Lucas and run out, but Aicha's guards would certainly catch them straight away. She had seen several armed men around the place the day before. She wouldn't stand a chance against them.

'I'll auction you tonight. My clients like a fresh woman.' She fixed her small brown eyes on Marie-Ange.

'An auction?'

Aicha nodded. 'Tonight. Yasmin will get you ready. I take it you know how to pleasure a man?'

Marie-Ange blushed violently and bowed her head.

'Never mind. If you don't, you soon will.' Aicha let out a cackle. 'They're all the same really, with the same basic needs. I do cater to special requirements, but we'll see about that when you've been with us a few days.'

'What about my son?' Marie-Ange gathered Lucas up and pressed him against her.

'I'm sending him to my sister in Kouba. She looks after my whores' children.'

'I don't want him to go away, please.' She held Lucas more tightly.

'You think a brothel is a good place for a child? You want him to see his mama naked with a man? Or several?'

Marie-Ange gave a strangled cry as the reality of her situation became agonizingly clear. She collapsed on the bed and rocked Lucas against her. What was to become of them, she wondered, kissing his cheek.

Aicha stood up and said something in Arabic to Yasmin. Then she gestured to Lucas. 'Say your farewells now. If you please me, and if you please my clients, you can visit him next week on Saturday. But if you give any trouble, it will be a while before you can see him again.'

Lucas cried as the woman grabbed hold of him and sat him back onto the bed. Marie-Ange smiled through her tears. She didn't want to alarm her son any further.

'It's going to be all right, my love. I will see you soon. You'll be fine…'

'Go now.' Aicha dismissed her with a flick of her bejewelled hand.

A man started singing outside again just before nightfall. It was the same melodious, repetitive chanting she had heard that morning. Marie-Ange gazed at the darkening sky already dotted with stars. A bright crescent moon shone above the town. It was evening already. In a few moments she would be sold at an auction. A man would pay to spend the night with her. She would have to…She put her hand in front of her mouth and rushed to the bucket to be sick.

Yasmin came in and gestured to follow her. Marie-Ange wiped her mouth with the back of her hand and walked, unsteady, towards her.

'Has my little boy left for Kouba? Did you see him? Was he all right?' she asked, clinging to the young woman's arm as her voice choked with tears.

Yasmin nodded. 'Yes, he was. Don't cry. Aicha's sister is good with children. My girl is there, too. She says Salima treats the children well.'

Marie-Ange swallowed her tears and let go of Yasmin. 'You have a daughter? How old is she?'

Yasmin counted on her fingers. 'My girl is eight. She's called Baya. Come now. It is time.'

The corridor was full of women talking and laughing, some of them just young girls. They swirled around in their colourful dresses. Tonight the doors and curtains were wide open, and Marie-Ange peered inside the small bedrooms as she walked past. The women were readying themselves for the clients, clasping chains around their necks and shiny bangles on their wrists and ankles, lining their dark eyes with khôl pencil and reddening their cheeks and lips with rouge. Marie-Ange wondered what they were talking about. They sounded like exotic birds, chirping away, happy and cheerful. Yet they were prisoners here, their bodies abused night after night. How could they stand it?

She entered a hot, steamy room.

'We have a hammam,' Yasmin said, disappearing behind the scorching hot mist. She instructed Marie-Ange to undress, and then picked up her gown and undergarments before pointing to a bench where Marie-

Ange sat down. She felt dizzy and the heat didn't help.

'You lie down.' Yasmin rubbed scented oil into Marie-Ange's shoulders and back in light, long strokes. The sensation wasn't unpleasant, but it was like being prepared for a sacrifice.

'Go in the bath now.'

Yasmin handed her a large piece of cloth and gestured for her to follow to the next room. Two women were reclining in a large bathtub. Yasmin spoke to them in Arabic and argued for a couple of minutes before the women reluctantly stepped out of the tub. They glanced at Marie-Ange with hostility. One of them made a sign with her fingers. Yasmin shouted at her and put her hand in front of her face, palm out, several times.

'What did she do?'

Yasmin shook her head and muttered. 'She's a bad woman. She sends evil eye.'

Marie-Ange washed and then rubbed rose-scented ointments on her body and oil in her hair. She would do everything Aicha wanted. She would lie with a man tonight, and every night after that. Tomorrow she would start learning about the layout and the running of this place, about the habits of the guards and the other women. She would bide her time. The following week, she would be able to see Lucas. And then, she would escape. There had to be police authorities she could turn to in Algiers. Perhaps even Monsieur Deval, the French consul if he was still in post, or representatives of the French army.

She dressed in a flimsy, transparent, red dress Yasmin supplied and slipped her feet into a pair of red slippers.

'You have beautiful hair,' Yasmin said, looking admiringly at Marie-Ange's golden curls which lay thick and shiny on her shoulders and down to the middle of her back.

She took a stick of rouge and brushed some on Marie-Ange's lips with her finger, and a little on her cheeks, too.

Then she stepped back, looking pleased with her efforts.

'We go now.'

They walked down to the ground floor and across several reception rooms where women sat around on large, colourful cushions, drinking and smoking a long pipe which reminded Marie-Ange of Uxeloup Malleval's opium smoking contraption. They finally reached a room with two dozen chairs and armchairs dotted around.

'You go and stand over there, but first, you drink this.' Yasmin handed Marie-Ange a small glass of tea. She gave her a smile and a pat on the shoulder.

Marie-Ange drank the whole glass. It tasted of mint and something else—something exotic and spicy. She hoped it was drugged, so all her senses would be annihilated and she would feel no shame and no fear. She followed Yasmin's instructions and stood facing the chairs. Almost immediately she heard men's voices outside. They were here. They would watch and bid for her and then…

She closed her eyes and breathed deeply. She had to go through with it, for her son's sake. She kept her eyes shut tight as the men came in and took their places on the chairs. Then, Aicha greeted her clients.

'Gentlemen, thank you for coming,' she said. 'We start our auction now. I want the lucky bidder to have a full night's enjoyment of our new lady.' She tugged at Marie-Ange's dress. 'Open your eyes,' she ordered sharply.

The room was full of men. Some wore European clothing, some French or English uniforms. Others wore Arabic clothing. But all had their eyes fixed on her. Bottles and glasses were handed out as well as cigars and pipes. Marie-Ange felt strangely detached from the scene now, as if she was watching it from above.

As she skimmed over the audience, she recognised the small, dark-haired man who was on the Maltese ship. The man she had seen in Catania. He was still wearing his cheap grey suit and was staring at her from his seat, a smug grin on his face. She frowned. Who was he and why did he keep following her? And why was he not with the other hostages?

She swayed and several men laughed.

'What did you give her? I hope she won't fall asleep in bed!' One of them shouted.

Aicha started the bidding at three hundred dinars. Hands shot up, voices called higher prices, cigars were lit and more bottles of liquor consumed. A shrewd businesswoman, Aicha circled around Marie-Ange incessantly, lifting her dress to expose an ankle, then a thigh; patting her bottom through the transparent dress; pulling the fabric onto her shoulder to bare one breast, tease a nipple; touching her hair and toying with her curls.

The atmosphere heated up as the bidding reached one thousand dinars. The room was getting very hot. The men's faces became blurred and disappeared in a fog of tobacco smoke. It was hard to breathe. Marie-Ange blinked and shook her head, then put her hand on her throat. She felt sick.

A tall, dark-haired man dressed in a black suit came in through the back door. She must be dreaming now, she thought, as she watched him lean forward and talk to someone in the audience. Although she couldn't see his face through the thick tobacco smoke, everything about him, from the colour of his hair to the way he moved reminded her of Hugo.

'Two thousand dinars, but I want her at my house,' the man called. Dear God, it was his voice.

Her heart stopped. Gasping with shock, burning with shame, she put her hands up to hide her face. As she struggled to breathe, she felt she was falling and everything went black.

Chapter Twenty-Nine

'I'll take over. Get your hands off her. I don't want her all bruised and damaged.'

It was his voice, again. He lifted her into his arms, and instinctively she rested her head against his chest. Her cheeks scraped the metal buttons from his jacket. The dream felt so real she didn't want to wake up.

'Monsieur, I want to up your bid to two thousand-five hundred dinars,' another man urged with insistence. He had a strong Italian accent.

'Too late. The bidding is closed and I believe I won.'

'Three thousand…you can get all the whores in Algiers for that price.'

'Let me through,' he ordered.

She felt his arms hold her more tightly against him.

'I don't usually allow women out of my establishment. Make sure you bring her back by eight tomorrow morning. Any longer and it will cost you.' Aicha's shrill voice was right next to her.

Marie-Ange shook her head and sighed loudly. She didn't want Aicha in her dream. Just him.

'Yes, of course. Now move out of my way, both of you.'

She was lifted into a carriage. The door closed and she heard him give an order in Arabic. His arms were still around her. She felt his lips kiss her hair.

'Everything's fine, don't worry, my angel,' he whispered in her ear. The stubble of his cheeks prickled her skin. This was the best dream she had ever had. A smile on her lips, she drifted back to sleep.

There was water nearby, a fountain maybe or a waterfall. A light breeze rustled tree leaves and tall grasses and carried their fragrance into the night. A woman laughed close by and hummed to the soft cords of a zither. A blue moonlight bathed the large bedroom that opened onto a garden. Marie-Ange touched the white muslin curtains floating around the bed. Her throat was parched and the crystalline sound of water nearby was so enticing it was almost torture. She tried to get up but her head spun too much, and she lay down onto the bed again. She wanted to sink back into her wonderful dream but she knew she must wake up. Whoever had taken her to this house would soon be back and demand what they had paid for.

She heard footsteps. The shadow of a man stood in the doorway. Her heart started beating wildly.

Hesitantly, the man walked over to the bed and Marie-Ange recoiled, covering herself with a sheet.

'Marie-Ange, are you awake?'

It was his voice. Was she still dreaming?

'I'm not sure...' She replied with hesitation, staring wide-eyed as he approached the bed.

He sat next to her on the bed. 'You're safe now. It's over.'

She pressed her hands to her heart. 'So I am awake? It's really you?'

His face was partly in the shadows but his eyes shone in the moonlight. He smiled and leant forward to touch her hair.

'Never, in my wildest dreams would I have imagined we would meet again, here in Algiers.'

Her heart leaped into her chest. Then she remembered something he had once said, a lifetime before. 'You said you never dreamed.'

He shrugged. 'I said a lot of bloody stupid things.'

She bent her head. 'How did you know I was there? In that...place?'

'Pure luck. I happened to be at the Dey's palace tonight for a briefing when the guards came into the courtyard with a group of women. One of them reminded me so much of Sophie I had to go over and take a look. It was her indeed. She was badly shaken and barely coherent, but she managed to tell me your ship had been captured and you had been taken to some woman called Aicha.'

He paused. 'I know of Aicha and her establishment. It has a certain notoriety here in Algiers. I hope I got there in time, before…?' His eyes were full of questions.

'Just about. Where is Sophic now? What about my aunt and my cousin? They were taken, too.'

He looked surprised. 'I did not know you had relatives with you. Like I said Sophie was barely coherent.'

Marie-Ange explained how she happened to be on the Maltese ship with Agata and Giulia.

'I'll deal with them tomorrow. The Dey has a lot to answer for. He is in blatant violation of the peace treaties he signed. He obviously thinks they are not worth the paper they're written on.' He took her hand and brought it to his lips. 'You will stay here with me from now on. We'll get Sophie and your family out in the morning.'

'No. I must go back to Aicha.'

He frowned. 'Whatever for? If you have left any of your belongings there, I promise I will replace them for you.' He sounded impatient.

'No, you don't understand. If I don't go back, Aicha will…' Now that the time had come to tell him, she didn't know if she would be able to. She could hardly breathe.

'She will harm my son—our son.'

He withdrew his hand. 'What?'

She inclined her head and swallowed hard. 'He is almost two and a half years old. His name is Lucas.'

The silence between them was filled with tension.

'You are telling me I have a son,' he said at last.

She nodded.

He pulled back and narrowed his eyes. 'And you didn't think I had the right to know about him before now?'

'Well, I…'

'Did you bring him up as Norton's son?' He clenched his fists on his thighs.

'No, I did not,' she protested. 'I left Christopher long before Lucas' birth.'

He seemed to relax a little. 'Why didn't you tell me? Why didn't you write to me, for God's sake?' The intensity of his stare made her shudder.

'I was going to tell you,' she started to explain.

He stood up abruptly. His eyes were hard. 'We'll talk later. Let's go and get the boy now. I won't have my son spend another minute in that place.'

'Lucas isn't at Aicha's. She sent him to her sister in a place called Kouba.'

Hugo took a deep breath. 'I know it. It's a village about ten miles from town. We need someone who can get us inside the woman's house, someone she knows. The last thing I want is to create a commotion in the middle of the night, alert villagers or even guards.'

'Yasmin might help. She has been looking after me. Her daughter lives there too,' Marie-Ange explained.

'We will fetch her first then. Get changed while I sort things out. I think there are clothes in there.' He pointed to a wardrobe in a corner of the room and disappeared into the garden.

Marie-Ange found an ankle-length skirt and a stripy white and blue blouse which she slipped over her flimsy red dress. She wondered who the clothes belonged to. Maybe they belonged to the woman who was laughing and singing in the room across the courtyard? She tried not to think about Hugo's reaction to her news. He was angry, very angry. She hoped he didn't despise her, or worse. She couldn't bear it if he hated her. For now she must focus on getting Lucas back.

She walked across the patio in the moonlight. The night sky glittered—black velvet pricked with thousands and thousands of stars glittering like diamonds. She had never seen a night sky so beautiful. She stopped at the fountain to cup some water in her hands and drank until her throat was no longer parched. Then she washed her face. She heard men's voices. A curtain was pulled back and Hugo came out of a room followed by a young man in dark blue trousers and tunic.

'Marie-Ange, this is a friend. Sheikh Zentar. He's going to help us.'

The man bowed deeply in front of Marie-Ange. 'We will take the calash for the women,' he said.

'Thank you Zentar. I won't forget this.' Hugo nodded sternly.

His friend stepped forward and clasped his hand on his shoulder. 'This is nothing, *Ahar*. I'm glad I can help.'

A few minutes later, they were on their way to the lower town and Aicha's establishment. Hugo and Marie-Ange waited outside the brothel while Zentar entered to fetch Yasmin. The young woman's eyes opened wide with surprise when, a short while later, she stepped into the calash and saw Marie-Ange.

'We're going to Kouba to get Lucas,' Marie-Ange explained. 'Can you help us?'

'You want to get your boy now? Aicha will be angry.' Yasmin shook her head, making all the charms and medals pinned to her veil jingle. Then she sat back and added wistfully. 'She will be very angry with me, too.'

Marie-Ange realised what she was asking Yasmin to do would put her and her daughter in danger. 'Then why don't we get your little girl, too? You don't have to go back to that place ever again,' she told her.

Yasmin joined her hands together. 'I can stay with you? And Baya stays, too?'

Marie-Ange nodded and the two women linked arms.

The truth was she had no idea if Hugo would agree to help Yasmin and her daughter. She didn't even know what would happen to Lucas and her.

They stopped on the outskirts of Kouba. It was only a small place. A few streets lined with flat-roofed houses, a square with palm trees, a fountain and a washbasin. The minaret of a mosque was barely visible in the darkness. A few dogs barked close by, but there was no light in any of the houses. Yasmin leant forward and spoke to the driver of the calash in Arabic, pointing to a side street. Marie-Ange jumped out and gestured to Hugo, who rode over to her.

'Is there anything wrong?' he asked, bending down slightly towards her.

'We are getting Yasmin's little girl too,' she said, standing on her tiptoes and putting her hand on his leg.

'But…' A deep frown creased his forehead.

'Please. She's only eight. We can't leave her there. You know as well as I do what will happen to her. And Yasmin will not be able to go back to Aicha's if she helps us.'

He straightened up and nodded.

Salima's house was tucked away behind a line of palm trees at the end of the village. Zentar and Hugo slid down from their horses. The calash driver jumped down, drew his pistol and walked around the house to guard the back door.

'I'll keep watch from here,' Zentar whispered.

Hugo helped the two women step down from the carriage, and then spoke to Yasmin. 'We'll try a soft approach first. Offer the woman money, hopefully, we won't need to use anything else.'

Yasmin looked terrified as she knocked on the door. Even though she smiled to reassure her, Marie-Ange too was anxious. A woman's voice answered from behind the door. Yasmin said something in Arabic and the woman replied with a harsh voice.

'She doesn't want to open the door.' Yasmin turned to Hugo.

'Then we'll use a little persuasion.' Hugo shoved a few gold coins into Yasmin's hand. 'Tell her she can have fifty dinars if she lets you see your daughter now.'

Yasmin nodded and spoke again. The woman behind the door laughed. There was a brief silence, followed by some clinking noises as the door was unlocked. A suspicious face peered in the doorway. Yasmin showed her the coins she held in the palm of her hand and Aicha's sister opened the door wider, enough for Hugo to stick his boot in. He pushed the door open and walked into the house. Then he put his hand over the woman's mouth and spoke a few sharp words in Arabic. Her eyes opened wide, and he released her.

'Go with Yasmin and get the children,' he told Marie-Ange. 'Madame and I are waiting here.'

Yasmin took a candle that had been left burning on the table and led the way to a back room where a half-a-dozen children of all ages were sleeping on mattresses on the floor. Marie-Ange knelt down and carefully lifted the thin blankets to peer at the children's faces. Yasmin pulled a girl out and lifted her into her arms. Marie-Ange looked again, fear tightening her chest like a fist. Lucas wasn't there. She ran back to the front room.

'Where is my son?' She shouted, panicked and clutching the woman's gown.

Aicha's sister shrugged. Hugo grabbed her shoulders and spoke to her harshly in Arabic. She said a few words and pointed to the door.

'She says a man came for him earlier. He told her he was taking the boy to the harbour,' he translated, turning to Marie-Ange.

'Which man? Why did he go to the harbour?'

Hugo spoke to Aicha's sister again. She shook her head and raised her hands in the air.

'Go back to the palace with Yasmin,' he said as they walked out of the house. 'Zentar and I are riding to the harbour now.'

He jumped on his horse but instead of following Yasmin into the carriage, Marie-Ange ran to him and clung to his leg.

'Let me come with you,' she pleaded.

'No,' he answered. 'It may be dangerous and you'll be in my way. Aicha's sister said the man was armed.'

'But you won't know him. And he won't know you! Please,' she insisted.

His mouth twisted into an angry grin.

'You are right. I don't even know what my son looks like.' He extended his hand and she grabbed hold of his arm so he could hoist her up behind him. 'Hold tight,' he said before spurring the horse on the road to Algiers.

Chapter Thirty

Hugo rode hard and fast behind Zentar. Clinging onto his waist, Marie-Ange's heartbeat echoed the thumping of the horses' hooves, prayers for Lucas' safety and questions about who had taken him and why whirling in her mind.

The sky was getting lighter already by the time they entered Algiers. The dawn dew felt like mist on her skin. In the lower part of town a few men staggered around, shouting and singing as taverns closed one by one.

Hugo spurred the horse down a lane towards the harbour. Smooth as a mirror, the sea reflected the grey dawn sky.

In front of them, Zentar drew reins. 'I shall get the harbour master. If you start at this end of the jetty, I will work from the other side.'

'There are too many ships. How will we know which one he is on?' Marie-Ange cried in anguish.

'We'll find him,' Hugo said calmly as he helped her off the horse. 'From the description the woman in Kouba gave me, we are looking for a small, dark-haired man with a scruffy grey suit.' He frowned. 'Actually, it reminds me of the man who tried to buy you back from me last night.'

Marie-Ange gasped. 'He was on the Maltese ship. I thought it was odd he should be at Aicha's and not with the other hostages. I saw him in Catania several times these past few weeks.'

Hugo raised his eyebrows. 'Do you have any idea who he is?'

'No.' She shook her head.

He surveyed at the dozens of ships moored along the

quays and let out a sigh of frustration. 'Not long before daybreak. We must hurry.'

He tied the reins of his horse to a pillar. 'There should only be fishermen getting ready to go out at this time. Any larger ship must have the go ahead from the customs officer and the harbour master before setting sail.'

They ran to the end of the jetty where fishermen loaded nets and baskets onto small boats. The man's voice she had heard before started singing as the sun appeared beyond the line of the horizon.

'Who is singing?' she asked, slightly breathless, as they ran along the quay.

'The muezzin, calling the faithful to prayer,' Hugo answered. 'Can you see anything?'

There were so many boats. Lucas could be anywhere. It would take hours to search them all even with Zentar and the harbour officials' help. Her eyes caught sight of red sails being hoisted up. The chebec was still there. For some reason she couldn't fathom, she felt drawn to it.

'The pirates' ship is over there,' she said.

Hugo frowned. 'That's strange, it looks like they are about to set sail. I wonder if…'

He pulled his pistol out and darted forward. She ran behind but stumbled in her red slippers. She kicked them off and carried on barefoot. Standing on deck, one hand casually resting on the banister, was the man they were looking for.

'He's on board!' Marie-Ange pointed to the chebec.

Alerted by her shouts, Rachid appeared on deck and immediately gave an order for his pirates to start firing. Hugo hid behind a pile of coiled rope, gestured for Marie-Ange to do the same. Peering out from behind the ropes, he took a few shots at the ship. Two pirates collapsed, one fell from the netting at the top of the mast into the harbour. The chebec's sails filled with wind and it pulled away from the jetty towards the high seas.

Zentar and half a dozen guards jumped into a boat and rowed towards the pirates. Oblivious to the shots being fired at him, Hugo dived into the harbour's dirty waters. Then grabbing hold of a rope dangling at the rear of the chebec, he climbed on board. From his small boat Zentar shouted something to Rachid in Arabic. An argument between the pirates and the Italian man followed before Rachid gestured to his men to hold their fire and the ship turned back towards the harbour.

By then Hugo had reached the banister. He climbed onto the deck and disappeared into the cabin, only to come back a few moments later with a screaming bundle in his arms.

Lucas! Relief washed over Marie-Ange like a tidal wave. She almost stumbled down to the ground as the tension that had kept her moving for the past few hours melted away.

The chebec moored alongside the quay with a bump and Hugo jumped down, holding Lucas as if he was the most precious thing in the world. Marie-Ange ran to them and held her hands out for Lucas who knotted his arms around her neck.

'Thank you! Thank you!' She told Hugo breathlessly, pressing the little boy to her heart.

He didn't speak but watched them, a wistful expression in his eyes.

'That was close,' Zentar said when he joined them on the quay. 'A few minutes later, and we would have missed them.'

'You stopped them just in time. What did you say to them?' Hugo asked.

'I told them who I was and said they would never be allowed back in Algiers if they sailed away with your son.' Zentar looked at Lucas and Marie-Ange, and then laughed whole-heartedly. 'What about that, *Ahar*? You now have your lioness and a cub.'

395

Hugo didn't answer. He raised a tentative hand to Lucas' cheek, but withdrew it without touching him. His eyes hardened. 'Can you take them back to the palace for me? There are things I need to do.'

He turned round and walked in long strides towards the pirates who were deep in conversation with the harbour officials. He seized the small Italian man by the collar, lifted him off the ground and dragged him away.

'Where is he going?' Marie-Ange tried to hide her disappointment. She had hoped they would go back to the palace together and that Lucas would meet his father at last. 'He seems angry.' Fear clutched at her heart again. What if he never forgave her?

'Don't worry,' Zentar replied casually. 'I think I understand. He's angry all right, but with himself. He thinks he failed you and won't rest until he has answers about who is behind your son's abduction.'

He smiled and his warm brown eyes lit up. 'You do you realise what you have done, don't you? In one night, you have given him everything a man can ever wish for.'

Zentar hailed a carriage to take them back to his palace on the hilltop. They drove through the gate and came to a halt in the courtyard where they were immediately surrounded by a horde of servants.

'I don't understand. Does Hugo live here?' Marie-Ange asked before stepping down.

'He stays here with me when he is in Algiers. The rest of the time, he has his own estate in Bou Saada, in the south.'

'Bou Saada?'

'It's an oasis town at the gates of the Saharan Atlas. I will leave you in the care of my staff for now.' Zentar smiled. 'Don't worry about *Ahar*. He will be back soon.'

'What do you call him?'

Zentar's eyes lit up. '*Ahar*? It means mountain lion. Saintclair saved my life two years ago. He rescued me from an ambush.' His face became serious. 'There were traitors in my clan who sought to get me killed. Saintclair stood between them and me. He is the bravest man I have ever known. One of the proudest, too.'

The sea breeze freshened and shadows lengthened as the evening set in. On the patio Yasmin, Lucas, and Baya played at chasing ants with sticks. Footsteps echoed onto the tiled floor and Marie-Ange raised her eyes. Hugo leant against the white wall, arms crossed on his chest, casting a huge shadow across the ground. He looked at her and the children with an expression she couldn't fathom.

'I need to talk to you,' he said at last. 'I know who is behind the events of the past two days.'

He unfolded his arms and walked to Lucas. Kneeling down beside him, he searched in his pocket and took out a large blue marble. The little boy's face lit up, and he grabbed hold of the bauble with a squeal of delight. Hugo smiled and ruffled his son's dark hair. Marie-Ange felt her throat tighten. Now that they were side by side, the resemblance between father and son was striking. They had the same bright blue eyes, the same dark hair, the same stubborn line around the mouth. And the same devastating smile.

He looked up. Marie-Ange stood like a figure from a dream, immobile and basking in the last sunrays of the day. Her hair was golden, her skin glowed and a pensive smile lingered on her lips. He swallowed hard. She was no dream. She and the boy were real.

'Come with me,' he said.

They walked through the garden, brushing past brightly coloured bushes and flowers.

'What do you know of your husband's movements?' Hugo stopped near the thick, scaly trunk of a palm tree.

She looked at him. 'Christopher? Do you think he's

397

behind all this?'

'I know he is. The Italian man told me. His name is Alphonso Vittori, by the way. He's a petty crook, although he calls himself an agent. He was hired by Norton to stalk you in Catania and abduct you. He arranged for Rachid and his corsairs to capture the ship. The plan was to keep you and Lucas captive until…' He breathed in and squared his jaw, '…you were malleable, as the bastard put it. He was supposed to take you and the boy to Malta where Norton would be waiting. However, Vittori and Rachid's greed got the better of them. They decided to take all the passengers to Algiers as hostages and sell you to Aicha for a hefty price. Vittori would then buy you back at the auction—supposedly for one night—before sailing to Malta with you.'

He sighed. 'That's why he panicked when I turned up at the brothel and outbid him. When he failed to buy you back from me, he went to get Lucas. He was going to feed Norton some lie about you getting killed during the capture of the ship.' He paused again. 'I didn't think I would ever say this but I'm actually thankful to that weasel. If he had followed Norton's instructions, God knows where you'd both be by now.'

Marie-Ange closed her eyes briefly. 'I haven't heard from Christopher since I left him, two and a half years ago. He threatened to come after me and my child when I least expected it. It looks like he carried out his threat.'

'Do you know where he has been the past two years?'

She shook her head.

'Robert wrote he was dismissed from the Royal Navy and travelled a lot.' She looked up to Hugo. 'So he is in Malta? Where exactly?'

'Vittori claims he has no idea where he is hiding, but he said something about a family wedding…and your father.'

Her eyes opened wide in shock.

'My father wasn't in Catania to meet me, as planned.

He did not even send a note to explain his absence to his superior at the Order. They thought he had been delayed in Trieste.'

'Trieste?' Hugo frowned. 'That's where Fouché lives now, among a court of faithful agents who have vowed to help him return to France. Do you think Norton is in Trieste, too?'

'I don't know, Hugo, but I must find my father. I am worried about him.'

'We will. We are leaving for Malta tomorrow. I secured the ransom for your relatives and for Sophie. They will be free in the morning. I also met with my superiors and requested some leave pending my resignation.'

She put her hand on his forearm. 'You are resigning from the army. Why?'

'It's no big deal. I have been meaning to leave for a long time.' He sighed. 'We'd better go back for now. Zentar has prepared a feast in your honour.'

There was so much more he wanted to say but he couldn't find the words. His behaviour had been despicable. He had abandoned her and their child to seek fortune in a far away land. How could she not hate him? Hell, if she didn't, he hated himself enough for the two of them.

She had to talk to him while they were alone. She gathered the courage to put a hand on his arm. 'No, wait! I want to explain why I didn't tell you about Lucas.'

He squared his jaw and narrowed his eyes. 'Go on.'

She dropped her hand by her side. 'I should have told you when you came to Wellcombe Bay. I wanted to tell you, but you were leaving for Algiers. You said you wanted freedom and adventure. I loved you too much to bind you to me when you had made it very clear you did not love me.'

She took a deep breath. 'You had a right to know.

399

Please forgive me.' Her voice broke and she turned away, unable to look at him.

'Forgive you?' He took hold of her arms to pull her close and glared at her with those intense blue eyes.

She held her breath.

'I am the one who should beg forgiveness,' he said, his voice harsh. 'I am the one who was too damned stubborn and proud to speak out that day, when I finally understood why I hadn't been able to forget you—and God knows I tried! Why the very thought of you drove me insane. Why I wanted you, still so much, even though you had chosen to return to your husband.'

He bent his head, lowered his voice. 'When you refused to implicate Norton in your statement, when you protected him, I figured he still mattered to you, so I did not say anything.'

'It wasn't Christopher I was protecting,' she protested. 'It was Robert. He had just started at the Naval Academy, and I did not want him mixed up in his brother's disgrace.'

He took a long, deep breath.

'And so I am the biggest fool that ever lived,' he whispered. He looked at her again, his eyes warm and soft. 'What I wanted to tell you that day, what I should have told you was that…' He took a deep breath. 'I love you.'

It was like the sun shining into her heart, lighting her from inside. She stood on her tiptoes, held her hand to his cheek. He took hold of her fingers and kissed them lightly. They remained silent as the last rays of the sunset died down and the blue hour engulfed the gardens, turning them into a dreamland of transparent light and delicate shadows. He bent down to kiss her, brushing her lips softly until they parted. Wrapping his arms around her waist, he pulled her against him until it felt like they were melting into each other. He cupped her face and stared into her eyes.

'Will you live with me in Bou Saada when we return from Malta?'

She smiled dreamily. 'Oh yes, I will live anywhere as long as I am with you.'

He folded her into his arms again and buried his face in her hair.

'I came too close to losing you and my son, so soon after finding you. I am not letting either of you out of my sight, ever again. That's a promise.'

He was holding her so tight she could hardly breathe, but it was the most exhilarating feeling in the world. She lifted her face towards his. There were shadows under his eyes. His cheeks were covered with rough, dark stubble. She ran her fingers along the line of his shoulders and clasped them tightly behind his neck, pressing herself against him. With a groan, he bent down and kissed her hard.

'I have waited almost three years for you. I want to take you to bed. Now,' he whispered breathlessly against her mouth before his lips trailed along her throat. Her body responded to his caress, her skin tingled all over, and a warm sensation spread through her. She wanted him too, but she pulled away.

'Later…first let me introduce you to your son.'

The Maltese ship left Algiers shortly after dawn. After Hugo complained to the French consul, Hussein Dey took the wise decision to free all the hostages. Marie-Ange watched the town disappear in the morning mist, floating above the sea with a mixture of elation and apprehension.

Hugo came up behind her. His arms encircled her waist. 'We'll be in Valletta tomorrow afternoon,' he said. 'I will have to speak to the English authorities about Norton as soon as we get there.'

She reclined against his chest with a sigh of contentment. She should be exhausted. They'd had very little sleep these past forty-eight hours, yet she had never felt so alive. Hugo bent down, lifted her curls, and kissed her neck. She blushed as his caress brought back the endless, burning heat of the previous night.

The banquet Zentar organised in her honour had been magnificent. Sword fighters, fire eaters, dancers, and musicians transformed the evening into a magical feast. Lucas had fallen asleep on her knees, and when she left the party to put him to bed, Hugo followed. Silently, he captured her hand and led her away. Once in the seclusion of his room, he feverishly slipped her blouse off her shoulders to cup her breasts in his hands, caressing her nipples with his thumbs until she moaned. He pulled her skirt up and pinned her against the wall, lifting her so she could wrap her legs around him. He had hastily untied his breeches, gripped her hips, and driven deep into her, whispering wild promises, swearing heated oaths. He had nipped at her throat, licked and kissed her breasts as the relentless force of his thrusts slammed her back against the wall again and again. Together they had shuddered and cried out as they finally reached the peak of their passion.

Later Hugo carried her to the bed, discarded his clothes, and they clung to each other and made love again, burning with the same haste, the same fever. He had taken her breath away with his caresses, stifled her cries under his kisses, and given her everything he had to give.

When it was over, he had buried his head in her neck and held her tight against him.

'I don't want to fall asleep. I am too afraid to wake up and find that none of this is real, that you were never here and my son doesn't exist,' he whispered. 'And that I will be going to Bou Saada on my own.'

'This is real,' she had said softly, wrapped in his arms, 'and it is forever.'

She asked him about Bou Saada and he talked about his small estate, his plantations of fig, olive and palm trees. He spoke of his house with its enclosed garden and fountains.

'It will be our heaven, my angel, I promise.'

If Algiers looked like giant white steps climbing up a hill, Valletta was a magic city built out of gold. Basking in the afternoon sunshine, houses, buildings, and churches glowed with warm, honey shades.

'It's beautiful!' Marie-Ange exclaimed.

'Isn't it?' Aunt Agata nodded, standing next to her. 'You will like the *dei Conti palazzo*. It's in the centre of town, on *Strada San Giorgio*.'

She turned towards Hugo who was talking with the captain of the ship and gave him an appraising glance.

'Colonel Saintclair looks like a good, strong, reliable man, even if I still have some reservations about your rather…unconventional situation.' She put her hand onto Marie-Ange's. 'It is nothing short of a miracle you found him in Algiers, dear. I dread to think what fate awaited you in that place. As for Giulia and me, and your friend Sophie, we might have remained captives for weeks, waiting for our ransom to be paid.' With a smile she added, 'Look at Lucas. It's like he has known his father all his life.'

Sophie had just walked out of the cabin and handed Hugo his son. Today he didn't hold him like a fragile ornament, but instead threw him into the air, making the little boy squeal with excitement. Marie-Ange walked across the deck, and together they watched as the ship sailed into Valetta's great harbour.

'I need to speak to the English officers in charge of policing the island,' Hugo said when they docked. 'I don't know how long I will be.' He bent down to kiss her and ruffled Lucas' hair. 'I'll see you later.'

Marie-Ange watched him speak with a customs officer who pointed to a fort near the entrance of the harbour. He then disappeared among the horde of passengers, sailors, luggage carriers, fishermen and street merchants crowding the quays. Two English soldiers came on board to take Vittori away. On the quay a young man waved excitedly in their direction.

'Matteo!' Giulia called and waved back. 'Quick, let's go down.' She gathered her skirts and rushed to throw herself in her fiancé's arms.

Marie-Ange was disappointed to see her father wasn't there. She hoped Baldassare was still in Trieste, and he would make it on time for Giulia's wedding. She couldn't help the feeling of anxiety gnawing at her, all the more now that she suspected Christopher had something to do with her father's absence.

Two carriages took Marie-Ange and her party to the palazzo. From the street it looked just like a prison with high, square towers and thick walls pierced with small barred windows. Marie-Ange, however, forgot about the forbidding exterior once they drove through the gates. Set in lush, colourful gardens, it was a vast, honey coloured stone building, with archways and wrought iron balconies.

They were greeted on the front steps by Agata's husband—her Uncle Paolo—and her father's brother, Alessandro. Tall and wiry, with clear blue eyes and a crown of grey hair, he was very much like Baldassare.

'I must speak to you, Uncle Alessandro, on a very urgent matter,' she said as he welcomed her into the palazzo.

Alessandro showed her into his study where she immediately set out to explain her fears about Christopher, the danger he posed to her and her son, and her uneasiness regarding Baldassare's prolonged silence. She was just finishing when an English officer was shown into the study. The officer looked hot and uncomfortable in a thick red jacket, black breeches, and high riding boots. Beads of sweat rolled down his face when he took his hat off.

'Major Harris,' he announced, clicking his heels together. 'I am here to take a statement about Commandant Christopher Norton.'

Marie-Ange saw both her uncles exchange irritated

glances. They invited the Major to sit down.

'I understand your husband is some kind of agent, is that right?'

Marie-Ange nodded. 'He used to be. Didn't Colonel Saintclair explain the circumstances?'

'I did indeed listen to the French Colonel's somewhat extravagant allegations, but before we do anything we need to ascertain more facts.'

'Why, Major?' There was impatience in Alessandro's voice. 'We need to find this man, this Norton. You have his accomplice in custody, I believe.'

'Vittori, yes, but…'

'So what are you waiting for before searching the island?' Alessandro's voice was icy now.

'You have to understand that my resources are limited. I cannot spare more than a dozen men at present.'

Alessandro slammed the palm of his hand on the desk. 'I'll round up men from my shipyard to organise the search.'

'Oh no, I cannot let you do that,' the Major objected. 'I can't have gangs roaming the island. It might be seen as some kind of uprising and cause a disturbance.'

'So what do you suggest, Major?'

The English officer looked at Marie-Ange. He hesitated and his cheeks became a little red. 'Well, I think the best course of action is for you to show your husband you are here in Valetta and let him take the initiative. He is bound to make a mistake. Then we shall catch him.'

Marie-Ange bolted upright in her seat. 'You mean to use me as bait.'

'This is a disgrace!' Alessandro and Paolo exclaimed at once.

Major Harris raised his hands to appease them.

'It is the best idea given our lack of resources.'

'Has this man, Vittori, not said anything about Norton's whereabouts?'

The Major frowned. 'Unfortunately he was the victim of an...accident and is unable to help us.'

'What kind of accident?' Alessandro asked, raising his eyebrows.

The door of the study opened softly.

The Major blushed again. 'He fell down and knocked his head.'

'You mean your men beat him up and threw him down the stairs,' Hugo said, walking into the study. 'If Vittori doesn't die of his head injuries, he will be useless for days.'

'You didn't say he had vital information,' the Major snapped back.

'I didn't know the English knocked their informers unconscious before asking questions,' Hugo retorted, coming to stand behind Marie-Ange's armchair.

'I don't care much for your tone of voice, Colonel,' the Major replied haughtily. 'I remind you that you are here on English soil.'

Alessandro stood up so abruptly his chair fell back in a crashing noise. 'No, Major,' he interrupted. 'You are here on Maltese soil. The English may have appropriated it but this is still our island.'

'This is getting us nowhere, Uncle.' Marie-Ange sighed, rubbing her forehead to soothe away a throbbing headache. She turned to the British officer.

'I will do as you suggest, Major. It doesn't look as if we have much choice, anyway. Presumably, you will assign a few men to my protection when I am out of the palace?'

Hugo placed his hand on her shoulder. 'What is this about?'

She turned her head up towards him. 'I will explain later, Hugo.'

'I will send two of my best men at precisely four o'clock. Madame, you are doing the right thing.' The major got up and put his hat on.

He nodded to Alessandro and Paolo, and as an afterthought reluctantly bowed to Hugo before leaving the study.

'You are very brave, Marie-Ange,' Alessandro said. 'Your father will be proud of you.'

Hugo stood before Marie-Ange and pulled her up gently.

'Are you going to explain what you intend to do? I hope this isn't what I think it is.'

'I am going to take a walk into town,' she said with mock insouciance. 'You are welcome to accompany me.'

Chapter Thirty-One

'This is madness, Marie-Ange. You make an ideal target standing here on the piazza.' Hugo sighed impatiently. He took her elbow and led her under the shade of one of the palm trees that lined the promenade.

'I am not here to hide behind a tree,' she replied, lifting her chin up. 'I do not want to live the rest of my days looking over my shoulder, waiting for Christopher to strike.'

She scanned the crowd of passers-by taking a leisurely stroll across the square, the open top carriages speeding past, and the busy stalls where women sold fried tomato pasties or tumblers of lemonade on the corner of the street.

'I wonder what he is waiting for. All this walking around isn't achieving anything except to show him you're here too, and that I'm closely guarded by two British soldiers.'

She indicated the men in uniform who had trailed after them all morning, as they had for the past five days.

'That's assuming he is watching, of course. Major Harris' plan doesn't seem to be working.'

'Major Harris is an imbecile,' Hugo retorted. 'If only I could take a few men out with me and organise my own search.'

She put her hand on his forearm in a soothing gesture and stood on her tiptoes to kiss his lips. 'I know he forbade you to interfere,' she said. 'What a pity Vittori couldn't give any more details.'

The Italian agent employed by Christopher had died from his injuries the day before. During his prolonged agony, he had mumbled repeatedly about an abandoned lighthouse but Major Harris deemed the information too vague to be acted upon.

'Do you know how many lighthouses there are on Malta?' he complained. 'Then there's Gozzo and Comino, and the smaller islands. I can't waste any of my men's time on such unreliable information.'

'We'd better get back. Giulia's wedding parade starts shortly and I have to get ready.'

'I don't want you to go.' Hugo frowned. 'I would be happier if at least I could walk alongside you. I don't like this custom of keeping men and women apart during the procession. It makes me nervous to leave you surrounded only with women and children.'

She smiled reassuringly. 'There will be a big crowd there, and you and the men will only be a few paces behind. I can't imagine that Christopher would risk being caught up in a wedding party.'

Hugo was being overprotective, she thought as she watched him frown again. If he had his way, she would be locked up in the palace all day. She knew he was frustrated to be confined to the role of mere bodyguard. And although he hadn't said anything, she could see he was hurt by her relatives' reluctance to accept him. Alessandro and Paolo might be grateful he had brought Agata and Guilia back safely to Malta, but their rigid social conventions prevented them from welcoming him whole-heartedly within the family. Hugo had been given a room in a faraway corner of the palace. The only time he was allowed to spend alone with Marie-Ange was during their walks around Valetta, and even then they were escorted by Major Harris' men.

'I have to attend Giulia's *il-gilwa*,' Marie-Ange insisted, opening her white sunshade and rolling the carved ebony handle between her fingers. 'It is the tradition to wish the bride and groom good luck.'

The only concession she had made was to leave Lucas with Sophie at the palace. She wouldn't take any risks when it came to his safety.

When they returned, they found the whole dei Conti residence in effervescence. Servants were already laying the banquet for the evening wedding reception and arranging fresh flowers on the terraces and around the gardens. A constant stream of traders delivered fresh produce to the kitchens, causing a traffic jam of carriages and carts on the drive.

'I wish you would reconsider,' he said again, caressing her cheek with his finger. 'I wish there was more I could do…I'm no use to anybody here, even to you.'

He bent down towards her and kissed the corner of her mouth. 'And I wish we could be alone.'

Her cheeks grew hot as his finger trailed slowly down her neck. She too yearned for time alone with him.

'Soon, we will go to your house in Bou Saada,' she whispered. There at last, they would be free to love each other.

He wrapped his arms around her waist and pulled her against him before kissing her hard on her mouth. 'Be vigilant this afternoon,' he said when he released her.

She nodded and climbed the stairs to her room.

On the first floor excitement among members of the bride's party had reached fever pitch. Housemaids ran along the corridors fetching ribbons, hot irons, gloves and stoles, glasses of water laced with lemon juice and honey, handkerchiefs sprinkled with essence of lavender to soothe frayed nerves…

One of Giulia's maids rushed over to Marie-Ange.

'Madame, the lace mantilla you ordered came while you were out. I put it in your room. And Master Lucas is asleep in the nursery.' She curtsied and ran back along the corridor.

Marie-Ange frowned as she walked to the nursery to

give Lucas a kiss. She hadn't ordered anything. No doubt her Aunt Agata had taken care of it for her. She tiptoed to Lucas's cot but he was fast asleep. He didn't even stir when she caressed his hair and kissed his cheek.

Back in her room, a small parcel awaited her on the bed's red silk counterpane. She opened the wrapping and carefully pulled out an intricate white and black lace mantilla.

'Beautiful,' she whispered, unfolding the delicate fabric. A piece of paper fell on the rug. She picked it up absent-mindedly and put it on the bedside table. The bill, she thought. She would give it to her aunt later.

She undressed to her corset and chemise and splashed some cold, rose-scented water on her face and arms. The light blue dress she was to wear for the wedding was laid out on a stand. There was a knock on the door and Sophie came in.

'That veil is exquisite,' she remarked, pointing to the lace mantilla.

'A present from Aunt Agata. Can you fasten the dress for me?'

Sophie helped her dress and arranged the veil on her hair.

'Will you look after Lucas this afternoon?' Marie-Ange asked, pulling a pair of white lace gloves on. 'I will spend time with him after the ceremony.'

Sophie nodded and leant out of the window. 'The wedding guests are outside already. Giulia is coming out now. She is so pretty! She and Matteo are so much in love. I do wish them luck.'

She smiled wistfully and a shadow drifted over her face. Uxeloup's shadow. Neither women ever spoke of him, but they hadn't forgotten the relentless obsession which precipitated his death and which had almost killed Marie-Ange.

Marie-Ange walked to Sophie and squeezed her hand.

'I'd better go, or I will be late.'

Outside, the bride and groom waited under the red and white wedding canopy which would be carried by four men to the church. The dei Conti women, relatives and female friends lined up behind them. They were followed by the men and by musicians who launched into a solemn march as the procession started.

Marie-Ange smiled at Giulia, radiant in an ivory coloured dress covered with tiny pearls. Glancing over her shoulder, she saw Hugo at the back of the procession. He stood out, tall and broad-shouldered in a formal black suit and as always, the sight of him made her heart beat faster. She longed for the day when they would be in Bou Saada, living as man and wife, even though they could never be married as long as Christopher was alive. A dense crowd lined the streets, clapping, cheering, and throwing flowers as the procession walked past.

As they approached the church, a movement in the crowd caught her attention. Several men seemed to be pushing their way from a side street towards her. Suddenly fireworks exploded all around the procession. The noise was so deafening people dispersed in a panic, screaming and running in all directions, pushing and shoving in a desperate bid to move away and avoid getting burnt. Women fell down and were stamped upon. Marie-Ange lost sight of Giuilia and Matteo as she was enveloped by acrid smoke which prickled her eyes and made her cough and gasp for breath. She felt a sharp tug at her sleeve. A small woman with a harsh, deeply lined face framed with black hair was staring at her.

'Please help me,' she said, yanking her arm towards a side alley. 'My child is hurt.'

The woman's fingers gripped Marie-Ange's arm like claws. Marie-Ange looked around for any sign of Hugo, her uncle, or any other member of the dei Conti household but all she could see were shadows running in the smoke.

'Come, please.' The woman walked fast, pulling Marie-Ange into a side street. Sounds of a horse coming at speed from behind made her glance over her shoulder. A rider charged in her direction, his head covered with an old-fashioned black tricorne hat and the lower half of his face hidden under a dark scarf. Before she could move out of his way, he bent down towards her, extended his arm, and scooped her up, flinging her across the horse like a sack of grain. Her mantilla flew behind, got caught in a wrought iron gate. It ripped and fell off on the cobblestones. She screamed with terror but her assailant pinned her down. His hand pressed heavily on her back as he manoeuvred his way out of the town's narrow alleys, hardly breaking his speed. Her head bounced against the horse's side as it pounded the cobbled streets, and then started down the coastal road.

She bit her lip and tasted blood. '*Runaway mara, runaway wife,*' the man said loudly every time they rode past people. Stifled against the horse's coat, her cries were too weak to be heard. Nobody would have helped her anyway. If she was a fugitive wife, she deserved whatever punishment her husband chose to give her.

At last, they stopped.

'Down.' The rider lifted her up by the waist and pushed her off the horse. She let out a cry of pain as she fell back onto the hard, rocky ground. Scrambling onto her feet, she blinked against the brightness of the sun and put her hand in front of her eyes. A lighthouse stood in front of her, at the end of a promontory surrounded on three sides by the turquoise sea. White frothy waves crashed on the rocks below with a thunderous noise.

'Who are you? Where are we?'

The man shrugged and pointed to the lighthouse. He gave the horse a kick, turned round and rode off.

She got up and looked at the lighthouse. Perhaps this was where her father was being held. Hope flared, but was replaced immediately by a dark fear. She was alone. The place seemed deserted, just seagulls circling over the waves, calling their mournful cry.

'I told you I would come for you.' A voice spoke behind her.

She turned around and narrowed her eyes against the sun. Christopher had his arms crossed on his chest, legs wide apart, his face twisted in a scowl. His pale blond hair shone in the sunlight.

'Did you enjoy the fireworks?' he asked. 'I thought I'd get it right this time, not like in Lyon. Remember? You reported everything I told you to your Capitaine Saintclair—or Colonel, whatever his title is now—didn't you? And together you got me dismissed and Fouché exiled.'

He took a few steps forward. Marie-Ange retreated until her back scraped against the wooden door of the lighthouse.

'There is nowhere for you to go, my darling wife.' He opened his arms. 'It's just you and me.'

She swallowed the lump in her throat. 'Where is my father?'

Christopher shook his head in derision and pointed to the lighthouse. 'In here. Dead. Or as good as, last time I looked.'

She put her hand in front of her mouth to stifle a sob.

'Oh, and I should mention that once I have disposed of you, I will take care of your brat and his father.' He threw his head back and laughed. He looked like a madman.

'Why are you doing this, Christopher? What do you want?' Her voice was shaking.

He raised his eyebrows. 'Me? I want to make you pay for ruining my life. Everything was going just fine for me until you and Saintclair turned up in Paris.'

'That's not true! I only wanted you to remember your past. I loved you so much. But you weren't the same man anymore. Everybody who knew you thought so, too. Robert, the servants at Norton Place...'

His face hardened and he narrowed his eyes.

'You turned them all against me. You dragged the Norton name in the muck and made me a laughing stock when you left. And then I was dismissed from the Royal Navy because of your statement. Even though it was anonymous, it didn't take long for my superiors at the Admiralty to work out I was the agent in question. As they were anxious to establish a good relationship with the new Bourbon regime, I was shown the door.'

While he talked, she pushed the handle of the door down behind her back and frantically thought about what to do next. Could she hide in the lighthouse or should she run down the track? There must be a village nearby, people who could help.

'Where do you live these days? In Trieste? Is that where you met Vittori?' she asked, in a bid to keep him talking.

He looked annoyed. 'I should have known the man was a waste of time. Yes, I am based in Trieste. It's where I bumped into your father a few months ago. He didn't know me, of course, so I was able to spy on him. That's how I learnt you were travelling to Malta for the wedding. It was the chance I had been waiting for. At last, I would have you and your child at my mercy.' He laughed. 'And now, Saintclair is here, too. It has turned out better than I could ever have imagined.'

He walked towards her slowly, a grin twisting his thin lips, clearly enjoying watching the fear in her eyes. He raised his hand to take hold of her, but she twisted her body away and he caught the sleeve of her blue dress instead. He gripped it so tightly it ripped, sending her tumbling down onto the ground. Her head slammed against sharp rocks.

'You won't escape, you know.' She heard him say and

everything went black.

When she opened her eyes, her head was throbbing with pain. Christopher was bending over her, so close she saw the cold glint of steel in his grey eyes. She tried to wriggle away, but he stamped on her dress to keep her still. Behind him a door creaked open, footsteps crushed the loose stones of the path. Someone had walked out of the lighthouse. Someone she struggled to recognise.

Baldassare. His face was battered and gaunt, his eyes swollen and almost shut, his clothes torn and caked in blood and dirt.

'Father!' She cried in anguish.

Christopher straightened up and turned round sharply. 'What? You're still alive? I thought you'd be maggot food by now.'

'You are not going to hurt my daughter, Norton,' Baldassare said.

'Do you think you can stop me? Look at you. You can hardly stand,' Christopher sneered.

Baldassare shook his head. 'Not me,' he answered. 'My brother. He is here to take care of us.'

Marie-Ange wondered why her father was talking about Alessandro. She wanted to go to him, but she couldn't move because she was pinned to the ground by Christopher's boot stamping on her dress.

'I don't see anybody around. Do you?' Christopher pulled a knife out of his belt and walked towards Baldassare. 'It's time I finished with you.'

'No! Please!' Free at last, Marie-Ange scrambled to her feet.

And then she saw him. Standing against the sunlight, he was cloaked in black. A wide-rimmed hat covered his head. The figure moved silently towards them. There was something odd about him, she thought, something that whispered to her he wasn't like any other man. Yet she felt no fear as he approached.

'Here you are, brother,' Baldassare said. A smile appeared on his dry, cracked lips. 'It has been a long time.' His eyes rolled back and he slid to the ground, still smiling. Marie-Ange wept and ran to his side.

'Who the hell are you? How did you get here?' Christopher asked, his voice hoarse, as the man walked towards him. He winced and put his hand to his chest.

The man carried on without answering. Christopher's face was now distorted in a grimace of pain. He stepped back, fingers clutching his chest as if he wanted to rip it open. Still the man walked, pushing him closer and closer to the edge of the cliff.

'Who are you?' Christopher repeated weakly. He staggered, dangerously close to the precipice and the raging sea below.

The man lifted his hand and without ever touching him, pushed him over the edge.

Gasping in shock, Marie-Ange saw Christopher fall. She ran to the spot where he disappeared and peered over the cliff. His body lay broken on the sharp rocks below, washed by the surf. Looking up she stared into the man's eyes.

'You!' She breathed out. So they had been right all along! Baldassare, her aunt, Uxeloup, and Edmond Malleval.

'Our paths have never crossed before, Marie-Ange. I am glad to meet you at last,' the man said.

'How is it possible? How can you be…'

He put his finger on her lips and smiled. 'Some things are not meant to be spoken of.' Turning to Baldassare's body lying on the ground, he added, 'Your father was a good man. He served us well. He is at peace now.'

He smiled again. The same kind, thoughtful smile he had on the portrait at Beauregard.

'Till we meet again.' He nodded, touched the rim of his hat in a brief farewell and walked away into the blazing sun. Only when he was gone did she understand what she had found so odd about him. He hadn't cast any shadow on the ground.

Kneeling down next to her father, she put his head gently into her lap. His face was battered and bruised. He must have suffered so much, beaten and held captive without food or drink for days. Her fingers stroked his hair as if to soothe away his pain. It was too late. A feeling of desolation invaded her as tears fell down her cheeks. Her father was dead. She lost track of how long she remained sitting there, her face and neck burning under the fierce sunshine, her head throbbing with pain where it had hit the rocks before.

The thunder of a horse's gallop made her look up. Hugo drew reins and jumped down from his black charger in a cloud of dust before the horse had even stopped.

'Marie-Ange!' He ran to her.

She stood up and was immediately enfolded into his arms.

'You're hurt. You have a nasty gash on your forehead.'

He kissed her hair, her face. His hands were all over her arms, her shoulders, her back. 'Thank Heavens I found you.'

He looked down at Baldassare's body. 'Your father... What happened?'

'I think he suffered too much. His heart...'

He pressed her closer to him. 'Where is that bastard Norton?'

She pointed her chin towards the cliff. 'He fell. Or rather he was pushed.'

'You pushed him?' Hugo stared into her eyes.

'Not me. There was a man. Didn't you see him on the road?'

He shook his head. 'I didn't see anybody. Was he one of Norton's henchmen?'

'No. It was...' Should she tell him? Would he even

believe her?

'It was my mother's godfather,' she said in one breath, gazing into his eyes. 'Hugo, it was Count Saint Germain.'

He shook his head and smiled. 'You just imagined him, Marie-Ange. You did have a knock to the head,' he said, stroking her forehead gently with his finger. 'And you're burning hot. You must have heatstroke.' He pulled her into his arms again and cradled her tightly. 'Never mind how it happened as long as Norton's dead. Don't worry. I will speak to Major Harris when he gets here.'

Did he think she had pushed Christopher? 'Hugo, it wasn't me,' she insisted. 'It was Saint Germain.'

'Don't worry,' he said again. 'I'll sort things out.'

'How did you know I was here?' she asked.

'I found your mantilla in the street after the crowd dispersed,' he explained. 'I took it back to the palace and Sophie said it was a present from your aunt, but Agata didn't know anything about it. So I searched your room and found the note. You didn't read it, did you?'

'Which note?' She cast her thoughts back to earlier in the afternoon. There had been a piece of paper in the parcel. 'I thought it was the bill.'

'It was a note from Norton. Telling you to enjoy the day before…'

'Before?'

Hugo sighed. 'Before it turned into a mass funeral. Your aunt declared that the mantilla was the work of lace makers in Marsaxlokk. When Paolo said that there was a lighthouse on the promontory past the village, I took a chance and set off.'

He held her tight against him. 'And I found you.'

A dozen riders and an open carriage appeared on the road. Major Harris and his men.

'About time,' Hugo muttered as the English soldiers dismounted and the carriage stopped.

'Well, well…What have we got here?' They heard

Major Harris exclaim in a loud voice.

Hugo squeezed Marie-Ange's hand. 'Let me do the talking.'

They were married the following week. It was a small, private affair.

As she stood in Our Lady of Victory Church, Marie-Ange felt her heart was ready to burst. Why did she want to cry when she felt so happy, she wondered, biting her lower lip to keep it from trembling. Throughout the short service, Hugo listened solemnly and intently to the priest. He took her hand, entwined her fingers with his and fixed his gaze on her. All she wanted was lose herself in his blue eyes. She was slightly breathless when she said her wedding vows, but Hugo's voice was clear and strong in the near empty church.

Afterwards, the hint of a smile appeared at the corner of his mouth as he bent down slowly to kiss her. He lifted her hand and pressed it to his heart. 'Forever,' he murmured before his lips brushed hers.

They left in the evening for Algiers, their first stop on the way to Bou Saada. Sophie had decided to travel with them.

'I want to see this city of happiness for myself,' she declared.

Night was falling when the ship sailed out of Valetta's Great Harbour. They stood on deck, Lucas snug in Hugo's arms, Marie-Ange leaning against his side.

'Who's that waving at us?' Hugo asked, pointing to the figure of a man who was alone at the end of the jetty.

Marie-Ange peered into the thickening shadows at the silhouette of man cloaked in black. She saw him touch his wide-rimmed hat and bow in their direction.

'It's him,' she answered with a smile. 'He is wishing us good luck.'

Hugo turned to her sharply. 'Who? You mean...'

When he turned again, there was nobody there.

Marie Laval

For more information about **Marie Laval**

and other **Accent Press** titles

please visit

www.accentpress.co.uk

CPSIA information can be obtained at www.ICGtesting.com
Printed in the USA
LVOW07s1456050815

448963LV00001B/80/P